A TASTE OF SHADOWS

SYDNEY
WINWARD

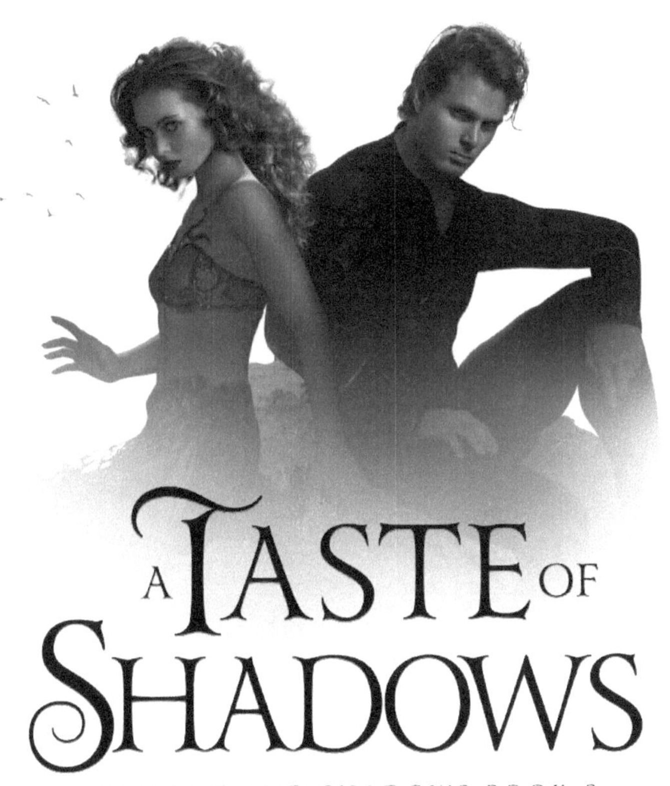

A TASTE OF
SHADOWS
SUNLIGHT AND SHADOWS BOOK 2

A Taste of Shadows

Cover Designed by MiblArt

Published by Silver Forge Books

Trade Paperback ISBN 978-1-7374854-3-8

Digital ISBN 978-1-7374854-2-1

www.sydneywinward.com

To my awesome parents who are always so supportive of my writing!

Books by Sydney Winward

The Bloodborn Series
Bloodborn
Bloodbond
Bloodscourge
Bloodbane

Sunlight and Shadows Series
A Breath of Sunlight
A Taste of Shadows
A Glimpse of Music

Lord Death Series
A Waltz with Lord Death

Novellas
Through Wylder Meadows
Root Brew Float
Yours, Sterling
On Silver Wings
Bloodmoon

Some days were so peaceful that they erased the burden of all the people she had killed.

Lyyli (Lie-lee) Ives stroked the surface of the water with long, delicate fingers. The fingers of a pianist, her adopted father had said, to match the willowy grace of her long dancer legs. Her reflection rippled in the water of the pond. Golden-copper hair and jade-green eyes scattered to the left and then the right.

Her mouth formed a serene smile as she touched the water like a friend she longed to never leave. It twirled and looped around her fingers as if playing like a hopeful puppy. It felt like a familiar cloak she wanted to embrace, always drawing her near but never fully inviting her inside.

"You seem to understand me perfectly," she used her hands to sign to the water. Her reflection mimicked the movement. "And I never have to speak."

She touched her throat, longing for the sound of her own voice. The last she'd heard it must have been a year ago.

The longing grew heavier and heavier with each passing second until it crashed over her. She gave into the desire, but not without caution.

Green and purple leaves rustled in a gentle breeze in the clearing a mile from her home. White clouds drifted past on a blue sky. Birds twittered in the trees, but animals were immune to her power.

Not a soul in sight, she dared to whisper her own name. "Lyyli." Lie-Lee.

Birds continued their calls. The wind rustled lightly through her hair. Peace. Tranquility. No one stabbed themselves. Jumped over the side of a cliff. Strangled themselves to death.

She released a long breath of relief and elation. Louder, she said, "What a lovely day." The sweetness of her voice cocooned her heart in security and warmth.

Her throat opened up like a blossoming flower beneath the first sunlight rays of morning, and she began to sing.

Magic lifted up around her, chasing the wind. Happiness settled deep within her as she sang about adventures and sword fights and dragons and love.

She lay back in the long, spongy grass, closing her eyes as she listened to her own voice. Foreign. Sweet. Rapturous. Wonderful.

The song slipped into melancholy as she poured out her heartache, loneliness, and even hatred for her twenty-three years' worth of a silent life. Her throat burned with emotion.

Tears escaped her eyes and trailed down her face. What she wouldn't give to end the silence.

Splash!

Lyyli's song ended abruptly as she bolted upright, only to find ripples traveling quickly across the pond. Wet blonde hair floated in the murky water before disappearing completely beneath the surface.

Astra! she screeched to her six-year-old adoptive sister, if only in her mind. She scrambled to the pond's edge and reached, but Astra darted away from help.

Her sister propelled herself downward until even her clothing disappeared.

She was drowning herself.

Panic gripped Lyyli's lungs and squeezed. Breath shuddered in and out with each gasp. She couldn't swim. If she jumped in, she might die as well.

Still, she backed up to give herself a running start. Her boots squelched through mud, slippery sticks, and then she threw herself over the lip of the pond and splashed into the water. Another gasp escaped her when the icy water climbed her legs, snagged her dress, and dragged her downward.

She splashed frantically, desperate for air. But when she quickly lost the fight, she dove beneath the water, blindly feeling for her sister. Her fingers brushed across reeds, slimy plants, and just as her lungs burned for air, her hand located fabric.

Her fingers closed around Astra's clothing, and she pulled until she wrapped her arms around her sister. Astra pushed her away, intent on drowning. Lyyli kicked and struggled to reach the surface. The dress she wore weighed her down like bricks tied to her feet. Coupled with Astra's fighting and her own soaked clothing…

They were both going to die.

Fire licked its way through her lungs. Clawing. Squeezing. Piercing. But with one last kick, her head burst through the surface, and she gasped in a breath of air. Astra no longer struggled. Instead, she lay limp in her arms.

Several times, Lyyli dipped below the water in her desperate quest to reach the shore. It only lay feet away, but no matter how much she kicked and struggled, she didn't know how to reach it.

Her arms and legs spasmed with fire, similar to the heat previously in her lungs. Fatigue settled in like a lulling embrace, and just when her body threatened to give up, two hands plunged beneath the water and grabbed her under the arms. They hauled both her and Astra to dry land.

She gasped in lungfuls of air, turning to find her older neighbor standing above them, his arms dripping water.

"Help me," she signed, her movement stiff and sloppy when an icy chill climbed her limbs. "Please, help me."

His eyebrows furrowed in puzzlement, not understanding her words. But still, he took Astra from her, bent her over his knee, and smacked her repeatedly on the back. Lyyli clasped her frigid fingers together and prayed to the heavens. *Please, save her. Please. I'll never speak a word again.*

After several long, torturous moments, Astra coughed and sputtered and gasped as she expelled the water from her lungs.

And then she lay still again. If it wasn't for her sister's shaking hands and chattering teeth, Lyyli would have feared the worst.

"Can you walk?" her neighbor asked. "I can't carry you both on the horse."

She shook her head and pointed in the direction of the house before she slumped backward on the grass, body exhausted. *Don't worry about me. Get my sister somewhere safe and warm. Far away from me.*

But she couldn't say it out loud. Otherwise, he would become a victim of the unforgiving pond as well.

The man cradled little six-year-old Astra in his arms. "I'll be back for you."

She closed her eyes and listened to his footsteps squelching through the mud and then the grass, followed by a nickering horse nearby. Steady hoofbeats moved in the direction of the farm.

Lyyli's entire body ached, but she couldn't risk her neighbor returning for her. Limiting contact with others was one of her biggest priorities in life.

What sad, pitiful priorities.

Her arms shaking, she pushed herself to her feet and swayed before catching herself against a nearby tree. With one shivering foot in front of the other, she stumbled back home. She entered the house just as the neighbor began to leave.

She signed, "Thank you."

It seemed he understood her this time, as he nodded, shoved his hat onto his head, and slipped out of the house.

Uncontrollable wailing greeted her in the somber farmhouse. Color leached from the walls. The world tilted one way and then the other. She stumbled toward the open door at the end of the hallway, but her adoptive father stepped out suddenly to stop her from entering, shaking his head.

"It's best if you don't go in," he murmured, shutting the door quietly behind him until it clicked.

Her trembling hands shook as they spoke. "Is she…" She paused, not able to say the word.

He frowned, but when he shook his head, relief flooded through her. She leaned against the wall, closed her eyes, and heaved a deep sigh. But then halted mid-breath. Although a simple, breathy sigh wouldn't cause damage, if her voice became audible in the slightest, she could kill a man.

"You did this, didn't you?"

"I'm sorry," she signed over and over again, tears spilling down her cheeks. "It was an accident. I didn't know she followed me to the clearing."

"Were you talking to yourself?"

She shook her head and made the sign for "singing."

"We're lucky she's alive. You know what has happened to countless others who have heard your voice."

"I know." If she used her voice, she was sure it would have been layered with misery to match her expression.

He ran his hand over his stubbled jaw, averting his gaze as if to avoid looking at her. "You can't stay here anymore. It's too dangerous. We're sending you away."

Lyyli latched onto his arm, pleading with her eyes to try and make him understand. She unlatched just enough to sign. "I swear I will never speak or sing again. I swear it."

Her father sighed, his shoulders slumping with defeat as he leaned down to kiss the top of her head like he had since they'd found her on their doorstep when she was only three years old. "It won't be for good. But no one can help you here." He picked up a piece of paper, an application of sorts, completely filled out. They'd been planning this for a while... "We were going to wait to bring this up, but it's just too dangerous for you to stay here any longer. Take this to Skaad. It's an application to enroll in the school there. You will learn to control your ability."

She briefly skimmed the paper and frowned as she pointed to a passage near the top. *Darkest Star Arcane Academy is open to all types of fae and humans. The first classes are scheduled to start in the autumn.*

Repeatedly, she pointed to the word "autumn."

"True," he said, acknowledging her point. "It doesn't start for another few months. But you need to leave. Perhaps the archmage will take you in for a time."

At the sound of her adoptive mother weeping in the next room, her entire body slumped in defeat. He was right. She needed to leave. Otherwise, the next slip-up might actually kill one of the people she loved.

Though, it seemed as if the only options that remained available to her were this school or finding a husband.

No one in the human kingdom of Frisia would take her for a wife despite hers and her parents' efforts to find her a match. So many suitors had already turned her down for her "muteness." There was nothing for her here. Not a husband. Not a family. Not a happy, meaningful life.

Perhaps the only way to live was to leave. If there was any possible way the archmage could help her, she would owe him her whole life.

"Who is the archmage?" she signed as she scanned the paper again.

Just as she spotted the man's name, her father said, "Lord Killian Graves. He's a Shadow Fae, the Lord of the Skaad province."

Lord Killian must be old, she decided, if he planned to open up a school. She wouldn't be surprised if he retired his title to his heir in favor of becoming the archmage. Either way, she knew she should go. She *wanted* to go. To leave. To escape. To flee.

Not forever. But perhaps for a good, long while.

A knock on the front door startled her, and she took to shivering against the wall as she watched her father open the door to reveal a gangly man holding a hat to his chest. "I'm here to pick up your daughter. Miss Ives, was it? The other passengers are waiting in the wagon. We need to depart immediately."

The blood drained from Lyyli's face. *Already?*

A part of her wondered if her adoptive parents had packed for her during her trek back to the house to get her out sooner rather than later.

Once again, without looking her in the eye as he passed, her father picked up luggage just around the corner and handed it to the man. Tears of betrayal cascaded down her face. This was her father. The man who had raised her. If he wouldn't keep her, then who would? Lord Graves would throw her out on the streets. She would have nowhere to go.

She schooled her expression into a stoic mask to hide her pain before she knocked on the door to the room she shared with her little sister.

"Go away!" her mother screamed. "Leave. Be gone."

The final knife slashed across her heart and left her to bleed dry on the floor of the home she'd grown up in. Her mother… Her sister… Her father…

Her father at least had the decency to reach for her as if to pull her into an embrace, but she ducked beneath his arm and slipped outside, pulling the front door shut between them. For a moment, she leaned back against the wood warmed by the afternoon sun, her eyes closed as she reined in the feeling of hurt and betrayal and loss.

Finally, she took one step away from the door but paused when she heard her father's muffled sobs. He wasn't weeping for Astra. But for *her*.

"Come on, lady," the man from earlier said with a motion of his head toward a waiting wagon filled with men, women, and children. A piece of long, yellow grass stuck out from his mouth. He took it out for a moment to spit on the side of the road. "We don't have all day."

Her heart continued to bleed as she clambered into the wagon and wedged herself into the corner between a young boy and a woman. Before she even sat down, the wagon lurched forward and threw her off balance. She barely caught herself against the wooden railing.

Several minutes passed before the low hum of conversation struck up around her. She kept her gaze on her lap, although she felt more than one pair of eyes watching her.

"Do you like to play games?" the boy asked, his wide, brown eyes staring up at her. "I know a game where I say a word, and you say another word that rhymes with it."

Heavy regret added to her despair. She shook her head and patted her throat, attempting to say she couldn't speak. His face fell moments before he asked the other person next to him to play instead.

Lyyli turned her attention to the passing scenery. Green trees. A gentle river. Sparse houses. At what point would her surroundings cease to appear familiar? How was she to reach Lord Graves? What was the school like? Did she have enough money to make the journey? What about tuition? She doubted her parents could afford it. And she had very little saved herself, the money packed with her belongings.

Perhaps her parents never intended to help with costs. They expected her to make her own way, and they wanted her gone.

Despite her heartache, she hoped Astra was all right.

After an hour, the wagon slowed to a stop beside a field of waist-high green corn stalks, and the man with the grass in his mouth rounded to the back of the wagon. He pointed to her and motioned with his head for her to get out.

"You will board another wagon headed to your destination. The others will continue on. Come on then. Hop to it."

She obeyed, and barely managed to leap off the wagon with her luggage before it lurched forward again. Dust kicked up in its wake, but after it rounded a bend in the road, it disappeared completely from sight.

She turned toward the fork in the dirt road, and to her horror, found three men advancing toward her. No other women or children had gotten off with her.

Turning on her heel, she attempted to flee, but one of the men grabbed her and wrenched her arms behind her back. Tears stung her eyes at the pain of someone else securing her wrists with rope. They pushed her forward, and without the use of her arms to keep her balance, she stumbled and hit the dirt road face first.

"Good job, boys," a man with a deep voice said, followed by the crunching of shoes and a cane on gravel. A pair of pristine black boots stopped a foot away before a stout man crouched over her. A hand with fingers covered in jewels grabbed her chin and angled it awkwardly, forcing her to turn onto her side to keep her neck straight. "This is her?"

Fear catapulted her heart into the boughs of the highest tree in the kingdom when she found herself staring back into yellow eyes tinged with black. They weren't normal. The pupil was a thin slit as if she stared into the eyes of a snake rather than a man.

She struggled away from him, but he held on tight enough to bruise. Terror guided her as she opened her lips to speak, to kill them all, but the man pressed something to her mouth.

She gasped and writhed against the foul fumes on the cloth, but all too quickly, her body became limp, including her mouth. Words refused to escape her throat. She was powerless.

And very much alone.

Another man heaved her inside a carriage, her entire body draped across one of the seats with one leg hanging off and brushing against the cold floor. The man with the yellow eyes sat across from her, simply staring at her with fascination.

The carriage jolted forward, and she wished she could either use her voice or fall into a deep, merciful slumber. But she could only stare and blink sluggishly. Nothing more.

The man smirked as he laid a fancy silver-and-black cane across his lap. "Well, my Mute Songbird. You and I are going to have a lot of fun."

Lyyli tried to cry out for help, but her body refused to obey. She was trapped in an immobile, mute prison with no way to escape.

illian Graves slammed the carriage door shut as agitation twitched in the intensity of his blue eyes. The startled driver jumped in the seat, and one of the horses flicked its tail and snorted.

Without stopping to apologize, he stomped up the graveled path to his estate, wincing against the brightness of morning as the sun began to rise. As a Shadow Fae, he stayed up all night and slept through the day. But the meeting had gone on for so long…

At the reminder, he scowled at the green vines dotted with pink and red flowers climbing the wall of his large estate. He ran long fingers through tussled honey-blond hair. He ignored the beautiful gardens and dense foliage surrounding his home in favor of a glare toward the curved mahogany doors standing in his way of refuge. Two servants opened the doors and bowed as he stalked into the estate.

He ripped off his gloves and threw his hat and coat onto a table. The moment he stepped into the comforting solace of shadows created from the banister, his magic washed over him like starlight on a glassy pond. He became the shadow, allowing it to pull him through its current up the stairs and down the hall. Only when the shadow chain broke in front of his bedroom door did he return to his solid form.

The feat exhausted him after such a long night at the Lords' meeting in Inuwa, Lord Beelek's province. His anger melted into frustration as he slipped inside his room. He slumped into a chair beside the window, pulled off his shoes, and threw them aside with greater force than necessary.

"An empire?" he growled, next shucking off his neckcloth. "Are they idiots?"

The shadow kingdom of Katalle had always been ruled by Lords. Ten different Lords for ten different provinces. It balanced power. It made each an equal. But at the meeting today, Lord Auer dared to suggest someone rule over the Lords to create an empire. And half the members had agreed to it!

Idiots. The lot of them. Thank the shadows the vote needed to be unanimous to make it happen. He had no intention of tipping the scale in the opposite direction. At least for now, it remained balanced.

A light, hesitant knock on the door.

"What?" he barked but then grimaced guiltily as he crossed the room and opened his door with an apologetic look on his face, overly aware of his half-dressed state. The serving girl's face turned pale as she wrung her hands together. "What is it?" he tried again, this time softer.

"My apologies, my Lord," she said, dipping into a hasty curtsy. Her cheeks flamed red as her gaze traveled from his bare feet to his half-buckled belt to the top of his undershirt that dipped low enough to reveal his chest. But then her gaze snapped back to his, and the pale fear returned. "Your mother… The Dowager Graves has been asleep since yesterday morning. She won't wake. We have tried everything. It's as if she's awake but dead—"

Killian took off running down the hallway, down a flight of stairs, up another flight, and into the north wing of the estate. His heart pounded and his head throbbed. He burst into his mother's bedroom, only to find her lying on the bed.

Still.

Unmoving.

Two female servants scurried out of the way as he approached. Her face was pale like in death. But her chest rose up and down with each steady breath.

With careful movements, he prodded her upper neck with his fingers, checked her abdomen for swelling, and he even glanced inside her ears, mouth, and nose.

Nothing unusual.

"What happened?" he demanded. He found a pile of clean cloths and a basin of water on the bedside table, dipped one of the cloths in the water, and placed it on his mother's hot forehead. He felt her pulse to find it beating quicker than it ought to.

"We don't know," the head maid said as she fussed over his mother's bedsheets. "My husband found her unconscious in the garden after you left on your trip. He thought she might have fallen and hit her head."

Next, his gentle fingers moved to his mother's head, and he probed her skull. No bumps. No lacerations. No swelling. He pulled her eyelids open. Like all Shadow Fae, her vertical pupils narrowed into tiny slits when exposed to the daylight.

He recalled every ailment he'd ever studied and every magical curse. He was frightened because he didn't know what this was.

"Have you summoned the doctor?" he asked.

"Yes. He has never seen anything like it."

Killian squeezed his eyes shut and rubbed the sudden ache in his temples. What was this? Magic? Poison? An extreme fainting spell?

"Where is your husband? I want to know exactly where he found her unconscious."

The head maid led him out of the room and downstairs into the foyer, where the head Shadow Fae butler, Emil, waited stoically by the door as if expecting them. Three of Killian's four female cousins who lived at the estate huddled in the corner, eyes wide as they spoke in hushed voices. They all wore nightgowns covered in robes, hair wild and eyes sleepy.

When he stepped foot outside the double glass doors leading to the garden, he shrank back into the shadows of the estate.

"Argh," he groaned as he swatted the air in front of him, but nothing changed. Daylight still pierced his eyes like searing anger. "It's too blasted bright outside. I can hardly see a thing."

"My Lord, would you like me to fetch the human gardener?" Of course, the human slept at night and awakened during the day. They were strange. But other types of fae did the same thing.

"No. I'm fine." Yet, his eyes watered profusely. He swiped the involuntary moisture from one eye and then the other before accepting a hat from Emil to shade his eyes. To hell with his blue fae eyes. Although those with darker eye colors like brown and gray still struggled with the light, blue topped them all. He was practically blind during the day. Unless it was cloudy. And today was *not* cloudy. It was blue and detestable.

When his eyes adjusted somewhat, he continued on a path around the estate and further into the gardens. Flowers of all colors, shapes, and varieties popped up around them. Most closed their petals as the sun rose higher in the sky and later blossomed in the moon's presence.

At last, they stopped in front of a large honey locust tree. A table his mother used for tea sat beneath the tree, and the moment he stepped near it...

Dark magic descended upon him like a chilling winter. Frigidness latched onto his foot, climbed up his leg, and sent a deadly shiver down his spine.

"Do you feel that?" he murmured to his butler.

The other man shook his head. "Magic, I presume?"

Without answering, Killian ventured toward the table and inspected it closely. A splash of tea remained unwiped from the surface, and he leaned in closer to sniff it. Chamomile.

"We left this area untouched," Emil said from where he stood beside an arch with purple wisteria climbing it—his mother's favorite. "We assumed you would want to take a look."

He ran his fingers through the spilled tea and rubbed them together before smelling it again and peering closer. No hint of poison. No residual magic.

"Was she wearing anything unusual?" he asked as he continued to inspect the surrounding area. "A piece of clothing? Jewelry? A hairpin?"

"Ah." Emil grimaced and stared down at his feet. "Yes. A hair comb. My wife thought it might be a gift from a suitor. A few have been coming around, so we didn't think more of it."

"Who was on the property? One of her suitors?"

The butler shrugged and grimaced again. "I apologize, my Lord. Whoever it was didn't show their face to us. No one outside the family or the regular servants have been by for over a week."

"Where is the hair comb now?"

The man blinked several times, the shadows from his eyelashes falling over the sunken wrinkles in his face. "With one of the girls, if I remember correctly. Your cousin, Charlotte, took it."

Killian swore under his breath and squinted against the bright light as he darted out from the shade of the tree, ran across the lawn in his bare feet, and stumbled up the stairs to the bedrooms. Instead of knocking, he burst into Charlotte's room...

...only to find her face as white as her nightgown, a stark contrast against the dark, wooden floor where her body lay. Her eyes were closed, dark lashes brushing against a curtain of death. A river of dread slithered through him. He approached slowly, watching for any sign of life.

Someone screamed in the doorway. Killian jumped a foot in the air and spun around to find his other three cousins staring at Charlotte, the youngest with her hands clamped over her mouth. She must have been the one to scream. "Hells, Mia!" he growled, rolling his shoulders back and crossing the remaining distance between himself and his unconscious cousin. "You scared me."

Emil pushed his way through the wailing and sniffling cousins, his expression grave. "Is she gone?"

"I don't know."

He stooped down and pressed his fingers against her neck to feel for a pulse, lowering his ear to her mouth. The slowest pulse. The faintest exhale.

And then he spotted a flash of blue and green tangled in her dark hair. He began to dig through the curtain of tresses but thought better of it at the last moment. A handkerchief at the vanity caught his attention, and he used it as a barrier between him and the object as he snatched it out like a viper attacking a mouse.

As if the threads of a noose snapped, Charlotte inhaled sharply.

But she didn't wake.

His cousins rushed toward their sister, elbowed him out of the way, and left him to his own devices as he scrutinized the hair comb. Blue and green gemstones climbed the silver comb like beautiful, dangerous ivy. Raw, dark power pulsed through him.

The magic was powerful. And if he hadn't attuned himself to intricate magic over the years, he might not have felt it weaved into the seemingly harmless object.

Who possessed such magic?

He turned on his heel toward the door, but Mia's scoff stopped him in his tracks. "You are just going to leave her here? On the floor?"

Right… What was he thinking?

With great effort, he hid his guilty grimace as he carefully stooped down, lifted Charlotte, and placed her on top of the bed. He never was great at considering other people's feelings. It was time-consuming and irrelevant to the task at hand. If he didn't catch the mage who had done this, they might not see whatever curse this was reversed until it was too late.

If it wasn't already too late.

A pit of fear churned in his gut as he remembered his mother's pale face and cold skin. And now Charlotte…

As head of the household and the mage of the family, it was his job to keep them safe.

His fingers drummed against his arm as thoughts and ideas whirled in his mind. He found himself climbing the steps to his private tower, two at a time.

Whoever had done this knew Killian would be absent for a short period. Not only that, but they managed to get close enough to his mother to perform the wicked magic. His best guess was whoever did this was someone his mother knew.

He burst through the door to his tower like a frigid flurry through a rattling window. Books, manuscripts, and scrolls lay strewn across his desk, scattered about his bookshelves, and some even wound up on the floor.

First, he crossed the room and closed the curtains to block out the offending light of day. Next, he picked out several different titles and laid them open on his desk. It was already piled high with open books, but what was a few more?

Under his breath, he murmured, "Magic, curse, enchantment…" He leafed through page after page, book after book. "What are you?"

Someone knocked on his door, startling him out of his search. His cousin, Johanna, peeked her head inside and smiled. "I thought you could use some khave. Heaven knows none of us will sleep well today."

His eldest cousin entered, holding two cups of the steaming liquid, and he gratefully took one from her and sipped at its sweet, energizing nectar.

Suddenly aware of his state of undress, he buckled his belt all the way, tucked in the remaining half of his shirt, and located a robe hanging on the opposite wall of the tower. Only after he threw it over his shoulders did he return to his desk. Johanna had already made herself comfortable in one of the armchairs against the wall. Thank the shadows she was more sensible and mature than her three younger sisters. She was the only one he would ever allow into his tower.

Like the rest of her siblings, Johanna's hair was a dark shade of brown, her eyes a smooth hickory, and her lips a pale pink. She crossed her legs where she sat and studied him over the rim of her porcelain cup.

"Just ask," he sighed, moving his attention to a scroll pulsing with dark magic. He rubbed his eyes, wishing he'd managed to sleep on the way back home in the carriage. But he'd been too angry to sleep.

"What do you think happened to Charlotte? To my aunt? I've never seen anything like it."

Although her expression remained calm, a deep fear collected in her eyes.

"Me neither." He picked up another book and opened it to a section about enchantment. Quickly, he scanned each page, searching for anything that mentioned some sort of sleep paralysis that placed its victim on the edge of death. By now, he had most of these books memorized. What more was he hoping to find?

A list of enchantments rolled across the page—sleep, paralysis, poison, death, forgetfulness, and many more.

Johanna snapped her fingers and grinned. "True love's kiss. Like in the fairy tales."

He lifted an incredulous eyebrow. "Those are *fairy tales*, Johanna. A waste of time. A way to fill children's heads with frivolous stories of make-believe. Besides, I'm not going to kiss your sister. Be my guest if you want to try."

As if wanting to ease the tense, serious atmosphere in the tower, she rolled her eyes at him and bounced her foot up and down as she continued to stare at him through the steam wafting from her cup. "Then who *will* you kiss? I have not seen you strike up any new courtships in many years."

He waved his hand in the air to push aside the topic and opened yet another book. "Another waste of my time. I have too much to do for a woman to tie me down."

"Are you talking about the school?"

Involuntarily, his gaze snapped to the architectural drawing tacked to the wall, depicting a cluster of large buildings with many rooms and windows. The construction was already complete, and in only a couple of months, the school would open. He'd already started accepting applicants—mainly Shadow Fae, though a couple of Sun Fae had applied as well as a few humans who wanted to learn more about magic and how to hone their own abilities.

Only a couple more months and his dream of teaching something he loved would be complete.

"Of course." He flipped through page after page of potion mixtures capable of bringing someone to the brink of death. If he hadn't found the hair comb in Charlotte's hair, would she eventually have succumbed?

"And you think no woman is capable of sharing your dream with you?" she asked, clearly not done with the conversation. "What about an heir? You will need one to pass down your title as one of the Lords."

With half his foot in the conversation and half in a book, he hummed a non-committal answer. "You are starting to sound like my mother."

"Your mother is smart."

A lump of dread clawed at his throat at the thought of his sickly mother, but he quickly swallowed it. She needed his intellect, not his wallowing.

He downed the rest of the khave, and energy surged through him only moments later. "I'll send for Sun Fae healers," he said, now scribbling a letter on a piece of blank parchment. "The ones in my circle are very knowledgeable."

"Killian." Johanna lifted a dark eyebrow while giving him a *you're avoiding the topic* expression. "If you're not looking for love, consider an arranged marriage. I know many influential ladies I can introduce you to. Some are acquaintances, others friends, and…perhaps a couple of cousins."

At the mention, his head snapped up and he scrutinized her, his gaze flitting over her wary face. She didn't mean… No, it wasn't possible…

Sure, cousins often married in Skaad, but it was more common to marry across provinces. To secure friendly alliances.

He shook his head and finished penning the letter. Obviously, she didn't mean *herself* as his potential wife. Johanna was usually more direct.

"There are bigger things to worry about than who will secure me an heir." He waved the half-dry letter in the air before pouring black wax and pressing the Skaad seal into the thick substance. "Such as making sure your sister doesn't die. Are you not worried?"

He noticed her fingers trembling as she took another sip of her drink. "I am immensely worried. But at least here I can be of some help."

With a roll of his eyes, he grumbled as he made his way toward the door. "By meddling in my affairs? The only help you are offering is distraction."

But as he passed by, she kicked him in the back of the knee. He yelped and glared at her before shutting the door soundly behind him. It was a shame he wasn't looking for a wife. She was the most tolerable candidate. But if he ever did marry, he wanted more than just *tolerable*. If he found someone he could love more than his studies, more than his magic, more than his school, he would consider marriage.

It wasn't worth it to him otherwise.

K have became Killian's constant companion over the next week. The lack of sleep brought him back to the days when he'd written his first book about dark magic at age nineteen and another only a year later about enchantments. But instead of straining his eyes to the brink of blindness, he found himself gnawing his fingernails to nubs and pacing a worn path in the wooden floor in his tower.

Both Charlotte and his mother still hadn't woken. Their bodies were slowly deteriorating as if caught in a web between life and death. It was as if a spider had injected its venom into them, and no matter what, they couldn't move while the insect sank its fangs into them and slowly sucked their blood.

There must be a way to fix this.

"Perhaps there is," he murmured to himself.

He ceased his pacing and opened his palm to reveal the sleeping draught he'd brewed earlier that morning. Purple liquid sloshed in the small vial. Tempting. Beckoning.

A lump of desperation formed in his throat, tempting him to use the one power he tried so hard to hide. No one knew about it. Except his mother. He'd made sure to keep it as one of his closest guarded secrets. If anyone found out about it…

Someone would kill him for it.

But if he continued doing next to nothing, he would lose both his mother and Charlotte. His family would never be the same.

In a moment of bravery—or perhaps foolish recklessness— he unstopped the vial, downed its contents, and hid the now empty glass container in a drawer. The world around him blurred. Browns and reds and greens and purples melded together in a dizzying array of colors. His body swayed one way and then the other.

He stumbled toward the cot on the other side of the tower and barely managed to lie down before sleep drowned him in darkness.

For as long as he could remember, he could be fully awake, even in slumber. His consciousness separated from his sleeping body as if he were a shadow. The essence of him slithered beneath the door and down a couple dozen stairs. He stopped in the hallway when Mia passed, not even looking in his direction. He was invisible, there but not quite there at the same time.

He allowed his essence to move more quickly toward his mother's room, floating through the air and joining with her own consciousness.

Only for a steel gate to block him. He attempted to enter her dreams with more force, but the harder he tried, the harder the magic afflicting her blocked him.

Next, he tried Charlotte's subconscious, with the same results. Frustration and confusion tumbled together within him. This wasn't normal, even for an enchantment. It was dark, powerful magic that blocked his own. A curse. A death sentence.

In the next room, his cousin Laureen slumbered. None too gently, he slammed into her own subconscious, half expecting for a wall to block his magic as well. But as he entered her dream, he stumbled across pink grass and barely managed to catch himself against a tree…

…made of sugar cubes.

Now wearing something resembling his fae body, he glanced around in wonder. Pink grass. Green skies. Trees and bushes made of sugary sweets. The thick, yellow pond nearby resembled lemon pudding. Bright-colored unicorns nibbled at the grass. And riding one of them…

"Killian!" Laureen shouted, waving her arms frantically in the air and completely unaware that he wasn't truly a part of her dream. "I'm headed to the jelly lake. Johanna is waiting for me."

But even as she kicked her unicorn forward, the creature's legs moved, but they went nowhere. One of Laureen's teeth fell out, followed by another. She stuffed them back into her mouth and gave him a grin. Her teeth fell out again, but when she attempted to put them back in, they wouldn't stay.

"Why are you just standing there?" she asked, now kicking the flanks of the unicorn with frustration written all over her face. "Johanna is waiting for you to kiss her."

"Huh?" he found himself asking before he managed to stop himself. He always made sure to tread cautiously in someone's dream. No one suspected his presence when he went along with the bizarre or even mundane. But if someone were to trap him in their mind, he feared he would be unable to escape.

"She says you are dragging your feet. She's tired of you dragging your feet."

Laureen ignored his puzzled expression and laughed triumphantly as she finally managed to gain some ground.

Only for the earth to crumble beneath her. She screamed as she fell, and the next moment, she was startled awake.

His essence was flung from her subconscious as her physical body bolted upright, chest heaving, skin glistening with sweat. But just as he started to leave, someone shook his body, and he slammed back to it. His eyes flew open to find Johanna shaking him awake. Behind her, daylight streamed into the room from the window.

Ugh. Daylight. He was getting tired of seeing it.

"What?" he asked groggily, as the effects of the potion hadn't quite worn off even though hours must have passed. Time moved differently inside someone's subconscious.

"The Sun Fae healers are here. They are apologizing profusely for the delay. Skaad is one of the furthest provinces from Heulwen. It took some time to arrive."

He rubbed the grogginess from his eyes and followed her into his mother's bedroom. Two Sun Fae had opened all the curtains, and he couldn't help but hiss and shield his eyes as he entered the room. One of the healers glanced up, which revealed a golden sun star tattooed on each of her cheeks. The other healer's arms were covered in tattoos from gold to silver to bronze and everything in between. Their kind tattooed their scars with colors and symbols to match. The only tattoos Shadow Fae got were usually the cursed kind. A curse marked the skin black either forever or until lifted.

So far, Killian had exactly zero tattoos, and he planned to keep it that way. No curses for him.

"Thank you for coming," he said as he shook each of their hands. "Lloyd and Tegan." If he remembered correctly. He nodded toward his mother. "How is she faring?"

The two Sun Fae shared a look. Golden healing light began to stream from the man's hands while the woman ushered him into the corner. Regret puckered her mouth. "We've been here a short time, and we've already seen what we need to see."

His stomach dropped. "Which is what?"

"This is a powerful spell, which can likely only be reversed by its caster. The threads of dark magic within her are so tightly woven that even we can't locate the ends to untangle them. I'm sorry, Killian. There is nothing we can do."

He nodded and crossed his arms tightly across his chest, expecting this answer but still not liking it. "I assume this will only get worse from here. Giving me an estimate, how long do they have left?"

"At most two months for your mother. We still need to examine Charlotte."

The stress of the situation shot his nerves through the roof. He channeled the energy into his balled fist, squeezing as tightly as possible until his entire hand turned white before releasing it. The stress remained, but now it was at least more manageable.

He didn't have two months to figure this out. In two months, he was supposed to open his school, and before then, he needed to get everything ready for his students and hired instructors. He couldn't deal with the grief of losing two of his family members while jumping straight into his lifelong dream of teaching. If he lost them, he would have to postpone opening the academy. Society would expect it. His own grieving heart would need it.

If he didn't figure out how to save them, he would lose so much. He refused to let it happen.

Again, he clenched his fist into a ball as they examined Charlotte and delivered the same results. Both Mia and Laureen began weeping. Johanna disappeared inside her room and didn't reemerge. But for him, there was no time to weep. He itched to do something, to alter this fate. If he could discover the mage behind the attack, he could get them to reverse it.

By any means necessary.

"Mother," he murmured in her room after everyone disappeared. He shook her shoulder. No response. "Give me some indication you can hear me."

Nothing. Not even an eye twitch.

"Who did this to you?" He paused, watching for any sort of reaction in the relaxed muscles of her face. "Family? An enemy? A mage?" Still no reaction. He peered closer and said, "I'm getting married tomorrow, Mother."

Her body remained still, every muscle unmoving.

A frown puckered his mouth as he straightened. "Ah, now I know you cannot hear me. You might have smacked me."

He crossed the room and stood before the open window, his hands clasped behind his back. Darkness crept across the sky like a welcoming breeze. Stars winked into existence, and with the absence of light, his eyes grew sharper. Each crisp edge of a leaf became clearer. The creek behind the estate shimmered beneath the starlight with colors beyond what the daylight could comprehend. The world stretched and yawned as it opened its arms to a wonderful, glistening existence. Blades of grass became straight and crisp. Flowers unfurled their petals to soak in the moonlight.

And finally, Killian didn't feel quite so blind anymore.

Rather, he felt unfettered. Free.

His gaze traveled from the creek, which glistened with a rainbow of color, to the Skaad Mountains silhouetted against a navy-blue background.

The momentary thread of peace snapped within him, followed by frigid cold as if the ice beneath his feet broke and dunked him beneath suffocating waters. The Skaad Mountains were dangerous, even for Shadow Fae. He'd heard tales of children wandering into the pass, only for their bones to float down the river months later. People who ventured too close either returned a completely different person or they didn't return at all.

His stomach churned as he recalled the myth of the witch in the mountains, who turned trespassers into animals, only for their own families to hunt and kill them and, ultimately, eat them for supper.

He believed the superstitions, at least to some degree.

A dark, dangerous power lived within the mountains. He sensed it. He feared it. He avoided it. He ignored it. He hoped if he left the witch alone, she would leave him and his people alone too.

Unless they ventured too close.

But what if…

He took a deep breath and exhaled shakily as he gripped the windowsill, his gaze glued to the dark silhouette. What if the witch could aid him? No other options remained if he wanted to save his family. At least no options that wouldn't take him months upon months to unravel. He had two months. No more.

Another breath exited his lungs, and with it, he hung his head. Was it a risk worth taking?

He peeked beneath his arm at his unconscious mother. So pale. So still. So much life left to live. Seeking out the witch was dangerous and perhaps even fatal. But he knew he would never forgive himself if he didn't at least try.

"You are lucky you have such a wonderful, loyal son," he said with a chuckle as he tucked the sheets around his mother and kissed her forehead. "I'll be back soon. You can count on it."

If only his trembling hands didn't betray his terror.

No one questioned him as he slipped out of the manor. No one stopped him as he saddled a horse made of midnight and shadows and packed very few provisions. And no one demanded to know his destination as he threw his leg over the saddle and kicked the horse into a trot. He glanced behind him when he reached the bridge arching over the creek only to find Johanna watching him from her bedroom window. The white silhouette of her dress stood out in the darkness of night.

As the horse trotted further from his home and closer to the mountain, he allowed his thoughts to focus on what he might face.

The witch.

Cunning. Ruthless. Tricky. Dangerous.

True, but he could also be those things.

After leading his horse through the forest and over another bridge, he slowed the creature to a stop and dismounted, his feet landing softly on the dirt path. The horse's red, ruby-like eyes blinked while its body shivered. It, too, could likely sense the foreboding danger of what lay within the mountain.

Taking a deep, steadying breath, Killian dug into his saddlebags and pulled out a ring inlaid with onyx gems and a potion made of midnight berries, moonlight, and a single fox hair. He dabbed the liquid with his handkerchief before spreading it onto the gems.

"*Ex praesidio per incantationes,*" he murmured.

The gems glowed hot like burning red coals and then ebbed into glimmering black once more. He slipped the ring onto his finger and immediately felt the protection the enchantment offered him. An enchantment to protect him from other enchantments.

Satisfaction overpowered his fear for a single moment. This particular enchantment was one of his own making. Blocking other peoples' magic was no easy feat—he only hoped his magic was strong enough to combat the witch's.

He tugged on the horse's reins, but the creature stubbornly tossed its head and pulled back. "No, you don't," he hissed, staring into its glowing red eyes. "You're coming with me."

The horse nickered and tossed its head back again, firmly planting its feet.

With a sigh of resignation, he glanced about. Crickets chirped in the undergrowth. Skaad birds fluttered in the boughs above, their razor-sharp teeth gnawing on branches. Several pairs of yellow eyes blinked in the darkness. Likely some benign creatures who liked to follow weary travelers through the woods. Or poisonous rabbits. He couldn't be entirely sure.

"Don't you dare get eaten," he ordered his horse as he loosely wrapped the reins around a low overhanging branch. "Not by trolls or demon birds or pixies." He shuddered at the thought of sharp pixie teeth tearing into his flesh. He patted the horse's flanks. "Behave."

A chill wind scattered gooseflesh along his arms and neck as he stepped out from the protection of the trees. The moment he tread over a trickle of a stream, a heavy weight smashed into his shoulders. The onyx ring burned his finger as it fought off the enchantment.

He staggered fully across the invisible barrier and gasped a breath into his heavy lungs. His head spun, confusion and disorientation threatening to topple him. The ring burned hotter and hotter until he hissed at the pain.

And then, just as quickly, the heat faded.

He blinked several times until a new uncomfortable sensation prickled his skin—the sensation of being watched.

Ignoring the feeling, he took several steps forward but stopped when the faintest blue light flashed only feet away from his face.

Sprites danced through the air in front of him, zipping one way and then the other, nearly invisible to the naked eye. Their giggles lingered in the air long after they disappeared. Despite his fear of what he was about to face, his intellectual mind couldn't help the desire from springing up like a bubbling fountain at the thought of studying the sprites. He'd never had the opportunity before because they weren't easy creatures to locate.

His pulse thundered in his ears as he produced a fairy crystal on a chain and murmured words to guide his way. "*Ducant me ad cor de pythonissam.*" *Lead me to the heart of the witch.*

The crystal glowed orange as if he held a lantern. Drops of crimson and yellow shimmered down from the sky like fiery snow. When it brushed against the ground, instead of catching fire, it disintegrated like ash in water. The flakes created a path forged of willpower and magic, leading up a path molded into the mountainside.

He glanced once behind him to make sure his horse hadn't been eaten yet. The creature's red eyes blinked once in the darkness before it lowered its head to snap its jaws around a mouse scampering by.

Another heavy wave of magic attempted to split his insides, but his onyx ring glowed to counteract the enchantment. He increased his pace, not daring to remain on the mountain any longer than necessary.

The further he climbed, the chillier the air became. The wind stilled, but a howl echoed nearby as if it relentlessly beat against the earth.

A movement from the corner of his eye chilled him to the bone. He spun around. Nothing. No sprite. No troll. Not even a mouse. An expanse of dark forest lay at the base of the mountain, and beyond he spotted distant lights from a nearby town.

He rubbed his hands up and down his arms in an attempt to warm himself, but the chill snuffed out every spark of heat in his body.

The trek led him to a flatter part of the mountainside. Large boulders converged on either side of him, creating only one way forward and only one way back.

"Gah!" he shouted, jumping a foot in the air when he ran into an incredibly detailed statue of a satyr. Stone horns stuck out of the top of his head, his mouth forever open in a scream.

With a shudder, Killian moved past and frowned as he encountered another statue of a man with a sword and a third of two women cowering against the wall.

"A strange collection," he said under his breath.

He traveled farther down the path, only for the cluster of statues to increase. The crystal enchantment he'd cast encircled a statue of a thin man, its light revealing an expression full of defiance before the trail ended completely, and the fiery light disappeared. In the statue's hand lay a dripping heart. Unlike the other statues, this man's eyes were unafraid. Rather, they contained hate and disdain.

Even more peculiar...

Killian moved closer as he scrutinized the man's mouth. The red imprint of lips marked the statue as if it had recently been kissed by a woman wearing lipstick.

His chest heaved with panic as he glanced back at the eyes, then at the stone heart in his hands, followed by the nearly imperceptible movement of what sounded like a very large snake behind him.

Basilisk.

He slammed his eyes shut and leaped out of the way just as something darted past his shoulder and crashed into one of the statues. Stone shattered. A serpent hissed.

He lost his balance and smashed into one of the boulders, but he didn't dare open his eyes. Using the rough surface as a guide, he trailed his hands over the boulders as he sprinted down the path as fast as his feet could carry him. A heavy slithering followed.

"Uh!" The word squeezed out of his lungs when he ran into a slab of rock and knocked the air out of himself. Behind him, he heard the serpent lunge again. He attempted to jump out of range, but then something sharp sliced through his arm.

Pain raged like the searing petals of lava flowers beneath his veins. An immediate sweat broke out on his forehead, and his muscles threatened to seize.

Venom. Basilisk venom.

This entire time, he'd been worried about what the witch might try to do to him. He should have worried about a venomous, stone-inducing snake instead. He'd had no idea it existed. Otherwise, he would have come prepared.

Pebbles beneath his shoes caused him to slip, and he found himself skidding through a blind, foreign maze with a dangerous creature on his tail. A vial of potion that could cure most poison lay within his bag. But then what? Get poisoned again? Eaten? Turned to stone?

He squeezed his eyes shut even tighter when he heard the creature dart ahead of him. Foul, venomous breath hit his face like a cloud of powder, enticing him out of fear to open his eyes. He ignored the enticement and ducked in the opposite direction. His shoulder bumped against rough stone before the ground beneath his feet transitioned from dirt to lush grass.

His heart raced faster and faster along with his pumping legs. He reached for a dagger tied to his belt, and with the hilt securely in his hand, he swiped blindly in front of him.

Think, Killian, think!

Basilisks were susceptible to their own venom, wounds created by iron weapons, and mirrors. He never thought he'd face a basilisk in his lifetime. He never thought to prepare for such a predicament.

The creature now wove around his legs like a predator playing with its prey. He could feel its gaze on him, daring him to open his eyes. He didn't. Instead, he swiped at the creature with his dagger.

It only connected with air.

His forehead burned hotter. His legs wobbled like jelly. His throat burned for air. But he kept running as fast as his long legs could carry him.

When he heard a splash of water in the distance, he sprinted toward it. Water was the only mirror he had at his disposal. If this didn't work, he was going to die.

Before he reached his destination in the darkness of his closed eyes, the ground beneath his feet caved. A yelp escaped him but was soon swallowed by a hiss uncomfortably close to his ear. He fell. Down…down…down…

Splash!

His body crashed into frigid water, quickly submerged by an unforgivable chill. He attempted to claw his way to the top, and he barely managed to gasp in a lungful of air before something solid and heavy smashed into him.

Heavy stone that could only be the petrified basilisk pushed him down until it pinned him to the bottom of what he thought might be a lake. Mud and rocks dug into his spine. Water teased his mouth and nose as he tried not to scream as fear gripped him with claws as sharp as blades. He pushed and heaved and struggled against the weight of the stone. It refused to budge.

Burning embers of agony pressed against his lungs, demanding air. No amount of struggling would free him. He was dead if he drowned. He was dead if he stared into the eyes of the snake. He was dead if the venom remained in his blood for even one more minute.

He dared to open his eyes.

Water blurred his vision, but the giant basilisk was visible through the dark haze. The length of the creature from its maw to its tail was pure stone. It pinned his torso to the lake's floor, as well as one of his arms. His entire body now burned as the venom coursed through him. No amount of wriggling liberated his pinned arm, so with his free arm, he reached for the shadows.

As if enjoying watching his torment, the shadows leaped out of reach with every pull of the current. He strained his body at an awkward angle, clawing for just a single shadow. His body shuddered in agony and began to give up when one of the shadows reached out to him instead. The moment it touched his skin, he grabbed a hold with his magic and melted into the shadow.

He shadewalked across the lake floor from shadow to shadow until he broke the surface of the water. He gasped in lungfuls of air and hauled himself out of the water before flopping onto his back.

His chest heaved for oxygen. His blood boiled in his veins.

Every movement agonizing torture, he dumped his soaking pack onto the ground and scattered the contents against the rocks. Gems and vials and a damp notebook fell out. He located a vial with blue liquid, uncorked the bottle, and downed its contents in a single swallow.

His body trembled and shuddered and writhed where he lay on the ground. He coughed and choked and forced himself not to retch as the anti-poison snuffed out the fire. Little by little, the blaze calmed into a flame, which settled into a warmth and then a chill.

He trembled both from the cold and as his fear caught up to him. His teeth chattered. His limbs shivered. And then, as if he suddenly found himself lying in front of a fire, warmth chased away a fraction of his frigid misery.

"I am greatly lacking in entertainment these days," a voice said, and his eyes flew open only to find himself staring at a glowing orange globe hovering over him. "I will allow you to sit by my fire."

The orange globe began moving away from him, taking its warmth with it.

As fast as his trembling fingers would allow, he packed his belongings and limped after the orb.

He'd never felt more foolish in his life.

He was too exhausted to care.

The orb led him to the mouth of a cave, and with each step, the wild mountain became something out of a storybook. Vines climbed the walls, moving slowly as if they were alive. Glowing butterfly wings flitted on branches growing across the ceiling. Yellow flowers sprouted on the cave floor in each of his footprints.

Finally, he reached a cozy room within the cave. A square dining table stood off to one side, and on the other lay a roaring fire inside what appeared to be a hearth. Two oversized chairs made of forest twigs sat in front of the hearth. He eyed them warily. After the incident with the basilisk, he didn't dare sit on something that might come alive and strangle the breath from him.

He wanted to get off this mountain as soon as possible.

"I assume you must be the witch of the mountain," he said to the empty air. "My name is—"

"I know who you are, Lord Killian Graves," the voice echoed again on all sides of him. Smooth. Silky. Dangerous. "Don't think I haven't noticed your offered peace, as I have given you the same in exchange. Unless someone happens upon my path on their own."

Laughter followed her statement. His shivering returned.

A slight scuffle behind him alerted him to someone's presence. He spun around, only for his eyes to harden.

A beautiful woman sauntered toward him, raven black hair falling to her waist. Her dress showed off most of her shoulders, and a slit in the material traveled all the way up her thigh.

He tore his gaze away and pushed his sopping wet hair out of his face. His clothing dripped water on the ground, and for a moment, he lamented over his soaked notebook. He never went anywhere without a notebook, and supposedly that meant to the bottom of a lake as well.

"Your basilisk nearly killed me."

The snake's venom continued to wither inside him until it remained as a pounding reminder in his skull.

The witch grinned as she stroked the delicate wings of a butterfly with a long, red fingernail. "It made for an interesting pet."

"One that killed your lover, I presume."

Her fingers stilled. "A lover. A grave mistake. He tricked me. Cut my heart out. And then sacrificed himself to the basilisk so I may never recover it. If he thought it would kill me, he was wrong." She glanced up with a sultry smile on her face. "Tell me, Lord Killian, do you know what it's like to feel *nothing?*"

He imperceptibly shook his head and backed up as she advanced on him until she trapped him against the wall.

"Would you like to find out? I can make your inevitable grief over your mother's fate disappear."

At the reminder, his heart panged as if the witch had reached inside his chest and plucked his ribs like melancholy harp strings. "What happened to her?"

"Every answer comes with a price." Her laughter echoed throughout the cave. He flinched. "I will give you two choices. Both come with interesting consequences. Choice one." She stroked the tip of his pointed ear with her fingernail. "I can tell you what happened and by whose hand, but the price would be your life for hers. Or Charlotte's. I will allow you to choose who to save."

A shudder ran down his spine as he yanked his head away from her touch. "And the second option?"

Another laugh escaped her as she threw her head back to expose her neck. He admired the man who managed to cut her heart out. It took guts. The witch was dangerous to hold so much power.

At last, she steepled her fingers together and offered him a devilish grin. "You get to decide. I'm interested to find out what you ask for."

Words swished through his mouth as he considered her offer. If he asked for something small and seemingly inconsequential, it would serve him more in the long run. It wouldn't be as quick of an answer, but it would be enough.

Mindful of every word he spoke, he said, "I ask you to give me the power to communicate with my mother."

"Wouldn't you rather have the power to bring her from the brink of death?"

"No. For you to give me this power, something of equal value must be taken in return."

"You seem to be well-versed in magic." Now her fingertips ran up the length of his arm, and in one fluid motion, she ripped off the lower half of his sleeve to expose his forearm. She latched on tight to his hand, a pact in the making. "I agree to give you this power. Do you agree to accept the loss of what I take from you?"

"Which is what?"

Her mouth broke into an amused grin. "I will tell you for another small price."

"Will I get back whatever you take?"

She paused, placing a finger to her lips in contemplation. "Perhaps. If someone takes your heart like mine has been taken, I will consider it."

For a long moment, he studied the fire burning in her eyes. This was a gamble, and in the end, he just might lose. He released a shuddering breath and shook his head. Whatever the consequences, he accepted them. Besides, he doubted anyone could take his heart. This trade would likely be permanent. "I agree."

A surge of power slammed into him hard enough to buckle his knees. His head spun sickeningly, his stomach churned moments before he turned his head to the side and vomited. Pain slammed into his eyes and skull before fiery agony crackled up his arm, originating from where she touched him. And just when darkness began to pull him under, the pain ceased, and he found himself stumbling through wild floor vines. The plants tangled around his legs and tripped him, and he smashed face-first into the ground.

He groaned with disorientation. When his world stopped spinning, he glanced down at his burning forearm. A black marking threaded its way from the base of his wrist to his elbow. A curse. The damned witch cursed him. But what did she take in exchange?

Another groan escaped him as he staggered to his feet, only to find himself at the base of the mountain where he'd originally started. His horse snorted only feet behind him, but as he glanced at the creature…

Shock rippled through him in waves, the next stronger than the last. The horse's eyes were a dark gray. The flowers that were originally purple on the forest floor were now gray. And the sky…

Gray.

A thousand different shades of white, black, and gray surrounded him.

All the colors…they were gone.

By the time Killian rode back to the estate atop his horse, his hair was a wild mess, his clothes were ripped and rumpled, and his body ached something fierce. The world around him pressed down on him in an array of gray, successfully disorienting him in a way that disconnected him from his surroundings. The witch had taken the colors from his life. How annoying and utterly inconvenient. He would have to start labeling everything by color, from his potions to his inks and even his clothing. He would have to recognize plants and herbs by their shape and smell rather than their hue.

How would this affect him as the archmage?

"Focus, Killian," he told himself. "One issue at a time."

The blush light of dawn crawled across the sky like an irritating, relentless worm. He should have asked the witch to do away with daytime altogether. He wondered briefly what the magic might have cost for such a feat. Or if the feat was even possible.

Weariness settled on his shoulders as he handed the reins of his mount to the stable hand before trudging toward his home. All he wanted to do was lay down and sleep for a few days. But every minute wasted was another minute his mother and Charlotte moved closer to their deaths.

With the intent to avoid notice, he slipped into the house from the side doors and ambled quietly across dark gray wooden floors, past a shiny black piano, and across a gray rug embellished with gray designs and gray tassels threaded on the ends. What color had the rug been before? He couldn't recall.

"Killian!" Johanna gasped.

He spun around to find his cousin leaping out of her chair beside the piano, her eyes wide. His first instinct was to hide his cursed arm behind his back, but he paused when he noticed streams of light purple waving over Johanna's head before it disappeared like smoke from a candle.

What in the shadows...?

"What happened to you?" she demanded as she marched toward him, grabbed hold of his elbow, and yanked his arm out from hiding to reveal the black etchings crawling across his skin.

Now a sickly yellow floated above her head, only to remain as she studied the curse. What were these colors?

His heart pounded a hopeful rhythm, and he couldn't help himself as he stared. The witch promised to give him a way to communicate with his mother. Were these colors associated with Johanna's thoughts? Or something else?

"Something terribly inconvenient. Nothing more." He pulled his arm out of her grasp and smoothed down his frayed and untidied shirt. Saving any dignity that remained was impossible at this point. "Do you ever sleep?"

She raised an eyebrow. "Do you?"

"Apparently not." He chuckled and raked his fingers through his hair stiff with dried lake water. "I'll need another cup of khave. It's going to be a long day."

"I'll make some for you."

Pink ribbons of light floated above her. He cocked his head as he tried to make sense of it. "I hate to be a bother, but what are you thinking right now?"

Instead of answering immediately, her cheeks flushed a darker gray. "N-n-nothing. I am just worried for your welfare, is all."

"Huh."

The pink wavered, promptly joined by the previous sickly yellow.

He reached into his pocket and produced his notebook but frowned to find it damp through and through. He needed another notebook. And quickly to allow him to record his most recent findings.

But most of all, he needed to find out what these colors were. Immediately.

"Killian," she said, more forcibly this time. "What happened? Where did you go?"

He studied her closely as he answered. "Sought out a witch. Fought a basilisk. Nearly drowned. Got cursed. But you might not believe me."

Her mouth fell open, and although she stood still, colors flew out of her at an alarming rate. Light purple, sickly yellow, a darker purple, pink, and red.

"You did what?" she whispered.

It seemed she did believe him after all.

Oh!

The colors weren't thoughts at all, he realized with a start. They were *emotions*. Light purple must be surprise. Sickly yellow represented worry. He wasn't sure about the rest. But it was a start.

"Thank you," he gasped. He kissed her cheek before he flew up the stairs and slammed his door shut behind him. Quickly, he discarded his clothing in favor of something new and comfortable, making sure to tie a handkerchief over his wrist to conceal the remnants of the curse that poked out of his sleeve. He wasn't sure what color the cloth was. It could have been purple or blue or green, and he'd be none the wiser.

When he flew back out of his room and toward his mother's with a dry notebook in hand, he leaned precariously over the railing. Two of his cousins glanced up at him as well as several servants. "No one is to disturb us," he announced to the room at large. "Not for any reason. None."

Without a backward glance, he slipped into his mother's bedroom and closed the door behind him. It was empty save for her lying pale and unconscious on the bed. For a moment, silence echoed across the walls. Depressing. Hopeless. And dreadfully gray.

"Mother," he said finally. Blue tendrils of emotions caught his eye, yet she didn't move. He guessed sadness and recorded it in his notebook. "So, you *can* hear me." Light purple. Surprise. "You and I are going to have a conversation. I desperately need your help. I can see your emotions. Pour everything you have into this. Help me understand through the way you feel."

Red-orange.

He puzzled over the color for a moment as he scratched it down. Acceptance? Agreement? Fear? He wasn't sure. He left it blank.

Leisurely pacing back and forth across the room, he asked, "Think of something that makes you happy. Think about it really hard, and don't let any other emotion interfere."

Yellow tendrils burst out of her. Not just a small wisp but a river of bright color. He noted the color next to the emotion. Together, they went down the list of bigger, easier-to-read emotions before moving on to the harder ones like hurt and excitement. Turquoise and orange. The tricky thing was many closely related emotions were slightly different shades of the same color. It made for an arduous morning.

After an hour of this, he rubbed his eyes, all too close to falling asleep on his feet. But at least the witch had held up her side of the bargain. She managed to take the colors from his world and transfer them to emotions.

Several more emotions remained on his list. He fought to stay awake, but he may not get another chance to communicate with his mother like this. He couldn't put it off.

"Next on the list..." He tapped the end of his quill several times against the word. "Passion."

A plethora of emotions became wisps over her head, the strongest color being red-pink. Embarrassment.

"Now, don't be embarrassed, Mother," he chuckled. "I need a completely full repertoire if I am to face what's ahead. So either you will reveal it to me, or I will corner an unsuspecting serving girl in the hallway and find out that way."

Of course, he would never do such a thing, and perhaps his mother knew it because angry red tendrils escaped her. Anger? Or...

Passion.

He frowned as he tapped his quill against his notebook. "Anger and passion are the same color. And who in the shadow's domain are you thinking about? Father?"

Olive green.

Hissing between his teeth, he jotted the color down. "I'm going to say that color is guilt. One of your recent suitors?" She had several who came by, some visiting more often than others. He began listing their names. "Max? Paul? Marvin?" The colors ranged from disgust to hate to indifference. "Lord Blom?" Red again, though he assumed it to be passion rather than anger. He simultaneously chuckled and made a teasing vomiting sound. "Oh, Mother. Really?"

The color emanating from her became a green-yellow, which he assumed was annoyance. If she'd been conscious, she might have flicked his nose and rolled her eyes and then sent him to do some menial chore.

The next color, he tried to ignore, pretending like he didn't see the dainty yellow threads as he jotted furiously in his notebook. It was, undoubtedly, curiosity. The yellow stubbornly remained.

"Stop," he sighed as he sank into a soft, velvety chair, positioning himself in a way so that his long legs dangled over the arm. "There is no one special in my life. You know that."

Unfortunately, the yellow continued to probe.

"Really, Mother. No one."

He could almost hear her next words accompany the blue of sadness. *Because you don't let anyone in.* They'd had this conversation before, and each time, he tried to sidestep the topic.

"I can't let anyone in," he said, now feeling a little foolish for seemingly talking to himself. "I have too much to do and not enough time to do it."

Then slow down.

He didn't dare believe the shade slightly darker than sadness was pity. All his life, he always concentrated on his next project or what more he might learn.

"I can't." He sighed and leaned his head back to stare at the ceiling rather than her emotions. "Now of all times is not the time to entertain your wishes for me. Moving on." Rubbing the fatigue from his eyes, he sat up straight in the chair and leaned his elbows on his knees, staring intently at his mother's still form. "I am going to figure out who did this to you."

Black as rich as coals slithered out of her mouth as if it didn't have any other place to escape. Fear.

"I have already discerned this is someone you know. Someone who knew I would be gone. Was it anyone in this household, including servants?" Nothing. No emotion at all. "Was it a friend?" Still nothing. "Someone in my circle?"

Tendrils of black fear gushed out of her mouth.

"Now we are getting somewhere." He tapped his quill against his notebook as he stared intently at her. "Someone powerful and dangerous." He began listing the ten Lords. Half of them incited fear. But then, all too suddenly, her emotions stopped.

"Mother!" he gasped as he shot out of his chair and straight to her side. He checked for breathing and a pulse, finding both weak. But she was still alive. He must have exhausted her with his probing questions.

He called for a servant to watch over her as he passed the rest of the night in fitful slumber, and only when the sounds of a rousing household reached him did he wake. He needed to see Johanna immediately.

One foot out the bedroom door, he froze when he realized something equally perplexing, horrifying, and flustering.

Pink.

The only emotion he hadn't been able to decipher from Johanna the previous day was pink. It was somewhere in between embarrassment, timidity, and love.

Infatuation.

"Oh no," he breathed, continuing down the hallway and descending the staircase. Johanna was infatuated *with him*. This changed everything. And perhaps not in a good way.

Shadows reached for him with every step, and he allowed them to grab him and pull him into their embrace for a quick moment before he found himself shadewalking from the staircase to the parlor where his cousins enjoyed a light breakfast.

The moment he entered, he received several emotions ranging from surprise to hope to…infatuation. He couldn't look Johanna in the eye without witnessing the pink tendrils of emotion escaping her.

He cleared his throat and pretended to adjust his cuffs. "Johanna. I know you've been handling correspondence in my mother's absence. Have we received any social calls lately? Invitations?"

All at once, silverware clattered to porcelain plates, followed by surprised, blank stares.

"You rarely receive visitors," Laureen pointed out. "Or accept invitations."

"Then it's time to remedy that."

Johanna jumped up, disappeared from the room, and moments later returned with a stack of paper and envelopes. She said, "A couple of social calls. A dinner invitation. I didn't open this one. I assumed it might be an application for Darkest Star."

Before she finished the list, he snatched the envelope out of her hands and ripped it open in eager anticipation. He scanned the paper. *Lyyli Ives. Age twenty-three. Human.* When he flipped the paper over, his blood curdled. Scrawled across the entire page in large, desperate handwriting were two words—HELP ME.

His eyebrows furrowed in puzzlement as he folded the paper and tucked it into the inner pocket of his vest. What could a human possibly be in desperate need of help for? He would look into her application later. Right now, two other people desperately needed his help.

"And a masquerade," Johanna finished. "Lord Auer is hosting the ball tomorrow at midnight."

His chest squeezed with hope, and for a moment, he wondered if he'd see the emotion reflected in a mirror. "Yes to the ball." Both Mia and Laureen jumped up and down and squealed, all while Johanna smiled calmly. "Allow me to rephrase that. Only I will go. And Johanna will accompany me." He regretted the words immediately. Now that he knew how she felt about him, it wasn't a good idea to go anywhere with her alone. But he needed her help to pull this off, and he didn't dare take either of the other girls. They would ruin this.

"Why don't we get to go?" Mia whined.

Laureen tugged on his sleeve, her chin trembling with faux sadness. To accompany the motion, a tendril of turquoise mixed with red leaked from her essence. Disappointment and hatred. Fine. She could hate him. He didn't particularly care.

"Johanna gets to do everything," Laureen complained. An envious green burned bright above her head.

"That's because Johanna doesn't whine every time she doesn't get her way. I'm trying to save your sister. You will only interfere."

"But Killian…"

"Enough!" he snapped. He pinched the bridge of his nose to ward off the growing ache of fatigue. "After we save Charlotte and I open my school, I don't care how many balls you go to. This will not be one of them."

Mia stomped her foot and stormed away. Laureen dropped into a chair facing away from him, sulking as she stared out the window. They were both acting like children. To her credit, Mia was only fifteen, but Laureen was seventeen. Charlotte was nineteen, while Johanna was twenty-one. He was eight years older than her at age twenty-nine, but sometimes it felt like decades separated them.

Turning to face Johanna, his gut churned uncomfortably at the sight of pink, red-orange, orange, and yellow. Infatuation. Confidence. Excitement. Happiness. "Go pack. We'll leave as soon as possible to arrive on time."

"How long will we stay?"

His gaze drifted in the direction of his mother's room. "As long as it takes."

K illian spent the entire day's carriage ride sleeping, pretending to sleep, and being wrapped up in a book about herbal remedies. He tried very hard not to speak to Johanna, but unfortunately, when he lifted his head to glance outside at the darkening skies, she spoke up as if waiting for an opportunity to converse.

"I've been thinking…" she started with a playful expression. "You should marry a Sun Fae."

He gave her a scathing look. "Never. I *never* want to see daylight again. There's a reason marriages between Shadow Fae and Sun Fae are extremely rare."

Sun Fae drew strength from the sunlight, while Shadow Fae drew strength from the moonlight. The two of them weren't compatible. They were like opposite sides of a coin, and they preferred to remain that way.

Propping his foot up on the bench across from him so one knee remained slightly bent to hide his activity, he pulled out Miss Ives' application and opened it.

"You are plenty old enough to marry now," he said slowly, cautiously. "Why don't you search for a husband during this masquerade? That way, we'll have more of a reason to be there."

As hard as he might, he couldn't ignore the streams of color escaping her from the adjacent corner of the carriage. Each emotion came and went too quickly for him to grasp. However, she maintained a cool facade.

"Unlike you, I would love to marry. Though, I'm curious. What would it take for you to change your mind?"

The hope leaking from her felt like vines choking him around the neck, squeezing tighter and tighter until he struggled to breathe. Still, he shrugged one shoulder and released a burning breath. He didn't dare answer. No reason to give her any hope at all.

As the stars glimmered in the skies above, his eyesight thrived in the growing shadows of the carriage. He studied the application with renewed interest. Lyyli lived in Frisia, one of the human kingdoms, in a small farming town. Very little else was written on the application. None of her interests, reasons for enrolling in the school, or what classes she would most like to take. No magical capabilities. No background in magic or future career interests in magic. She was the plainest candidate he'd had thus far, and he'd turned other candidates away for less.

But...

Careful to avoid drawing attention to his movements, he flipped the paper and read the words HELP ME over and over again. The ink had dripped before drying, and small spatters lay across the page.

How perplexing. Who was this woman, anyway?

Equally strange was the way the ink dripped. Either she was sloppy with handwriting, or…

His eyebrows furrowed as he brought the paper closer to his face. The ink might not be ink at all. Perhaps it was paint.

He folded the paper so only a corner showed with the ink, and then he presented it to Johanna. "What color is this?"

She narrowed her eyes at him as if she thought he was mocking her before lowering her gaze to the paper. She gasped. "Is that blood?"

Blood.

His stomach churned with queasiness as he added the piece of information to the growing perplexity of a puzzle that was this application. This woman, Lyyli, wasn't just an average human applicant.

Then what was she?

"I'm trying to figure that out," he answered quietly. Thankfully, Johanna didn't get a chance to reply when the carriage hit a bump just outside Lord Auer's property. He gazed out the window at the shimmering magic barrier surrounding the fortress-like estate.

"What is that?" Johanna whispered, her eyes wide right as they passed through the barrier. Nothing happened, except the magic trickled through him like the faintest shock.

"It's a magical wall meant to give the caster information about who passes through. It's a very useful talent of Lady Auer's, although irritating."

"Why irritating?"

"Because it makes getting close to her husband difficult. She will always know who enters and exits the estate. It's useful and expected for parties or large gatherings, though off-putting to those with whom he is trying to form an alliance. They trust no one."

"Neither do you."

"True." He grinned as he continued to watch as the fortress grew larger and larger with each passing moment. "Speaking of, put this on." He draped a bracelet made of onyx around her wrist and clasped it. "No one will be able to enchant you, and if they try, you will know it. Never take it off while we're here."

She reached across the carriage and touched his knee. "What's my role here?"

Trying not to grimace, he shifted in his seat so her hand dropped from him. He couldn't marry his cousin. Sure, she was pretty and tolerable and respected his dreams, but it wasn't enough. He doubted he would find anyone who would be enough.

"Johanna," he said seriously, meeting her eye as he tied on what used to be a silver and black mask that covered half of one side of his face and the opposite eyebrow. It was now black and light gray, lacking all color. "What I'm going to do here is dangerous. I may make enemies, and if I'm caught, I'm sure I'll be subjected to something far worse. You will be my partner when I need you and my alibi when I'm gone. Listen to conversations and glean what you can. We are trying to catch a would-be killer, who I assume is both dangerous and powerful. You can still back out and return home with the carriage. I can go in alone."

"No." Dark tendrils of hair cascaded over her shoulder as she shook her head. "My aunt and Charlotte are important to me. I won't allow them to die. But I would like you to be transparent with me. What do you know?"

She tied on her own mask, a slim metal constructed of who knew what colors and feathers sprouting on one side of her face.

"I cannot tell you. If you are caught by a potential enemy, you are safer not knowing what I do."

Or at least what little he *did* know.

Although she squirmed in her seat, she didn't argue.

The carriage pulled up in front of the fortress, joining a dozen other teams of shadow horses and carriages. When their carriage stilled, the door opened, and Killian stepped out first. He extended a hand to Johanna and helped her out before tucking her hand beneath his arm. People stared as they passed and whispered behind feathered fans the color of black and a few different shades of gray. Surprise and curiosity greeted him. Everyone below his station curtsied or bowed.

"Why are they whispering?" Johanna asked quietly.

"Because." He adjusted his mask, cursing the fact that he couldn't see color. He missed it like someone might miss a limb. "No one expected to see me here. They are now expecting I will stir up trouble."

"Will you?"

"Of course, my dear." A wicked smile grew across his face as he glanced sideways at her. "I am not some weak Lord who will run away with his tail between his legs. I plan to remind them why many are wary of me."

She gripped his arm tighter as they climbed the steps leading to the entrance. "How? Will you hurt anyone?"

Hopefully not.

With his opposite hand, he tapped his temple. "Knowledge of the mind is a thing to fear itself. I can confidently say I know more about dark magic than anyone in this fortress. People don't like that."

"They consider you a weapon."

He kept his eyes forward, though he watched his surroundings carefully. "A dangerous one."

The knowledge he harbored in his mind made him a dangerous man to cross. Whoever enchanted his mother and cousin must be someone confident they could get away with it.

Finally, they entered the fortress. Gray stone walls were lined with torches and old furniture. A servant guided them down a long hallway with a dark gray carpet stretching from one end to the other before they stepped into a spacious ballroom. Three large chandeliers hung from a high ceiling. Thick, lavish drapes hung from floor-to-ceiling windows. An assortment of food and drink decorated long, rectangular tables. Shadow Fae from all across the kingdom filled the ballroom. From the forests of Adderwall were Shadow Fae with antlers on top of their heads, many decorated in a beautiful assortment of ornaments. From Sigmar were the horned fae with tails as sharp as swords. Aside from the Shadow Fae shapeshifters, everyone else looked like him—

pointed ears and narrow-slitted pupils. Though in the low light of the room, his pupils might look more like a human's when they were larger.

He nodded to Lord Jannick across the room, who acknowledged him with a slight dip of his head. Next to him stood Lady Feist. She was one of the ten Lords, though the only lady Lord, as her daughter could not inherit the title, and her grandson was still too young to become a Lord at age three.

He casually steered Johanna to the front of the room to greet their host. Lord Auer stood next to his wife, greeting guests. The stout man's laughter shook his belly and emanated through the room.

The swish of skirts drew his attention to the young lady who stood to Lord Auer's right. His gaze traveled up a full skirt made of slim feathers in a variety of different shades, a bodice of intricate beadwork, and sheer sleeves at the shoulders. Long hair cascaded over one shoulder, leading up to a slender neck, and her face was covered by a harp-shaped mask that reminded him of a cage. The moment their eyes met, it was as if he tumbled over the edge of a cliff, but instead of crashing, he kept falling and falling and falling.

A thousand butterflies crawled through his stomach. His heart squeezed inside his chest. The young woman was beautiful. And as he approached, she never took her eyes off him. Ribbons of pink and yellow escaped her, giving away her curiosity and interest in him. But all too quickly, the ribbons turned blue and black. Sadness and fear.

Tearing his gaze away from her, he kissed Lady Auer's knuckles and gripped Lord Auer's hand in greeting.

"What are you doing here?" Lord Auer asked, and even without his twitching eye, the green-yellow colors he gave off indicated his blatant irritation.

Killian grinned, amused by the man's reaction. "Well, I was invited. No?"

"O-o-of course," the man stuttered, now shifting from one foot to the other. "Only, I heard about your mother. My deepest condolences. I assumed you would not make it." Nervousness.

"Oh, I wouldn't miss this magnificent party. Though, I hate to intrude on your hospitality…"

"No, no. Of course not. Stay as long as necessary." Anger.

Interesting. The man didn't want him here. Why?

He turned to face the beautiful woman, and his stomach flipped again when he met her eye. Her lips formed a sweet shape, like the pinkest rose in bloom on a summer evening. "Will you not introduce me to your companion?"

"Ah. My prized jewel for the night. Lord Killian Graves, allow me to introduce you to my Mute Songbird."

The woman's eyes widened behind her harp mask at the mention of his name. The light purple of surprise accompanied the action.

He took her hand and slowly brought it to his lips, never once taking his eyes off her. She was gorgeous, even without colors to show him what she truly looked like. "You are lovely."

She signed, "Thank you," with her opposite hand, and he suddenly felt foolish when he realized she might actually be mute. Or deaf. Out of all the subjects he'd studied, sign language was not one of them. He knew only a few of the basics.

"Can you not speak?"

Lord Auer answered for her. "She cannot speak, but she has the loveliest singing voice. You'll hear it soon enough." And just like that, the man turned to greet the next family in line.

As soon as Lord Auer's attention left them, the Mute Songbird gripped Killian's hand tighter, her eyes wide while a deep red emotion cascaded out of her. Desperation. She signed something into his hand with her open palm beneath one hand, one thumb pointed up.

She repeated it again, her eyes begging for him to understand.

"I'm sorry," he murmured with a frown. "I don't know what you're saying." And he had no way to learn. Not here and not now, at least.

His eyebrows furrowed in puzzlement. If she could sing, how could she not speak? Was it an enchantment? A curse? Something else entirely?

The deep red desperation gushed out of her as she signed something else, but her hands dropped quickly when Lord Auer glanced their way. The red transitioned into the navy blue of despair as she lowered her gaze to the floor.

"It was lovely to meet you," he said quickly as he dipped his head and stepped back, though he made sure to enunciate in case she was deaf and needed to read his lips. "I look forward to hearing you sing."

Once again, he threaded his arm through Johanna's and led her away, but he swore he felt the Mute Songbird's gaze on his back in his retreat.

And he did his best to ignore it. Yes, she was a beautiful woman. But he was not here to dance the night away in a pair of slender arms nor engage in a tryst. There was no time for that.

"Lord Auer is acting strange," Johanna murmured close to his ear. "He's not happy to see us."

"No, he's not. The question is, why?"

They made their way to the refreshment table, and just when Johanna picked up a chocolate truffle, he smacked it out of her hands. She stared at him incredulously.

"Sprite dust," he explained as he pointed to another on the table and the sheen coating the top chocolate layer. "If you want to keep your wits about you, don't eat it."

"Then what *can* I eat?"

He scanned the vast selection and found one delicacy layered with sponge coral, which brought out the happiest emotions in a person. Ember weed topped another treat, which imitated fire in the mouth and caused actual flames to shoot out someone's nose. A third refreshment was covered in mersalt, which turned someone's skin either green, blue, or pink for a short amount of time.

"Here," he said as he picked up an unembellished tart. "This seems safe."

But the moment she took a bite, antlers sprouted out the top of her head. He clapped his hands over his mouth at her shock, and despite reaching for self-control, a snort managed to escape him. "If you eat one, you might as well eat them all at this point."

"Oh dear," she gasped as she touched the antlers, which only made him laugh harder at the irony. "How long does this last?"

"Probably only a few minutes." Others around him blew fire from their nostrils or walked about with tinted skin like the Mer Fae. He'd met a few merfolk in his lifetime, but they were tricky to spot. When on land, they walked about on human legs. When in the sea, they swam with a tail and fins.

He lifted two crystal flutes of bubbly liquid, took a quick sniff of the tart apple scent, and sipped the drink. Bubbles popped and fizzed down his throat, but otherwise, no other aftereffects made an appearance.

"Lord Graves, it's good to see you here," someone said, and he turned to face the very man that inspired scarlet emotions from his mother.

"Good evening, Lord Blom." Killian lifted his goblet to his mouth to hide the knowing smirk attempting to grow across his face. "The party is a bit dreary without my mother here. Wouldn't you agree?"

The man cleared his throat and itched his nose right above his bearded lip, all while streams of passion, embarrassment, and fluster escaped him. "Indeed. How is she faring? I am told visitors are not allowed to see her."

Unfortunately, his smirk grew too large to hide behind his flute. "If she was awake, I'm sure she would make an exception for *you*. You are a dear friend of hers, no?"

Lord Blom cleared his throat again, this time itching the bristles on his cheek. "Of course. Do you know what happened? Was she really enchanted?"

Genuine concern rippled out of the man, and Killian relaxed. Lord Blom was not responsible for this. "Yes. Though, I've heard true love's kiss sometimes works against enchantments. Perhaps you should give it a try."

He left the man gawking after him as he began to cross the expansive ballroom, weaving in and out of the crowd and toward another influential family. However, a small hand grabbed his and pulled him into the center of the room in the empty space below Lord Auer and the dais he stood on. The hand belonged to the Lord's youngest daughter, only about nine years old.

Involuntarily, his gaze flitted to the Mute Songbird, only to find her watching him already. Those eyes… They were captivating. And that mouth…

He forced his attention away.

"Will you show me a magic trick?" little Aiyasha asked, and a sudden excitement swept through the room as a dozen other children laughed and ran in his direction, forming a semi-circle around him. It seemed the masquerade wasn't just for adults after all.

A laugh escaped him as he tugged on one of her braids. "Fine. But only one. You stand here. And you, stand here. Hold your arms out. Yes, just like that."

He lined them up, each with their hands outstretched so their shadows connected one with another. He did his best to ignore their growing audience, each with emotions ranging from curiosity to wariness to excitement.

"Are you ready?" he asked the children, and they gave him a collective nod. "Are you sure?"

"We're sure!" they shouted, followed by giggling and restless arms.

With a grin growing across his face, he made a show of holding his breath until his cheeks bulged, plugged his nose, and then he jumped straight into Aiyasha's shadow.

And disappeared as if he'd jumped into a pond.

He shadewalked quickly from one shadow to the next and reappeared at the end of the line as if he popped straight out of the ground. The children shouted excitedly and clapped with joy, followed by more clapping from their still-growing audience.

Killian bowed, feeling a bit silly when he'd accomplished such an easy feat. But when he attempted to back away, the people around him began clapping in unison and chanting, "One more. One more. One more."

With a grimace, he glanced back at Lord Auer, who urged him to continue with a wave of his hand. By now, the entire ballroom had grown quiet, and now all eyes rested on him. Did Lord Auer not provide any means of entertainment other than the musicians? He was a teacher, not a performer.

But perhaps, tonight, he could be both.

The idea gave him a bit of a thrill. He loved teaching, even the impromptu kind.

"I was not expecting to put on a show tonight," he said, and the floor rumbled with laughter. He couldn't help his own smile from appearing. "But I suppose I must oblige."

Dozens upon dozens of people watched him behind masks and fans and feathers. Slowly, he sauntered before his audience as he spoke, his arms folded behind his back. "Magic is all about balance. To take, you must give. And vice versa. It is a never-ending cycle of equilibrium."

"We want magic, not a lecture!" someone in the audience shouted. More laughter rumbled through the room.

He shook his head and chuckled. "If you ask a teacher for a performance, you get a lecture to go with it. I need a volunteer."

Several people raised their hands. He turned in a full circle to select his participant when his gaze once again fell on the Mute Songbird. Although she didn't volunteer for the job, he held out a hand toward her. She inhaled sharply, followed by light purple streams of surprise. And then the sickly yellow of anxiety. After she glanced at Lord Auer, he nodded his permission. She lifted her skirts and stepped carefully down the steps of the dais. When she slid her hand into his, unexpected butterflies gathered in his stomach, begging for release.

With her at his side, he turned to face his audience again. Using his finger, he drew a line from his breast to his navel. "Every person is born with a well full of magical potential. Some are born with the well filled. Others must learn to fill it themselves. A good amount more will never learn to even locate their well.

"There are two types of magic—what you are born with and the magic you learn. Just think of all that untapped potential! Magic is in the very air, in the very fibers of the earth itself. And when you tap into it, it becomes a part of you."

He swallowed as he held up a hand, placing his middle finger and thumb together while reaching inside his own deep well of magic. All his planning and sacrifices in the last week had all led up to this point. He needed to shadewalk faster than he'd ever shadewalked before.

He snapped his fingers.

And every light in the ballroom snuffed out.

The audience cried in surprise as the room became pitch black. Streams of emotions escaped them from surprise to fear to amusement to worry. But he ignored them all as he melted into the shadows and shadewalked the entire perimeter of the room, weaving in and out of shadows in a matter of seconds. Attuned to his magic, he recognized a few harmless charms worn by people in the audience, a couple of protection spells. But the most important of everything he found was the three people wearing enchanted items. Lord Blom. Lady Feist. And the Mute Songbird.

Around her neck was a necklace with large, sparkling gems in a few different shades of gray.

He had no idea what any of these items did, but their bearers made it on his list of possible suspects of whoever had hurt his mother.

Just as quickly as he left, he returned to his spot beside the Songbird. In the darkness, no one had noticed his few seconds of absence.

Magic flowed through his arm from the light he'd taken from the room. It pooled in his upturned hand, glowing like starlight. "Ooohs" and "Ahhhs" rumbled through the audience.

"Miss Songbird, will you do me the honor of blowing on my palm?" Each word from his mouth he enunciated, and he made sure light illuminated his face—most importantly, his lips. He still couldn't tell if she was mute or deaf.

Streams of color escaped the woman, emotions ranging from fluster to excitement to worry. She leaned closer, and the moment she blew a long breath onto his hand, butterflies escaped his palm like bubbles on the wind.

A surge of delicate wings imitating starlight shot out from him and fluttered about the room. His audience laughed gleefully as the butterflies flew around them. One of them landed on the Songbird's mask, slowly flapping its wings. A large smile grew across her face, and another wave of butterflies fluttered in his stomach rather than in the air around them.

He forced himself to tear his gaze away when the audience clapped enthusiastically.

"Thank you. Thank you." He bowed several times and called out over the excited crowd. "If you are interested or know someone interested in learning more about magic, don't hesitate to apply to the Darkest Star Arcane."

All at once, the light returned to the room, and the butterflies disappeared.

Lord Auer clapped slowly and stepped down from the dais. Although they were both Lords, Killian stepped off to the side. Auer was the host, after all.

"Your understanding of magic never ceases to amaze me, Lord Graves."

Killian nodded in acknowledgement, though he carefully watched as ribbons of fear fluttered above his head. Fear and anger. And a little bit of yellow-green annoyance.

Continuing, the man gestured to Lady Songbird. "May I introduce to you all tonight's lovely guest, the lady with the most beautiful voice, the Mute Songbird."

A polite round of clapping filled the room as the lights dimmed, and sunshine rained from the ceiling to shower Lady Songbird in specks of light. He glanced to his side to find a Sun Fae working his magic. Slow and steady.

But when he turned his attention back to her, dread sank to the bottom of his stomach. The woman wasn't just anxious to be standing in front of a crowd. She was downright terrified. Her emotion was the blackest black he'd ever witnessed—a color he'd never seen before in his life.

The musicians struck up a slow tune, rich and heavy with feeling. And when Lady Songbird opened her mouth to sing, his lips parted in surprise. The most beautiful melody escaped her mouth, a song filled with hope and longing. Her voice transfixed him, gluing him to the spot as he gazed at her in awe. There were many sounds he adored—midnight rainstorms, wind rustling through tall grass, chimes tinkling in the breeze. But none of them held a flame to the beauty of her voice. Of her song.

He hissed when his onyx ring burned his finger. His eyes widened as he looked from the Songbird to those around him. Yellow streams of happy emotion escaped each person, not even a flicker of another emotion to accompany it.

Everyone in the room was being enchanted.

By the Mute Songbird's voice.

Across the room, Johanna met his gaze with wide, fearful eyes. She didn't seem to understand what was going on, but she likely understood to some degree when her bracelet must be burning her the way his ring did.

He didn't hesitate.

He hurried across the room, grabbed Johanna by the elbow, and tugged her into the hallway. He didn't stop leading her away from the ballroom until they escaped the sound of the woman's magical voice entirely.

They stopped when they reached an indoor fountain in a circular room with high ceilings made of glass. He sat down on the edge of the fountain and rubbed the enchantment from his eyes.

"I've never seen anything like that," he murmured as he twisted the ring on his finger and studied the way the onyx glowed like waning embers. "Stay away from her, Johanna. She's powerful. And dangerous."

Johanna's hands trembled as she held them to her heart. "What will you do?"

"I don't know yet. I wasn't expecting this."

"Expecting what?"

He ran his hands over his face again, grateful for the way the fountain drowned out most other sounds, including the addictive voice. "I don't *know*. Something isn't right here. I need to find out what. Johanna..." Hesitation left him as he squeezed her hand. "You need to leave. One misstep, and you might not be the same again."

"And what about you? I can't leave you here on your own. I won't go."

"Cousin, you're being..." Foolish? Stubborn? Infuriating? Brave? But as he looked her in the eye, at the resolution therein, he knew she wouldn't go unless he dragged her into a carriage himself. "Fine. But go to your room. Stay there all night and don't leave."

"What will you do?"

"The same."

He released a long breath and gazed at the glass ceiling overhead. A full moon shone brightly through the glass, glinting off the fountain of steady water. At the edges of the room, vines and flowers climbed trellises that reached for the night sky. Everything was black, white, and gray. Would he ever get used to this curse?

After escorting Johanna to her temporary chambers in the fortress, he found his own. As a Lord, he was given one of the larger chambers. A bed lay on one side of the room and an oversized armoire on the other. His favorite piece of furniture was a desk that took up a good portion of the wall nearest the window.

It was a desk he would undoubtedly use during his stay here.

Just outside his door, the sound of cloth ripping accompanied a loud *bang* against the other side of the door moments before a piece of paper slipped underneath.

He strode toward the paper and picked it up, his heart dropping to his toes as he unfolded it.

HELP ME.

Sure enough, as he opened the door a crack to peer into the hallway, he caught a glimpse of a feathery skirt disappearing around the corner, trailed by two armored guards.

As quietly as possible, he closed the door and pulled out the application he'd received only yesterday. The handwriting matched. Lyyli Ives was the Mute Songbird.

He wasn't sure whether to feel concerned, afraid, or triumphant. A dangerous weapon had just been laid into his hands, and he didn't know whether it could help him or hurt him.

But one thing he knew for sure... His plainest candidate for one of his students at Darkest Star had just become his most interesting.

ears trailed down Lyyli's face as she stared blankly at her closed bedroom door from where she sat on the bed. Her body, now in her day gown, which was really a nightgown in the human world, sagged wearily against the wall as if nearly all of her energy had been drained from her song. No one had died, and she supposed she had Lord Auer's necklace to thank for it. But she felt empty. Hopeless.

Agonizingly sad.

She missed her family in the month she'd been a prisoner here. She mourned for the hopelessness of her future. She dreaded what Lord Auer might force her to do next.

She shifted on the bed, and with the movement, the chains binding her wrists rattled against the floor. At least the chains were long enough to allow her to move somewhat freely throughout the room.

"You put on quite the show tonight," a voice said from the corner.

Her hands flew to her throat to keep herself from screeching in fright. Her gaze froze on the figure bathed in shadows. In the darkness of near dawn, firelight crackled across the room and illuminated the man's face.

Like the first time she'd laid eyes on Lord Graves, her stomach took a tumble down a staircase, and her heart quickly followed. He was achingly handsome. Bright blue eyes. Tousled blond hair. High cheekbones. Pointed ears. Inquisitive mouth. And he was tall. Much taller than her. Although she'd initially found Shadow Fae pupils disconcerting, they didn't bother her anymore when she was constantly surrounded by similar people.

"Don't sneak up on me. Ever," she signed. But he only stared at her in confusion. His bottom lip worked its way between his teeth as if he were trying to learn the language just by watching her.

And she didn't miss the way he kept one foot in the shadows, ready to escape with whatever power he had used in front of the children at the masquerade. Smart man.

Slowly, he pulled out the piece of paper she had slid beneath his bedroom door earlier. She'd feigned tripping, ripping her dress in the process. And she hadn't been entirely sure if it was the right door.

He flipped it over to show the two words scrawled across the page. "This is concerning to me, especially now that I find you in chains. Even more concerning when I've seen your handwriting before." He pulled out another paper and opened it to reveal her application for Darkest Star Arcane. It hadn't been easy to slip it in the post without Lord Auer's knowledge. "Is this your blood?"

She nodded, mimicking writing and then shaking her head.

"You had nothing else to write with," he interpreted with a thoughtful expression. "Why did you write to *me?*"

A huff of frustration escaped her. Surely, he'd never had to deal with someone who, in trying to speak to him, would end up killing him instead.

Spreading her fingers, she tapped her thumb against her forehead.

"Ah." He grinned. "I know that one. Father. Your father asked you to write to me?"

A wave of sadness and hurt washed through her. She turned her gaze to the fire in the hearth.

Lord Graves took one hesitant step out of the shadows and then another. To her surprise, he placed a small notebook, an inkwell, and a quill into her lap. She didn't hesitate as she began writing, grateful for a way to communicate quickly to him her predicament.

My adoptive father sent me away. Sent me to you. I— She paused, her emotions wavering before continuing. *I almost killed my adoptive sister. He thought you could help me with...with this.*

He picked up the chair beside the desk and placed it in front of the bed, sitting only a couple feet away. His eyes held her captive. No one had ever given her such intense focus before.

Fluster rattled her hand for a mere moment before she forced it to remain steady.

You are young, she wrote. *I expected someone...much older.*

A devastating grin spread across his face. Then, all too suddenly, the night's chill was swept away by the heat crawling beneath her skin.

"I'm older than you, to be sure. You're closer to Johanna's age."

Disappointment crashed her flailing heart to the compacted earth as she remembered the beautiful woman draped on his arm earlier tonight. *Your wife is beautiful. How long have you been married?*

His eyebrows furrowed as he stared at her words. "Huh?" Finally, his head snapped up, and he once again met her gaze. His face turned a shade paler. "You think Johanna is my wife? No, no, no. She's my cousin. Well, that's not to say cousins don't marry in Katalle. But no. We're not married. I'm not married at all, actually."

He ran a hand down his face and took a deep breath. She couldn't help as her lips twitched in amusement at his fluster.

"Let's move on. I don't want to get caught in here." He leaned his elbows on his knees and studied her again. "Tell me about your magic. And these chains. Tell me why you need help."

Her fingers moved furiously as the quill scratched across the paper. She told him about how her voice killed people. She told him about how she had been on her way to seek him out when Lord Auer had captured her. She told him about how the necklace she wore tonight muted her power to only influence people's emotions rather than kill them.

"Did I hurt you?" she signed, worry knotted in her stomach. But when he didn't respond immediately, she wrote the question on the paper.

Shaking his head, he replied, "You can't easily hurt someone who was already prepared for battle."

His relaxed posture unnerved her. Only her father had ever been relaxed in her presence. *Aren't you scared of me?*

"I admit I'm a little nervous, knowing what you can do. But I signed up for this. To teach and guide those who need my help." He leaned back in the chair and studied her again. She wondered what he saw. What wasn't he saying?

You know a lot about magic, she wrote, her chains rattling as she moved. *Take away my voice for good so I can't hurt anyone else.*

He swallowed as he stared at the words for a beat too long. "For good? You never want to speak again?"

She shook her head. *I'm too dangerous. I have killed people.*

"How many? On purpose?"

Accident. Her chin trembled, tears brimming in her eyes as she wrote the next part. *I don't want to say how many. Too many.*

Strangers. Friends. Neighbors. A boy she'd loved. No matter how careful she was, she could never manage to be careful enough.

"Lyyli, this is important for me to know. Were you born with this ability or cursed?"

Born. But I can't know for sure. I was left on my adoptive parents' doorstep when I was three years old. They took me in.

"And they've never heard your voice?"

I've been careful. But I like to think someone protected them from me. Just in case.

Slowly, he reached out to her but hesitated, his fingers inches from her chin. "May I touch you? I have a good idea of what I'm looking for, but I need to make sure."

After several loud, flustered heartbeats, she nodded.

His gentle hands prodded her jaw, then moved lower to her neck. Heat blossomed through her as if his fingers created fire rather than shadow and starlight. Her entire body flushed from her head to her toes. For a moment, his fingers trembled, but he quickly shut his eyes and continued probing her neck.

His eyelids only opened halfway as he took her arm and turned it one way and then the other way. And when he opened his eyes all the way, he released a shuddering breath as his gaze traveled to the space just above her head.

Another flash of heat washed through her as he cradled her face in his hands and peered closer, now studying her eyes. Her heart fluttered so fast that she would never be able to count the beats even if she tried.

He touched the curve of her ears last, leaning close enough for her to feel his breath on her skin.

When he dropped his hands and leaned away, she immediately noticed the lack of heat. Then, he pointed to the notebook, indicating for her to write.

"Your Darkest Star application says you are a human."

It was a statement, not a question. Her puzzled brows furrowed together. *I am.*

Again, he stared at her as if trying to solve a particularly confounding riddle. "Humans are capable of performing spells, incantations, and more, but they are never born with magic. Ever. You are not a human."

Confusion dragged her heart through the mud. She blinked several times, but the seriousness of his expression never diminished. Of course, she was a human. She looked like a human. Ate like a human. Dressed like a human. Lived with humans.

I must have been cursed then, she wrote. It was the only other explanation.

But still, he shook his head. "Did you know the Ocean Fae like to pierce their body with jewelry? At some point, you had piercings all along your ear. Most have long since closed up. I would inspect more of you just to be certain, but, well..." He grinned. "That would be highly inappropriate."

She blushed to the roots of her hair.

Lord Graves grimaced and cleared his throat as if he'd surprised himself by his own comment. "Sorry. What I mean is...my best guess is you descend from merfolk. Can you breathe underwater?"

She lifted her hands to protest but dropped them slowly and shrugged. She signed, "I can't swim."

This time, he seemed to understand her meaning. "But you've been in the water. What happens when you bathe?"

Her last blush still hadn't dispersed, but now another layered on top of it. *Nothing happens.*

"Nothing at all? You don't grow fins? Your skin doesn't change color?"

No and no.

"Huh." He sat back in his chair, the lip between his teeth doing more puzzling. He tapped his fingers against his leg for several moments before he shot out of his chair and crossed the room in a couple of strides. A few seconds later, he returned with the basin of water sitting on the table near the door.

Gingerly, he picked up her hand and placed it in the water. When nothing happened, he scooped water and brushed it along her arm. Still nothing.

She jumped when he snapped his fingers. "Saltwater. You are not a freshwater fae. I will return in a few minutes."

She blinked, and then he was gone as if he'd never been there in the first place. A wave of relief washed over her as she clutched his notebook to her chest. For an entire month, she'd felt afraid and alone. Lord Graves was an ally. One she knew she could trust. She'd heard about his mother and cousin, about the enchantment bringing them closer and closer to their deaths. Despite having to worry about his own problems, he was worried about *hers.*

Curiosity pricked her with its needle as she ran a finger over the leather binding of the notebook. The book was small enough to fit in a pocket or reticule. If he had it on hand tonight, did that mean he always kept it on his person?

The room remained empty and quiet aside from the crackling logs in the hearth. Not able to contain her curiosity any longer, she opened the notebook and flipped through the pages.

Her breath caught in surprise. The pages were filled with Lord Graves' elegant handwriting, his thoughts, feelings, and discoveries scrawled across each page—including the margins.

A smile curved her lips as she traced one of the passages with her finger. '*Note to self: NEVER inhale dried blottberries again. I sneezed my brains out for the entire night and then some.*'

Another passage read: '*Wild blouts may look cute, but I have discovered their set of fangs. NOT CUTE. RUN FOR THE HILLS.*'

An actual laugh escaped her, but then she clapped her hands over her mouth and glanced wildly around her. Thank the stars. Lord Graves was nowhere in sight.

She flipped the page, and her eyebrows furrowed as she scanned a list of colors. Each one shared a line with an emotion. How strange… Did emotions have colors? What kind of research was the archmage doing?

"All right," Lord Graves said. She jumped at the sound of his voice and hurriedly flipped to a blank page in the notebook. "I tried to recreate the thirty-five grams of salt to a liter of water ratio found in the ocean. The cook is going to wonder what happened to all of his salt."

He repositioned the chair so the firelight cast a longer shadow on the floor. He stood rooted to the shadow as if he expected this to go horribly wrong.

Lyyli took a deep breath and focused on keeping her mouth and throat shut. "I'm nervous," she signed.

The archmage's mouth puckered as he lifted his gaze to the space above her head again. What did he see? "It's fine to be nervous. You've lived your entire life as a human. I can't imagine it would be easy to find out you were something else entirely. Hypothetically speaking."

Yet, judging by the confident and all-too-excited look on his face, he was not expecting to be wrong.

A flush crawled through her body as he took her hand and gazed at her earnestly. "Are you ready?" he murmured the same words he'd spoken to the children but with a softer tone. She nodded. "Are you sure?"

She squeezed her eyes shut and swallowed. Her father had said Lord Graves might be able to help. Putting her faith and trust in him was another matter entirely. Still, she nodded again and slowly opened her eyes.

Never in her life had she stepped foot in the ocean, such was her fear of water. So when he placed her hand into the saltwater, she inhaled sharply when a tingling sensation rippled through her. Not unpleasant. But new. Different.

Her eyes widened, and her body became rigid as she watched her skin tone shift from ivory to the blue of a robin's egg. Silver-blue fins sprouted from her wrists to her forearms as if they had been hiding beneath her skin the entire time. Silver streaks cascaded through her copper hair like a shimmery waterfall. She touched her neck, only to find gills that hadn't been there a minute earlier.

Shock crashed down on her. Her heart accelerated. Her breathing came in rapid gasps.

Lord Graves took hold of her shoulders and forced her to look into his eyes. "Are you going to unhinge?" he asked with a cautioning tone. "Warn me now so I can shadewalk."

Closing her eyes, she took several deep breaths and somehow managed to shake her head. This was fine. Everything was fine.

But when she felt her arm fins brush against her leg, she opened her mouth as the shock tumbled over the side of her calm dam. Lord Graves shadewalked out of the room right as she released a muffled scream, which she attempted to bury into the crook of her arm.

She was…she was…a mermaid! Without a tail, at least. For now. How had this happened? How hadn't she known? She should have known. And now she felt like a fool. A crazed, shocked, fool of a mer.

After several minutes, Lord Graves returned with an air of caution, right as the effects of the ocean water began to fade, and her skin returned to its normal hue.

"Are you all right?" he asked. True concern lay within the depths of his eyes. He approached slowly as if she were a wild animal who might open her mouth and doom him to an untimely death.

"No," she signed before gesturing to the entirety of herself.

He lowered himself into the chair once again, and the way he placed his hands on her upper arms helped steady her emotions. A river of calm washed through her. She wasn't alone in this. He was here to help. She trusted him. He was the *only* person she could trust.

"Lyyli," he started to say but then pursed his lips. "By the way, I hope you will think of me as Killian when we are out of school boundaries and as the archmage at school."

Surprise rippled through her. Did this mean he planned to accept her into the Darkest Star Arcane? To help her with whatever this was? Whatever it meant?

He continued. "There are several types of mer. Freshwater. Deep-sea ocean. Tropical. Arctic. Open ocean. And…sirens."

Her eyes widened, and not able to take any further surprises tonight, she released a long breath and leaned back against the wall. She wrote in the notebook, *I am a siren?*

"Perhaps." He tapped his fingers against his lips. "Both water fae and land dwellers consider sirens a threat. They have been hunted for centuries. I thought they were extinct. But now I suspect otherwise."

She leaned more heavily against the wall as the information sank in. Killian—a pleasant shudder raced down her spine just from thinking his name—had been able to figure out what no other person had. And in a matter of minutes. Perhaps Lord Auer knew. But for someone as young as Killian to know so much?

He was smart. Smarter than she'd expected.

A door slammed in the antechamber, causing both of them to jump. In a matter of moments, Killian returned the chair to the desk, dumped the remainder of the saltwater out the window, and snatched back his notebook and quill.

Panic set in when the footsteps came closer and closer to her door. "Don't leave," she begged with her hands. "Please, don't leave."

He must have read the panic in her movements because he paused just before he stepped into the shadows. Keys rattled on the other side of the door.

Although he said nothing, he gave her a regretful look before he dropped into the shadows and didn't return.

The door swung open.

The dread in her heart dropped to the very pits of hell.

Lord Auer.

"Touch me, and I'll kill you," she said aloud, startled by the foreignness of her voice. She'd rarely heard it herself unless whispered in a secluded space.

Whatever enchanted her voice to kill those around her dissolved into his ring. The ruby glowed bright red before settling into the color of blood. Cold. Lifeless. Cruel.

Fortunately, he'd come alone to fetch her. She didn't want to accidentally kill an unsuspecting maid or servant.

Ignoring her threat, he strode across the room accompanied by several thumps of his cane with every step, unlocked her shackles, and replaced them with a rope tied around both wrists. She struggled against him, clawing and kicking and attempting to bite. But he was strong. Much stronger than her feeble attempts to escape.

The man tugged her along. She dug in her heels but only managed to scuff up her bare feet against the wood. Slivers stabbed through her feet. Tears of pain pricked her eyes, but she never stopped struggling.

Not again. Please, not again.

She opened her mouth to call for help but closed it just as quickly. No one could help her. They would sooner find themselves at the end of their own blades than rush to her aid.

"You stubborn chit," he growled as he tugged a little too hard when they reached the hallway. She lost her footing and tripped onto her hands and knees. Not even a moment of reprieve passed before he began dragging her through the empty corridor. Her chambers were located in a secluded wing just above the dungeons, and no one—neither maid nor guard—passed by more than once a day.

At the end of the hallway, Lord Auer threw open a door, the metal creaking open and slamming against a dark, cool stone wall.

And he began dragging her down the steps.

Each unforgiving step dug into her back and clawed at her clothing. Loose rocks tore through her legs, creating a trail of blood into the descending darkness. Pain shot through her body, and she found it increasingly difficult not to cry out or whimper. When she attempted to find her footing, more pain shot through her feet where the slivers dug into her skin.

She dared to speak in a whisper. "Please don't make me do this. You said it wouldn't happen for another week."

His face was barely visible in the darkness. As they passed beneath a missing brick in the wall that allowed moonlight into the narrow staircase, his yellow snake-like eyes glowed for a fraction of a second.

For a moment, she thought he wouldn't answer, but then he said, "I have no choice but to do it *now*. I had not anticipated Lord Graves' arrival. He always seems to know everything. I don't know how he knows so much, but the fact that he's here and not with his mother can't be a coincidence. We're doing this tonight. Before he starts meddling and poking around."

He frowned as if he'd said too much. People often did around her. When she couldn't speak outright, people wrongly assumed she couldn't communicate at all, or in some cases, that she couldn't hear them speak. They wrongly assumed their secrets were safe.

Lord Auer unlocked another door and threw it open. This time, he helped her to her feet. More tears of pain filled her eyes when stabbing agony roared through her soles. How could something as small as slivers cause so much pain?

She froze as she trained her gaze on the opposite side of the room. Firelight from a torch flickered across the stone walls, a rectangular stone altar with three daggers resting side by side, and…

Terror seized her as she spotted three people kneeling on the ground, hands tied behind their backs and sacks over their heads. She scrambled toward the exit, but before she reached the door, Lord Auer slammed it shut and locked all five of them inside.

"Siren song and self-sacrifice from the sun, moon, and ocean," he said, roughly placing his hands on her shoulders and spinning her to face the three masked people. One of them remained stoically still. Another swayed on his knees as if drunk. The last whimpered, her voice muffled by the sack over her head.

Lyyli's hands trembled when she realized what they were. Fae. Shadow, Sun, and Ocean.

Ocean. Like me.

Again, she spun around faster than he could catch her. She tugged on the door handle, and when it didn't budge, she pounded her fists against the thick metal. The echo reverberated through the room.

Lord Auer tugged her back and pinned her against the wall with a strong arm to her neck. Air struggled to enter through her crushed windpipe. She clawed at his arm, his hand, his face. But he only pressed tighter.

"Sing, pet," he growled, spittle hitting her face. When she still fought him, he bellowed inches away. "Sing!"

Her lungs burned. Darkness spun dizzily in her head. Still, she managed the slightest shake of her head.

He released a yell of anger and threw her to the ground. Air rushed back into her lungs, but when she hit her head against the solid stone, she involuntarily grunted in pain.

Eyes flashing wide, she scrambled back against the wall just as the three masked prisoners darted in unison toward the waiting daggers.

Silent tears fell down her cheeks as she squeezed her eyes shut and plugged her ears to block out the gruesome sound of blades stabbing flesh. Warm flecks spattered her face, her clothing, her feet, but she kept her eyes closed.

The prisoners remained quiet. Not a cry of pain, not a wail of agony, as they delighted in their own deaths.

She unplugged her ears, only for silence to greet her. She didn't dare open her eyes.

Heavy heartache pressed down on her until she struggled to breathe. Remorse and grief punched her in the gut, all while talons of self-hatred dug into her skull. She had done this. Her voice had killed these innocent people.

A shudder shook the stones below her feet as if a beast opened its jaws to yawn. But all too suddenly, the earth remained still.

"You may return to your room," Lord Auer said in a voice devoid of emotion as he unlocked the door. "A guard will be waiting at the top of the stairs to escort you to your chambers. A bath will be waiting. And don't stray anywhere else."

She numbly stood and scrambled up the rough steps on pained, slivered feet. She was a monster. A disgusting viper of a monster. If only the blades had been turned toward her instead. If only her voice disappeared forever. If only she had been born a regular human and not a siren, if that was truly what she was.

If only…

The fortress was quiet.

But not just the quiet following a long evening of drinking and dancing. It was a foreboding kind of quiet. Like the stillness of a battlefield after the last man fell. Like the eerie silence of the minutes after a violent snowstorm. Like the shock of an unmoving body after they took their last breath.

Killian opened the shutters in a secluded hallway and leaned on the windowsill. Streaks of gray colored the sky, the light slowly seeping from swaths of clouds and making way for the beginning of another night.

How much time had passed since he'd seen color? The frightening thing was he was getting used to it. Would he ever see color again? He'd gladly go without color for the rest of his life if he could save his family.

He frowned as he rubbed his arm where his sleeve concealed the black etchings. What did he know thus far? Lord

Auer didn't want him here. Lyyli had the ability to sway emotions. What else? How did it connect?

"Killian." Someone touched his arm. He jumped and spun around, only to find Johanna at his elbow. She wore a silk scarf around her head as if trying to conceal her identity. Plumes of pink and yellow escaped her at the sight of him. He *must* change that. Any marriage they would have would be comfortable, but not fulfilling. Could she not see it as he did? Perhaps if he put someone else in her path…

He ran a hand through his hair. He was solving three problems too many at the moment. Why did he feel the need to add another one to his plate?

She pulled him into the corner and murmured, "I believe I have some information you might find useful. I overheard Lord Jannick speaking to Lady Feist. They are being coerced to be here, and they'd rather be anywhere else."

"Coerced?" Confusion rattled his brain as he tapped his fingers against his arm. "In what capacity? And why?"

"I don't know." She shook her head regretfully. "I don't make a very good spy."

He tapped her chin and smiled. "Get enough pieces and solve the puzzle. No? I'll look into the situation. Thank you for informing me."

Turning away, he strode down the hallway with purpose, bounding quickly down the steps, past servants rousing for the night, and down the stone steps leading to the expansive gardens. Should he ask permission to steal a couple of flowers from the garden?

Probably. But he was never great about asking permission. Or respecting others' privacy, for that matter.

A trickle of fear wormed its way through his heart. He needed to infiltrate Lord Auer's dreams. Perhaps his wife's, too.

Still, the thought caused anxiety to spur his heart faster.

Dozens of varieties of flowers greeted him as he entered the seclusion of the gardens, as well as several dozen scents mingling together from bitter to sweet to sour.

And they were all gray.

"Drat everything," he growled to himself. He studied a dark gray flower with black thorns the length of his thumb. Next, he rubbed a light gray petal between his fingers. Several more recognizable plants and flowers resided in the garden's next section, such as roses, butter wisps, and chamomile. But he could not discern between colors. Different roses contained different properties for potions and elixirs. More importantly, the purple rose, when crushed, could amplify the power of truth serum.

"I hate you, witch," he mumbled under his breath. He swore he heard chuckling inside his head.

He leaned closer to a rose and sniffed its fragrance. Sweet but with a hint of mint. He guessed it was a green blossom rose, though he could easily have mistaken it for light purple or even yellow with how light the shade of gray was.

With a careful, scrutinizing eye, he moved further into the rose garden, his feet making hardly a sound on the brick walkway. "Purple rose, purple rose, where are you?" He paused beside a medium gray flower, staring intensely at its open petals. It could be orange. Maybe even pink. Perhaps even a medium purple.

He plucked one of the petals and sniffed. Sweet.

He nibbled on the end. Bitter. Like an orange peel.

"Orange rose, you can't fool me. Where's your sister, Miss Purple?"

Someone sniffed behind him.

"Gah!" Killian spun around and melted into the shadows just as he spotted the hem of a light-shaded dress. He popped up in another shadow only feet away. Lyyli sat on a bench, staring wide-eyed at him while she wrung a handkerchief between her hands. He placed a hand over his frenzied, startled heart. "I apologize. You frightened me. Gut reaction."

But then he noticed the dark blue of despair, the turquoise of hurt, the sickly yellow of anxiety, and the regular blue of sadness. The space around her eyes looked an odd shade of gray as if she had been crying until he showed up.

She stood and moved quickly down the walkway. Away from him.

Away...

From him?

She reached the entrance of the hedge maze when he gathered his wits. He dropped into the shadows and reappeared in front of her, catching her by the arms. A new river of tears trailed down her face, the sheen glinting beneath the reflection of the languid fountain behind them. She turned her face away, averting her gaze, though she didn't try to flee again.

"Lyyli... What's the matter?"

She didn't answer.

He nearly rolled his eyes at himself. Of course, she didn't answer! He was a fool who really needed to learn sign language.

After a few moments, she signed something to him, both despair and fury escaping her in an angry outburst of emotion. He bit his lip as he attempted to decipher the meaning. But then his blood burned with heat when she slipped her hand into his vest, her touch gentle against his chest.

He dumped ice water over his head, if only in his mind, when she pulled out his notebook, quill, and ink. Her hand shook as she scribbled on a blank page.

His heart sank.

You knew Lord Auer was using me, yet you left me to face him alone. You're the only person I can trust, but I don't know anymore.

He ran a hand over his stubbled face, staring down at her words and then at the hurt in her expression. Not just hurt, but pure betrayal.

"I thought it was only a servant at the door. I didn't know it would be Lord Auer," he rasped. "I am so sorry, Lyyli. I didn't know. I didn't know…"

He forced me to kill—she silently hiccupped when more tears continued to fall—*three people. Take me far away from here. I beg you.*

The shock of her words rattled his heart. Without another word, he pulled her into his arms, not a flicker of fear for his own safety as she sobbed silently into his chest. His body trembled with regret as he held her close, as if by pure determination alone he could chase away her demons. "I cannot. Not yet, at least. Knowing what you are to him, taking you would be considered an act of war between provinces. There will be more lives at stake than just the ones who have perished by your voice already."

She clutched his shirt, her body shaking even more than his. He held her tighter and moved them deeper into the shadows of a hedge and away from anyone who might happen upon them.

"That's not to say I won't try to help you," he murmured, horrified over what she might have gone through last night. "I swear *on my life*, you will not be forced to kill any more people. I will find a way to ensure your safety. In a more diplomatic way. I have a lot of power as a Lord, and I will use it to keep you safe."

Although she continued to hold tight to him, she signed, "Thank you," a few times and then rested her head against his chest.

He froze at the intimacy of it.

The effort to comfort had flipped on its head and turned into something...else. Her warm body pressed against his, fitting nicely inside his arms. Despite his height, her willowy figure reached just below his shoulder. It felt...nice...to hold her. To protect her.

Slow down. His mother's words echoed in his mind, words he'd heard time and again. He'd thought he understood them. But now?

He swallowed as he slowly lowered his chin to rest on top of her head, heart pounding like wild trolls in pursuit of a stag. His mother had never meant for him to stop being ambitious or to stop reaching for the next star. What she meant was to stop and enjoy life's little moments.

Such as holding a beautiful lady in his arms.

Lyyli released a shuddering breath and leaned further into him. His heart raced. His mind emptied of everything except the sweet floral scent of her hair. The splashing fountain became a slow trickle as he focused on each of her slowing breaths. His surroundings became a haze of black and white and gray.

Until he only saw her.

Student!

His mind shouted the word, and he crashed to his senses as if he dunked himself into an icy lake. Lyyli was going to be his student. Holding her like this…it was inappropriate.

He shifted with the intention to step away, but her face contorted in pain. One of her hands flew to her neck, another to her side, and she stood awkwardly on the outer edges of her feet.

A bruise peeked out from the collar on her neck. A spot of blood seeped into her dress at her side. And her feet…

"You're hurt." Searing, hot anger shot through his body. "Did Lord Auer hurt you?"

She closed her eyes and nodded. She signed something with her hands and then pointed to her feet.

"Let me take a look." With one hand wrapped around her waist to take some of the weight off her feet, he helped her sit on the rim of the fountain before he swiveled her around so one foot lay in his lap. He slipped her shoe off to reveal the graceful arch of her foot, her slim toes, and the slivers embedded beneath her skin.

He sucked in a breath between his teeth. "I don't have tweezers on my person, but I do think I can get these out. Will you allow me?" When she nodded, he unbuttoned his vest and dug inside his pockets. His notebook pocket currently lay empty, as Lyyli still held onto it. Two other pockets contained small glass vials of potions and elixirs. He pulled out one of the elixirs and unsheathed a small knife with one edge sharp and the other blunt.

Lyyli snatched her foot away from him.

He gave her a reassuring smile as he swirled the liquid in one of the vials. "This is a mild, topical numbing elixir. Good for toothaches, headaches, and slivers, in your case. It shouldn't hurt. I'll try to only use the blunt edge of the knife."

After a few moments of hesitation, she gave him back her foot. He dabbed the elixir with only one of his fingers onto the bottom of both feet. Otherwise, he might not be able to feel his hand while he did this. She winced before her face relaxed as the pain dissipated.

Turning his knife, so the blunt edge faced her skin, he carefully began pushing slivers from her feet. His eyebrows furrowed in concentration, and when he pulled out one particularly large splinter, he grimaced as he held it up for her to see. It had to be about two inches long.

She pointed to his book, giving him a questioning look.

"Sure, you can look through it. It's mostly just my silly ramblings and observations."

She shook her head slowly as she wrote on a page and faced it toward him. It read: *I think you are funny.*

Heat shot from his toes to his cheeks and only managed to grow hotter when ribbons of pink and yellow wafted out of her. He glanced to the side in a lousy attempt to hide his flush, but his eyes widened in horror when he gazed at his own reflection in the fountain.

Only to find pink and yellow ribbons wafting from himself as well.

He splashed the image away with his hand, but when the water calmed a fraction, the color remained.

A nudge from Lyyli's questioning foot seemed to ask, "What is it?"

"Ah! Nothing." He covered one of his ears with his hand. Heat burned the pointed tips. But as he glanced at her again, she only tipped her head curiously.

He relaxed.

But only slightly. Although she didn't see emotions like he could, he was shocked at the revelation of his own. They mirrored hers. Infatuation and happiness.

Student. Student. Student.

He drilled the word into his brain. And on top of it…*siren.* She was dangerous to get close to, especially because he didn't know how to protect himself from her voice. His enchanted onyx ring would quickly break under such immense power, his magic no match against hers.

To distract his thoughts, he blurted the first thing to come to mind, "What color would you consider your hair to be?"

He inwardly cringed. What was wrong with him? A beautiful woman happened upon him, and suddenly he could think of little else.

She gave him an odd look before she absently ran a strand between her fingers. *Golden copper*, she wrote.

"And your eyes?"

Another odd look, but her mouth twitched as if she thought he was trying to humor her. *Jade green.*

His gaze roamed across her hair and face as he attempted to imagine her with that coloring. Simply looking at her took his breath away, every black, white, and gray inch of her. "You are stunningly beautiful." His breath hitched, and his hands froze around her foot. Had he said that out loud?

Judging by her rosy cheeks and tendrils of pink infatuation and red-pink fluster—yes, he most certainly had.

He scratched his nose to save himself from his own embarrassment. "Probably a siren thing."

She shrugged one shoulder and tucked a strand of hair behind her ear. Though, he didn't miss the twitch of her mouth as if she tried not to smile.

Clearing his throat, he slipped her shoes back on and helped her stand. She wobbled and collapsed against him. Silent laughter shook her shoulders as she pointed to her feet and then at his vest.

"You can't feel your feet." Despite his fluster at her nearness, his own grin spread across his face. "The numbing effects should wear off soon. I only wish I had something else to help with your other injuries." His fingers hovered over her neck, but he didn't touch. "I can summon a Sun Fae healer."

Shivers of black fear escaped her as her gaze darted to a distant spot in the gardens. He followed her gaze to find two guards standing watch. Although she stoically shook her head against his suggestion, she clutched his arm tight as if afraid he would slip from her grasp if she didn't cling to him.

Familiar voices echoed over the hedges. Lord Auer and his family, if he remembered correctly. He started toward the sound, but Lyyli dug in her feet, frantically shaking her head.

He gave her a regretful look. "I promised to offer you protection. This is how I will do it. Trust me, Lyyli. Please."

For several long moments, she searched his face as if trying to find deceit. But finally, she nodded. Her fingers trembled against his arm, but she didn't fight him this time as he led her in the direction of the voices. Lyyli's two guards trailed further behind.

"Strength," he murmured to her just before they rounded the corner of the garden.

At a large, round table sat Lord Auer, his wife, his daughter, his son and his wife, and their two young children darting in and out of a pair of lilac trees.

Conversation hushed. Lord Auer's eyes nearly bugged out of his head as his attention snapped from him to Lyyli, arm in arm. Surprise. Anger. Fear.

Everyone else smiled welcomingly.

"Good evening," Killian said, grinning from ear to ear as he stopped short of the table. "I just learned the wildest thing. I thought I recognized this beautiful gem," he gestured to Lyyli, "at the masquerade last night, but I couldn't be sure. Without her mask on, I am now certain. This is Lyyli Ives! How fortunate I was to run into her here."

"You know her?" Lord Auer gawked, all while red tendrils of anger escaped him while he stood and leaned forward on the table. "You must be mistaken."

"I'm not. Her father is a friend of mine." The lies rolled off his tongue. This was the only way to keep her safe without starting a war. Or becoming a target—if he wasn't one already. "The family has come for supper a few times. I received her application for Darkest Star two months ago." Yes, it was an exaggeration. "I'm looking forward to having her in my classes come autumn."

More gawking. More anger.

"Would you look at that?" Lord Auer's heir and Killian's friend, Lorenz, said with a grin. "A beautiful reunion if I ever saw one. Come. Pull up a chair. We were just having brunch."

However, Lord Auer wasn't finished. "She has no magical abilities. She cannot even speak. Therefore, she has no business at your school."

"Pray tell. What business has she here?" They sat, and he reached for two biscuits. One for himself and one for Lyyli, though her trembling hands remained hidden beneath the table, her eyes downcast. "Yes, she has a lovely voice but a desire to learn magic."

The man finally sat, though furious tendrils of red leaked out of him as he fumed.

Killian casually spread butter across a biscuit as if he weren't sitting at a table with a dangerous man and a mermaid scared out of her wits. The black tendrils of fear betrayed her.

So many things about Lord Auer rang warning bells in his head—using Lyyli, suggesting an empire, the fact that the man clearly didn't want Killian there judging by his peeved emotions. Although he didn't know for sure if Lord Auer had anything to do with his mother's unconscious state, he planned to find out.

"I was expecting Miss Ives to arrive at my estate and attend Johanna." He paused and waved the knife nonchalantly in the air. "They are nearly the same age, you know. But recent events within the family happened and then Miss Ives never showed up." He laughed, his eyes full of mirth as he tipped his head toward Lyyli. "You should have told me you were stopping to sing for Lord Auer. I almost sent a search party after you."

"An enchanting voice," Lady Lorenz said, her fingers clasped together as she stared almost dreamily at Lyyli. "Lord Graves, where have you been hiding her?"

To give himself a moment to compose an answer, he stuffed half the biscuit in his mouth, all while Lord Auer glared daggers at him. "I had no idea she could sing. An interesting turn of events." He leaned across the table to bring more attention to himself rather than Lyyli. "Your Ladyship, what's that in your hair?"

Under his breath, he murmured an incantation as he reached behind her ear and pulled out a flower with a long stem. Everyone at the table clapped delightedly, and Lady Lorenz beamed with happiness as she accepted the flower from him.

"You are wasting your talents on happily married women," she laughed as she cast an adoring look at her husband, who returned it wholeheartedly. "Rather, you should focus your efforts on the half-dozen women who gazed dreamily at you last night."

Huh? What women? Was she exaggerating, or was he oblivious?

Lorenz burst into laughter as he smacked the table, making the silverware rattle, and Killian couldn't help but chuckle awkwardly at his own expense. "What was the saying, Killian? When Shadow Fae start sleeping during the night? I remember when you said that to me last year about finding a wife."

"Well…" He scratched his head, now a tumble of awkwardness and nerves. What was wrong with him? His collar suddenly felt too tight, an unbearable heat scathing him within. He was overly aware of Lyyli's presence beside him. "I did say that after we had a little too much to drink."

"So, you didn't mean it?"

"No, no. I meant it."

"Right. Because you have too much to study." He clicked his tongue. "Killian, Killian. Always with your nose in a book. Or some kind of dangerous, carnivorous flower." He laughed again at the reference from when Killian had gotten his entire arm stuck inside the mouth of a malifious plant. Lorenz had to hack it to pieces before it released his arm with only minor burns as a result.

Lorenz's wife asked, "What are you researching at the moment? I'm sure we are all curious to know."

It took a large amount of effort to keep himself from taking Lyyli's hand beneath the table. She still hadn't eaten anything, and she wouldn't raise her gaze to her abuser. All he wanted was to wrap her in his arms again and make her pain go away. That and punch the daylights out of Lord Auer.

At the thought, he caught sight of himself in the reflection of his knife. Red anger streamed out of him. His nostrils flared. But otherwise, he hid his emotions well.

"As you know…" He poured himself a glass of nectar and did the same for Lyyli, taking a small sip before he answered. "Most of my attention has been on the school this past year. I do have a side project, however. I've become increasingly interested in enchantments."

His heart thrummed in his neck as he reached into his pocket. This could either help him or doom him.

Careful to only touch the cloth wrapped around it, he set the hair comb he'd found in Charlotte's hair onto the table, watching Lord Auer's reaction. The man's eyes widened, but his expression otherwise gave no indication of recognition. His emotions, however, swirled all over the place.

Surprise. Anger. Annoyance. Fear.

Sadness.

Lord Auer's gaze shifted to his two grandchildren, who laughed as they chased each other around the garden. They fell in a heap in the dirt and began piling rocks around their feet.

"What a lovely piece," Lady Lorenz said as she reached for it. Killian took a risk and didn't stop her. But before she touched it, Lady Auer smacked her hand away.

"You shouldn't touch things you don't understand," the older woman chuckled nervously. "Lord Graves just said it was enchanted. No?"

No, he hadn't.

He frowned at the dangerous hair comb. Why hadn't he thought to question his mother about the Lords' wives? If only he'd had more time with her. But he quickly replaced the frown with a smile to mask his transparent emotions.

"This enchantment is quite the puzzle," he said as he secured it in the cloth once more and tucked it inside his pocket. "There is some strong magic involved."

Lorenz opened his mouth as if to say something, but then a servant approached and bowed low to both Killian and Auer. "My apologies, my Lords, but Lord Galish has arrived."

"Great." Lord Auer clapped his hands together and pushed himself from his chair. "That makes ten. Lord Graves, I hope you will humor me with this impromptu meeting. With all the Lords here, I thought we could resolve several issues we left untouched last meeting."

Reluctantly, he stood. He held out a hand to help Lyyli to her feet before tucking her slender fingers around his arm. "The ten of us met only weeks ago. Is there really such a dire need, Auer?"

"Humor me, Graves. Be in the great hall in one hour."

He began leading Lyyli away, and with his back turned, he quietly mocked Lord Auer by repeating his words in a whiny voice.

Lyyli slapped her hand over her smile as if trying to keep a laugh from escaping.

"Honestly," he gasped the moment they were out of earshot. "Do I look like I'm twelve to you?"

She shook her head, her grin only growing larger across her face.

His breath shuddered in his lungs. Holy shadows... She had a beautiful smile.

Student!

Releasing a long breath, he delivered her back to the gardens where her guards trailed further behind. He leaned in closer to murmur in her ear. "He won't hurt you without thinking twice about it now. I'll find you later to give you another form of protection. I'll just need...one of these." Carefully, he separated a single thread of hair from her head and plucked. A wince of surprise flitted across her face, but the smile quickly returned to her mouth.

The soft strand rolled between his fingers before he tucked it safely in his breast pocket. Golden copper, she'd said. What must she look like with such coloring?

He kissed her knuckles and bid her farewell, taking the long way back to his room through the other end of the garden he hadn't explored. Most of the flower shapes were recognizable in their gray form, but none were roses.

What an inconvenient curse. He never realized how much color had aided him in the past until a witch had stripped it from his vision completely.

He climbed the stairs to his chambers but paused when he spotted something lying at the base of his door. Each footfall created little sound as he approached cautiously, only for a whoosh of surprise to escape his lungs.

Surprise and…fondness.

A soft smile tugged on his lips. Two roses lay on the ground, complete with thorns and petals. A tangy sweetness greeted his nostrils as he picked them up and inhaled. Purple. These were purple.

"Lyyli," he whispered, realizing she must have heard him in his wanderings through the garden looking for the evasive flower. He glanced back and forth across the hallway. Several people ambled about, but she wasn't one of them.

And then he slipped into his room with a smile still on his face and the flowers tugging on his heart as if the two were connected by strings. For a single moment, his life stood still. It wasn't bleak, filled with black and white hopelessness. But it was warm and happy.

For just one moment.

If terror had a name, it would be Mel Auer.

Lyyli stood in the corner of the great hall, trying to make herself as small as possible to avoid notice. She wrung her white-gloved hands together and then smoothed her thin blue skirts just to give her hands something to do.

One by one, Lords and Ladies began to file into the room, talk and laughter echoing off the grand ceilings. Gazes flitted her way and then darted somewhere else as if they found her stillness uninteresting. One gaze, in particular, pressed down on her as if she were caught in a mudslide and couldn't break her way to the top for air. Lord Auer watched her carefully, more so since Killian had arrived.

Not able to withstand his snake-like gaze for long, she moved to the window and brushed thin, gossamer curtains aside to peer into the darkness of night. A long stretch of green grass stood between the fortress and the shimmering wall of magic that prevented her escape. And just beyond that…

Freedom.

If Killian couldn't take her somewhere safe, she would find a way to help herself.

A despairing breath fogged the window, and she absently dragged a finger through the haze to form a picture of wide oceans and warm beaches.

Three.

That was the number of times she had tried to escape already. But the moment she passed through the shimmering barrier, Lord Auer knew it immediately and sent men after her. Three escape attempts. Three beatings. The next time she found an opportunity, she would leave for good. Somewhere no one could find her. A place everyone would be safe from her, and she would be safe from them.

She gazed at the image she'd drawn of the ocean as it slowly melted away against the warmth of the torch-lit great hall.

The ocean...

She was mer. Killian had mentioned she should be able to breathe underwater. She'd felt her gills, her arm fins, and the way her entire body had shifted to welcome the change from human to mermaid. If she could just get to the ocean, perhaps she could rid herself of this horrible existence of fearing and killing and running.

And Killian.

Her stomach twisted with premature grief as she turned her head to the round table in the middle of the room. Nine Lords and one Lady were seated at the table, talking amongst themselves.

As if feeling her gaze on him, Killian lifted his head and offered her a warm smile. Butterflies erupted in her stomach. Heat pierced her cheeks. She liked the Shadow Lord. A lot. He was kind and helpful and attentive and completely endearing.

And unmarried.

At the thought, she ripped her gaze away and fingered the jeweled necklace at her throat. Never again. She refused to risk Killian's life by striking up anything that resembled a courtship. No matter how much she wanted it. He *saw* her like no one else ever had. He *knew* what she was capable of, yet he treated her kindly, even though she was vastly beneath his station. He deserved far more than a premature death.

It was all the same. She killed almost everyone she got close to.

Then why did her traitorous heart wish to see his smile directed at her once more?

Killian's soothing voice jerked her out of her spiral of despair as it rose above the others, and instantly the room quieted. "Lord Auer, since you called this meeting, why don't you conduct today?"

"It would be my pleasure," Lord Auer replied as he tapped a stack of papers against the table to align them. As a couple of servants set about filling goblets with what looked to be water, he continued, "First, I would like to congratulate Lord Blom on his daughter's engagement."

Congratulations and clapping rounded the table, and as they conducted business, she returned her attention to the window, and more specifically, to the shimmering ward. The ward had to have a weakness. No one could possibly be powerful enough to keep it up constantly. Right?

Unless…

Her breath fogged the glass as she peered closer. If she could just figure out how the ward was erected in the first place, she could damage it and slip through unnoticed.

But then what? The ocean wasn't too far from here, but it would still take her many hours on foot just to reach it. If someone discovered her absence, was she fast enough to outrun someone in pursuit?

Not to mention her shackles during the day when she and everyone else slept, and her two guards who kept watch constantly. Was she brave enough—or perhaps cruel enough— to kill them with her voice in order to escape to freedom?

She shook her head and sighed despondently. No more killing. Ever. She could not stomach it. She would rather endure the shackles than take another life.

"Graves," Auer said, snapping her attention back toward the meeting. "Another point I wished to discuss. Your school."

Killian's body tensed, but his face remained expressionless. "Yes?"

"I know I am not speaking only for myself when I point out the obvious." Auer's yellow eyes flashed dangerously like a snake about to strike. "How are you to continue with your Lordly duties if you are busy teaching and running a school? It is my suggestion to retire your title to your heir. Wait…" He paused, his lips smirking. "You don't have one. Might I suggest we all place suggestions for an heir on the table and choose?"

"Now, wait a moment." Killian rose from his chair, both palms flat on the table. "You are vastly wrong if you think I can't handle all my responsibilities. I'm not the only teacher at Darkest Star. And this is not how this works. You can't just vote me out of my title without a nine-to-one ratio. It would have to be unanimous."

"Then let's take a quick vote. All in favor of Lord Graves relinquishing his title should he go forward with his position at the school?"

Seven out of ten hands raised.

Seven.

And judging by Killian's shocked expression, he had not anticipated the turnout. Although Lyyli didn't know much about politics, she couldn't help but wonder how many people Lord Auer had to bribe or threaten to receive such a large voting turnout.

"So many?" he choked.

The only Lady seated at the table, one of the two who had not raised their hands, waved an arm toward Killian. Bangles clinked together as her arm moved, and her gold earrings flashed in the candlelight. Likely in her sixties, the woman had not lost any beauty with age. Gray streaked through dark brown hair. Wisdom lay within deep brown eyes. She exuded elegance and poise with every movement.

"Perhaps, Lord Graves," she suggested, "you might appease the masses by finding a suitable wife. You have no wife and no heir. Your familial line lacks strength. Your title dies with you."

Murmurs of agreement rounded the table.

Lyyli's gut churned with unease as her hopeful fancy for the Shadow Lord broke like a brittle, dried leaf and scattered with the wind. *Suitable wife.* That was something she would not make. In fact, she didn't even make the list for suitable courting material. Why did the thought twist her heart?

Slowly, Killian lowered himself back into his chair and crossed an ankle over his knee. "Very well. I will find myself a wife and have an heir and even a spare. But I am fully capable of all my duties as Lord and mage."

Her heart twisted further.

"See that you are," Lord Auer grumbled, not appearing even slightly happy as the Lady's suggestion was received by nods of approval. He motioned with a hand, and several more servants bustled out with drinks and refreshments. "We'll take a short break and resume in fifteen minutes. In the meantime, enjoy the food and a brief musical piece."

When the man motioned to her, she stood rooted to the spot as ten pairs of eyes swiveled in her direction. Intense fear churned within her gut, and she only wished to either flee from the room or hide behind the cage of a mask from the masquerade. If Lord Auer's enchantment didn't hold, all of these people would die.

Including Killian.

As she forced one foot in front of the other to stand in the front of the room, she met the resolve in Killian's eyes. His jaw was set with stubborn determination, almost as if to say, "You can't hurt me."

Yes, I can, Killian. You have no idea the true power of my voice.

Perhaps *she* didn't even know the true power of her voice, but she had witnessed firsthand how fast it could kill someone. She'd witnessed it again and again and again.

And again.

A harpist wearing a golden gown the color of her instrument joined her at the front. Lyyli's gaze slid longingly to the window. She could still refuse. She could run instead of subject these people to her voice and Lord Auer's enchantments. But at what cost?

A chill raked over her as her gaze slid to Lord Auer. Threats lingered within his yellow eyes. Not just a beating if she refused to comply. But perhaps something far worse.

She eyed the crystal goblets at the round table. If she could just smash one and take the glass to injure herself instead of these innocent people...

Her two guards stepped closer to her as if sensing her inner turmoil. They stood only a few feet behind her now.

Please forgive me, she begged silently as she clutched her hands to her heart. Fear and shame tackled her on either side, but the audience still waited expectantly. What they didn't know was that her magic was about to make them all much easier to manipulate and control. She also feared it might be part of the reason why so many of the Lords were trying to vote Killian out of his title.

The harpist plucked several beautiful notes, and then Lyyli began to sing.

> "Where the bells are dancing silver
> And the straw is twirling gold

There we will meet, my two hands for you to hold."

Emotion lodged in her throat at the melancholy song of loss and heartbreak, but the power of her voice began to take effect. Instead of inspiring tears or frowns, her audience smiled joyfully. All except three of them, including Killian and the Lady.

"From the ashes, you will rise
Free of soot and dirt and cold
Once again, we touch the stars, each shining light for us to mold."

The jewels of the necklace burned the skin at her throat as the enchantment threatened to break under the astronomical weight of her voice. Hotter. Hotter. Hotter.

Just one more verse. It's all I can do.

"Death never raises scythe again
To cut the fragile ties
Of red lips grown so pale and cold, no longer its demise."

A gasp escaped her as the stones of the necklace shattered and scattered across the floor, leaving a searing burn in their wake. She swayed on her feet and clamped her mouth shut, refusing to utter a single noise without the protection of the enchantment.

Killian's chair scraped against the ground as he stood, but he made no move toward her when a round of applause lifted into the air. Her audience smiled, filled with unnatural joy after hearing her song.

But Killian...

He didn't smile. Rather, concern lay within his blue eyes. How was he not affected by the song? He should be swimming in happiness, blind to the dark terrors of the world, and especially to the terror sitting only feet away from him.

But...no one was dead.

A wave of relief crashed over her, and she was vaguely aware of one of her guards steering her out of the great hall. Only then did she realize her world spun. The walls became gelatinous waves, the floor ripping out from beneath her like slippery carpet. And when the ceiling came within view of her dizzy mind, a darkness collapsed on her.

Everything became quiet and still.

Killian's expression settled into a serious concern as he watched Lyyli sway on her feet. She only made it to the exit before she collapsed entirely, one of her guards just barely catching her before her head hit the ground.

He inhaled sharply and leaped to his feet, dashing in her direction. But Lord Auer quickly stepped in his way. No emotion—nothing at all—escaped Lyyli as her limp form was carried from the room and disappeared behind the corner. Was she…dead?

No, she couldn't be.

The thought spurred panic within his heart. He stepped into Auer's shadow and shadewalked around him, only to appear a foot away. He resumed his dash after Lyyli.

Lightning quick, Auer grabbed hold of his wrist and squeezed hard enough to inspire an involuntary whimper.

"We're not done here," the man said in a low growl.

"Lyyli—"

"Is fine. She has fainting spells every now and again." Auer stepped closer, and for the briefest moment, Killian thought he spotted sympathy in the man's eyes. If it weren't for the confidence of triumph leaking from his emotions. Manipulative bastard. "Return to your seat. There is one more matter to discuss with the Lords present."

Killian shifted his gaze to the empty doorway, his gut churning with trepidation and his mind whirling with concern. For a flicker of a moment, he didn't doubt that if he looked into a mirror, he might find a wide array of confusing emotions leaking out of himself.

Swallowing the lump of dread in his throat, he nodded and returned to his seat. Worry gnawed at him despite the calm expression he kept painted on his face. He crossed an ankle over his knee, but when his leg bounced up and down with nervous impatience, he placed both feet on the floor. It grounded him. At least long enough to sit through whatever business came next.

Many of the eyes that had previously stared at him now swiveled to Lord Auer as he clapped his hands to get everyone's attention. Silly smiles lingered on many faces. If only he could smack them right off and dart after Lyyli without repercussion.

"Right then," Auer said. "Let's resume. I would like to take another vote before concluding the meeting. By raise of hand, how many of you would like to turn Katalle from ten provinces to a strong, reigning empire?"

This again? Killian resisted the urge to roll his eyes and tapped down his rising anger. At the last meeting, five people had voted in favor of the empire. The idiots. Only weeks had passed since the vote. Surely, nothing would change.

However, his mouth fell open as, one by one, each Lord raised their hand. Only he and Lady Feist kept their hands in their laps.

His eyes widened in shock as he glanced across the table to meet Lady Feist's eye. Anger, fear, and disappointment rolled off her like a slippery log tumbling through a marshy bog.

What was happening? How was this possible? Surely, no one was daft enough to follow through with this ludicrous plan.

Lyyli...

Her name tumbled through his mind as he touched the onyx ring hugging his finger. It protected him from enchantments. He knew for a fact that Lord Blom and Lady Feist wore similar enchanted items after discovering them during his party performance, which likely protected them as well. Had the others been affected by Lyyli's voice?

"Well," Killian said as he stood and straightened the lapels of his coat. "This meeting has been most enlightening." He threw a knowing glare at Lord Auer, and although he said nothing, a quiet understanding passed between them. Auer knew he knew.

And because of it, Killian would find a way to destroy him. Diplomatically, of course. But without concrete evidence, he had nothing more than Lyyli's testimony and his own conclusions.

Red and black streams of anger and fear oozed out of the other Lord.

Without so much as another word, he stalked out of the room. Not to check on Lyyli. Not yet. What he needed was more information.

He absorbed into the shadows and waited. When Lady Feist took leave of the great hall, he followed slowly, creeping along the shadows as she made her way down the hall. Finally, she stopped in a shadowy nook of the fortress furnished with potted plants and cushioned chairs. Most interestingly, Lord Blom soon joined her.

The man hunched his shoulders with shame, refusing to make eye contact with the Lady.

"You gave in to his threats, didn't you?" Lady Feist accused without preamble, her voice a low hiss like a snake about to strike. "Why didn't you stand up for yourself like we planned?"

Lord Blom's expression fell in defeat. "My daughter is getting married. If I don't comply, a terrible fate will befall her fiancé. I can't do that to her. I can't take away her happiness."

"You are a fool."

"I know. But he struck me at my weakest point."

These two were allies, Killian realized. Perhaps the only ones he might find within the Circle of Lords. Between Lord Auer's threats and Lyyli's voice, Lord Auer was slowly gaining control over the ten Lords.

He revealed himself, slowly stepping out of the shadows. The other two went rigid, eyes wide as they realized their conversation had been overheard. But he held up a placating hand, all while he stared back at them with a serious expression.

"Eavesdropping on a Lord is a serious offense," Lady Feist sniffed.

He nodded. "Yes, but this is a serious matter. It seems we all have a common enemy." He held out two hands. "I have set up wards in my bedchamber to prevent such eavesdropping. Shall we move this discussion there?"

They eyed him warily. Lord Blom spoke. "Wards? Or traps?"

Appealing to the Lord's affair with his mother, he growled, "I am starting to believe that man has enchanted my mother so deeply that if I do not find a way to release her, she will die within the month. Do not think for a single second I am here under friendly circumstances."

After sharing a long, contemplative look, each of them took a hand. The exertion to shadewalk the three of them to his chambers was great, and by the time they appeared before the hearth, he gasped in a breath and reeled from the energy spent.

Shadewalking himself was no problem and took little energy unless traveling long distances. Shadewalking others took too large a toll on him. He didn't do it often, nor did he like to.

"I am sure we have all come to the same conclusion," Lady Feist said as she crossed the room to the complimentary spirits on the corner table and helped herself to a drink. She poured the liquid into a glass and threw it back faster than a sprite in flight. "The vocalist is some sort of witch. She must be disposed of."

Freezing dread shot through his veins at the thought of Lyyli's skin becoming cold and pale in death. To never again see her tentative smile. For her to die before tasting the air of freedom.

He braced himself against the wall and took several ragged breaths. Then, shaking his head, he corrected, "Lyyli is a victim. Not a threat. She is held captive against her will to do Lord Auer's bidding. I am trying to help her, not doom her to an unjust death."

The Lady lowered herself delicately on one of the armchairs and peered at him over the rim of her once-again-filled glass. "I see. You are attached to the Songbird."

"N-n-no. I'm—"

"Enough to take her as your bride?" She smirked as she tapped her long fingernails against her glass. "That would solve two of our problems with one swing. You will save your title and keep her out of Auer's grasp. What do you think, Blom?"

Lord Blom eyed both of them warily, but as if he wanted to steer clear of a likely argument, he remained silent and crossed the room for his own drink.

A blazing flush spread throughout Killian's body, from the tips of his ears to his burning toes. He felt like he slipped off a cliff and plunged straight into a volcanic river. He'd never intended to take a wife. But today...

He frowned through his transparent blush. Today proved he could not keep on this path of teaching without making a few changes. Albeit life-altering changes.

A wife? What women did he even know who weren't twice his age? And were unattached? His cousins. Lyyli. And…

His mind drew a blank.

He couldn't marry Lyyli. She was to be his student *and* she was a dangerous siren. And Johanna… She was the obvious choice at such short notice. But to cross that solid boundary he'd created between them made an uncomfortable pit form in his stomach.

Scratching his head, he sighed as he sank into an armchair across the hearth from Lady Feist. "Speaking of problems… How long do you think I have before I need to marry?"

Leaning against the wall beside the window, Lord Blom answered. "Best to do it sooner rather than later with these types of things. A seven-to-two ratio is not looking favorable for you."

Killian leaned forward with his elbows resting on his knees. He steepled his fingers together and rested them underneath his chin, deep in thought. "This is all connected. I just know it. My mother's poisoning. Lord Auer trying to vote me out of my title. The proposed empire."

He lifted one finger. "First, we need to figure out who he wants to replace me with." He held up another finger. "Second, we need to learn who would be at the head of this empire. If it's Lord Auer himself, or someone else entirely."

"I don't know if I can find out the second," Blom said as he swirled the liquid in his glass and continued to stare out the window. "But I think I can get the information out of him for the first. If he thinks he's swaying me to his side—"

"You're already halfway there," Lady Feist muttered into her glass. Blom still heard it and glared, though the shame he felt was transparent only to Killian.

"I can't afford to lose my title." He now leaned forward with his elbows on his knees, a pleading look in his eyes as he caught the Lady's gaze. "More harm than good would come of it. I need the ladies at court to know…" He choked on the rest of the sentence until his stomach churned with so much dread that he barely held himself back from vomiting. This wasn't what he wanted. Never was. "…that I am looking for a wife."

Another smirk lay hidden behind the glass filled with liquor. "Consider it done. By tomorrow night, you will be the most eligible bachelor in the ten provinces."

This time, vomit began climbing his throat, and he quickly stood and placed a fist against his mouth to stop it from escaping. He paced about the room, taking deep breath after deep breath.

"What's the matter with you, boy?" Blom gaped, his eyes trailing his movement across the room. "Anyone else would be ecstatic to be in your position."

He shook his head and finally stopped pacing when his stomach calmed a fraction. How could he possibly make them understand? "I only wanted to marry if I found someone I loved more than my ambition. And now I fear I will be forced to marry a stranger."

Lady Feist, at least, offered him a sympathetic smile. "What means more to you? Your title or who you marry?"

It didn't matter what meant more to him. What mattered was what he thought was right. Only his title offered him enough power to fight back against whatever Lord Auer was planning.

Instead of answering, he turned the conversation on the other man, a widower, to direct their attention elsewhere. "How long have you been having an affair with my mother?"

Lord Blom choked on his drink, coughing and sputtering and pounding a fist against his chest. Through his watering eyes, he gasped, "How did you find out? We weren't going to tell you."

"It doesn't matter how. What matters is I know. How long? Before or after my father died?"

"After. I swear by the evening shadows. Several years after."

"Good." He paused for a moment as he remembered the passionate and happy emotions escaping her days ago. "You seem to make her happy. That's all that matters to me." The wilting roses stashed in the armoire dragged his attention back to his newest tasks. Another long night, and perhaps even a long day, ahead of him. "I have some work to do. Perhaps we can speak again tomorrow night."

Lady Feist set her glass down on the table and sauntered to the door. "*If* you have time. I have a feeling your time might be a commodity. Starting…now."

When she slipped into the hallway, he nearly dry heaved. He had no time for this. There were a thousand other things he needed to do, and finding a wife would only be a hindrance.

Blom started to follow, but he paused with one foot in the room and the other in the corridor. The grief was unmistakable on his face. "I won't get to say goodbye, will I?"

"I don't know," he answered quietly. "I haven't received word that her state has worsened. I'm hoping for the best."

With a quick nod, Blom slipped out of the room, and slowly, Killian closed the door behind him. His heart ached, but there was no time for grief either. He had work to do.

He slipped a hand into his vest pocket and pulled out the strand of Lyyli's hair he'd taken from her head. Next, he dug into his luggage and sifted through several small boxes containing jewelry, cufflinks, and even a hairpin. Although enchantments weren't his specialty, he never knew when he'd need to use one. This particular enchantment wasn't to harm or poison or confuse. It was to protect.

He pulled the lid off a box and gazed down at a pair of dark gray earrings the size of peas. Were they blue? Green? Purple? He couldn't remember.

But they would do perfectly.

Again, he reached into his luggage and pulled out a slim, rectangular box the size of a large book. He set it on top of the table and carefully opened it to reveal twelve different vials in two neat rows filled with a variety of elixirs he'd created himself. One vial lay half-empty, as he'd already used one dose for his onyx ring. Hopefully, he wouldn't need the second dose.

Cold glass met his finger as he slid it along each vial. Gray, gray, gray.

"Why can't inanimate objects have feelings?" he muttered to himself, blowing out a frustrated breath. A wisp of hair lifted beneath the huff. "Then it might be easier to discern between these."

Rather than inspecting each beneath a light to gauge their possible color, he slid aside the false panel at the top of the box, and his cheat sheet fell out. He unfolded the paper and grinned, thanking his past self for such a guide. If he found himself in another color predicament, he would ask Johanna for help.

"Ah, the connection elixir," he murmured as he plucked one of the vials out of the padded velvet. A woodsy aroma greeted him as he unstopped the vial. Perfect.

He located a bowl within his luggage and a thin, wooden spoon. Lyyli's hair, two pairs of earrings, and then the entire vial of elixir. The concoction hissed as it immediately absorbed the piece of hair, and only after a minute of stirring, he added his own hair.

"*Tueri et conseruare.*"

A chunk of magical energy escaped him like a rush of breath. He braced himself against the table at the unexpected draining sensation. The room spun in circles, and he squeezed his eyes shut until the dizziness passed. More magic than he originally anticipated drained from his well. A chill rushed through him as if a blizzardy wind burst through the window and bathed him in its flurry.

The moment his head ceased spinning, he scooped the earrings out of the mixture and placed them back into the small box, tucking it safely inside his vest.

He needed more pockets, he decided. He carried far too much of an inventory on his person.

Next, he carefully picked up the roses and brought them to his nose. The tangy sweetness greeted him, a scent which he now associated with Lyyli.

A worried knot formed in his stomach as he got to work plucking the petals and mashing them inside a mortar until it turned into a mushy substance, the start of a truth elixir. How was Lyyli faring? Would Lord Auer see to her care? Or would he continue to mistreat her?

At the thought, he crushed the petals harder and faster. He'd made her a promise to protect her. But he couldn't do it until this was done.

At long last, when the maidservant finally left her room in the late hours of the night, Lyyli lethargically lifted a hand and touched the burned skin along her collarbone. She winced at the pulsing heat of pain.

Had Lord Auer's magic done this? Or her own siren powers?

The chains around her wrists rattled as she buried her face in her hands. If only she could contact her father, but she dared not put them in harm's way.

How many sirens had been used or hunted down before her? How many lives had been lost? How many countries had fallen? She was slowly watching Katalle fall, and part of it was her own doing.

Knock knock.

The quiet, hesitant rap on her door inspired a wave of panic to gush through her. She remained still as she laid on her side, keeping her face toward the wall. Had Lord Auer come to force her to kill again? Perhaps with a new enchanted piece of jewelry to combat her power. How could she fight back? If she sang and managed to focus her power on the man's ring, could she break the enchantment held within it?

The door creaked open and shut just as quickly, followed by silence.

"Lyyli," a familiar voice murmured. "How are you faring?"

She bolted upright, twisting in her chains until she spotted the tall man at the far end of the room. A strand of blond hair fell over blue eyes riddled with exhaustion. His lips puckered with concern, his eyebrows furrowing moments later as he surveyed her up and down.

"Killian," she signed by giving him the name sign of "Mage" with a "K."

He produced his notebook from his vest pocket, and she eagerly reached for it. When he also handed her the familiar quill, she glanced at him expectantly.

Despite his weariness, he grinned. "I enchanted the quill. As long as ink remains in the inkpot in my room, the quill should go on writing without it. Go on. Give it a try."

Her mouth quirked to the side, overshadowed by doubt. But when she ran the quill along the paper, a trail of ink followed. Her entire soul lit up.

So now you care about my privacy? she teased, eagerly writing in the book as she referenced him knocking on the door rather than shadewalking into the room. She only wished she had quicker and more satisfying means of communicating, but she would settle for anything for a chance to talk to him.

He shrugged sheepishly as he crouched to her level. "I am trying to be better at respecting privacy. I admit I don't care much for it. It's often a frustrating waste of time."

She tipped her head as she surveyed him with a long, lingering glance. He was different from any other person she knew. He took an analytical approach to life, caring more about solving riddles and learning answers than he did about people's feelings.

"That came out wrong," he murmured as he ran a hand across his face. "I don't always say things tactfully."

I like your honesty, she wrote. *Your straightforward approach to life is refreshing.*

Once again, he shrugged one shoulder before he dug his hands into his tired eyes. "I think plenty of people would disagree with you. I have made many an enemy with my honesty."

Not me.

His throat bobbed up and down as he swallowed, staring at the page for a beat too long. His gaze then drifted to the chains around her wrists. "I have something for you. It doesn't feel right to give it to you with your hands bound. I think I can shadewalk you out of your bindings. At least for a time. Care to escape the fortress for a bit? I don't think anyone will catch us if we're careful."

Hope blossomed in her heart like the first buds of spring as she nodded enthusiastically. She cared little about her state of undress. Freedom meant far more to her than propriety.

However, a moment of guilt pinned her where she sat as she watched him move sluggishly with exhaustion. She wanted to tell him to rest. To not worry about her. But she was selfish for wanting to be out of her bindings, to want to spend time with him, to want his protection.

He opened her armoire and began digging through her clothes before he paused, stepped back, and held his hands up. "My apologies. Privacy."

Amusement crinkled the corners of her eyes as she wrote, *A frustrating waste of time?*

Warmth settled deep in her soul as he chuckled under his breath. "Exactly. Time is a valuable asset. I am searching for a cloak for you to wear. The night is somewhat chilly."

Using a finger, she pointed to the far end of the armoire. Excitement, nerves, and hope bounced through her chest. She no longer felt the cold bite of the chains. She no longer despaired, if only for a blessed moment.

Killian draped her cloak over his arm and then instructed her to lay her wrists against the mattress so they wouldn't make noise when they fell after they shadewalked. His steady hand gripped her elbow, and it was as if time froze as he gazed into her eyes. Mere inches separated them. If she wanted to—which she really, truly did—she could stand on her toes and meet him in a kiss.

"Don't scream." His soft words brushed past her ear. "It helps if you close your eyes."

And then they fell.

Or rather, it felt like falling. Her stomach lurched. She lost control of her limbs as if swept away in a raging river. Darkness crawled across her eyes, entered her nostrils, and when she opened her mouth to gasp, shadows slithered inside like dark wispy snakes.

She clung tighter to Killian, but he wasn't solid anymore. *She* wasn't solid anymore.

Just as her heart raced with panic, she gasped in a lungful of fresh night air and stumbled several feet. Killian caught her around the waist before she managed to face plant onto the cobblestone walkway. Her hands trembled. Her teeth rattled with shivers.

A thick cloak fell across her shoulders, and moments later, warm arms enveloped her and crushed her against a warm chest.

"I should have warned you about the side effects of shadewalking." A grimace layered Killian's voice. "I apologize for not having the emotional foresight."

Despite her teeth rattling her brain, she smiled within the safety of his arms, knowing he was unable to see it. *I don't mind,* she thought as she breathed deeply and inhaled the scent of forest and curiosity.

Only when her shivering subsided did he push her away, much to her disappointment. But the feeling quickly faded when he reached into his vest and popped open a small black box. She inhaled sharply at the glittering emerald earrings twinkling beneath the moon's glow.

"Beautiful," she signed.

He plucked one of them from the black velvet cushion and twirled it close to his face. "This is my protection to you, as promised. As long as you wear it, it will give you the means to contact me."

Her heart beat incredibly fast as he gently took hold of one of her ears and slipped the earring through a hole at the top of the ear that must not have closed up completely.

"Think of it as a magical, one-sided tether," he continued, oblivious to her racing pulse as he slipped the other through the opposite ear. "If you pull on the thread, I will feel it and come to your aid."

"How?" she signed. Her fingers reverently brushed the pieces of jewelry, her heart cherishing the beautiful gift he'd given her.

He paused and studied her for a moment, but as if he realized what she asked, he answered, "There are two ways. The first is to use your own magic. Envision a thread connecting you to me through your earrings. Then imagine yourself pulling on it. If you can't figure it out, another way is to coat the earring in your own blood. A drop is only what you will need."

Her hands conveyed her gratitude. "Thank you."

"Of course. I only wish I could do more." He glanced back at the fortress while biting his lip, and disappointment seeped into her soul. The last thing she wanted was to return to that awful room, willingly walking back into her shackles.

However, her heart leaped in surprise when he returned his attention to her, his smile bright as he offered his arm. She hesitated.

"It has been a long while since I've been able to enjoy the quiet stillness of a beautiful night. Care to join me for a leisurely walk?" He held up his opposite hand as if about to make a vow. "I swear I will not take samples of any plant life we come across. Nor will I stick my face in any unknown species just to see what will happen. I also promise I will not bore you with my insatiable thirst for magical discussion."

A giggle threatened to rise up her throat, but she quickly pressed it down and instead hid her smile behind her hand. She picked up the notebook and quill, scratching, *I find your magical discussions fascinating. I would like to learn more.* She tapped the end of the feather against the paper as she contemplated her next question. *What is the scariest magical creature you have come across?*

Rather than taking his offered arm, she slid her hand into his, fingers intertwining. He inhaled sharply, all while warmth spread between them at the intimate contact. His long, slender fingers wrapped snugly around hers. Thrilling sparks shot from her fingers up her arm and jolted her heart into a frenzied rhythm. Her entire chest burned with warmth at the shocked fluster growing across his face. She shouldn't get this close to him. She knew she shouldn't. But for a moment, she was selfish. Just a short walk. She might not get another chance.

"I…uh…um…" He released a long breath and glanced down at the notebook as if he'd forgotten the question. "Right, magical creatures. I've come across plenty of nasty critters. Some worse than others." But when she gently tugged on his hand so they began walking side by side beneath the romantic moonlit night, he grew quiet.

She risked a glance at him to find his mouth moving silently as if struggling to find his words. With his free hand, he rubbed the back of his neck.

The quill and notebook sat awkwardly in her free hand as she curled her fingers to look like claws and bared her teeth, a questioning reminder in her eyes.

Slowly, a smile replaced the fluster on his face. Amusement twinkled in the blueness of his eyes. His elongated pupils had grown large enough to nearly push all of the blue out entirely.

"Most of the scary critters I have come across are no larger than my head. But the few times I have actually been terrified for my life…" His shudder entered her hand. "I was in a part of the desert, studying the magical properties of the stadenis cactus. A redonadren bird landed on one of the spikes. Too late, I realized what it was."

She squeezed his fingers to bring his attention to the questioning look in her eyes.

He answered, "Alone, these flesh-eating birds are relatively harmless. But part of a flock, they're extremely dangerous. And they always travel in a flock." His expression lit up with terror but also excitement as he told the story, his free hand gesturing through the air along with it. "A swarm flew above me. I dropped all my equipment and ran. There were hardly any shadows, so I couldn't escape. They swarmed me. I got cut up pretty bad, and I might have suffered worse if it hadn't been for the Sun Fae I had been traveling with who fought them off. My magic was useless in the desert."

The connection of their hands remained as he lifted one of his sleeves to reveal a scar across his forearm. "I haven't ventured to the desert since that excursion. Perhaps I will return one day, but next time I plan to be better prepared."

Take me with you, she wanted to say but held her tongue.

Sweet warmth passed through her as she touched one of her earrings. What would it be like to have a man like him in her life? Sweet. Attentive. Caring. Smart. Focused. Safe.

Both hands shook uncontrollably as she attempted another question inside the notebook. *Are you really going to get married? To whom?*

Envy and hurt and hopelessness and more envy battled one against another inside her heart. She hardly knew Killian, yet she felt like she knew him better than almost everyone she'd ever met, and she felt like he knew her. Tangible happiness slipped through her fingers when she realized he would marry another, and she would return to her own hopeless existence. She wanted so much more.

She swallowed the hopelessness and gave in to the rise of determination, even though she knew she shouldn't. She didn't know how yet, but she wanted to fight for the future hovering just out of reach. A future with happiness and acceptance and…Killian. If he took away her voice for good, she would never be able to hurt him. Maybe she didn't have to escape to the sea. Perhaps the escape and the beautiful life she wanted were right in front of her.

"I can't keep up with you," he said as he stopped walking and held her at arm's length. "Just give me a moment."

"Keep up with what?" she signed, but of course, he didn't understand.

His attention lingered on the top of her head, and when he finally lowered his gaze to look her in the eye, she swore she spotted a flush growing across his face. Though, in the darkness, she wasn't entirely sure. Her eyes didn't work as well as a Shadow Fae's at night.

Clearing his throat, he answered, "I must marry, yes. To whom? I don't know. I'm not exactly happy about it."

And just like that, her hope began to deflate. "Why?" she signed, and this time he understood.

He released a long sigh, and they began walking again. Only then did Lyyli glance around at their surroundings. Large, overhanging trees created a private space on the far side of the Auer property. Glowing blooms ranging from pink to blue to even glistening black blossomed on all sides of them, drinking in the moonlight. A cobblestone walkway stretched through a winding path, and they were blessedly alone. No guards. No courtiers. No danger.

Just Killian and Lyyli.

They sank onto a stone bench as he answered. "I admit I am afraid my studies, ambitions, and dreams will suffer if I take a wife. That's mostly what I have against the idea. I have worked too hard to throw away my dreams."

Her fingers trembled as she braved her next words in the notebook, still holding fast to his hand. She wanted to fight, and she had limited opportunities to do it.

If you were my husband, I would single-handedly fight off the redonadren birds so you could study your cactuses.

Surprise flitted across her expression as he released a full-belly laugh. The sound created a tingle of awareness where their skin touched from their fingers to their wrists. He had a beautiful laugh.

Also, she had been serious. Why was he laughing?

His eyes glinted with amusement as he leaned forward on his knees and turned his head to the side to look at her. "I don't doubt for a single second that you could manage the feat with such a voice."

If he thought this was a game, then fine.

Her lips twitched as she fought off a grin, the quill scratching in the notebook.

We would sit by the fire on a cold winter night, and you would tell me all about your magical discoveries, and I would teach you sign language to make conversing easier.

"I do need to learn sign language," he murmured as he plucked a long, red flower from a green vine climbing the trellis beside him. She watched as he inspected it closer, the conversation seeming lost between them. But quickly, he grimaced and stuffed the flower inside his pocket. "I apologize. I promised not to take any plant samples tonight. The red snapper, I believe it is, is good for protection against lightning strikes. I would like to add it to my collection. When I travel to the rainy region, it will come in handy."

He ran a hand over his face and groaned. "I am rambling again."

She released his hand as another bolt of determination washed over her. She could not attract his attention if he did not look at her in his daze of distraction.

So, she grabbed either side of his face and turned his head until the surprise in his eyes became visible. Then, she released him to sign, "I would never take your dreams away. We could share them."

But of course, he didn't understand her. Besides, she knew she was being too forward with a man far above her station, one she only recently met. But if he must marry, then she wanted a seat in the competition.

"Lyyli, I don't understand."

Frustration boiled inside her cauldron of despair. All too easily, fire lit the underside of the cauldron, boiling and bouncing and sizzling. At home, she'd never experienced the issue of not being able to properly communicate. The notebook and quill weren't satisfactory enough.

If she didn't place herself in the competition now, she might not get another chance.

Slow with her movements, she placed a hand over his heart and then touched the same hand over her own.

"*Oh.*" He leaped up from the bench and shook his head, squeezing his eyes shut. "No, no, no. Miss Ives, you are misinterpreting my intentions. You are my student. I absolutely, under no circumstances, cannot court my students."

The declaration kicked her in the stomach, knocking the air from her lungs. She reached out to the trellis to steady herself. Her cauldron of despair bubbled up again. Despair for a bleak future filled with monsters, abuse, and unintentional killing. Despair for something she wanted, only for it to dissolve between her fingers. It didn't matter what she wanted. She was a monster. A killer.

A siren.

Monsters didn't get happy endings. No matter how much they wished for it.

She shifted her body away from him and rested her forehead against the trellis, her eyes closed. The rancid stink of the red snapper filled her nostrils, but she didn't bother to move away. An ache flared within her chest. It had no right to live there, especially with how short her acquaintance had been with Killian.

Or rather, Archmage Graves.

She supposed she needed to get used to the name. After his rejection, she had no plans to attend Darkest Star. There was no escaping Bramwick.

No one would help her. Not even the person she had put her trust in.

Right now, someone was bound to have noticed her absence. Perhaps Lord Auer was out looking for her right this second.

She took one earring out and started on the second but stopped when Lord Graves said in a whispery, melancholy tone, "Don't. They are for you."

"There is no point," she signed, counting on the fact that he couldn't understand her. "You can't protect me. Won't. What good will these do?"

Heart aching, she finished taking the second out and placed both on the empty space beside her on the bench. How could she possibly believe someone like her, with unknown origins, someone who lived on a farm, could possibly court or even marry a Shadow Lord? His cousin, Johanna, would make him a much better match.

"Lyyli..." His voice escaped as a husky whisper. She didn't dare meet his eye.

Take me back to my room, she wrote and quickly pushed the notebook aside.

What future did she have? Her father had sent her away. Being around anyone was dangerous. Lord Graves couldn't help her. Or perhaps he was too afraid to try. Lord Auer was a dangerous man.

No future existed for her. At least not one worth living.

Come morning, she would escape.

Or die trying.

The only good thing about having the ability to kill people with her voice was that she couldn't talk. Especially when she didn't want to.

Lord Graves dropped her off at her room, and at her request, the bindings remained on the bed rather than around her wrists. He lingered in the shadows, and she felt his eyes on her back, but only moments later, he disappeared.

Her shoulders drooped as heartache crashed over her head. She'd never hoped so much for something. Only to be rejected. And oh, how it hurt.

Taking a deep breath, she squared her shoulders and clenched her jaw with determination. Outside the window, the pink blush of dawn crept across the sky. The Shadow Fae in Bramwick would soon fall asleep.

She gave one last look at the closed door on the other side of the room before she pulled open her window and glanced out. Two stories stretched between her and the ground, the wall slick with very few footholds. If she slipped…

Survival was not likely.

She stripped her bed of two sheets and tied them together before she threw them over the side of her windowsill. Drat. The makeshift rope reached only halfway to the ground.

White fabric fluttered in the light breeze as she reeled it back up. She threw her armoire open, quickly dressed in a lightweight frock, and began tying the other dresses to the end of the sheets, making sure each knot was secured. By the time she finished, the sunlight rays of dawn had cast its net over the earth. The ward shimmered in the distance, catching the light like sparkling ocean waves.

Reminded of her ultimate goal, she tied one end of the rope to the leg of her bed and threw the rest over the side of the window. Her jaw ached from the determination she trapped between her clenched teeth, but she ignored it as she took a deep breath, threw her legs over the side, and clung on tightly to the rope.

It held.

For a moment, her body swayed back and forth with the breeze as she struggled to plant her feet against the outer wall of the fortress. Her heart raced. Her arms and fingers burned with the agony of holding her body so high above the ground.

But finally, her feet found purchase against the wall, and slowly, hand by hand, foot by foot, she began to descend.

Growing up, her adoptive mother had told her stories of princes scaling towers to save their princesses from fire-breathing dragons, or wealthy women escaping an arranged marriage by climbing out their window either aided by a trellis or a rope.

The stories made the feat sound easy.

This was not easy.

Each inch of her body trembled with fatigue. Twice, she stopped when a breeze buffeted her body to the side. Her feet scrambled against the slick rock, and just when she managed to gain hold again, she glanced down.

Dizziness crashed down on her at the sheer drop to the ground. Just one mistake could break her neck. She had never attempted this feat before. But then again, she'd never been so desperate to escape.

Her breathing grew fast and ragged as she barely held her panic at bay. She resumed her descent, her arms shaking with the effort.

Riiipp!

A scream lay on the tip of her tongue as the ground came at her alarmingly fast. The makeshift rope jerked as it caught on a few desperate threads.

Smash!

Pain ripped through her shoulder as she hit the fortress wall. Black shrouded her vision like ebony clouds in a tempest sky. Her hands lost their remaining grip on the rope, and she fell the last several feet to the grassy knoll with a *thunk.*

Lyyli groaned but quickly shut her mouth. Even the slightest whimper could kill a man.

Slowly, the darkness faded from her vision, and she found herself staring up at fluffy white clouds crawling across a bright blue sky. One by one, she moved each extremity. Fingers. Arms. Feet. Legs. Torso. Neck. Only her shoulder ached from the impact of the fall.

She pushed herself into a sitting position, wincing when the action pained her. No one rushed to her aid. No one was within sight, and thankfully, everyone within the fortress must not have been looking out their windows.

Pain flared again as she wobbled to her feet. None of her mother's stories mentioned the heroines falling in their escape attempts. She already made a poor princess. The role of a fumbling, mute prisoner suited her much more.

Not daring to dally any longer, she limped straight toward the shimmering ward on the outer edge of the fortress property. She didn't bother hiding. The Shadow Fae likely wouldn't be able to spot her easily in broad daylight. She also didn't dare to waste time attempting to steal a shadow horse. The beasts were terrifying, and she'd likely lose a hand sooner than she would coax one of them from the stables.

Each step she took toward the ward strengthened her resolve. Her limp became less pronounced. The pain in her shoulder began to ebb.

She stopped inches before the ward, watching the shimmer of pink, purple, orange, and blue glimmer in the sunlight. Just beyond it? Freedom.

****

Killian rolled over in his bed, pummeled his pillow, and rolled over again as guilt and regret ate at him. He had never in his life felt as if he'd messed up more than he had last night. He wasn't sure why Lyyli had taken him so much by surprise when she'd silently confessed her intentions toward him. He'd seen every one of her emotions, for shadow's sake! How daft was he?

He sighed and dropped his head against the pillow again, running his hands down his face as a waterfall of shame fell across his shoulders. So much time had passed since he'd focused on courtship. His first reaction to the mention of it with Lyyli had bound him in panic.

Her bright eyes and joyous smile and feminine grace filled his thoughts, pushing him even farther from sleep. The delicate arch of her neck. The soft curve of her jaw. The silky strands of her hair.

His heart thumped harder as he recalled every second in her presence. The furtive smiles. The shared secrets. The *easiness* of her company. The woman was lovely in every facet of the word.

"Idiot," he murmured to himself, tossing over onto his back and staring at the ceiling. He had approached the line of courtship without any prompting, without any hesitation, without even realizing he'd done it. And the second Lyyli had named what it was?

He'd pushed her away.

"The biggest idiot," he corrected himself as he swung his legs over the side of the bed and dug his palms into his eyes.

But…she would be his student.

Students be damned!

His legs suddenly itching to move, he crossed the room and threw back the curtains to gaze outside into the brightness of day, much to the discontent of his watering eyes.

He'd made a mistake. He knew it now.

Would Lyyli give him a second chance?

A long shape caught his attention on one side of the towering fortress walls. It was difficult to make out within the haze of daylight, but when he squinted his eyes, he thought he spotted a thin white, black, and gray rope hanging from a window.

Panic caught in his throat when he recognized the willowy figure scaling the walls. "Lyyli!"

****

"Faster than a doe in flight," Lyyli dared to whisper to herself as she bounced on the balls of her feet, gazing with trepidation at the shimmering barrier before her.

If she could only reach the forest this time, she would have a greater chance at obtaining the goal of freedom. The forest, and then later, the ocean. None of them would be able to follow.

Her heart raced, blood flowing quickly through her veins. She let out a long breath.

And then she began to run.

The ward's magic trickled over her as she crossed the barrier. Her cloak billowed out behind her in her flight. Grass and mud squished beneath her boots with every frantic footfall. She would make it this time. She had to.

The space between the fortress and the woods seemed to stretch on forever, as if every time she glanced up from her feet, she found herself in the same spot. Her lungs burned with the effort, and when she glanced behind her...

A surge of relief spurred her faster. The fortress grew smaller with each passing moment. She would make it. She would make it!

Alarm shook through her when a large man appeared out of nowhere in front of her, and before she managed to swerve away, his arm made contact with her throat.

Her feet flew out from beneath her, pain coursing through her throat as she landed hard on her back. Air rushed out of her lungs. Black stars fell across her vision, swiftly followed by yellow.

Yellow like a snake.

"No, no, no!" she shouted as panic clawed past the agony climbing her neck. Her nails raked across the grass as she scrambled to her feet, but just as the soles of her shoes found purchase against the slick grass, Lord Auer kicked her in the stomach. She flew backward and smashed once more against the ground, and this time she wasn't able to get up as he placed his large, dirtied boot against her collarbone.

His weight crushed her bones, her lungs, until she feared either one might give out. She clawed at his boot, but it continued to pin her to the ground.

"Where are you going, might I ask?" The thin black slits of his pupils struck a chord of fear in her heart. She nearly expected his tongue to flicker out of his mouth like a cobra's.

"Get off me," she sobbed, glancing around to find the field empty save for the two of them. "I have done enough! Release me. I beg you."

He shook his head, his weight pressing harder on her until another sob escaped her throat. "Sirens only have two existences—to either become slaves to their master's bidding or to die by the sword. I'm showing you mercy. Under my wing, no one can kill you."

"Killian will find out. He'll stop you."

"I don't give a shadow's arse about what Killian might do. He's complicated matters, but if I tell everyone you've run away? Or stage your death? He can do nothing if he thinks you're dead."

And then what? Her soul cried with the injustice of her situation. Surely, Lord Auer would lock her away deep beneath the fortress like a prisoner. A slave. No one would know where she was. Not even her family.

"You are a cruel man." Her quivering voice betrayed the bravery she tried to project.

"No, my Mute Songbird. I am not cruel. But I do what is necessary to survive."

"I hate you." She spat on his boot.

Lord Auer cocked his head to the side and studied her in amusement. "And your burning hate matters to me why?"

Tears of pain and despair leaked from her eyes as she began to sing. It was a folk song from back home. Her wavering voice muddled the words, but the melody drifted upward, her siren power leaking from every note.

The man's ring glowed bright red to combat the effect of her voice. The acrid smell of burning flesh came moments before he hissed and staggered backward. He flicked his hand through the air as if the action might put out a fire, but the ring smoldered hotter still. His eyes widened as if suddenly realizing the danger he was in. Either he would lose his finger, or the ring would shatter, putting him at her mercy.

She struggled to her feet, slowly backing away as she continued the song. Fear and regret coursed through her. She had no choice but to kill Lord Auer. But...she'd never killed anyone on purpose. Even if this felt more like self-defense.

In only a couple of strides, Lord Auer crossed the space between them and raised his fist, likely with the intent of knocking her out just as the jewel in his ring shattered. Her song ceased abruptly as she cowered beneath his blow, throwing both hands up to protect herself.

Clap!

The force of the blow never struck her. Instead, she peeked her eyes open to find another person standing protectively in front of her, Lord Auer's fist caught inside his hand. Her eyes widened.

Killian.

And then her surprise quickly turned into alarm. Had she continued singing for another second, he would be racing toward his death. He must have shadewalked to get to her.

"Has nobody taught you never to strike a woman?" Killian grunted as he tossed Lord Auer's fist aside.

"She's no woman," Lord Auer spat, cradling his blistered and blackened finger against his chest. "She's a monster."

Killian took a step backward until he stood directly in front of her, near enough for her to close her trembling fingers around his thin, white tunic. "When you tell yourself that, does it help you sleep at night?"

Lord Auer's terrified gaze darted between them. "You don't understand. She's…she's…" He lowered his voice. "A siren."

Her fingers continued to tremble, and as if he could feel it, Killian reached behind him and gripped her elbow reassuringly, without turning his back to the enemy. "I do understand."

"*How?*" The Shadow Lord's throat bobbed up and down with fear as he glanced at her, but he turned a glare on Killian, nonetheless. "You can read minds."

"I cannot. But it wasn't difficult to put the pieces together." He released her and stepped forward, brandishing a small dagger from his belt. Her heart quickened when she thought he might use it on Lord Auer.

No bloodshed. Please. I cannot stomach any more.

Never mind that she had been ready to take Lord Auer's life herself.

"Hurt her again," Killian said in a low, threatening voice, "and I will consider it an act of war between our provinces."

"Over what?" the man scoffed as he gestured to her. If only she had her own knife, then she would swipe his grin right off his face. But then…bloodshed… "Over a girl with a pretty voice?"

"Pretty face. Pretty voice. Sure. But also the woman I'm in a very serious courtship with. If you touch another hair on my potential bride's pretty head, it will be war, Auer."

Both hers and Lord Auer's jaws simultaneously fell open in surprise. Courtship? Serious? With her? But…but…what about what he said only last night? That she had misunderstood his intentions? That he would never court a student?

Her blood heated and then cooled in rapid succession. What he said must not be true, just another way to protect her. He didn't mean it. But she desperately wanted his words to be true.

However, when he turned slightly to look at her, every pore in her body heated again beneath the questioning truth of his gaze. Momentary shock pulsed through the furnace within her at the foreign strangeness of his eyes. Blue surrounded the thin black slits of his pupil when exposed to the sunlight. They weren't terrifying nor snakelike. More like a feline. Strange. Different. Beautiful.

And then she noticed the red around his eyes. As if he'd been crying.

No…not crying. He couldn't see in the sunlight. They were on the verge of watering.

"You are a fool, Graves. She'll rip you apart in your sleep."

He opened his mouth as if to reply, but a low growl from behind cut him off. Lyyli turned.

And stifled a scream.

Killian's reflexes took over as he grabbed Lyyli's wrist and threw her behind him just as large, black talons lashed out and struck his shoulder. An involuntary cry of pain ripped out of his mouth as he collapsed to the ground. His hand reflexively reached for the wound...and came back covered in sticky blood.

His gaze darted toward the horrifying beast on four legs, twice as big as a horse and something in between a lizard and a feline. The sharp end of its long, thrashing tail swished back and forth while its frill flared out around its face. A rattling hiss escaped between sharp, unforgivable teeth. Its eyes gave a similar glow to the variety of strange shapes and symbols emblazoned on the creature's chest.

A blanket of dread fell across his eyes. This creature... It couldn't be... It wasn't possible...

It lunged at him again, and he grunted when agony rippled across his shoulder as he scrambled out of the way. The talons missed him by mere inches.

"Lyyli, get back to the fortress!" He swayed dizzily as he once again stepped between her and the creature. He didn't wait to find out if she obeyed him. He reached into his pocket, pulled out a vial full of what he remembered to be black powder-like sand, and then after speaking a few words under his breath, threw the vial against the creature as it charged at him again. The glass shattered, and sand burst in all directions like a cloud of smoke.

The beast shrieked, flailing its head as it backed up, but the black, shimmering cloud followed it. Temporary blindness. It wouldn't buy him much time, but it would buy a little.

"What did you do?" Killian shouted at Lord Auer, grimacing against the fire in the gashes in the shoulder. "What have you done?"

The older man gasped in each breath, perspiration dotting his brow as he backed up toward the fortress. He clutched his left shoulder as if *he* were the one who'd gotten attacked. "I didn't do this… I don't think… I couldn't have…"

Fear oozed out of the man.

To his dismay, Lyyli hadn't moved from her spot behind him. Infuriating woman. Yet, he admired her resolve to stay at his side. Foolish but brave.

"Get back to the fortress," he said again, now watching the beast sneeze, growl, and attack the black cloud.

Lyyli pointed at his chest, concern rippling out of her.

"Go get help." He widened his stance, his only sharp weapon the knife in his hand. "Don't worry about me. I have an idea. I think."

The solution would only be temporary. Frighteningly temporary. But he couldn't let the beast roam free only to attack innocent people.

Thankfully, she listened to him this time as she turned and darted toward the fortress she had been running from only minutes earlier. The creature snapped its head in the direction of her flight, and despite the black cloud trapping it in a daze, it bounded after her.

Killian swore under his breath. The ancient beast was after the siren. Why?

Magic pooled at his core, and he grunted at the pain the effort caused him. He latched onto the thin shadows cast by towering trees and skittered through them, just barely fast enough to outpace the reptilian feline. He jumped out of the shadows, grabbed Lyyli by the waist, and pulled her back into the shadows with him just as the creature swiped its gleaming talons. They popped out of the shadows at the base of a large, leafy tree a small distance away.

He sagged against her, accidentally pinning her against the trunk when his world spun sickeningly. Shadewalking another person took too large a toll on his body. Blood continued to soak through his clothing as the metallic smell filled his nostrils.

Her soft, warm hands found his cheeks, gripping him tight and shaking him gently. He expended far too much effort as he pried his eyelids open to find her gazing back at him with large, distressed eyes. Only a couple of inches separated their faces, but when he tried to focus on her, he swayed again.

A curse word escaped under his breath. Venom claws. Always venom! He needed to speak with whatever evil gods made such evil creatures.

With fumbling fingers, he dug into a pocket and retrieved a light-grayish vial. "What color is this?" he murmured as his vision blurred in and out of focus. A huff of frustration escaped his mouth when she signed something. He didn't have time to guess what she said as the creature released another deafening roar and turned in a full circle in the middle of the field. Searching. Hunting.

Quickly, Killian unstopped the vial and poured the contents over his wounded flesh. He hissed at the acidic burn. "Nope," he gasped and pulled out a second vial of a similar shade. "Wrong one."

This time when he poured the liquid over his wound, a pulsing relief pushed the majority of the agony from his body as the elixir dragged the venom out of the gashes. His vision slowed into a languid tilt, and with a start, he realized his forehead rested against Lyyli's.

"Apologies," he murmured as he stepped back, squeezed his eyes shut, and when he opened them again, he was ready. It took several tries to locate his pocket until his swirling world finally came to a halt. He pulled out the jewelry box and thrust the two earrings into her hands. "Hold these for me. I need this box."

However, as he took several steps out of the trees, his knees buckled underneath him, and he landed hard on his side. Despite the danger, despite bleeding out, embarrassment heated his cheeks. What a pitiful sight he must be to Lyyli!

The creature shook the remaining dark cloud from itself, narrowed its eyes on Auer where he struggled to stand, and began advancing.

"Demon spawn!" Killian shouted, effectively pulling the beast's attention away from Auer. His world jolted suddenly, and he stumbled sideways. When his world tilted the other way, he gave up his attempt to stand and instead sank to his knees.

As the beast began to advance on him instead, he opened the earring box and began to chant in a low murmur. "*Quae sigillum captionem.*"

The magic within his well escaped like a rushing exhale, pouring into the small box in his hands. It drained every last drop, and just when the exertion threatened to knock him unconscious, the magic now inside the box began to reach out to the beast.

Like a strong tide, the magic sucked it inside, and he snapped the box shut.

He inhaled a gulp of air, a shiver running through him at the horror of his depleted magic. He'd never given so much before. He was lucky. The spell could have taken some of his life force instead of all his magic. His magic would regenerate within the next several nights, but until then, he wouldn't be able to seal the box completely.

Which meant no one could open it without releasing the creature.

Soft hands wrapped around his arm and helped him to his feet. His heart flip-flopped inside his chest when he met a pair of beautiful eyes—concerned beautiful eyes. Lyyli placed her hand over his heart as if to ask after his wound.

"It's not feeling great," he answered honestly, wincing as he rolled his shoulder. Blood continued to soak his clothing. It needed a bandage. A large one.

He caught her hand in his, mesmerized by the graceful curve of each joint, yet her palms were rough rather than smooth like an idle lady's. Warmth radiated from her fingers and into his as if a small spool of sunlight tethered them together. For once, he didn't mind the sun.

"Graves!" Auer gasped, the distraction effectively severing the connection of the sunlight thread between them.

When he turned, alarm shot through him to find Auer on his hands and knees in the middle of the field, clutching his left shoulder.

After a few stumbling attempts, Killian reached the man and hefted him to his feet. His shoulder screamed in protest when the fire of agony slithered through the gashes in his flesh. The elixir worked to pull out the remaining venom.

They stumbled forward, and in both their weak states, they nearly collapsed to the ground. Surprise jolted through him when Lyyli took Auer's other side and helped support him as they hobbled toward the fortress.

She would help Auer of all people?

He swallowed his rising emotions as he realized the depth of her goodness. How could a siren possess so much compassion? Even for the man who had hurt her?

As they neared the fortress, several guards burst outside into the sunlight, recoiled, and then when they spotted the three of them, moved forward with haste.

"What happened?" one of the guards asked as he took in Killian's blood-soaked tunic and Auer's feeble state.

"I believe his heart is failing him," he answered, his breath coming out as labored puffs. "Find a healer."

The guards took Auer from them, and the moment they stepped foot inside, they were met by a flurry of panicked activity. Guards, physicians, and family were awakened and running to and fro with bandages, cloths, and more. Had anyone seen what happened? Had they seen the beast? Heard it?

Auer disappeared down the hallway while one of his physicians motioned Killian in the opposite direction. When the woman was about to guide him inside a room, he stopped short at the door as panic surged through him. His curse mark… If the physician tended to him, word might spread. His reputation would suffer.

"No," he grunted as he took a step back, glancing behind him. Lyyli still trailed him, her hands to her heart as she stood only several feet away. "Lyyli will see to my wounds. No one else."

The physician bowed and walked away, but not before leaving behind a bowl of water, clean cloths, and bandages. The moment the two of them stepped inside the room, he closed the door behind him with a resounding *thud*. The silence of her company held the tension together in the room.

"Why?" she signed. "Why me?"

"Because...because..." He scratched his head before falling into a chair, exhausted and in pain. Lyyli quickly pulled up a chair in front of him, gently took his hand, and cleaned the blood from his skin with a damp cloth.

Instead of answering the question, he took out the jewelry box and turned it in his opposite hand. "You can't just destroy strong magic like this. You can either transfer it or contain it. Nothing else will do."

Frustration burst out of her as she signed something to him, and yet again, he didn't understand. He echoed her frustration.

If only she could speak. If only he knew her silent language. He vowed to learn it.

He pulled out his notebook and quill. A splash of blood seeped into the corner pages, but Lyyli either didn't notice or didn't care as she eagerly opened it and began to write.

Do you sleep with this?

He pressed his lips together to try to hide his amusement at her disbelief. "Of course, I do. Either in my pocket or on my nightstand. Sometimes I wake up with an idea, and if I don't jot it down quickly, I will forget."

For several moments, she simply stared at him before she shook her head and sighed. *You are strange.*

This time, his amused grin broke through his self-control. "Me? *You* are a fish on legs who can't swim. Need I say more?"

She clamped her hand over her mouth, and with her other hand, she hastily scrawled, *Don't make me laugh. It will be the death of you.* Her smile fell, and her expression sobered.

Although she didn't write in the notebook, her doubtful and insecure emotions spoke for her.

"I apologize." He grimaced and glanced away from her, staring at a dark spot on the curtains covering the window. "I can't say I'm well-versed in courtship. Quite the opposite, actually. It interested me somewhat in my younger days before..." He swallowed as he finally admitted the truth. "Before my father died. After, I was thrown into the role of Shadow Lord, and I put so much focus into my duties and magical studies. There was no time to court. It became a distant desire and managed to vanish completely over time."

He lifted his head to find her studying him curiously. "I hadn't meant to hurt you last night. I simply needed time to think about this."

But I am your student, she wrote. *There is nothing to think about.*

"Yet," he corrected. "You are not my student *yet.*" Hesitancy and hope streamed out of her, though she remained still, the washcloth in the bowl completely forgotten as she watched him with wary eyes.

He felt utterly powerless as his body reacted in completely foreign ways to her hopeful gaze. The pulse beneath his veins beat faster and faster. A flush burned the tips of his pointed ears.

"I-I am probably not an easy man to court. I have secrets. I have ambitions. I get distracted easily—"

The tips of his ears burned hotter when she placed a finger against his lips before writing in the notebook—a notebook which probably needed to be replaced soon with something with more room. She turned it to face him.

And I accidentally killed the only boy I ever courted. Her expression fell. *I am not easy to court either.* But then she rolled her eyes. *What are we doing, talking? You are clearly in pain. Take off your shirt so I may tend to your wound.*

His fingers hesitantly reached for the first button. Then the second. On the third, he paused. "I have secrets, Lyyli. I don't think you will be particularly happy about this one."

He watched as curiosity, confusion, and trepidation became tendrils of emotion above her head. And then he finished unbuttoning his shirt. He grimaced at the pain encompassing his shoulder, and with Lyyli's help, they managed to slip his injured arm out of the sleeve.

She inhaled sharply, her eyes wide as she stared at the black curse etched onto his skin from his wrist to his elbow. Although she said no words, didn't even sign, she pointed. Her curiosity now mingled with fear.

"A secret," he grunted. "Might be temporary. Might be permanent. When Shadow Fae get cursed, it leaves a mark on their skin."

The black of fear slowly disappeared, though her trembling hands betrayed her as she dipped the cloth back into the water and dabbed at his wound. He hissed at the pain rippling through his shoulder.

"If we are to court, you deserve to know," he continued, teeth clenched through the administration. "You mustn't tell a soul. Promise?" Lyyli nodded, her eyes wide. Green, she'd said they were. They were beautiful as black and white. He bet they were breathtaking with color. "I needed a way to communicate with my mother, so I visited a witch." She dropped the cloth as surprise shot out of her, but she quickly resumed her task. "The witch took away every strip of color from my eyesight. Everything I see is black and white and gray."

Now she paused, staring into his eyes as if looking for the evidence.

"A-a-and she gave me something else in its stead." He swallowed as he gestured to his arm. "Please don't be too angry." He paused long enough to steel himself. "I can see emotions through color. I can see every single emotion you're feeling right now. Every single one since the moment we met."

Again, she dropped the cloth, but instead of picking it up, mortification burst out of her like an exploding star. She covered her face with her hands, but not before he noticed the shade of gray of her face growing darker with a blush.

Mortification. Embarrassment. Shame. Anger. More embarrassment.

"Don't be embarrassed," he murmured quietly as he reached out to her, but his fingers hovered inches away. "Your emotions have not changed my opinion of you."

She dropped her hands from her face and wrote angrily in the notebook, followed by a red burst of color. *All this time? Tell me everything you saw. I deserve to know.*

He picked up the wet cloth and dabbed at his wound just to give his hands something to do. Scathing heat burned him, and he squeezed his eyes shut for a few moments. "Umm...you are sad all the time. And afraid. You feel relief and gratitude when you are around me. And...umm..." He coughed into his hand. "Pink," he said quickly before moving on. "You get anxious and fearful in front of a crowd. A bit of despair mixed in with your sadness."

Lyyli's eyes widened, followed by surprise and trepidation as she leafed through the pages of the notebook and stopped on a particular page. He watched as her eyes moved as she skimmed the contents of the page.

And then she froze.

Moments later, she dropped into a chair, her face in her hands again. Embarrassment. Mortification. Without looking at him, she flipped the book around and pointed to the word "pink" on the emotions-color page.

Pink: infatuation.

He grimaced apologetically, but she probably didn't see it with her fingers covering her face. "Yes, I am aware you are fond of me romantically. But remember when we sat at the pond? I saw my own reflection. And…pink. You aren't the only one."

Slowly, she removed her fingers from her face and gazed back at him. Being honest about his feelings set him on edge as if he stood before a cliff, and just the faintest of breezes might knock him over the side. When was the last time he'd confessed something so terrifying? Probably never.

His palms began to sweat, and he subconsciously wiped them on the knees of his trousers. She didn't reply. Rather, she stared at him as the light purple of shock, the pink of infatuation, the yellow of happiness, and the faintest trace of black fear escaped her.

"I am not sure why you are afraid." He wiped his palms again. "Will you please explain? I am riddled with anxiety over your unspoken thoughts about my confession."

At last, she picked up the quill, her hand trembling as she wrote, *I am terrified I might kill you.*

"Ah." He nodded while wearing a frown. "A legitimate concern. And before you ask again, I am *not* taking away your voice."

She breathed in a slow, deep breath and let it out just as slowly. Suddenly, her eyes lit up, followed by furious scrawl.

I am able to speak around Lord Auer. His enchanted ring allows it. You can enchant something as well.

The hope in her eyes struck him in the gut as he gave her an apologetic smile. "I am flattered you think so highly of me as being capable of such strong magic. Whoever created the enchantment has a well of magic deep enough to penetrate the force of a siren's voice. Either that or..." He trailed off, swallowing at the terrifying possibility.

She softly nudged his uninjured shoulder as if silently prodding him to continue.

"Or...whoever is responsible for the enchantment is finding another source to sustain such strong magic. There are such items in the world. Some of the darkest of magic. Illegal magic. If you kill someone and trap their magic in a powerful enough item to sustain it, the feat is possible."

His mind whirred with the terrifying possibility. Such items were rare and most thought to be destroyed.

The whirling thoughts in his mind halted suddenly as Lyyli dabbed at the skin around his wound and then his neck, and when her fingers stilled, he found himself gazing into her warm eyes. His heart pounded against his ribcage. His body flushed with heat.

He didn't doubt pink streams of infatuation fluttered out of him like a kaleidoscope of butterflies. It had been so long since he'd surrendered himself to these feelings. So long since he'd allowed himself to focus on courtship while he pushed his studies aside. He'd forgotten how pleasant the warmth smoldering in his core was.

"I was thinking," he murmured, his voice breaking the tender silence. Guilt churned inside him as he realized he was putting courtship above his priorities for his mother, but then he reminded himself he needed to keep his title to keep his power. They were both important. "I want to take you to the ocean tonight if you will allow me. I will teach you how to swim, and you can fully discover who you are as a mer."

The sickly yellow of anxiety made an appearance over Lyyli's head. She signed something, but the black emotion over her head interpreted her words for him.

"What are you afraid of? Change? The truth? The water?"

She nodded to all three.

"I won't let you go. I promise."

Before Lyyli was able to answer, the door on the opposite side of the room burst open. Johanna entered with a Sun Fae at her heels. At seeing them together, Johanna's face contorted into unease.

"Get out," Johanna snapped to Lyyli.

"Johanna," Killian growled a warning. "That's no way to speak to her."

"Please leave," she amended, though her glare remained fixed to her expression. "He's in good hands now."

Starting a fight now between two people he cared about while he was injured was a horrible idea. So instead, he offered Lyyli a warm smile. "Thank you for your help today. And...pack your things discreetly. None of us will stay here any longer. Especially not you. I'll take you to my home. No one will know where you've gone."

Her eyes widened, and slowly, she spelled out with her hands A-U-E-R.

"Auer is in no position to keep you here. I already told him where I stand with you."

With one last glance toward Johanna, she dipped her head and scurried out of the room. A tense, uncomfortable silence rippled in her wake.

As the Sun Fae quietly tended to his wound, saying nothing about the curse marking his arm, Johanna stood with her hands on her hips, giving him an accusing glare. "You told me she was dangerous. You told me to stay away."

"She *is* dangerous, yes. But she's not the assailant I previously thought her to be. I like her." His gaze challenged hers, and he braced himself for the inevitable pain he might cause her with his confession. Johanna was his cousin, and that was all she could be. Even if he had to weather more storms with Lyyli.

Slowly, Johanna's fists melted from her hips as surprise and a tinge of hurt waved above her head like a flag of defeat. "I heard a rumor you were looking for a wife. Is she...?"

"On the list? Yes. Or rather, she is the list." He leaned back in his chair, sighing at the cool relief running through his shoulder as the Sun Fae magic touched him.

"Why?" Johanna asked quietly. "What kind of wife would she be for you? A Shadow Lord. She can't even speak."

He ran his fingers through his hair as he frowned. Johanna was right. Lyyli couldn't speak. She was mer. A siren. The faintest sound from her lips could kill him.

What was he doing?

His shoulders slumped as her rationale muddled his mind. He'd finally taken that step forward in courtship and felt as if she just pushed him so he stumbled backward. Auer's words came to mind. *You are a fool, Graves. She'll rip you apart in your sleep.*

How had she not accidentally killed her adoptive family, even from something like crying out in her sleep from a nightmare? Or a stubbed toe?

If she was any other woman, mute or not, courting and even marrying her would not provide an issue.

"I'm fond of her," he replied lamely. "Isn't it enough?"

The breath from Johanna's mouth escaped as a sigh. "I don't know, Killian. But you've always taken your duties as a Shadow Lord seriously. Would she make a good Lady?"

He remained silent because he didn't know the answer to her question. Lyyli had lived a life full of fear, with a focus on trying to keep others safe from herself rather than going out and taking the world for her own. She hadn't had the opportunity to delve fully into life. But he wanted to give her that opportunity.

Frustration pricked his eyes. He had so much to do and so little time to do it.

For the first time in his life, he didn't know what to do next.

Johanna gave his uninjured shoulder a kind, reassuring squeeze. But instead of hounding him more on the subject, she asked, "How is your shoulder?"

He glanced down to find the gashes closing beneath the Sun Fae's administration. The dark lacerations had turned into faint lines, which transitioned into silvery scars. Thankfully, neither the Sun Fae nor Johanna questioned him on the curse trailing up his arm.

"Much better. Thank you," he breathed to the fae healer. "Johanna, we'll leave as soon as possible. It's time to see how my mother is faring."

Because if anything, he'd learned something both useful and dangerous. Lord Auer may be the puppet, but someone else pulled the strings.

Lady Auer.

He thought back on when he'd shown her the enchanted hair comb. She'd known it was dangerous without him saying much about it. And the moment Lyyli had stepped out of the rippling barrier of Lady Auer's ward, Lord Auer had come after her. Lady Auer was the puppeteer. He was sure of it.

And he could not afford to be wrong.

An awkward tension descended upon the carriage like dark clouds gathering in preparation for a thunderstorm. Lyyli didn't need to see emotions to sense Johanna's displeasure with her company. The woman turned her body toward the window, not once looking her way.

Lyyli desired to cut the tension with a knife or with a kind word. The feat proved impossible with no way to communicate.

Instead, she sat on her hands as her insecurity ran wild. She didn't belong here. As a siren, a mer, and the daughter of a farmer, she didn't truly belong anywhere. But especially not in a Shadow Lord's carriage.

She bit her lip as she gazed out the opposite window, watching as the dark scenery jostled by. Silver-tipped birds darted past the window. Blooms of oozing red flowers and delicate yellow moonbeams climbed the long, wild grass. A creature with sharp teeth and long ears bounced from tree to tree. Up above, a large, round moon twirled and shimmered as if trying on a gown of starlight in front of a mirror.

"What are you?" Johanna asked suddenly, making her jump in her seat. Her gaze darted to the other woman and then to where Killian lay sprawled across the seat opposite them, deep in slumber. Even curled up, his long legs protested the lack of space the carriage offered.

"Mermaid," she signed, a sigh waiting on her lips when she thought communication might be hopeless. But when Johanna's eyes widened, so did hers.

"A mermaid," she breathed. "I have never met one."

Lyyli's hands spoke rapidly, desperate for conversation in a language she spoke well. "You understand sign language?"

Johanna nodded and signed as she spoke. "I work with underprivileged children at an orphanage. A sibling pair is deaf. I learned it to better communicate with them." She paused and cocked her head to the side, now studying her more carefully. "Be honest. Have you bewitched my cousin with that voice of yours?"

She shook her head. "No, never."

Across from them, Killian snorted and rolled onto his back before lying still. Johanna now spoke only with her hands as if afraid he might overhear. "I know you bewitched everyone at Lord Auer's ball. Killian could have experienced the same fate."

"I promise I didn't bewitch him."

Johanna snarled and struck a fist against the side of the carriage, jolting Killian awake. But she paid no heed to him as she continued to sign. "It isn't fair for you to slip into our lives and take what I've been trying to get for several years. You can't take him. You just can't."

Tears rolled down the woman's face, the sight creating a pit in Lyyli's stomach.

Killian croaked, "What's going on? Did something happen?"

With a shake of her head, Johanna said out loud, "Go back to sleep. We're just talking."

He didn't.

Lyyli hesitantly reached out to touch Johanna's elbow to bring her attention back to her. For once, she took comfort that Killian couldn't understand sign language. "You love him?"

Johanna sighed and shook her head, not answering for several long seconds, and even then, she answered with her hands and not out loud. "You don't understand. I am the eldest of my sisters. I must marry well. I will never marry better than a Shadow Lord. I am fond of him to some degree and have held onto the hope that Killian would choose to marry someday, and the best match would be me. You have ruined this. How can I ensure my sisters all marry well now?"

Lyyli had seen the way Johanna often looked at Killian. The woman was likely lying about her feelings, or at the very least, downplaying them.

Frowning, Lyyli played with a strand of her copper hair, running it through her fingers as she thought through the issue. She had finally found an opening for her own happiness, and she was too selfish to throw it away so easily. In the end, things might not work out with Killian.

The thought struck a hole through her chest.

Glancing across the carriage, she met his eye. Confused. Concerned. His mouth opened and closed as if he wanted to say something, but something held him back.

At last, she replied to Johanna. "I did not mean to upheave your life. I'm sorry."

"That's it? You're sorry?"

"What else would you have me do? I don't want his title or his influence. He's kind and attentive and sweet. I would settle for just him, and I don't want to walk away." She subconsciously touched the earrings in her ears, the ones from Killian. She'd put them back in and hadn't taken them out.

Johanna chuckled as she wiped her eyes. Out loud, she said, "It's not easy to get a read on your personality until you talk." With her hands, she said, "He has told me similar things about you. He never sought out a wife. I suppose the right person had to entice him." She hung her head before wiping away another tear. "I will have to look elsewhere for good matches."

For several moments, Lyyli sat on her hands and bit her lip. What could she possibly do or say to fix this? Why must she trample on someone else to get what she wanted?

However, Johanna continued speaking silently as if not even waiting for her to answer. "He is not interested in me that way, and perhaps I only wanted his title. Like I said, the right person had to entice him." She turned her head and offered a watery smile. "At least you are kind. Killian deserves someone kind. And patient. *Very* patient."

A laugh began bubbling up her throat, and she slapped her hands over her mouth to keep it down. Johanna's chuckle took its place.

"Patient? Really?" Her fingers leaked sarcasm.

"Yes, really. Just wait until he locks himself in his tower for some project or another. He won't even remember to eat."

When both of them shot amused glances at Killian, he huffed. "All right, now I am certain you are talking about me. It isn't fair that I don't understand. Actually, it's downright rude to talk behind my back."

Lyyli signed to him, and Johanna interpreted. "We are talking to your *front*. You need to learn sign language. Someday you might not have a notebook to write in."

Again, he huffed and rolled his eyes as he reached into his vest pocket and waved his notebook in the air. "I always have it with me. *Always*."

She reached across the carriage, enjoying the way his breath hitched when she took his hands and helped him sign "notebook" and "always." He practiced a second time on his own, opening his hands like a book, mimicking writing, and then circling his finger through the air.

His warm smile shot heat straight through her core and into her cheeks. He said, "A couple hours remain until we reach the estate. Will you teach me more?"

Returning his smile with a tender one of her own, she signed, "Always."

They practiced over the next couple of hours, learning basic words and phrases. Johanna helped interpret for her, mostly because she could not see well in the dark like the other two, and she couldn't easily write in the notebook.

A breath of relief escaped her at how much easier it was to communicate this way. She elicited a laugh from Killian on multiple occasions, and the darkness in her own heart lifted simply at spending time with him.

The carriage stopped abruptly. Killian stepped out first, helped Johanna down, and held out his hand for her. Her heart raced as she slipped her hand into his, his fingers far rougher and more calloused than she expected of a Shadow Lord. What emotions did he see escaping from her?

Probably enough to send her falling back into a six-foot grave of mortification.

And then her eyes widened when she saw it.

The estate loomed over them, the most gorgeous structure she had seen in her entire life. Three stories stretched into the starry night sky, the outer walls covered in flowering vines that glowed beneath the moon's light. From left to right, the estate sprawled elegantly across the property, with far more windows than she could count. On the furthest right, a tower extended a smidge higher than the estate but still connected to the structure. Although the estate wasn't a castle, it still looked like something straight out of a fairy tale.

"I get to stay *here*? Are you sure?" Thankfully, Johanna interpreted her signing.

Killian nodded and tucked her hand inside the crook of his elbow before leading her toward the estate. "I would rather you stay here than remain at Lord Auer's mercy. Even if he *is* bedridden. You are free. You may do whatever you wish, go wherever you want."

Lyyli quickly signed to Johanna. "I thought he was trying to find a cure for his mother. Why are we here?"

She simply smiled and answered with her hands. "He has a reason for everything. I've learned not to ask questions. It only slows him down."

Servants opened the estate doors for them, and the moment they stepped inside, Lyyli's mouth fell open. Magnificent splendor stared back at her.

Tapestries of thread and silk hung from the walls. The furniture curved with elegant grace from the tables to the chairs to the bookshelves. And as she stepped farther into the entry room alone, she turned in a slow circle. A silver chandelier hung high above them, the glass reflecting the candlelight from the sconces and sending a rainbow of color sparkling across the walls.

The atmosphere felt warm and safe, nothing like Lord Auer's cold, unforgiving fortress.

She suddenly felt self-conscious of her simple clothing, unkempt hair, and slippers with a hole in the right sole. Again, she asked herself... *What am I doing here?*

Killian slipped off his coat and handed it to who she assumed to be the butler. "Make up a room for our new guest—Miss Ives. Make sure she's properly fed and taken care of." He murmured something close to the man's ear, and she thought she caught the word "mute."

After so many years of being called mute to neighbors, visitors, and more, the sting of longing never ceased to prick her heart. Longing for something different. Something normal. To speak without repercussions.

Two young women rushed into the room to greet them, each casting uncertain and wary looks toward her. Killian didn't miss a beat as he walked toward an elegant staircase and asked, "How are my mother and cousin faring?"

"The same, milord," a female servant answered with a curtsy. "Though they have both lost some weight, and neither has woken."

"Wonderful," he breathed a weary sigh. "If anyone needs me, I'll be in my tower."

He met her eye across the room and opened his mouth as if he wanted to say something, but then he turned and climbed the staircase, disappearing from view. A rush of uncertainty slammed into her as he left her with strangers in an unfamiliar, foreign world.

Taking a deep breath, she smoothed down her skirts. She felt uncertain and self-conscious, yes. But here, she was safe.

****

Killian's eyes burned with fatigue, the lack of sleep he'd suffered over the past few days catching up to him. He gingerly sipped on a cup of steaming hot khave as he piled his desk several feet high with numerous books, texts, and scrolls.

A knock sounded on the door, making him freeze. For a moment, his fatigue tried to catch up with his mind. No one spoke on the other side of the door to announce themselves.

Lyyli...

His heart sped up as he smoothed down his hair and straightened his clothing. "Come in," he croaked, cringing before he cleared his throat.

Sure enough, Lyyli hesitantly stepped inside, running her fingers through her hair all while nervousness leaked from her every pore. Nervousness. Uncertainty. Doubt. For a moment, he wondered if he exuded the same emotions.

"I...uh..." The tips of his ears burned as he surveyed the room. Stacks of books, vials, artifacts, and more littered every surface, even the floor. He cleared his throat again as he stepped around several potted plants he'd placed in the sunlight before he'd left and shoved a stack of books off one of the chairs to give her space to sit. "I'm suddenly embarrassed at how much of a slob I am. I swear I'm not usually this messy." A hiss escaped through his teeth. "That was a lie. I am the messiest person you will ever meet."

Her fingers moved to clamp around her mouth as if she barely held back a smile or perhaps even a laugh. The amused emotions cascading out of her betrayed her, however. His own nervousness eased a fraction.

Killian switched his weight from one foot to the other, wishing she could speak. If they married, what kind of marriage would they have? What about children? Would they be born as sirens or Shadow Fae?

He would never be thinking about this if the other Shadow Lords hadn't pushed him into it. But he found himself giddy. Hopeful. Excited.

He flexed his fingers awkwardly. *Do something, Killian!* But what? When was the last time he'd courted someone? Forever and a half ago. Perhaps he should just marry her and end his awkward uncertainty.

"You look nice," he blurted and then inwardly cringed. Nice? What was she? A show horse? Surely, he could come up with better compliments.

However, she simply twirled for him, giving him a teasing smile as she showcased the holes in the bottom of the dress. Her hair twirled with her, long tendrils escaping to her lower back. Despite the holes, despite her worn shoes, she was the most beautiful woman he'd ever known.

Would she mind if he doted on her with new clothing? Shoes? Jewelry?

He grinned wryly, amused at how quickly he took to the idea of courting. Perhaps the desire had simply lied dormant inside him until he found the right person.

Instead of sitting in the proffered chair, Lyyli explored the room, looking but not touching. After a minute, she stood in front of a large map stretching across the wall.

"I know I said I would take you to the ocean tonight," he said as he picked up a book and flipped through it. "Tomorrow. I promise."

She shrugged a shoulder and continued to study the map. Streams of melancholy blue replaced her previous amusement as she touched a small spot on the map in the human kingdom of Frisia.

"You are missing home?" he ventured.

A sigh left her lips as she nodded, still with her back to him. He frowned as he glanced from his work to her and back to his work. He might be able to spare a few minutes.

"Have a seat." He gestured to the empty chair before clearing off a second and scooting it close. The moment she hesitantly lowered herself onto the cushion, he dragged his finger from his throat to his stomach. "This is the location of everyone's well of magic. Close your eyes and try to envision what your well looks like. For me, I imagine a small pool of inky black. It ripples each time I touch it, each time I draw from it. Your own well is where your voice draws its power. You will need to learn to separate your voice from your magic. And—from what I've witnessed myself—your well is quite large. Larger than mine. Larger than…anyone's I've ever known. But it has its limits. I've seen that too."

When she gestured toward his chest, he pulled out his notebook and handed it over. She wrote, *Are you certain?*

He smiled and leaned close with his forearms resting on his knees. "No. I can never be certain of anything unless I study it long enough. I'm afraid I cannot risk it with you."

How do I find my well?

For the first time when speaking of her voice, hope blossomed from her person like a beautiful flower in bloom.

"May I touch you?" he asked, and when she nodded, he hesitantly reached out and placed his entire hand over her heart while his other braced against her back to straighten her spine. "Close your eyes again. Take deep breaths. And remember, this takes time. It's normal to practice this for months before you are able to touch your magic. But with you… Your magic latches onto your voice naturally, as I assume is common with sirens. You can already touch your magic. Not voluntarily, but your body has practice finding the well. Just listen to your body. When you speak, where do you draw from?"

After a minute of deep breathing, he released her and allowed her to practice on her own for a moment. His voice interrupted the stillness of the tower. "When I first started shadewalking as a young child, it wasn't easy to stop. The shadows would pull me in, and there were times when I couldn't escape. The longest I've gone trapped in a shadow was three days before my mother used a bottle of sunlight to dispel the shadows, and they spit me out. Shadewalking became a source of fear for a long time after my terrifying experience. But when you control your magic rather than allow it to control you, there is nothing to fear."

She opened her eyes and gazed back at him. Knots formed in his stomach, his tongue momentarily speechless. Several moments passed before he realized she'd written in the notebook. *You think I can control this.*

"I *know* you can." Or at least he truly hoped. There was also a possibility sirens simply couldn't be in the presence of anyone but another siren without killing them. But as far as he was concerned, no other sirens existed. "Most people have to learn how to turn on their magic. You must practice turning it off."

Taking her hand, he led her across the messy floor and to the window, pulling back the drapes to reveal the large expanse of his property. He continued holding onto her as he pointed to a spot near the edge of the property.

"The underground soldier barracks are just beyond those trees. I only have a couple handfuls of soldiers on the property while the rest are elsewhere. I can make sure it's empty for an hour or two a day. It will be safe for you to practice there."

"I can't see it," she signed, and he momentarily froze.

He ran his fingers through his hair, both worried and alarmed. "Forgive me. I forgot you aren't nocturnal. I didn't even consider…" His hand ran over his mouth before gesturing between them. "Will this even work? You sleep through the night."

Her hand shook as she wrote in the notebook, but he didn't miss her hopeful emotions. *My whole life, I've slept through the night. The past couple of months have been different. Strange but not awful. I can get used to it.*

Yet, she would be giving up so much. Far more than he would be giving up. "Why? Why take a chance on me? Why sacrifice so much?"

Because you see me. All of me. You don't fear me. You have already taught me so much about myself. Because my future looks brighter with you in it. Forgive me for being forward, but I will give up everything for this chance.

For a long time, he stared at her words, his heart racing faster and faster in time with his rising flush. He wasn't sure how to reply. He'd never been great at expressing his own emotions, not even when it mattered most.

At last, he dropped her hand, cleared his throat, and crossed the room to his desk before throwing a large volume open. His cowardly self needed to hide behind his books for a few minutes to give him time to think.

"I don't know if you noticed," he said, flipping page after page, "but the symbols on the beast that attacked us on Auer's estate looked familiar. Do you know what they are?" When she shook her head, he continued, "They are the symbols to resurrect something dead and usually something powerful. The amount of magic necessary to resurrect such a being is…" He blew out a long breath. "…astounding."

His pulse jumped in surprise when Lyyli joined him at the desk and rifled through one of the books. Hiding his smile proved difficult as they searched the books together for either the symbols or the creature.

What felt like hours ticked by, and he found her company more than pleasant. In fact, focusing on the task at hand was nearly impossible with her near.

Lyyli suddenly slammed a book down on the near-empty table before sinking into a chair, her head in her hands. He turned the book to face him, all the blood draining from his face as he read.

The galiphor was an ancient creature, one of three pets belonging to the Shadow Emperor a thousand years ago. The Shadow Emperor had been defeated and buried deep underground, along with his pets. A myth described the possibility of resurrecting such a powerful being with…

With…

A siren's song. A blood sacrifice of shadow, sun, and forest.

"Lyyli," he whispered, his head shooting up to find tears escaping through the cracks of her fingers. Her shoulders shook silently as she cried. "Did Lord Auer make you kill three fae?"

She nodded, her head still buried beneath her hands.

The air whooshed from his lungs as he leaned against the side of his desk. Auer's words echoed in his mind. *"I didn't do this... I don't think... I couldn't have..."*

It only proved that the man hadn't known what he was doing. But if Lady Auer truly was behind this, what was her goal?

"All right," he murmured, the tips of his fingers drumming on his desk. "Now we need to figure out if the Shadow Emperor is resurrected or just his pet. And if so...how to defeat him."

Several more confusing puzzle pieces clicked together. The votes on turning Katalle into an empire rather than ten provinces. If someone meant to resurrect the Shadow Emperor, the task would be easier if the Shadow Lords handed over their power rather than fighting against the change.

Guilt churned within his stomach when he realized Lyyli was still crying. How could he be so oblivious to her despairing feelings when they stared him in the face?

Quietly, he pushed away from the desk and sat on the arm of her chair before pulling her into his embrace. She shook against him, though not a single sound escaped her lips.

"It's not your fault," he whispered against her hair. "You had no choice. Don't blame yourself."

Yet, she placed her hand on his shoulder where the galiphor had scratched him.

He covered her fingers with his own and gave her a sincere smile. "I'm fine. It left a scar, but I'm alive. It's not your fault. Believe me, Lyyli."

She bit her lip through her tears, but finally, she nodded. His heart nearly burst out of his chest as she placed her damp lips against his cheek. She moved out of the chair and away from him far too quickly for him to grasp her around the waist and pull her back into his embrace for the scorching kiss he longed to give her. Instead, he watched as she slipped from the room and closed the door behind her.

Silence echoed in her absence, leaving the room far colder than only a minute prior.

A smile crept across his face as he touched his cheek, where her kiss still lingered. Although she could not speak, their connection burned brighter than ever. And he planned to follow the connection to find out where the road led him.

Staring at his own body as he slept never failed to unnerve him.

A chill crawled up Killian's spine as he watched his actual body sleeping slumped over on his desk, his hair a mess and spittle escaping the corner of his mouth and seeping into one of the open pages of a book. Thank the shadows Lyyli wasn't there to witness something so…embarrassing.

He reflexively reached out for the book to protect the pages from his own drool, but his fingers passed right through as if he were a ghost.

"Don't sabotage this for me," he said, pointing a stern finger at himself. "Lyyli can still change her mind about us."

Of course, he remained fast asleep. Lyyli likely slept as well. Or did she? The light of day streamed in from the window, and everyone except perhaps a few soldiers and the human gardener slept.

Closing his eyes, he took a deep breath and allowed a rush of focus to wash over him. Today, he couldn't be distracted because he planned to finally catch a would-be killer and find a way to save his mother and Charlotte.

The dangerous feat could kill him if he wasn't careful.

With one last breath, he allowed himself to slip from the room and drift on the wind. In only a few moments, he found himself in front of Auer's fortress. The ward surrounding the property rippled and shimmered. If he passed through, even in this dream-like form, would Lady Auer know he'd crossed the threshold?

He frowned. Certainly, no one was that powerful, especially a Shadow Fae in the light of day. He only managed this feat of magic himself because of the temporary magic-enhancing potion he'd taken before he'd fallen asleep.

In this form, he managed to circle the estate in a matter of seconds and stopped short near the back of the property. Several small breaks in the ward caught his eye. He didn't hesitate. Rather, he slipped through and snapped toward Lady Auer's dreams.

Only to slam into a wall of steel.

Killian's form shook, reverberating like a metal lid falling to the stone ground as the force of the impact knocked him off his feet and onto his back. He stared up at a gray stone ceiling, dark gray velvet drapes at the corner of his vision. The room spun as he attempted to gather his bearings, and after a few long moments, he stumbled to his feet.

Lord and Lady Auer slumbered beside each other in the bed. Auer's face was pale, beaded with sweat. His chest rose up and down rapidly with each breath. Thank the shadows the man was alive. Although he didn't necessarily like Lord Auer, and he or his wife were likely responsible for poisoning his mother, he didn't want to see the man dead.

Once again, he closed his eyes and allowed himself to slip into Lord Auer's consciousness. This time, no steel barriers prevented him from entering. In his weakened state, Lord Auer likely couldn't throw him back out even if he tried.

His breath escaped him as a cloudy stream of surprise as he glanced around at his surroundings.

Death.

Everything was dead and bleak on Auer's property in the dream, from the trees to the grass to the gardens. Flowers wilted. Trees shriveled up, their trunks and roots twisted into charred shapes. Dark clouds covered the sky, trapping in the stench of decay and misery.

Brittle grass crunched beneath Killian's boots as he slowly made his way toward the front entrance. The bodies of soldiers, servants, and nobles littered the ground, eyes staring vacantly at the sky. Instinctively, he searched each face, hoping no one he knew crossed his path despite this being a dream.

Yet, his stomach churned, a sour taste in his mouth as he recognized the bodies of Lady Feist and Lord Blom among the remains of a stone wall blasted apart. Stone and wood buried most of their bodies in the wreckage. He grabbed onto Lady Feist's arm in an attempt to hoist her body out but quickly paused.

This was a dream. Nothing more. A dark, morbid, chilling dream.

His breath fogged in front of him as he continued on, doing his best to ignore the death and carnage behind him.

However, a nagging worry pulled on his mind. No one's dreams were this detailed. Ever.

He glanced back at Lady Feist to find each gemstone of her bracelet dull and dusty, with one of her earrings ripped from her ear. Several rips tore the bottom of her dress to threads as if claws had raked over her before her death.

A shudder ran through him at the impossibility of it, at the disorientation of the dream appearing like real life. He forced himself to ignore it. He'd seen the state of the fortress during the daytime before entering Auer's dreams. It wasn't in shambles.

The clouds above darkened with each step he took toward the front of the fortress. The air thickened with dread, making each breath difficult to draw. The temperature plummeted as if he descended into the depths of a freezing cave, shivers wracking through him. He hugged his arms to his body, shocked at feeling the cold. He'd never felt cold or warm in dreams before.

"Focus," he said to himself, his breath a cloud of steam. "Find Auer."

The distant sound of voices caught his attention. He picked up his pace.

As he rounded the corner of the fortress, the bricks crumbling like dust in the wind, he spotted a familiar figure standing on the bridge.

Auer's clothing appeared as dull and lifeless as his expression, the ends frayed as if with age. He'd lost a few pounds, his tunic hanging off him rather than fitting snuggly. Both fear and resignation filled the man's eyes as well as...

Killian frowned as he watched the emotions escape him in bursts of color. Should he be able to see Auer's emotions in a dream?

Another chill stuttered through his body when someone else joined Auer on the bridge. He was a man but not a man. Large horns curved out of its head like a bull's. A tail whipped through the air behind it. Its skin was an ashy gray, though black and a lighter gray also rippled through it like lava. He stood a foot taller than Auer, snarling through sharp teeth.

"Where is she!" the man-creature shouted in Auer's pale face. "You promised to deliver the siren to me. Where is my bride?"

A pit formed in Killian's stomach when he realized he spoke of Lyyli, and he released an involuntary gasp.

The man swiveled around until large, beastly eyes trained right on him. Fear, despair, and an insatiable chill struck him like the blow of a mace. He stumbled backward just as the creature lunged toward him, moving with impossible speed. Hands moved toward his throat, but Killian slipped from the dream before the creature's fingers made contact.

He awoke with a gasp, his head shooting up from the book it had laid on previously. The bodily chill remained, violent shivers shooting through him. The tower walls seemed to close in on him. Trapping. Suffocating. He pushed himself out of his chair and stumbled toward the shadows.

In the next moment, he found himself in Lyyli's room.

She burst upright in her bed, her eyes wide as her gaze trailed over him.

His teeth chattered as he spoke. "I'm not sure why I'm here. I'm sorry. I'll leave."

He turned toward the shadows, but he breathed in sharply with surprise when her soft, warm hand tugged on his. She patted the bed beside her. He suddenly felt twenty years younger, seeking comfort after a particularly awful nightmare. Without hesitation, he slipped his shoes off and climbed beneath the sheets beside her.

He expected nothing more than the comfort of her presence, so when she pulled him closer and wrapped her arms around him, he nearly burst into tears of relief after...after what? Auer's nightmare?

No, it was no nightmare of the dreams but a nightmare of reality.

Lyyli smoothed his hair down, her fingers stroking with such tender care. He buried his face in her shoulder and closed his eyes as lingering fear continued to tremor through his body. Little by little, his shivering subsided as her warmth penetrated the frigid ice running rampant through his veins. His heart returned to a normal rhythm, and her sweet, floral scent grounded him.

Her slender waist rested beneath his hand, and he dared to wrap his entire arm around her, holding on tight. Their bodies fit perfectly together like a specially tailored coat. Everything about this felt...right. Perfect.

Happy.

The warmth in his chest grew to encompass his entire body, effectively pushing out the remaining cold. The entire world slowed until it froze within this beautiful moment.

He took a deep breath of her scent and let it out slowly, wanting to savor every detail for as long as possible.

One of her slender fingers stroked his nose as if asking to see his face. He reluctantly pulled away a few inches and rested his head on the pillow beside hers. Curiosity, worry, and uncertainty waved their colors above her head.

"I know I said I always have my notebook on me," he murmured, glad that her curtains blocked out most of the light of day from the room, "but I left it on my desk. I suppose I lied."

An amused smile broke across her face. Curiosity probed at him again as if she intentionally spoke to him in a way he could understand.

Sighing, he slipped his fingers into hers, giddy butterflies turning his stomach over in the most pleasant way. Their hands fit as perfectly together as their bodies. "I have another secret I wish to share with you. It's more dangerous than my last. Can I trust you?"

Lyyli nodded, her eyes wide as she searched his face. He swallowed as his gaze took in every detail of her. Shiny hair. Petite face. Small nose. Beautiful, curved lips. And her eyes...

He ran his thumb from the corner of one of her eyes, over her cheekbones, and across the delicate curve of her jaw. What he wouldn't give to see her in full color rather than black and white.

"I can dream travel, which means I can enter people's dreams without their knowledge. The only other person who knows is my mother. It makes me...a threat and would put me in danger should someone find out." He stopped to watch as her emotions flickered from surprise to curiosity to wonder. "I entered Auer's dream, but I don't think it was a dream. A part of me believes it might be the future. Or an alternate reality. I don't know what I saw, exactly. A creature that looked like a man, a bull, and a demon warped into one being. Everyone was dead. The creature wanted you for a bride. And when it looked at me...it's as if I became a block of ice."

He shook his head, blowing out a breath. "I realize how ridiculous this sounds. It's silly now that I say it out loud—"

Lyyli grabbed his face, gazing intently at him as she shook her head. She signed something he interpreted as, "Not silly." She then placed a hand over his heart and then tapped her head.

"You want me to enter your dreams?"

She nodded.

Resting his head against his hand, he studied her curiously. "Do you realize what you could reveal in a dream? Secrets, feelings, events, and more. On top of that, there's a large chance you won't even remember me being there." He lowered his voice as he mused to himself, "Unless I created a potion where you could control your own dream."

Frustration rippled out of her, likely stemming from wanting to communicate with him but not being able to. She used her hands to sign. He recognized "I have no," but the rest of the sentence flew over his head. Frustration rippled out of him too.

"I wish I had known I would meet you," he sighed, resting his head back onto the pillow. "Then I could have been better prepared for communicating."

He made the mistake of giving in to his heavy eyelids and Lyyli's enticing warmth. Just a few minutes. He would stay for just a few minutes, and then he would leave. If any servants caught him in here, gossip would spread like an infectious disease.

He yawned and opened his mouth in an attempt to say something, but sleep quickly pulled him into its safe arms, and he gave in all too easily.

flash of gold. A spin. A dip. A moonlit stroll. A
beautiful melody floating through the night. And a pair
of gorgeous blue eyes holding her captive with every
gaze, every glance.

Lyyli woke with a smile on her face as she attempted to
capture the most wonderful dream. But the harder she tried to
grasp onto it, the quicker it sifted through her fingers like sand
in a scorching desert. Killian had been in her dream. Or at
least she thought she recalled as much. And the rest?

She shook her head wistfully, wishing to savor every
moment, whether fictional or reality. It had been so long since
she'd been this happy. Years, even. Many years.

She shifted with the intent to sit but froze when she
noticed the strong arm wrapped around her waist and the slow
breaths near her ear.

Killian!

Panic raced through her heart as she glanced toward the
darkening window, her eyes wide. He had stayed the entire

day in her bed, arm wrapped around her, and bodies pressed close. Very close. Every curve of his body melded with hers, their feet tangled up together.

Her panic exploded.

What do I do?

Pretend to sleep. That way, he wouldn't know she had been awake all this time, which would force him to react to their intimate position first.

Her panic calmed into fluster, which calmed into determination. But the moment she slammed her eyelids shut, Killian's laughter rumbled against her back. Her fluster only grew when he whispered against her neck, "I can see your emotions. I know you're awake."

A raging flush swept from her cheeks down to her toes. She turned to face him but inhaled sharply when their faces were close enough for the tips of their noses to touch. She shifted away, her body still burning with a frenzy, embarrassment, and if she didn't lie to herself, even desire.

She pointed above his head, her gaze fuming as she silently demanded to know what his emotions looked like. It was only fair.

The most adorable sheepish smile appeared on his lips, even cuter with the sleepy slant of his eyes. "Shock. Embarrassment. And...umm...perhaps some excitement." When he dropped his lips to the thin fabric covering her arm, her fluster grew hotter than ever before. "I never meant to stay the whole night," he murmured against her shoulder, "only a few minutes. But I'm not going to lie... It's nice to wake up with you next to me."

Her heart squeezed in the most pleasant way at the blatant smoldering desire in his own eyes. She had no idea how her hands didn't tremble as she signed, "Kiss me."

For a moment, he paused before his gaze shifted just above her head as if seeking confirmation from her emotions. A playful yet devilish grin spread across his face. For a moment, a ripple of surprise ran through her. This was the same Killian who had refused to court a student? The same Killian who she'd assumed was inexperienced because of his lack of desire to court?

The breath fled her lungs as he kissed her shoulder, her neck, her jaw, and then his fingers intertwined with hers, pinning her arms above her head.

Her chest rose and fell with shallow breaths when he straddled her, a strand of his hair falling over his eye as his thin pupils grew larger with desire to match her own. No, Killian far outmatched her limited experience, but the fact that he was interested in *her* when he could likely have any woman he wanted ignited a fire within her belly.

Anticipation tingled from their intertwined fingers to every thread of her body as he lowered his face to hers. His warm breath caressed her mouth, and then only the smallest of spaces remained between them. She lifted her face to meet him, but they both froze a whisper of a breath away when someone knocked on the door.

Killian rolled off her and disappeared into the shadows as if he'd never been there in the first place just as the door opened. A maid walked in carrying a fresh pot of water, but she froze mid-step. The woman's gaze darted from Lyyli's disheveled appearance to Killian's boots lying at the base of the bed.

Lyyli's face filled with warmth as she launched herself off the bed and quickly kicked the boots beneath it. Thankfully, the maid simply placed the pot of water in the corner, curtsied, and scurried back out of the room.

The moment the door closed, she released a sigh and leaned with her back against the nearby wall. She shut her eyes, trying to recall the way Killian's hands felt in hers and how his near-kiss almost unraveled every knotted thread in her body.

When she opened her eyes, he was still gone, her only companion being the offending pot of water.

She smiled softly as she stared at the shadows Killian had dissolved into. She had no idea how she had caught his attention, but she was grateful for it.

****

Killian shook his head wryly as he descended the stairs two at a time in nothing but his socks and rumpled clothes. He had half a mind to banish all the servants from his estate after being unexpectedly interrupted but quickly reminded himself it was a foolish idea.

As he entered the dining room, a couple of servants served breakfast to Johanna, Laureen, and Mia, who sat at the table. Although Johanna simply peered at him over her porcelain cup, Laureen blurted, "You look awful."

Taking a seat at the head of the table, he fixed his sleeves and avoided eye contact. "I fell asleep at my desk."

The female servant leaning over his shoulder to fill his cup with tea twitched her mouth to the side, all while amusement poured out of her.

He frowned. "Do you find something funny?"

A sliver of surprise joined her amusement. "No, milord." However, a snort escaped her, and she quickly excused herself from the room. He watched as she disappeared, suspicious that she might have seen through his half-truth. Or even worse, perhaps she was the servant who had barged in on him and Lyyli in the first place.

He shook the worrisome thoughts from his mind and sipped the scalding tea, welcoming the distraction from the chaos currently battling inside his head.

"Good evening," Johanna said warily, but not to him. "I'm glad you made it to breakfast."

Immediately, his head shot up, followed by swift movement to his feet. Lyyli stood hesitantly in the doorway, hands clasped together in front of her. She wore a new dress, or perhaps one borrowed from one of his cousins. The dress hugged her slim shoulders and buttoned at the wrists like the current fashion. The patterned fabric tapered down to her narrow waist and spooled outward, though not all the way to the floor like it should. Her tall, willowy figure prevented the skirts from hiding the slippers on her feet.

She pulled at her skirts as if in an attempt to hide her ankles, the darker gray of a blush painting her cheeks as she glanced away shyly. When he finished gawking, his mouth twitched as he fought off a grin. She was usually much bolder than him.

"Good evening," he said as he pulled out a chair to his right. "I trust you slept well? It must not be easy accommodating yourself to a new location."

The beautiful dress accentuated her graceful movements as she took the offered seat. Her foot quickly kicked him beneath the table as if rolling her eyes at him. He tried not to grin at her playful jab while others watched.

"Thank you," she signed before directing a smile across the table at Johanna. The two of them traded a string of hand gestures, and then Johanna laughed, which effectively dropped the tension in the room.

"What's so funny?" he asked, glancing back and forth between the two of them.

Johanna smirked. "Lyyli was just commenting that you look like a team of horses ran you over. I told her it's your most natural appearance."

He directed his eye roll at Lyyli. "Hilarious."

"She's not wrong," Laureen chimed in, pointing at him with her fork. "I thought you wore those clothes yesterday."

"Yes, well..." He took a bite of a muffin to give him time to find the right words. "I'm also working day and night to save our family. I may end up wearing these same clothes for days as far as I'm concerned."

When Lyyli kept her hands in her lap, he reached across the table for the scones and held the plate in front of her. She rewarded him with a timid smile as she placed two of the scones on her own plate.

"Has anyone had any interesting dreams lately?" he asked, subtly watching Lyyli from the corner of his eye. She quirked her mouth to the side, her eyebrows furrowing as if trying to remember. But finally, she shook her head.

By the shadows... He sighed. All that romancing he'd done in her dream meant nothing if she couldn't remember any of it. He'd made quite an effort, too.

"Not that I can recall," Laureen mused.

Mia giggled. "I kissed a frog in my dream. He turned into a prince. If only it were real life."

"Why would you kiss a frog?" Laureen gagged. "Why would you think that's a good idea, even in a dream?"

"He turned into a *prince*," Mia argued back. "I'll kiss all the frogs for my chance at happily ever after."

As the two of them argued, he leaned closer to Lyyli and murmured, "I had a nice dream. I danced with a beautiful woman, and we may have shared a kiss or two."

Deep red-pink fluster exploded out of her as she snapped her head to the side to look at him. He didn't need to see color to know her entire face filled with a deep blush.

When she didn't even try to sign to answer him, he slid a piece of parchment toward her and a quill. The ink dripped as she wrote, *I don't remember.*

"I mentioned you probably wouldn't. Oh well. Perhaps there will be other opportunities." He grinned as the red-pink colors flew out of her again, and then he leaned closer, only inches from her ear. "I would like my boots back."

This time, she seemed to take her fluster in stride as she teased him back. She wrote, *They are mine now. You will never find where I've hidden them.*

He chuckled, still keeping his voice low. "They are much too big for you. Besides, I have ways of making you talk. Those purple roses you gave me? I used them to create a truth elixir."

And you would waste such an elixir on me?

"No." He shook his head, still grinning as he buttered a scone. "Your voice would kill me first when you inevitably answered. I know better. Rather, I think there are other tactics to get the answers I seek."

It had been such a long time since he'd been in such a flirtatious mood that he couldn't help but grin triumphantly when her face flushed again.

You are deplorable, she wrote, though her smile sullied her words. She caught his hand beneath the table, and this time, he flushed. The other girls carried the conversation for the rest of the meal, as he found himself momentarily speechless.

This woman might be my future wife, he thought, the situation surreal. Only a few days ago, he'd never considered taking a wife at all. At least not seriously.

Johanna interrupted his thoughts as she stood from the table, her expression solemn. "I must check in on Charlotte. Killian, promise me you'll help her."

He swallowed the lump in his throat and nodded. "I will."

Or at least I will try, he added silently.

The moment his cousin disappeared from the dining room, he pulled Lyyli to her feet and spoke quietly in a reverent tone. "Allow me to introduce you to my mother. I know she would love to meet you."

Together, they left the room, climbed the stairs, and after taking a deep breath, they entered his mother's bedroom.

Like last time, a welcoming darkness filled the room save for several candles on each bedside table. His mother lay still on the bed, draped in a thick coverlet. The candlelight illuminated the pale hue of her skin, so much like death that he dropped Lyyli's hand to check for a pulse.

She lived. But for how much longer?

"Mother," he said as he softly shook her shoulder. "Are you awake?"

Yellow ribbons of happiness fluttered above her head. A relieved sigh escaped his mouth.

He smoothed her matted hair back from her head, hoping a physician might take another look at her to assess her health. But in the meantime, he knew his words would lift her spirits. "I brought someone to meet you. Her name is Lyyli Ives. We met on Auer's property." Was it really such a short time ago? So much had happened since then.

But when his mother only reacted to his words with curiosity, he stole a glance at Lyyli and added, "We are courting."

Although a surge of happiness passed through him, his confession was met by disbelief wafting out of his mother. "She doesn't believe me." He laughed and ran a hand down his face. "Mother, she can't speak to you. She's...mute."

Anger.

"I don't believe it," he murmured, casting Lyyli an amused look. "She's angry at me because she thinks I'm lying. The one time I bring a woman home to meet her..."

Lyyli approached the bedside, and he watched her curiously as she took her mother's hand and signed something he actually understood into her palm using a hand-over-hand modified sign language. "*My name is Lyyli. It's nice to meet you.*"

Shock. Embarrassment. And then overwhelming happiness.

"She understood you," he said, motioning with his head to their hands. "Or at least to some degree. Keep talking." How was it even his mother understood some sign language? Why hadn't he made an effort to learn over the years?

The next thing she signed, he only understood "you" and "home," but whatever it was, happiness and pride gushed out of his mother seconds later, followed by overwhelming curiosity.

He tipped his head to the side, attempting to understand. "I think she wants to know more about you." His lips curved up in a wicked, coy grin. "Well, she's stunningly beautiful." Amusement rippled through his mother while Lyyli covered her face with her hands. He continued, trying to skirt around her being a siren. "She's a mermaid raised by human parents, and she has one younger sister."

Turning his attention to Lyyli, he asked, "What do you enjoy doing? Amidst all this madness the past week, I've never had the chance to ask. And please say it slowly. I'm horrible at sign language."

Smiling, Lyyli signed something he definitely didn't understand before mimicking riding a horse.

"Ah! Riding a horse." The next thing she signed, he guessed, "Painting."

She nodded her confirmation before adding the word, "Bowls." Then, she proceeded to mimic chores on a farm, such as collecting eggs, cooking, and milking a cow. "I also love cats," she signed.

"Cats?" He quirked an eyebrow at her. "I'm not fond of them myself. They knock over vials and sit on important paperwork. My mother has a couple of cats. They're probably quite different from the cats you're used to."

As if in answer to his statement, two glowing eyes blinked in the corner, simply watching them. The interruption helped put his mind back on track. "Mother, I think I figured out who did this to you. Think of fear for yes, happy for no, and confusion for I don't know." He took a deep breath. "Lady Auer."

Fear.

The black tendrils escaped her without hesitation. Fear. Panic. Hopelessness.

He released his breath and slumped into a nearby chair. "I thought so. She's cunning and powerful. Too powerful. But the question is...why did she target *you*?"

Lyyli rapidly signed, her eyes wide. He grimaced. "I apologize, Lyyli. I can't understand you. Can you use...smaller words?"

Amusement trickled from his mother at his request, and he couldn't help but roll his eyes. "Don't laugh at me, Mother.

I'm doing my best." More amusement. "I know, I know. I'm courting someone I can hardly communicate with." He traded a look with Lyyli. "She's special. You'll see. I can't wait for you to meet her for real."

Lyyli's entire face lit up with a blush as she scribbled in his notebook. *Lord and Lady Auer mentioned something the day you arrived. They had expected your mother's ailment to keep you away. I think they wanted you occupied elsewhere. Could they feel threatened by you?*

"Maybe…" he mused as he stood and paced across the room in long, unhurried strides. "They are trying to take my title away, which is no secret. They are manipulating people's emotions to agree to their demands." He grimaced when Lyyli winced. "It's not your fault. You had no choice."

She signed, "I feel bad." Yet, the small word hardly did justice to the wide range of colors wafting above her head. Guilt. Devastation. Fear. Sadness.

He closed the distance between them in a couple of strides and placed his hands on her forearms, giving them a gentle squeeze. "You were a victim. Remember, he can't hurt you anymore. You are safe here."

A tear trickled out of the corner of her eye as she signed, "I know."

Considering what had nearly happened this morning in her bedroom, he dared to lower his lips to her temple and give her a lingering, chaste kiss. However, when the action created a sense of longing for more, he forced himself to release her and step back. He also ignored the yellow happiness bursting out of his mother like overwhelming sparks of sunlight.

"From what I see," he continued, rubbing a hand over his ears where the pointed tips burned, "there are two options. One—I convince Lady Auer to fix the mess she created. Two— I brush up my studies on enchantments and figure it out myself." He sighed and ran his hand over his face at that option. Who knew how long it could take? Besides, the enchantment was powerful. He may not be able to match that vast amount of power. But…

His head shot up so suddenly, he winced from the unexpected whiplash. Lyyli stepped backward and shook her head as if she had already guessed his thoughts.

"Just hear me out," he pleaded. "Your magic was strong enough to break Auer's enchantment. What if it's strong enough to break this one as well?"

Four large, bolded words took up an entire page of his notebook as she turned it to face him. *I COULD KILL HER.*

"Could you?" He gestured to his mother and then to the window. "She can't move and won't be jumping out any windows. We'll take anything potentially sharp out of the room."

"No," she signed. Her determined expression indicated her decision was final.

After a moment, he swallowed and nodded. He was not like Auer. He would not force or pressure her. But he needed to say one more thing. "All I'm saying is your power has the potential to do good as well. I hope one day you won't fear it."

Without waiting for a reply, he crossed the room and squeezed his mother's hand. Although her body didn't respond, her emotions revealed both happiness and sadness. "I'll send a trusted advisor back to Bramwick with an official letter from me. No one will believe you are my key witness, but I'll find a way to make them believe it. Everything will turn out just fine. Just hold on a little longer."

Gratitude.

Then as if she succumbed to fatigue…nothing.

He checked her pulse and found it beat weakly but surely. A sigh whooshed out of him at the same moment his trembling muscles brought him to his knees beside the bed. Closing his eyes, he recalled the night his father had died. He'd died much too early after being thrown from a horse. The head injury he'd sustained hadn't been healable, not even by Sun Fae.

This moment with his mother felt all too familiar, filled with heartache and hopelessness. For the first time since his father's death, loneliness overcame him when he realized what he'd lose if he failed. Aside from his cousins, his mother was the only family he had left. All she had ever wanted was grandchildren. How could he have been so selfish and denied her that happiness? To spend her midnight tea with a daughter-in-law? To chase laughing grandchildren around the lawn? His own ambition had blinded him. And now, he feared he might be too late.

He started when Lyyli wrapped her arms around his neck from behind, offering him her silent comfort. Warmth burned bright in his chest when he realized he wasn't alone. Although he wasn't sure what to call his and Lyyli's relationship, he knew he wanted to pursue a future with her.

After several moments of comforting silence, he wiped the moisture from his eyes with the back of his hand and offered Lyyli a trembling smile as he stood.

"I have a very diplomatically nasty letter to write to Lady Auer, and then… Well, usually I retire to my tower for the night to work on my latest project, but would you like to accompany me to the ocean instead? I think this is…I think it will be good for you."

Her eyes widened momentarily before she bit her lip and nodded. It was time she reached out to the mermaid within her. He wasn't sure how much he could help, but he could try.

A sliver of worry pierced him, and he tried his best to push it away. In the ocean, he would be vulnerable. If Lyyli made so much as the slightest noise, it would mean his death. If she allowed her fear to control her, it would put them both in danger.

wish. Shhh. Swish. Shhh.

Lyyli's heart picked up its pace for an entirely different reason other than Killian's strong arms encircling her waist. The gentle lullaby of the midnight ocean sang in the distance, obscured by layers of trees, shrubs, and darkness. She strained her eyes, searching for the vast body of water she'd only ever heard about rather than seen.

Her arms shot toward the saddle as she lost her balance atop Killian's shadow horse, but before she slipped more than an inch, Killian tightened his grip on her.

"Eager?" He chuckled, the simple sound sending shivers of pleasure dancing across her arms. "You will be able to see it just around this bend. I admit, I haven't had many dealings with mermaids. I don't entirely know what to expect."

"Me neither," she signed. Both nervousness and excitement enticed her to lean forward in the saddle. The solid warmth of his chest nearly called her back, but the gentle, soothing waves sang a stronger lullaby with each rocking step of the horse. She *needed* the ocean, and now that it called to her, her soul called back. The mermaid within her cried out with burning anguish after being suppressed for so long.

She could wait no longer.

She slipped from the horse, her shoes striking the dirt path as she ran. Salty wind tugged her golden copper tresses from its bun. She breathed the air in, savoring the feel of it within her lungs. The dirt path transitioned into sand as she sprinted around the bend.

And skidded to a stop.

The half-moon rained down on the largest body of water she had ever seen. The surface rippled like sparkling white gemstones glittering with each wave before lapping against the sand. Water reached as if straining to touch her before getting pulled back to join the rest of the ocean.

With a sole focus in mind, she continued toward the ocean, but just before the water lapped her feet, a hand clamped around her wrist.

"Wait a moment." Killian's white teeth seemed to glow beneath the moonlight as he grinned. "You don't know how to swim yet. I recommend we approach this slowly. Perhaps start by taking off your slippers. Otherwise, you will lose them within seconds."

She glanced quickly at the empty stretch of beach with a covering of trees on all sides before she kicked off her shoes and began unbuttoning her dress. Killian's eyes widened, and he quickly averted his gaze to the sparse clouds above.

"I suppose I did not give this part much thought," he murmured, and she only wished he could see the teasing smirk growing across her face.

Her only desire was to throw herself into the ocean. Propriety took up very little space in her mind when the ocean called to her like…like…

A siren.

I'm a siren, she thought, pausing momentarily after she shucked her dress on top of her shoes. What would it be like to sing with the waves? To add her voice to the beautiful lullaby?

The wind tugged at her chemise as if beckoning her toward the surf.

She grabbed Killian's hands and placed them at the top of his shirt, silently asking him to undress. As much as she wanted to wade through the ocean, she also didn't want to do it alone.

Finally, he met her eye, the heat of his stare melting her like candle wax. One by one, his fingers unfastened each button of his shirt. She unabashedly watched as he slid one arm out of a sleeve, but then he paused for a moment before sliding the next one out.

A knot twisted in her gut as her gaze trailed up the black designs of the curse stretching from his wrist to his elbow. Three scarred gashes swept across his shoulder where the galiphor had sliced him with its claws.

How many times had this man saved her life? He not only saved her life, but he gave her a life to live. How could she ever repay him?

At the blatant black reminder scrawled on his arm that he could see each one of her emotions, she pointed above his head and signed, "I deserve to know your feelings too."

"Right," he breathed. When he unbuckled his belt, he paused as if expecting her to turn around. She didn't. Instead, he shifted to give her a nice view of his long back and broad shoulders. He stepped out of his trousers, but like her, left his undergarments on. "I'm feeling a bit nervous."

"Why?" she asked with her hands just as he glanced at her over his shoulder.

"You make me nervous."

Involuntarily, her fingers brushed against her throat. She bit her lip, once again faced with her terrifying ability to kill him with a single sound.

He shook his head and took a step closer, followed by another. "I admit I'm worried about your voice. But no...*you* make me nervous. In a rather...pleasant way."

Oh.

The tempo of her heart increased at his confession. She pointed at herself. "Me too."

"I know." His responding smile tied her insides into a hundred complicated knots. "I can see it."

A frigid and impatient salty spray misted her face. She inhaled sharply when her skin tingled along her arms, her neck, and her ears. Her skin tone shifted into a light blue as fins sprouted from her forearms. Moonlight rippled across her skin in a beautiful silver shimmer.

And her ears...

Tentatively, she reached up to touch the web-like membrane hugging the curve of each ear. Strange. Foreign. Yet natural.

She glanced up to find Killian not just staring at her but *admiring* her. His gaze swept across her face and lingered on her lips. When he stepped even closer, her heart tried to jump out of her chest in its frenzy.

But instead of kissing her, he bent down and scooped her into his arms. Her initial disappointment dissolved into fondness and warmth as she wrapped her arms around his neck and held him close.

Warmth and safety enveloped her.

At least until his feet and legs *sploshed* into the water.

She gripped him tighter, her eyes wide as the water climbed higher and higher up Killian's legs and then his lower waist as if eager to touch her. He murmured in her ear. "Are you ready?" When she nodded, he added, "Don't scream."

He dunked her completely into the frigid water from her head to the tips of her toes.

A string of panicked bubbles escaped her mouth when the skin from her waist to her lower legs tingled and tightened. Two legs kicked, and then what seemed to be only one. But it felt wrong. Her joints moved the wrong way, much more flexible than her knees and ankles, and at the end of where her feet should be…

The moment her head broke the surface of the water, she gasped in air. Panic clawed at her chest when a blue and silver-scaled tail stood in place of her legs.

"I have a tail!" she signed. The simple acknowledgement spurred her alarm faster. She thrashed in Killian's arms, spraying water in all directions. Her chest heaved with panic, and when her body moved with such foreign motion, she flailed and thrashed again.

A pair of arms tightened around her, holding her securely against a warm, solid chest. "It's all right," Killian soothed while his fingers stroked her hair.

Little by little, her thrashing subsided into exhaustion and misery.

For the first time since her adoptive father had sent her away only months ago, betrayal twisted her gut. But betrayal from whom? She didn't know. Life's unfairness crashed over her head—for the other half she'd never known about; for the voice she could never use; for so many opportunities she'd watched flash by because she was a danger to everyone around her.

Devastation and grief joined the betrayal, and her body began shaking as she silently sobbed into Killian's shoulder. Her body became limp, no longer willing to fight.

"Are you hurt?" he asked after a couple minutes of tears trailing down her face.

She shook her head and finally lifted her gaze to find him drenched with water, droplets dripping from his hair and into his face. Her lips cracked with the barest hint of a smile.

"I have a tail," she signed again, this time much calmer than minutes before.

"And it's a magnificent tail. I wish I had one."

The slightest effort on her part lifted the end of her tail out of the water. Iridescent blue fins shimmered as they caught the moonlight. The movement felt foreign but also natural. She tipped her head to the side, allowing her emotions to ask, "Why?"

Slowly, he began to turn them in a circle. She held tighter around his neck so they nearly touched cheek to cheek. He smiled. "I have seen so much of the world. Everything except..." He nodded to the dark water surrounding them. "I envy the door opened to you. I'll never be able to explore what lies beneath the ocean."

She'd never thought of this as an opportunity. While he might envy her new fins, she envied his eager mind.

Swish. Shhh. Swish. Shhh.

The gentle push and pull of the ocean waves relaxed her further, providing a sense of calm and...privacy. For a moment, she and Killian were the only two people who existed in the world.

"How are you feeling?" He smoothed back a strand of hair plastered to her cheek, his fingers skimming across the sensitive gills at her neck.

Her mouth twitched as she pointed to the top of her head.

"Right. Sorry." He chuckled and shook his head. "I already know how you feel. What I meant to ask is how can I help?"

You are doing so much already, she thought, though she had no idea how to say it in terms he might understand. Instead of answering, she locked eyes with him as they continued to move in a slow circle.

"I can't be completely certain, but..." He managed to keep a steady grip on her as he gently wiped one side of her face with his thumb and then the other. "I think your tears might be silver. They are the same kind of glimmer as your tail." He ran a hand over his chin. "Also, another guess. Your tail is purple."

A large smile spread across her face as she shook her head and spelled out with her fingers, "B-L-U-E."

"And your skin is...green?"

"B-L-U-E," she spelled out again.

"Blue," he murmured.

Her breath hitched when he pressed a feather-light kiss to her cheek, and she inhaled his scent of forest, curiosity, and saltwater as he kissed the other cheek. When he attempted to pull away, she tightened her arms around his neck and closed the distance between them. Their lips met in a soft but deliciously salty kiss.

A bubble of sound climbed up her throat, but she pushed it down and allowed a sigh to escape instead. Warmth traveled through her in the most pleasant way when he tangled the fingers of one hand into her hair and pulled her closer to deepen the kiss. She allowed her hands to slowly roam across his chest, over his broad shoulders, and then she twisted a strand of his damp hair around her finger. He tasted dark and mysterious—like shadows and magic.

Up until recently, most of the events in her life had been rather unfortunate. But tonight proved different. Killian's kiss, his touch, sparked a new life inside her. A warmth. A happiness. She never wanted it to end.

Salty spray crashed over their faces, forcing them apart. Panic jolted through her as she tightened her grip, her fingernails digging into his shoulders.

"I've got you." His sturdy hands supported her, providing her reassurance that the ocean wouldn't pull her under. "Just focus on me. I won't let anything happen to you."

Little by little, she loosened her grip until the blue of his eyes gazed back at her. He resumed turning in a slow circle.

Releasing a shaky breath, she allowed herself to relax in his grip and tilted her head back to admire the stars twinkling across the midnight blue canvas above. Her heart accelerated when he lowered her further until the refreshingly cold water claimed her back and most of her tail.

She squeezed her eyes shut as she handed her trust to him completely and let go of him. His hands continued to support her, but her arms now lay on either side of her, surrendering fully to the ocean.

"Do you know what the terrifying thing is about giving a bird its wings?" His deep voice broke the stillness of the night. Without opening her eyes, she shook her head. "The bird might fly away and never come back."

A soft smile spread across her face, her body relaxing even more as she opened her eyes to meet his worried gaze. She signed, "I will always come back."

"Always?" He seemed to remember her teaching him that word in the carriage the night before. "Are you certain?"

She placed a hand on his bare chest, right over his heart, and then she brought her finger to her lips and then flattened her palm against her fist. "I swear," the action said.

His expression turned thoughtful as if he contemplated something, but before she managed to question him, he slowly began to flip her over onto her stomach. Despite the panic running rampant through her belly, she chose to trust him.

"I will teach you how to swim. As a mermaid, your tail will likely do most of the work, but first, you need to trust your mer half. Your eyes should be able to see beneath the water. Your gills should erase your need to breathe through your lungs. When you are ready, try placing your face in the water."

Breaths escaping in shallow gasps, she plunged her head beneath the water.

And froze.

The world beneath the seemingly dangerous and dark waters appeared clear to her eyes. Small fish lazily swam past in a colorful array of blue, yellow, and silver. White seashells half-buried by sand shone beneath the rippling waves. And just beyond the sand lay a deep, dark blue ocean, waiting to be explored.

Her heart gave a start when she realized her head had been beneath the water for several minutes. The gills on either side of her neck pulsed slowly as they worked for the first time in her life.

Gratitude surged through her at Killian's undying patience. He was a magnificent teacher. His students would truly benefit from learning from him.

He taught her how to move her arms in large strokes, how to paddle with her hands, and how to most efficiently move her tail. And when she gained enough confidence, he let her go and allowed her to roam beneath the water at her own pace. At first, she stayed close to him, but then she ventured out farther and farther until the pull of the ocean created a chasm of longing within her. She longed to explore what should have been her home. She longed to discover who she was and where she came from.

But she swam back to Killian because she longed for a life with him more than anything else.

After he carried her out of the water, they both lay on the sand, gazing up at the stars as they waited for her tail to dry and for her legs to return. She turned her body to rest her head on his chest, listening to his steady heartbeat with his arm securely around her shoulders. They lay like that until the light gray of pre-dawn filled the skies, long after her tail transitioned into two legs.

For a moment, everything was perfect.

"We should get back," Killian said finally when pink added its hue to the sky.

Their backs to each other, they dressed in their dry clothes and walked back the way they came, but a splash followed by someone's voice caused her to spin to face the ocean.

"Little one," someone said in garbled words. A different language. Again, foreign, but she understood it.

Her eyebrows scrunched together as she studied the woman in the water. Shells adorned her red hair, her pink skin shimmered beneath the dawn light, earrings traveled up her right ear, and a small pearl piercing rested on the side of her nose. The mermaid stared back at her with wide, green eyes.

"Who are you?" Lyyli asked with her hands.

The mermaid simply tilted her head as if studying her and then tilted it the other way before speaking in the same garbled language. "You are your mother's age when she gave birth to you. You look just like her, Lyyli."

All the strength left her legs, and she nearly collapsed to the ground at the mention of her mother. She found just enough strength to take a step toward the water, but Killian gripped her elbow in warning.

As if just noticing him, the mermaid switched tongues, speaking with a heavy accent. "Who are you? Are you trustworthy? Do you know what she is?"

His grip on her tightened, and his expression hardened. "I am the Shadow Lord of Skaad. She is safe with me." He stepped in front of her, but Lyyli still craned her neck to glance at the woman.

"I don't have much time." The woman glanced back and forth over the water before her gaze found Lyyli's. "You and I are the last of our kind. My name is Eliel. I am your aunt." The breath halted in Lyyli's lungs. "When you were young…you were being hunted. I kept you safe for several years after your mother was killed. I thought you would be safer on land than in the sea, and I entrusted you to a farmer and his wife and used my magic to protect them from your voice. But when the danger passed, and I came back for you, you were gone. I've been waiting for you to step foot in the ocean to locate you through our shared blood, and you haven't until today."

The mermaid held up her hand, revealing the pearl ring sitting on her finger. She explained, "I had it enchanted to teleport me to your location. It only has a couple more uses after tonight."

Lyyli's head swam with uncertainty and confusion. The woman's features resembled her own. She knew her name and she correctly spoke of her adoptive parents.

"She's telling the truth," Killian murmured. "At least as far as I can tell by reading her emotions. She's feeling the same level of loss and devastation that you are."

Once her legs solidified with determination, she stepped in front of Killian to get his attention, pointed to her throat, and then pointed to the mermaid.

He seemed to understand because his eyebrows furrowed when he spoke. "I believe what Lyyli is asking is how can you speak without consequences when she is unable to do so?"

Eliel nodded once before glancing around them once more. "Practice. I had the good fortune of having my own mother teach me how to control my gift."

Gift...

"Curse," she corrected in an abrupt hand movement.

As if she understood, Eliel shook her head. "We exist to heal, to comfort, to inspire happiness in times of grief. Several of our kind chose to use our gift to destroy and kill in the past, and now we are almost extinct because of those who hunt us." She held her palms out placatingly. "Come back home with me. I can teach you everything you need to know. I can teach you how to speak, how to hone your gift, how to walk among humans and fae with confidence."

An invisible crack tore through her heart as she glanced from Killian to Eliel. This was something she'd always wanted all her life—to speak, to fit in, to live a normal life. But these past couple of weeks had meant the world to her. Killian had changed her life, provided her hope, and gave her a beautiful happiness she never knew could exist.

Silently, Killian watched what must be her emotions tumbling over her head. As if sensing she desired comfort, he lightly snaked an arm around her shoulders and absently played with the ends of her hair. "This is your choice."

She didn't need the ability to see emotions to hear the pain and longing in his voice.

Eliel continued, her heavy accent stretching across the space between them. "It won't be forever, love. In fact, I encourage you to return to land. We need to keep our kind from going extinct. It does not matter if you mate with a merman, a human, or a fae. You will give birth to one of us."

Killian's fingers stilled against her back, all while heat scorched her cheeks. She ignored the unbearable flush as she pointed to her aunt and then pressed a hand over her belly.

The mermaid smiled sadly. "I am getting older, love. I have taken many lovers, but I have lost all my pregnancies. I had all but lost hope until I sensed you within the ocean tonight." She held out her hand again. "Come home with me."

The pressure of Killian's still hand on her back kept her grounded to his side. She didn't want to leave.

Slowly, she shook her head. Killian's deadline to marry loomed over her head. She feared if she left now, she would lose him forever. She needed to think about this. To figure it out before committing to leaving for a time with this stranger.

Eliel dropped her hand, though she did not appear disappointed as if she expected the answer. "Lyyli, perhaps someday you will marry and have children of your own. Those children will be—" She paused and glanced around again before continuing. "—what we are. Their first cries *will* kill. Unless you learn how to help them and protect those around you. I ask you to think about my offer. When I sense you in the ocean next, I will come. I hope it will be soon."

Without another word, her aunt dove beneath the water, a green tail fin flicking the surface before she disappeared entirely.

The world stilled. Even the lapping waves quieted as she stared at the spot where the last of her kin had disappeared. Was she being foolish by choosing to stay with Killian? Was she allowing fondness and love to cloud her judgement?

Her eyes widened. *Love...*

Quickly, she swiped at the invisible emotions over her head, her gaze darting to Killian. But his attention remained intensely focused on the ocean as if watching for other merpeople to appear.

Only a hush remained.

"You are regretting your choice," he said suddenly, breaking the stillness of the night.

"I don't know," she signed. "I'm confused."

He studied her for a moment before holding out a hand, and she gladly took it. "Let's head back to my estate. A good morning's rest will do you some good."

As they headed back to where his shadow horse chomped on something crunchy and red, she glanced longingly back at the ocean. It gleamed beneath the pink and orange hues stretching across the sky, but even then, the water reflected the melancholy gathering in her heart. It called to her, sang for her to return.

But she remained silent.

yyli had been quiet ever since they returned from the ocean. Quiet even for her.

Killian frowned as he pulled his neckcloth particularly tight, nearly choking the air right out of himself. He recalled her lingering glances of longing as she'd stared out at the home she'd never known. Her emotions may have been a jumbled mess, but he couldn't deny that she wanted to return. A piece of her seemed to have gone missing since last night.

"What am I doing?" he growled to his own reflection, once again sending his valet away when he attempted to slip into the room. He was not in a mood to simply stand still while someone fussed over him. "Courting a mermaid? She doesn't belong here."

The deadline to marry hung like a dark, heavy rain cloud over his head. Could he truly marry a mermaid? A siren? Someone with a heart bound to the sea? Courting Lyyli was a dangerous and albeit foolish bet. If he continued down this path, would he lose, or would he win?

He groaned in frustration when he missed a button on his waistcoat and started all over again. What he *should* do was break it off with Lyyli and place a safer, more reliable bet on Johanna. His title, his family, his school, *everything* was at stake if he played his cards wrong.

"I can hear you being grouchy from the other end of the estate," a muffled voice said through the door.

With a frown, he stalked toward the door and swung it open to find Johanna smirking at him. "I am not grouchy."

"You are. I also came to tell you that Lady Auer is nearing the estate in her carriage."

He swore under his breath as he grabbed his shoes and his coat, awkwardly hopping into the hallway as he attempted to dress while moving. Johanna followed closely behind when he nearly stumbled down the stairs in his haste.

"Girls!" he shouted over the frenzy of servants scurrying from room to room with tea, refreshments, and last-minute cleaning. Two soldiers stood at the door, and from this vantage point, he spotted another dozen lining the drive in the front. Mia and Laureen appeared at the bottom of the stairs, faces flushed. "Good, you are dressed. Listen to me. You will not stray within eight feet of Lady Auer. Understand? And if she offers you anything, do *not* take it."

Chest heaving with exertion, he turned to Johanna just as he slipped on his second shoe. "We are to act civilly, but not without hostility. She knows what she's done. Do you have your onyx bracelet?"

Johanna nodded, revealing the gems secured around her wrist.

On the opposite side of the foyer, Lyyli stood with her fingers clasped, nervous streams of sickly yellow wafting off her.

"Lyyli." He crossed the threshold and took both of her hands, concern likely showing on every inch of his face. "She can't know you're here. Stay out of sight. *Promise me.*"

They had left the Auers' estate hastily, keeping Lyyli out of sight and notice. If Lady Auer found out Lyyli was here, he feared the knowledge might put her in danger.

She nodded and released a hand to sign, "I promise."

Clomping hooves stopped just outside, sending his heart shooting to the ceiling. He spun her around and gave her a gentle push, watching the back of her head until she disappeared from sight. Only then did he turn toward the door. Johanna joined his side while his other two cousins waited on the opposite end of the room parallel from them. Usually, it would be his mother by his side as head woman of the household, but Johanna was his eldest cousin while his mother remained "ill."

He dug into his pocket and handed the vial of truth elixir to a servant, the potion colorless and tasteless. "Dump this in a pitcher of water. Serve it as soon as possible." The servant scurried toward the kitchens.

Taking one last deep breath to calm the fury rising within him, he nodded to the soldiers standing sentry at the door. They opened the double doors, allowing the darkness of night to crawl into the estate. Along with something else dark and sinister.

Lady Auer climbed the stairs and entered his home with her head held high. She wore a dark dress—perhaps blue or purple or gray, he couldn't tell—with a matching fashionable hat and wrist-length gloves. She strode inside as if she hadn't just been accused of attempted murder of members of the aristocracy. As if her husband might not be lying on his potential deathbed.

"Because you have answered my summons in person, Lady Auer, I assume you are admitting fault."

The woman simply gave him a passing glance before her gaze continued to take in the room as if searching for something.

Or someone.

Dread climbed up his throat, but he swallowed it down in favor of a glare.

She began taking off her gloves but paused with the second halfway off her hand. "I thought you had four cousins."

He balled his hands into fists at his side. "Charlotte is afflicted with the same *ailment* as my mother."

She nodded, her head still held high as she scanned the room, both gloves now pressed inside one hand. When a serving girl entered with the pitcher of water and goblets, she served Lady Auer first and then himself. Lady Auer didn't drink until he did.

"Have you no guests tonight?"

"None," Johanna answered for him when he would have been forced to tell the truth under the elixir's influence.

Fighting against revealing Lyyli's whereabouts proved to be difficult.

The tension in his fingers increased as he squeezed them tighter. His heart pounded harder than ever as he carefully watched the top of Lady Auer's head, but no emotions escaped the treacherous woman. None at all. Not even a flicker of color.

Finally, her steely, unapologetic gaze found his. "Where is your mother? I will see what I can do."

Killian eyed her suspiciously. The woman wanted to help? After everything? There must be more to it.

"Upstairs." He motioned for Johanna and two soldiers to follow them up to the next level. One soldier walked in front of Lady Auer while the second trailed closely behind, each with a hand on their weapons. Killian watched her carefully. Should she make any sudden and unexpected movements, he remained ready to shadewalk Johanna to safety at a moment's notice.

They gathered in his mother's room, and simply seeing her lying still on the bed caused another wave of fury to cluster like a dark storm brewing within him.

Lady Auer pulled up a chair, and when she reached out to touch his mother, he clasped a hand around her wrist.

"What are you doing?" he growled.

"If you care about your mother's possible recovery, you will release me."

Black waves of fear escaped his mother. Panic, anger, and fear. His heart panged as he ignored her silent pleas for help and released Lady Auer's wrist.

The woman lightly touched his mother's arm and closed her eyes. Magic rippled through the air—dark and sinister and unforgiving. But most of all, powerful.

After several minutes, the magic flickered out. His mother remained still and unmoving, fear oozing out of her like a deadly disease. He watched her carefully, his gaze missing nothing from each matted strand of her hair to the rise and fall of every breath.

No change.

At last, Lady Auer opened her eyes and stood, pulling her gloves back on. "This is now beyond my power," she said in a flat tone, her expression lacking emotion, though her eyes were unrepentant. "My enchantment was meant to be permanent. There is nothing I can do."

Despair and anger pressed heavily on his shoulders as he followed her gliding figure into the hallway. He stood rooted to the spot as she descended the stairs. Anger and despair curled his fists around the edge of the banister. He wanted nothing more than to drive a sword into her chest, to make her pay for what she had done. But he was not a killer, no matter how much fury boiled in his veins.

His voice echoed across the foyer. "You will be held accountable for your actions in front of the ten Lords, and I will make sure your sentence is worthy of your crime."

She paused, her hand on the door handle. "Soon, it will not even matter." Without glancing back, she strode outside and disappeared from sight.

The weight of despair collapsed his chest as if every one of his ribs fractured in a hundred different places. The agony of failure and loss heaved in each trembling breath. Walls spun, and the floor shifted beneath them.

Despite the solid railing keeping him upright, he felt himself tipping as his despairing emotions collapsed his lungs. He gasped in a deep, agonizing breath.

And allowed the shadows to swallow him whole.

L yyli peeked out the filmy white curtains to watch as Lady Auer departed the estate in no apparent rush. Her unhurried footsteps followed the path to her waiting carriage she'd only just arrived in minutes earlier.

She pulled the curtain open wider to peer below. The woman did not look as if she cared to return quickly to her ailing husband, but her frustrated frown accompanied the glare she inflicted upon one of the shadow horses hitched to the carriage.

Lady Auer dropped her glove and halted suddenly. When a servant rushed forward to retrieve it, she stopped them with a motion of her hand. She stooped to pick it up, but all too suddenly, she glanced over her shoulder.

Lyyli breathed in sharply as she dropped the curtain and stepped out of view of the window, pressing her back against the wall as panic weaved into each frantic heartbeat. Had Lady Auer seen her?

Not until after the crack of a whip and clomping of hooves did she dare to peek outside again. The carriage disappeared down the road, and with it, leaving a sense of relief.

A knock at her bedroom door startled her, and she spun around just as Johanna entered. The devastation on her face stamped Lyyli's heart into the ground. The woman was one word away from breaking.

Instead of speaking out loud, Johanna signed. "Killian is…not all right. I can see how happy you've made him recently. Please go to him. He needs you."

With her heart already stamped to the ground, a team of invisible horses completely obliterated what was left as it crumbled with Killian's pain. So…his mother would die. As would Charlotte.

Her eyes watered, but she held back her tears. "Where is he?"

"I don't know." Johanna blinked several times as if damming her own emotions. "He could be anywhere. But in his state… I would say either his tower or the garden. The garden was his mother's favorite place to pass the time."

Was…

Killian's mother likely would never enjoy the garden again.

Lyyli hurried toward the door, but before passing through, she wrapped her arms around Johanna in a lingering embrace. Nothing she could say could fix this. It was the only thing she could offer.

Johanna's shoulders began shaking, and she ran from the room moments before a sob trailed after her down the hallway. More muffled sobbing escaped two other bedrooms, and she caught the head maidservant dabbing her eyes with a white handkerchief downstairs.

Slowly, Lyyli descended the staircase, her fingers trailing across a smooth, glossy banister. She stopped as her gaze traveled in the direction of Killian's tower, but some other power tugged her in another direction, a thread connected to the earrings in her ears. When she tugged on the thread, the flimsy string became a sturdy rope leading her toward Killian.

She exited the estate from the back doors opening into the garden, following the insistent tug on her enchanted earrings. Shadows came alive beneath the stirring of the breeze. Wind rustled trees and bushes, an eerie whistle when it seemed as if she might be alone in the vast garden.

But she continued to follow the thread past a garden table with empty chairs. She passed a stone fountain void of running water, the fish spurting air rather than liquid. Finally, she stopped at the mouth of a path tunneled by trees. Darkness awaited her down the path, and her mer eyes couldn't see more than a few feet in front of her in such intense darkness.

After several long moments of contemplation, she steeled her nerves and took a step into the darkness and then another step. A shiver ran up her arms when a breeze brushed her skin. The hairs on the back of her neck stood up, but when she glanced behind her, she only found darkness.

She increased her pace into the black void but stopped short.

A lone figure sat hunched on a stone bench, his head in his hands. His sniffling stopped, his shoulders freezing, but he kept his face hidden.

"I don't want company, Johanna," Killian croaked.

Lyyli bit her lip, uncertain whether she should turn back the way she'd come to give him privacy or to comfort him in his time of distress.

Beneath the shadowy trees, a patch of gleaming flowers caught her eye, the plant climbing like vines as if trying to capture moonlight on its petals. She carefully plucked one of them, watching as the flower pulsed like starlight in the midnight skies.

Approaching quietly, she placed the flower on his lap and stepped back with the intent to return to the estate. Killian's head shot out of his hands, their gazes locking across the space between them.

The light emitted from the flower reflected off the tears trailing down his face. A heaviness rested in his eyes, a sadness surely deeper than the darkest depths of the ocean.

Her heart ached at the despair he must be feeling.

She signed, "I read in your book that tears can be shared. You do not need to shoulder your heartache alone."

"I caught about half of what you said." His chuckle sounded more like a sob.

In case he didn't understand the preciseness of her meaning, she moved slowly as if he was an animal that might spook. She lowered herself onto his lap, wrapped an arm around his neck to steady herself, and then she caught one of his tears on her finger. The saltiness greeted her tongue as she licked the tip of her finger. In only moments, despair crashed down on her.

Not her own, but his.

Dark clouds of pain blocked out every inch of sunlight within her soul. Despair. Loneliness. Heartache. Loss.

The emotions contorted her expression with agony and streamed out of her eyes without her permission, soaking her cheeks. She felt his inevitable loss as her own, as if it were her own mother dying.

She wrapped her arms around him and buried her face in his shoulder as she took on half of his heartache. His shoulders shook beneath her, and then the shaking turned into sobs. He wrapped his arms around her, burying his fingers in her hair.

Together they cried as they shared the heartache, the loneliness, the despair, and she continued to hold him until his shaking subsided. He shifted beneath her, and moments later, she found him offering her a handkerchief.

She gratefully accepted and wiped her eyes and her cheeks. When she handed it back, he used it as well to clean his own face.

"Why would you do that?" he whispered against her hair.

Swallowing her trepidation, she placed a hand over his heart.

"I'm angry with Lady Auer too."

With a start, she realized he had misread the emotion. She slipped her hand into his vest pocket, pulled out the notebook, and skimmed its pages until she found the one listing each emotion and its corresponding color. Without the light of the flower illuminating the page, she would have been blind to its words.

Love, passion, and anger were all similar colors—red and dark pink. Instead of interpreting her answer as she loved him, he'd interpreted it as anger.

Perhaps now wasn't the right time to confess the workings of her heart anyway.

"How did you find me?" he asked.

She grabbed her ears where her earrings lay, the very ones he'd given her to connect them and protect her from Auer.

"Ah." He nodded with understanding. "I am glad to see you wearing them."

After a few moments of silence, she flipped through the notebook, trying to find a single spot of empty space. The entire notebook was filled, the last pages containing Killian's research on the galiphor.

Finally, she found an empty margin near the middle of the book and wrote, *Are you going to be all right?*

"I don't know." He shrugged, absently playing with the end of her lock of hair. "I can't quite take this in."

She flipped to the pages about the galiphor and signed, "How can I help?"

"By staying out of danger." He kissed her wrist, and then his lips lingered on her palm. Heat shot up from the earth, traveled up the length of her body, and filled her cheeks. By the responding twitch of his mouth, she knew he noticed the blush, even in the darkness. "Losing my mother will be hard enough. I don't want to lose you, too."

She stood abruptly to hide the way his words scorched her face like the sun beating against blazing hot sand. She smoothed her skirts and wiped her face one last time just to give her hands something to do. And when she turned her back to him, she inhaled a deep breath of disbelief.

All her life, no one understood her. People wanted to be rid of her. They sent her away to be someone else's problem. But Killian…

I don't want to lose you, too.

He *wanted* her. When no one else did. He *understood* her. Like no one else ever had. He was patient and kind, and like nothing she'd expected from the archmage of Darkest Star Arcane.

Afraid the realization would unravel her completely into a blubbering mess and risk his life with the sound of her voice, she signed, "I will be at the house if you need me."

Without waiting for an answer, she turned on her heel and hurried down the dark path. Her footsteps transitioned from a fast walk to a run, and only when she escaped the dark tunnel of trees did she gasp in a breath of air, her hands on her hips as she tilted her head to gaze at the twinkling stars overhead.

Two more of those stars would fade by the month's end. Dowager Graves and Charlotte. Although she didn't know of a way to break this enchantment, she knew one thing she could do.

With purpose in her stride, she entered the house, climbed the stairs to the second floor, and slipped into Dowager Graves' room. A servant curtsied beside the bed, finished her task of spooning water into her mouth, and left just as quickly.

Lyyli sat in the chair beside the bed, pondering what she wanted to say.

Finally, she took the woman's still hands and signed. "Let me tell you a story of how the fairy gained its wings."

247

tudy. Research. Preparation.

Over the next few days, Killian threw himself wholeheartedly into his books and magic. But while concentration and innate direction usually controlled his research, he found himself unable to focus when his mother lay in her room, Death standing over her with his sickle raised.

He rubbed his eyes at the new strain of tension, his focus once again dissolving when the pictures in the book on his desk blurred into a gray mess. Black, white, and gray melded together, distorting the image of what should be ribbons of gold, silver, black, and green.

"Argh!" he growled, overcome with frustration as he shoved the book off his desk and into a heap on the floor. Pages came loose from the binding and scattered across the ground.

For several long seconds, he stared at the mess of paper and one of the open books about sirens. He didn't have many books that mentioned them but tidbits of legends about their catastrophic power and tears capable of miracles. Though, Lyyli had already cried a few times, and nothing had happened.

Slowly, his anger evaporated into crushing despair. He rested his palms flat on the desk and hung his head as he breathed in and out slowly.

A few days until Lady Auer's hearing. It wasn't soon enough.

Tears slipped from his eyes and fogged his gray surroundings. Gray. Gray. More gray. The sacrifice had been for nothing. He'd lost his colors. He would also lose his mother, his title, and perhaps even his school.

He swiped the back of his hand across his face as the despair swirling within the confines of his heart transitioned into a determination of a sort he hadn't felt in...well...ever. The only thing his mother had ever wanted was to watch him marry and play with her grandchildren. There was no time to give her grandchildren, but perhaps he might provide her with some measure of peace and happiness before her death if he married.

Perspiration slicked his palms as he glanced toward the closed door of his tower. He had known Lyyli for only a couple of weeks. He feared asking for her hand.

He feared rejection.

He feared failure.

He feared making a complete fool of himself.

"I'm not ready," he whispered to the empty room. Though, as if the lone calypso plant growing in a pot in the corner heard him, its leaves shifted to open its jaws to catch his despair. At this rate, the plant would grow several feet within the next few months.

The strong, earthy scent of khave wafted past his nose from his half-empty mug on his desk. The brief hint of cinnamon jolted him further into the present, and he couldn't help but chuckle at himself.

"I am almost thirty years old. How am I still not ready for marriage?"

Again, only silence answered him.

Swiping his sleeve across this face to catch the remainder of despair and hopelessness, he strode across the tower, threw the door open, and jogged down the stairs. He needed to find Lyyli.

Several servants curtsied as he followed the string of magic connecting him to the woman in question. His eyebrows furrowed in puzzlement as the string led him in the direction of his mother's chambers.

He cautiously climbed the stairs, slowing when he found his mother's bedroom door partially open. The carpet absorbed the sound of his footfalls as he approached, and when he peeked his head inside...

He froze.

Lyyli sat beside his mother's bed, soft candlelight flickering across her animated face as she spoke silently into his mother's hands.

A smile slowly crept across his face as he leaned against the doorframe and watched, captivated by the way she spoke. Mostly, she signed into his mother's hands, and every few words or so, she'd take her mother's hands and positioned them into a sign that must have been difficult to portray otherwise.

Colors of emotion flew out of both of them. For Lyyli—the orange of excitement, the red-orange of confidence, and the yellow of happiness. For his mother—the yellow of happiness, and he interpreted the light pink as fondness. As if she were her own daughter.

His expression softened as he watched Lyyli's eyes light up as she signed something about spring leaves, followed by his mother's accompanying amusement. A grin spread across Lyyli's face, but it quickly froze on her lips when she glanced up and spotted him in the doorway.

Surprise, uncertainty, and worry replaced her previous excitement and happiness.

"Don't stop on my account," he said as he gestured for her to continue. "It seems as if you are both enjoying yourselves."

Relief filled her expression as she signed another sentence to his mother and then dropped her hands. To him, she signed, "I will continue the story tomorrow."

"A story, eh? About what?"

"Forest F-A-E."

She spelled out the second word.

It was amazing how much he was catching onto just by watching and paying attention. He was far from conversing in coherent sentences with her, but he planned to learn.

He nodded. "The Forest Fae are interesting. More mysterious than anything. I've only known a handful in my life."

"Who?" she questioned with the crook of her finger as her thumb rested against her chin.

"My father's childhood friend and his daughter. You may have heard of her. Nyana Everdon, half Sun Fae, half Forest Fae. She is—was—the Sun Fae queen."

Lyyli asked another question as he stepped farther into the room. He only recognized the word "death."

With a shake of his head, he answered, "No, she's not dead. But her husband was recently overthrown by his younger brother." He shuddered despite the warm summer air entering the room through the open window. "Good riddance. Trust me, you didn't want to find yourself in the same room as him."

The spoiled, pompous brat had physically abused one of Killian's own servants! He only wished he'd discovered the act before the man had left Skaad. However, it was safe to say Killian had made sure the man suffered from mild poisoning for three weeks straight. It was *almost* a shame Liam was now dead because Killian would have liked to have poisoned him several more times for justice's sake.

His heart pounded a deep, reverberating rhythm within his chest as he gazed into Lyyli's eyes. He knew how he wanted to do it now. How he wanted to propose. At the one place that made him the happiest.

"Are you busy?" he asked, stuffing his hands in his pockets to hide his nervousness. "Can I take you to Darkest Star?"

He should have been finalizing the classes long before now, but fate had dropped several boulders in his way instead.

Lyyli nodded enthusiastically, the large ribbon in her hair bouncing with the long tendrils of hair curling down her back.

Her hands flew excitedly in front of her as she animatedly spoke to him.

"Slow down." He chuckled, grateful for her excitement. "Meet me in the foyer. I'll be down in a minute. I would like a quick word with my mother alone first."

His entire body warmed when she stood on her toes to place a kiss on his cheek and then scurried out of the room. The moment Lyyli slipped out the door, and it clicked shut behind her, he released a tense breath. He slowly lowered himself into the chair Lyyli previously occupied, overly aware of his racing heart and warm cheek.

Absently, he reached out toward his mother's cat sleeping on the bed beside her and scratched beneath its chin, its hairless black skin stretching as it lifted its head to give him better access. Its fangs elongated as it closed its eyes in enjoyment. But he knew better. He might find those fangs in his hand if he wasn't careful.

"What do you think?" he asked his mother nervously. "Do you like her?"

Yellow slammed into him, so bright that he sucked in a breath and flinched away. When the flash of color subsided, he burst into laughter as his uneasy nerves relaxed. "I'll take that as a resounding yes." He bit his lip and wrung his hands together. "I know she's not...exactly what you may have had in mind for me...but I really like her, too. I'm going to..." He cleared his throat, the muscles in his forearms straining as he wrung his hands harder. "I'm going to ask for her hand tonight. Do I have your blessing, Mother?"

Instead of another bright flash of emotion, both yellow and blue swirled slowly above her head like two dancing dragons. Sad but also happy.

Weeping for joy.

Without a word, he took her fingers and squeezed, pressing a kiss to her pale hand. For several long moments, he bowed his head as he remained at her side. There was so much he wanted to say, but his tongue refused to work. He'd never imagined having to move forward with his wedding day alone. Without his mother.

It was bittersweet.

"I'm glad I have your blessing," he said finally. "I'm hoping Lyyli will say yes, but…I'm not so sure she will. She's a mermaid, Mother. What if she doesn't want to stay on land?" Even despite Eliel's encouragement for Lyyli to return to him on land, what if she preferred the sea?

Even more confusing, if they had children, they would be sirens. Would he be safe from their voices? Would his servants and family be safe? How could he be certain?

The light purple of surprise escaped her, followed by a light red-orange. Was that encouragement?

A barrage of colors followed, and Killian found it difficult to follow. It was a story—one he didn't understand. Perhaps about her and father's courtship and marriage? If only he could hear her words instead of only see her emotions.

"Thank you," he said, squeezing her hand. "I will let you know how it goes. Wish me luck."

Yet, as he slipped out the door, his anxiety turned his pulse into a flurry of activity. He couldn't forget the longing in

Lyyli's eyes when they'd visited the ocean. The image of pure bliss and freedom in her expression was forever branded into his memory.

Despair became a solid pit in his stomach, sinking lower, lower, lower, until it became a permanent fixture in his body. If he was a good, selfless man, he would let her go. But he didn't want to let her go. He wanted her here. With him. Forever.

What a strange, new desire.

Now his head was just as muddled as his heart. What was he supposed to do?

Lyyli fluffed her hair, smoothed her dress, and checked the mirror in the foyer in case something like a smudge of dirt or dried pastry lingered on her face. But instead, she found hope and excitement staring back at her from her reflection. Green eyes glittered with happiness. Her mouth set in a determined line.

With her fingers, she smoothed the worry from her brows. Despite what Johanna had said about not having feelings for Killian, she noticed the way she looked at him when he wasn't watching. With longing and sadness. As much as Lyyli liked Johanna, the woman was competition. And with a deadline looming over Killian's head—pressure to marry soon from the other Lords—she knew this was her only chance. She loved him, and she wouldn't give him up for anything or anyone. Not while she still had a chance.

She bit her lip as she glanced toward the drawing room where Johanna and two of her sisters lingered. Was she being too selfish by stepping in Johanna's way? The other woman was a born and bred aristocratic woman.

Lyyli was a farm girl.

Before she had a chance to answer her own question, Killian jogged down the stairs, a bright smile on his face.

Relief melted her core. She'd worried she wouldn't see his smile again.

He uncorked a vial of orange liquid and downed its contents before wrapping an arm around her waist. She glanced up at him questioningly.

Shaking the empty bottle, he explained, "This is an elixir to briefly boost the capacity of my well of magic, as well as fortify my magic against drying up. If I take you to the school by carriage, the trip will take hours. But shadewalking will get us there within minutes. Though, only at night when there are enough shadows to travel by."

When he held out his hand to her, she hesitated. Her first experience with shadewalking had been disorienting and unnerving. Did she want to shadewalk again?

But gazing into Killian's hopeful but nervous eyes squared her resolve. A marriage with him would mean taking risks and discovering the unknown. She couldn't balk at his magic now.

She slipped her hand into his, enjoying the warmth he offered with the simple touch.

But her pulse soon spiked when his eyes transitioned from blue to shadowy black as if his thin pupils had enlarged to cover his entire eye. They flickered with power, like wisps of black fog in midnight forests.

He pulled her into the shadows...

…and they disappeared.

The panic of losing her sense of self and her surroundings clawed at her throat. Only, she no longer had a throat. In place of her body was something as thin as shadows, as translucent as air, as hot as fire. She burned and quaked and cooled as her surroundings flashed by in a blur of black shadow and moonlight.

She reached out to touch the sinewy substance, but she was no longer whole. Instead, she was the shadow.

Shadows gently spit them back out on cobblestone. Lyyli inhaled a sharp breath, touching her hair, her throat, her torso. She found everything whole and intact.

Her gaze trailed from the red slippers on her feet to the seafoam green material of her dress. Once again, her fingers raked through her golden copper hair but froze as she took in her surroundings.

Slowly, her eyes widened as she turned in a full circle. She stood beside a large, circular pool surrounded by cobblestone and a magnificent garden. Benches lingered beneath shady trees while silver, purple, and blue flowers burst into bloom beneath the moonlight's caress. Several large buildings made of stone stood tall, forming a circle around the spacious garden. The moon hung directly above them, providing a gleaming light that reflected off the smooth surface of the pool.

Hesitantly, she reached out to the water and disturbed the surface with a finger. Water rippled with the movement, momentarily distorting the moon's image.

"Incredible," she signed, turning in another full circle. "It must cost a fortune to attend the school."

Killian tilted his head to the side, studying her for a moment before he answered. "It's not as expensive as you might think. My aim is to teach students, not pad my pockets with their coin. Though, I do pay my staff well."

A smile spread across his face as he took a deep breath and let it out. "This is my home. I have never felt as if I belonged anywhere more than I do here."

Satisfaction glimmered in his eyes, and she wanted to see the school the same way he did. She climbed onto the stone lip of the fountain and turned in a circle with her gaze trained on the moon overhead. The stars spun with her as if dancing in tune with her heart on its dusky canvas.

Nostalgia slammed into her as she remembered the late nights she'd spent with her sister gazing up at the numerous stars overhead as they lay on a blanket in the field. She missed her family. Immensely. Did they miss her too?

She held in a yelp when her foot slipped on the smooth edge. Killian caught her by the waist, never taking his eyes off her as he gently lowered her to the ground. Her lips twitched in amusement when a bare foot touched cold cobblestone. She'd lost a slipper.

And then her pulse jumped to her throat when he lowered himself onto one knee. She stared at him, eyes wide as his mouth opened, closed, and opened again.

In the end, he cleared his throat, picked up her errant shoe, and slipped it onto her foot. "Don't want you to go without your second slipper. I still have a lot to show you. Come on."

She followed behind him as he led her toward one of the buildings, her face hot with embarrassment. For a moment, she'd thought he was about to propose. How silly of her! How could she have thought that, despite the dangerous hope swirling in her core?

Humiliation burned hotter in her face when she remembered he could see every one of her emotions. If he so much as glanced at her, the workings of her heart would lay on a silver platter for him to peruse at his leisure.

Stop feeling! she screamed at herself, but her emotions continued to tumble out of her despite her plea. She couldn't remember the last time she'd been more mortified. He had probably known what had gone through her mind when he'd knelt.

She pressed her lips tightly together as she watched him run his fingers through his hair and fiddle with the ends of his sleeves.

To put the strangely awkward moment behind them, she pulled out her own notebook from her dress pocket and wrote. *How much will it cost me to attend?*

They paused in front of a greenhouse so tall that it touched the midnight clouds. Foggy glass panels revealed luscious green plants and a variety of foreign flowers from orange to silver to blood red.

Killian rubbed the back of his neck, finally meeting her gaze. The blue in his eyes shimmered in the darkness like a cat crouching in the shadows.

"It's not something we need to discuss right now. How about tomorrow?"

Reluctantly, she nodded. She knew she could never afford to attend the school. Not in her wildest dreams.

Biting her lip, she ran a hand up her arm and cupped her elbow self-consciously as she gazed up at the magnificent structure looming above her. She had no idea where she stood with Killian. He had not tried to kiss her since they returned from the ocean. Perhaps this competition for his affection had been doomed from the start.

The greenhouse door opened suddenly, and she jumped when she found a slender man with dark skin and eyes a molten copper, hidden behind a pair of spectacles.

"A-a-archmage," the man stuttered as he wiped his foggy spectacles on his tunic. "I-I-I had no idea you were paying a visit. I-I-I would have cleaned up. It's a mess in here."

"Professor Laugen." Killian gripped the man's hand. Laugen apologized under his breath for his dirt-covered hands, which he also proceeded to wipe on his tunic. "It's an impromptu visit. I hope everything is going well as the start of the school year approaches."

The man nodded. "Splendidly. And who is your guest?"

"This is my...umm...well..." Killian cleared his throat. "Lyyli Ives. I'm giving her a tour of the property. She's likely to become a student at Darkest Star."

"Oh?" The professor adjusted his spectacles and gazed at her curiously. His copper eyes seemed to pierce her with his scrutiny. Until now, she hadn't noticed his long ears peeking out from brown hair. They drooped the slightest bit. A Forest Fae. "I see you have the mark of the earth upon your brow. What do you do that gets your hands dirty?"

She wrote in her notebook and turned it to face him. *My family are farmers.*

"Ah." He nodded and finally stepped aside to allow them inside the greenhouse. If he was curious about why she didn't speak, he said nothing of it. "I don't doubt you have a great grasp on soil and how to create healthy crops. Good. Good. I do enjoy when students already have a background in my area. I do hope you will take a class or two from me."

A rush of humid air hit her the moment she stepped foot in the greenhouse, along with a collage of scents ranging from sweet to sour to rancid. She gazed in awe at the vines climbing trellises attached to each wall, reaching toward the moonlight beams entering through the glass roof overhead.

Leaning over a cluster of pink blooms, she inhaled their fruity scent. But when she approached white flowers within a garden box, Killian quickly grabbed her elbow and steered her away.

"Poisonous," he explained, nodding toward the patch of white petals. "You must first soak them to neutralize the poison and then pluck the petals while they are damp to get to the sweet, healing center. If prepared correctly, you can create healing tonics or just as easily create a poison."

He cleared his throat, scratched his head, and then pulled at his cuffs again. Was he...nervous?

"Excuse me. I wanted to check on the progress of the thornwart vines."

Perplexed, she watched his retreating back disappear behind a large cart filled with green herbs until it swallowed him completely. He was not acting like himself. Had she done something wrong?

Discomfort balled in her stomach as she entertained the idea that he might have brought her here to end things with her. Before they really even truly began.

To hide her growing unease, she turned her back and studied several potted fruits. They were round with white spots, growing on a vine similar to a tomato. She didn't dare inhale it nor touch it.

Professor Laugen sidled up next to her and plucked one of the fruits, popping it into his mouth. He chewed for a few moments, grimaced, and swallowed. She inhaled sharply in surprise when his skin turned a light shade of orange.

"It's not done yet." He wiped his mouth on his sleeve, leaving behind a purple-blue streak. "These fruits are great when adding to a transformation spell, but you have to get them just the right level of sweetness."

She tore her gaze away from his orange skin and scribbled in the notebook. *Where are you from?*

The professor moved onto the next row of plants, leaned in close, and squinted. "Archmage Graves sought me out in the forests of Andanara. When he offered me a teaching position at the school, how could I refuse? I get to do what I love all day, and someone pays me to do it!" His laughter echoed off the glass walls of the greenhouse, but then he coughed and fidgeted with his spectacles. "Of course, I get to experiment with a new variety of species in Skaad. I suppose I just couldn't help myself."

He produced a thin knife and scraped the fine hairs off a leaf, quietly muttering to himself as if forgetting her presence.

She slipped away to find Killian doing much of the same. If she could laugh, she would. But instead, she settled for a smile. When he glanced up, she gestured to the green blossom hidden within the green foliage.

His answering smile spiked her pulse through her veins. "It's the flower I used to create the elixir I drank to enhance my magic."

After spending a moment writing in the notebook, she turned it to face him. *Why don't you take the elixir all the time?*

"Because it completely destroys me the day afterward." He bent at the waist to examine the flower closer, running his fingers over the silky petals. "Either I will sleep an entire day through, or I will be non-functional in body and mind. Even khave can't counter its effects. However, I am aiming to create an elixir to help someone recover quicker from using too much magic at once."

He straightened suddenly and snapped his fingers. "I just remembered a book I have in the mage's quarters. It may lend me information about the galiphor and whatever beast I saw in my dream. Come on."

He threaded his fingers through hers, and moments later, the shadows swallowed them.

****

Killian was a frazzled mess.

Perspiration slicked his palms. His heart refused to stop hammering against his ribcage. He fidgeted and fidgeted some more, and when his hands didn't have enough to do, he rifled through book after book, creating a mess of pages on top of his desk with no spot of wood visible beneath the mess he made.

His gaze jumped over pages, but when his blood scorched a trail of lava through his veins, he couldn't think clearly.

The only way to hurtle over his immense anxiety and discomfort was either propose or drop his endeavors entirely.

Taking a deep breath and holding it for the count of five, he slowly turned around to face Lyyli within the archmage's quarters. She calmly explored the large, circular room, and he couldn't help but watch as she ran her fingers over the glowing flowers climbing up vines toward the stars shining through the ceiling made of domed glass. In the middle of the room stood an enormous bed. She trailed her fingers along the fabric and moved behind the wall it rested against, only to come back out wearing the archmage's ceremonial robes.

Despite her height, the robes drowned her, the fabric pooling at her feet as she spun in a circle. A large smile spread across her face as she pulled up the sleeves to uncover her hands, only for the fabric to conceal them once again.

Drowning in his own clothing, she next moved to the curved shelves that fit snugly against the wall, each filled to the brim with potions, elixirs, and ingredients. He watched as she picked up a vial, peered close at the shimmering liquid inside, and then set it down again.

He remained rooted to the spot, transfixed as she set the robes aside and continued her exploration toward the writing desk. Her slender fingers opened each drawer and closed it again, but then her emotions lit up with joy and curiosity when she seemed to spot something inside.

His throat closed up as she pulled out a music box, the lid decorated with a small tapestry of unicorns within wild woods.

"That was my mother's." His words escaped as little more than a raspy whisper. Her gaze darted up to meet his. "She gave it to me when the last brick was laid to finish the school." A wry yet amused smile pulled up on his lips. "She told me it was a trinket passed from female to female down the Graves' family line to bring luck and happiness on a wedding day."

A shaky breath left his lips when he realized this was the perfect opportunity to propose. He wrung his hands together and took several steps forward but stopped when blue streams of sadness escaped her to go along with the downward pull of her lips. When her gaze lifted, her sadness and worry slammed him in the gut.

She pointed to herself, shook her head, and then pointed to the unicorn.

Realization drove another fist into his gut. The unicorn symbolized purity and innocence. Her written words from a while ago echoed in his mind. *I accidentally killed the only boy I ever courted.*

She was not a virgin.

Perhaps it should have bothered him, but it didn't. It didn't change anything.

He shrugged and took a step closer and then another. "And neither am I. It doesn't matter."

Yet, her sadness remained as she wrote in the notebook and turned it to face him. The explanation was long.

I grew up alone. I had my family, but they didn't understand me. Not really. They were afraid of me despite how much I knew they loved me. We moved a lot because of the trail of bodies I left behind. When I got older, we settled on farmland. I was alone. Neighbors refused to look me in the eye. I was treated like someone who was invisible, like someone who didn't matter. No one tried to communicate with me until he came along.

For once, I was loved and accepted. And I killed him too.

The depth of her heartache nearly broke him in two. He could only imagine how lonely her life must have been, how desperate she must have been to dispel that loneliness.

Despite how anxious he was to propose, he took the music box from her, ignoring the beautiful ring nestled inside—a ring meant for his intended—and wound it up. A tinkling melody chirped from the box. Like forest sprites giggling as they raced through a waterfall. Like stars twinkling as they twirled their silver gowns. Like a gentle breeze weaving through clusters of leaves.

He set the box down and held out a hand to Lyyli. Tears shimmered in her eyes as she wordlessly slipped her hand into his and allowed him to pull her close until her head rested against his shoulder, his chin resting on the top of her head. Together, they swayed back and forth to the melodic chimes, holding each other close.

When it felt as if his entire world was falling apart around him, her stability kept him grounded. She was the only thing that made sense in a world filled with heartache, grief, and uncertainty.

He wanted to keep her.

So desperately.

The last note filled the quarters. Yet, they continued swaying as if the music never stopped. He found himself lost in her gentle touch. In the sweet, floral scent of her hair. In the warmth burning bright within his chest.

Warmth.

Happiness.

And something else he wasn't sure how to name.

"I swear I had a good reason for coming here." He chuckled as he finally stopped swaying with her. "But I seem to have forgotten what it was."

When she lifted her head from his shoulder, he inhaled sharply at the confusing mixture of emotions melting off her. Dark pink. Red. Yellow. Orange.

Dark pink?

What in the shadows was that emotion?

Thoroughly destroying the romantic tension between them to fuel the curiosity of discovery, he reached into his pocket, pulled out his notebook, and flipped to the page of colors. He trailed his finger down the page and stopped near the middle of the list.

Dark pink—love.

He dropped his notebook in his surprise, his pulse spiking when he stooped to pick it up. Lyyli's hand touched his shoulder, her eyes inquisitive as if to ask after his well-being.

He opened his mouth to reassure her when he caught sight of his own reflection in the mirror across the room.

Dark pink burst out of him like fireworks during the winter solstice.

He raked his fingers through his hair. How had this happened? Sure, he was fond of Lyyli. But love?

Yet, the proof stared him back in the eye from the mirror. Dark pink swirled above his head like smoke dancing in the wind. He couldn't recall ever falling in love before. Was this what it felt like? Warmth. Happiness. Gratitude. Desire.

Realizing his jaw had dropped, he snapped it closed and stood abruptly. But when he turned his head to glance at Lyyli, he found her only inches away, concern still written on her face. She couldn't know. Even as panic over the foreign emotion being discovered coursed through his veins, he wanted to hide it until he managed to figure it out himself.

She couldn't know. He wouldn't tell her.

Fear, uncertainty, and worry clouded the dark pink wafting above her head. She gazed at him directly in the eye and signed three words he recognized far too easily. "I love you."

Heat scorched his ears as he stared wide-eyed at her. All coherent thought fled his mind as he turned into a pile of brainless mush. His lips parted. Yet, no sound escaped.

The longer he stared, the darker the color gray stained her cheeks. He needed to say something. Anything! But what?

Her hands trembled as she wrote in her notebook, and he watched as the words took shape. *Of course, I understand if you don't feel the same way. It hasn't been very long, and—*

He startled even himself as he smacked the notebook out of her hands before she finished the sentence, cradled her face, and transferred the scorching heat from his ears to the point where their lips met in a searing kiss.

Drawers rattled as he backed her into the desk. He knew he should have stopped the kiss then and there, but he felt powerless against his own desire as she threaded her fingers through his hair and pulled him closer. He lifted her onto the desk, and her legs wrapped around his waist, trapping him.

A passionate wave crashed over him as he fully surrendered to her touch without a fight. A part of his brain flashed in warning, but warning for what? He wasn't sure. All he knew was he wanted more.

His hands trailed up her thighs, over her hips, and to her shoulders. He paused, finding the slightest sliver of restraint.

But as Lyyli began unbuttoning his shirt and running her hands over his chest, his sliver of restraint melted to the back of his mind as a groan escaped his mouth. He unfastened the top three buttons on the back of her dress, just enough for the fabric to droop low enough to reveal bare shoulders.

Stop!

His mind shouted the word as another warning flashed across his vision. Something was wrong. But he snapped his eyes shut and ignored it. He bunched up her dress to her thighs, leaving a trail of kisses from her jaw to her throat to her shoulders. Her skin was soft beneath his lips.

He wanted more.

He *needed* more.

Lyyli pushed his shirt off his shoulders, and it fell to the floor. She hooked her fingers under his belt and pulled him closer until not even an inch remained between them. A haze of desire fogged his mind. He needed her kiss. Needed her touch.

Needed her voice.

The shock of the realization gave him enough willpower to break away from her. He shook his head in an attempt to clear the fog, but the moment her lips kissed his neck, the fog returned, thicker than before.

He picked her up with her legs still wrapped around his waist and stumbled blindly toward the bed. He tripped over the corner of the bed frame, and they both crashed into soft sheets, tangled in the other's embrace.

The kiss deepened in a feverish need, a tangle of limbs, of hot breaths, and a desperate desire. He unfastened another button on the back of her dress and then another, kissing every inch of exposed skin. And when she loosened his belt, the voice screamed at him again.

Stop!

He mumbled the word against her lips, but the sound was lost in their kiss. Waves of need beat against him as if they dragged him beneath the surface of imaginary waters. His lungs tightened. His chest squeezed.

Air refused to enter him no matter how hard he tried to reach it. He clawed frantically to reach for air, but he only managed to dig his fingers into Lyyli's shoulders, kissing her with more frantic urgency.

His chest screamed with agony. Foggy pleasure mixed with desperate fear. Black seeped into the corners of his vision like shadows slowly burying him within its inky grave. They crawled across his body, entered his mouth and nose, and stole the air right from his lungs. The heavy weight crushed him until one rib snapped. And then another.

Agony ripped across his torso, and yet he needed more.

More.

More.

More.

It was as if his body threw out one last attempt at survival before the shadows buried the last smidge of moonlight in his eyes. He used the last remaining bubble of air within his lungs to plead with her. "Stop."

Her hands pushed him forcefully away, and he hadn't the strength to catch himself as he rolled off the edge of the bed and landed hard on the floor with a *thud*. He clawed back to the surface, and the moment his head broke for air, he gasped. Pain ripped through his chest, and he barely managed to crack his eyes open to find his skin discolored from the bruising of cracked bones.

His ribs truly were broken.

Lyyli hovered over him, her eyes wide as she clutched her dress to keep it from falling off. Fear, panic, sorrow, and immense regret wafted over her head. As the shadows dispersed even further, he gasped in another breath and winced at the agony ripping through his ribs. Slowly, his head stopped spinning. The darkness dispersed. And his eyes focused enough to find tears trailing down Lyyli's cheeks.

She rushed away only to return with a glass of water and a wet cloth, which she placed on his forehead.

Otherwise, she didn't touch him.

"I'm sorry," she signed over and over again. "Please live. Please live. Please live."

A groan escaped him as he rolled over onto his side, and he couldn't help the wave of nausea churning in his gut. He retched.

When the nausea subsided, he lay on his side for a moment as the remainder of the fog in his mind dispersed. He suddenly understood what it felt like being a sailor lured overboard by a siren before she dragged him to the depths of the sea. He'd been a willing participant, happy to die in her arms.

Lyyli was more dangerous than he'd realized. She didn't need to use her voice to use her magic to kill. A kiss worked just as well, destroying him from the inside out. A marriage with her would never work.

Unless...

A different kind of agony squeezed his chest. He'd heard the saying before, "If you love someone, let them go." But until now, he'd never understood what it meant.

"How many men have you kissed?" he mumbled as he managed to sit up. But when nausea returned at full force, he sat back against the bed. Her chin wobbled as she held up two fingers.

"And the first one died." He squeezed his eyes shut to prevent himself from seeing her emotions. If he witnessed them, he wasn't sure he could do this. Their first kiss had been gentle and sweet. She hadn't used her magic then, even unknowingly. The passion between them must have sparked it.

He took a deep breath. "I think...I think you need to go. Back to the ocean. Back to your aunt. You can't stay here."

yyli stared at Killian, her hands held to her heart to both keep her dress from falling off her shoulders and to keep her heart from bleeding out. She'd almost killed him. With a *kiss*! If she'd allowed the kiss to go on any longer than it had, he would be dead.

The horror of it ripped her soul wide open. She was afraid. Of herself. Of what she could do. What she had almost done to the man she loved.

Heartache rippled down her face, warm and wet and filled with despair. Killian kept his face buried in his knees, his eyes shut.

He didn't want to see her emotions.

He was sending her away.

For good.

Despite her efforts, the blood from her heart seeped out between her fingers and dripped onto the floor. When she glanced down, she almost expected to find a pool of red. Yet, the floor remained unblemished.

Everyone always sends me away. I have no place. I am a danger to everyone around me.

But Killian didn't want her words. He didn't want her apologies or her explanations or...or her love.

Otherwise, he would look at her. By averting his gaze, he was also blocking out his ears.

"It's for the best," he whispered.

She swiped the tears from her eyes and spotted the purple bruises on his side. She'd broken his ribs. *With her kiss.* What other damage might she have done? What more damage could she have done if she hadn't heard his quiet plea for her to stop?

"Forgive me," she signed, but her words fell on deaf ears.

Shame and despair pricking her conscience, she slipped behind the changing screen in the corner of the room, her hands trembling as she buttoned up her dress. She likely missed the top button in her haste as she spun around and ran past him, where he still sat shirtless on the floor. She heaved open the door and slammed it shut behind her. She swore she heard him calling her name in her flight, but she didn't stop.

Tears blurred her path as she ran down stone steps, escaped into the fresh night air, and kept running, her feet leading her blindly forward. She yanked the earrings he'd given her out of her ears and threw them to the ground. Killian would never find her again. He was safer without her in his life.

She never should have sought him out from the beginning. He had enough to worry about without her adding to his injuries.

Her surroundings flew past in a blur of green, black, and gray. A vine tangled around her ankle and nearly tripped her. She yanked her foot free but lost her shoe in the process. Cobblestone transitioned into dirt, and she lost her balance long enough to lose her second shoe.

Yet, she kept running.

After several minutes, her chest ached with the exertion, but she refused to stop. Not until she put as much distance between her and Killian as possible.

The forest shadows swallowed her in a single bite as she continued her flight through the trees. Branches clawed at her. Vines and dirt snagged the hem of her dress. As she took the path through thorny bushes, the fabric of her clothing ripped. One of the larger thorns caught onto her skirt. She thrashed and flailed until she yanked herself free. Her dress tore.

Still, she didn't stop.

Minutes passed, or perhaps hours, when a thick cloud of salty air entered her burning lungs. She breathed in deeply, desperate to feel the saltwater with each inhale.

Instinct drove her bare feet faster. Dirt became sand that squished between her toes. She pulled her dress over her head and threw it into a cluster of palm trees. Her petticoat nearly tripped her as she dropped it to her ankles. She stumbled over the white, slippery fabric before kicking it aside and continuing her flight toward the ocean. The saltiness of the air grew stronger with each passing moment, with each step she took forward.

Next, she untied her corset and shucked it off, finally stepping out of her bloomers until she stood on the beach with nothing but her skin in the pale light of dawn. She gazed out over the calm ocean waters with longing and desperation. She didn't belong on land. No one wanted her here. She was a danger to all. But perhaps she might find a life of solitude beneath the waves.

"I am not a human," she signed to the empty beach, not daring to utter a single word, even when she thought herself alone.

Slowly pulling out the ribbon from her hair, she discarded the very last thing that tied her to this world.

"I am a mermaid."

Taking one step into the water, her legs solidified into a tail, and she fell into the foamy water with a splash.

The moment the cold water rushed over her, she glanced up to find two yellow eyes glowing from the shadows high in a tree. The yellow eyes blinked before the creature leaped from the branch and soared toward her. Sharp yellow teeth oozed black liquid while blood coated its outstretched talons.

Despite her care to always remain silent, she screamed.

****

"Drat!" Killian said under his breath, followed by several curses. He held Lyyli's earrings in his palm, the thread connecting him to them dying slowly like a fly caught in a spider's web.

He swayed on his feet, his head spinning and a wave of nausea churning in his gut. His broken ribs burned like fiery embers, each breath he took painful beyond belief.

Leaning against a nearby tree to take some of the weight off his weak, trembling legs, he scanned the area to try to figure out which way she'd gone. "How could I have messed this proposal up so badly?"

Now completely dressed, he mentally checked off all the mistakes he'd made in the past hour. Yet, he'd meant what he'd said. Lyyli needed to go home to learn how to control her magic. What he *hadn't* meant was for her to run off in the darkness without him, without aid, and attempt the feat herself.

And perhaps not before they'd made some sort of arrangement for her to marry him first.

"Drat it all!" He kicked the tree with his boot in his frustration, only to wince at the new pain flaring up in his toes. He still wanted Lyyli as his wife. If he'd only been lucid enough to explain. If only she hadn't run off so quickly.

Now he didn't know which way she'd gone.

"Are you looking for your newest recruit?" Professor Laugen said behind him as he wiped his hands on an already dirty cloth. The man adjusted his glasses and nodded toward the path leading west. "I've never seen a look of pure heartbreak before. What did you do? Deny her entrance into Darkest Star? I rather liked her."

"No." Killian raked his fingers through his hair. "No! Of course not. This is a more...personal matter."

The professor paused before his lips pressed tightly together. "Uh-huh. In that case, good luck. I've never known a man who could fix a woman's heart after crying *that* much. I think I'll stay here and dig your grave."

"Funny." Killian rolled his eyes but worry gnawed at him. The darkness was filled with creatures Lyyli wouldn't understand. Creatures that could eat her or tear her to bits if she wasn't careful. And because of her human upbringing, she wouldn't know what to expect or what to look out for. Where could she possibly have gone that was west?

He nearly banged his head against the same tree he had kicked.

The ocean.

Of course.

His worry gnawed harder. If she stepped foot in its waters, he might never see her again.

His shadewalking power leaped away when he reached for it. He chased it around within himself, but it darted into shadow after shadow until the feat exhausted him. The elixir should have given him enough power to shadewalk a great distance at least one more time. Lyyli had drained him.

Completely.

"I need a horse," he said exhaustedly. "Please tell me I might acquire one here." He couldn't remember for the life of him if the stable master had arrived on the property yet.

The professor nodded his head in the direction of the stables. "I think there are a few. But the stable hand is a human. He takes care of them during the day."

Before the man finished his last sentence, Killian stumbled in the direction of the stables. A sense of urgency guided his feet forward as he slammed open the doors to find himself staring back at several pairs of unblinking eyes in the darkness.

He only dared to waste enough time to bridle one of the horses before he jumped up and rode the creature bareback. When dizziness threatened to topple him over the side, he squeezed his eyes shut for several moments before kicking the beast forward. The shadow horse galloped ahead with impeccable speed, heading west toward the ocean.

With each passing moment in the blur of black and gray of his surroundings, he dreaded the fast-approaching sunrise. The light would blind him to his environment and make travel dangerous.

"Come on," he urged the horse faster down the trail but inhaled sharply when he spotted something caught on a tree. He pulled back on the reins, earning himself a disgruntled snort from his mount as it ground to a halt, nearly throwing him off.

When the jerky movement settled, he leaned forward and snatched a piece of fabric off the brambles of an unforgiving bush.

Memories of the passionate encounter with Lyyli in his chambers flashed across his mind as if he held her bunched-up skirts in his hands all over again. Soft silk. Elegant lace.

The air squeezed from his lungs, his chest tightening. The pressure increased until it felt as if someone took hold of one of his ribs and bent it at a dangerous angle.

He cried out with agony as the rib snapped, and not able to stay upright through the pain, he tumbled over the side of the horse and landed in a heap on the dirt floor. For several long moments, he focused on breathing as he stared up at the dawn light above. Another rib had cracked. Which meant...

Horror pulsed through each thunderous heartbeat as he rolled over with a groan of agony. Lyyli's magic still flowed through his veins. It was slowly killing him.

He was dying.

For several moments, he stared at the light of early dawn visible through the leaves shifting with the wind overhead. He felt useless. Powerless. Like a grain of sand buffeted by the ocean's current, not knowing up from down. Just when he tried to tackle one problem, another one surfaced.

Fire erupted in his side as he pulled himself into a sitting position, gasping with the effort. He had two choices—return home and try to figure out how to cure *himself,* or attempt to locate Lyyli and hope she might reverse the damage done to his body.

Only a couple of problems bared their teeth at him like guard dogs to the sanctuary of good health and prosperity. Lyyli might not know how to reverse the damage. He also might not find her in time.

Shock rippled through him, not from the realization of his imminent death. But from the thought that Lyyli's little sister had heard her voice. The girl was dying as well.

If she wasn't already dead.

Determination forced him to unsteady feet. He painstakingly climbed onto the patient horse, crouching low to prevent himself from falling off again.

A feminine scream.

"Lyyli!" he gasped, kicking the horse forward.

Branches snagged his hair. One of them scratched his cheek. But he continued to cling onto the horse's mane as the creature thundered through the trees, across rocks and sand, and finally burst onto the beach.

Killian slowed the beast to a rickety stop before dismounting. He stumbled through the sand before he lay eyes on a gigantic, winged beast swooping down from the skies as it dove for its prey in the water. When it missed, it swooped upward, only to spiral downward to try again.

Someone splashed in the water in their desperation to get away but was unsuccessful when the creature dove again. Familiar symbols glowed on its beak, similar to those of the galiphor.

For a moment, shock rooted him to the spot. Whatever these creatures were, they were after Lyyli. Why? To kill her? Or something else?

The ocean water garbled her next scream, kicking his panic into gear. He didn't dwell on why he wasn't trying to end his own existence after hearing her voice. Rather, he leaped into action.

A small portion of magic still coursed through his veins, enough for him to snatch a branch from the ground as he stumbled toward the surf.

"Ignis!" he shouted, and the end of the branch burst into flames. He planted himself between Lyyli and the winged beast, waving the fire in front of its face. The creature screeched, flapping its powerful wings so the gust nearly extinguished the fire. It attempted to fly around him, but he waded deeper into the water to keep himself and the fire as the only barrier to the mermaid in the ocean.

Another screech escaped the bird's mouth. It flew closer, only for Killian to wave the fire in its face. It squawked and turned in the opposite direction, flying away from them until it became a small black dot in the lightening sky.

"Lyyli," he gasped finally as he dropped the branch, the fire hissing as the ocean water extinguished it. He splashed through the water as he attempted to locate her. Finally, he found her clinging to a rock jutting from the water.

And she was naked.

Her long hair covered the portion of her breasts that the rock didn't. Her eyes were wide, her knuckles pale from clinging to the rock.

He kept his gaze glued to her face as he splashed toward her, and only when he wrapped his arms around her scaly, bare waist did she start signing frantically. He caught bits and pieces of her words. "Heard...voice...death."

"Shh, shh. It's all right," he tried to soothe. "I heard your scream, but it didn't hurt me. I'm fine. Well...for now."

"How?" she asked as she trembled against him. She wrapped her arms around his neck, not at all ashamed of her state of undress.

Like a mermaid. A real mermaid. From what he knew about them, males wore nothing from the waist up, and the females were depicted in the same way in paintings and books.

He blinked several times, trying to push the thoughts from his mind as well as trying to keep his gaze from dropping lower.

It was not easy.

"I will tell you in a minute. For now, that creature can come back, and I don't want us to be here if it does."

With a whistle to gain his horse's attention, he trekked away from the ocean and into the thick trees with the beast following at a distance. Every step stole from the reserves of his energy until his feet dragged in the dirt. Exhaustion threatened to collapse him as the elixir started to wear off entirely.

Lyyli's tail dried, and as it transitioned into two legs, he found himself carrying a *very* naked woman in his arms. She didn't seem to care, but only held him tighter. As if...as if he were a safe place for her.

He coughed, overly aware of her smooth skin against his fingers, the softness of her body pressed against his. Heat climbed to his ears.

Both his self-control and energy near to crumbling, he set her down, averting his gaze to the trees above them as he pulled off his shirt and handed it to her. After a few moments, he dared to glance at her. The hem of the shirt touched her upper thigh, barely covering anything higher. The top portion of the shirt fell off one shoulder while the sleeves drowned her arms.

She rolled them up to her forearms.

His self-control once again threatened to crumble at the sight of her wearing his clothing. But even now, he had more self-control than he had at Darkest Star without her magic flaming what passion already existed.

Waves of dizziness and nausea crashed over him as his energy drained further. He collapsed to his hands and knees.

A soft, tender hand touched his shoulder. Although he wanted to glance up at her, he instead fought off ripples of nausea.

"Your magic," he coughed. A groan escaped him before he collapsed onto his side. "Your magic is still in my body. It's killing me. I think that's why your voice doesn't affect me further."

He sensed rather than saw her lower herself beside him before settling his head on her lap. Her voice escaped as a raspy whisper as she spoke. *Out loud.* "Killian, I am so sorry. Forgive me. Please, forgive me."

A sigh of contentment left his lips. He took a deep breath and let it out slowly, relaxing at the sweetness of her words. The sweetest sound.

"You have the most beautiful voice I have ever heard. Will you sing to me? Please."

"I could kill you."

"I'm already dying."

She paused for a long moment, and when she spoke again, her voice cracked. "I never meant to hurt you. I can never forgive myself for this."

Wearily, he grasped onto her hand and attempted humor, if only to cheer her up. "I know you didn't. For what it's worth..." He managed an exhausted smile. "I will never forget that kiss for as long as I live."

"Why? Because it sucked the life out of you?"

He shook his head the slightest bit, wincing when the action created a pounding ache against his skull. He touched her knee and stilled when he found it bare, once again overly aware she wore no clothes except the shirt from his back.

But she didn't flinch away or react. He dared to draw circles on her skin with his thumb. "No. Though, I derangedly enjoyed every moment of life-sucking bliss." A low groan escaped him as he shifted onto his back and tipped his head to the side to look at her. Devastation and regret gazed back at him. "Because it made me happy. You make me happy."

Lyyli exhaled a sad sigh and shook her head as she looked away from him to stare at the trees. "You are still under whatever spell I accidentally put on you."

"I've been put under plenty of spells in my lifetime. This is not one."

Again, she shook her head and refused to meet his eye. "I'm a mess, Killian. Perhaps what I want is not what is best for you."

He didn't answer when a wave of dizziness crashed over him in the form of Lyyli's magic. Excruciating pain pressed on his ribs, and with each second of pressure, he began to lose consciousness.

His words escaped as a rush. "I don't have much time. My body will crash from using the elixir. But Lyyli. Listen carefully. I came to warn you. Your magic is still running through my veins. Your sister is likely facing a similar fate. You need to go home. You need to—"

His next rib cracked, and his world turned dark.

omething between a wail and a sob escaped her mouth when she heard the next *crack* just before Killian's body went limp. *Stop!* she willed her magic, but it was as if it continued to climb through his body like deadly vines snuffing out every flicker of his essence.

She had to stop this. But how? The only person who might be able to help her lay unconscious in her lap, and her aunt could be ten leagues away in the sea for all she knew.

Dread crawled through her in the form of creeping ice. Cold. Dark. Inescapable. Killian thought her sister was in danger. But it had been months! Astra could be dead by now, and she would have had no way of knowing.

But what if she wasn't?

What if she had recovered and perhaps knew of a way Killian could recover, too?

Determination gave her the strength to climb to her feet. She hooked her arms beneath Killian's and dragged him toward the shadow horse. In the daytime, the horse's body was translucent, its outline barely visible beneath the light of morning.

As if sensing her urgency, the animal laid down. She hesitantly reached out to touch its back.

Despite its translucency, the creature was solid.

Her arms shook with the effort it took to drag Killian's body. Not only was he tall, but he was heavy. A grunt escaped her mouth as she used far too much effort to drape him over the horse, folded in half. Upon rounding the horse, she tripped over one of its legs but barely caught herself. The creature snapped at her in warning with long, pointed teeth. But otherwise, it remained still.

Carefully, she ran her fingers through Killian's hair, over his shoulder, and then took the reins in her hands.

"I'm so sorry," she whispered before she didn't dare speak again. At least Killian's legs were long enough to balance his weight. But she wasn't sure how to transport him without jostling his ribs.

The horse stood slowly as if aware any sudden movement might throw its rider off its back.

Hours passed as Lyyli led the horse in the direction of her parents' home. Blisters dotted the bottoms of her bare feet as she traversed rough roads and rocky terrain. She winced as a particularly sharp rock dug into her toe and split the skin. But she kept walking, remaining vigilant of her surroundings.

Dense, green forests transitioned into thin trees as they entered the human lands of Frisia through the backroads to avoid notice. A familiar, wide river provided her direction as she followed it from sparse trees to vast farmland. By the time they reached the main road leading into her hometown, dusk fell, splashing red, orange, and yellow across a blue canvas.

Dirt caked the bottoms of her blistered and bleeding feet, climbing up muddied ankles. Saltwater coated her hair, causing it to lay stiff against her shoulders. Killian's shirt barely covered her, and she hoped they wouldn't run into anyone else on the road.

"Ughhhh," Killian groaned.

Her heart leaped into her throat as she spun around to find him pushing himself up from his folded position on the horse. His eyes were bloodshot, his usually pale face red from hanging upside down for hours.

She rushed over to him, touching his face, his bare shoulders, and then her fingers lightly skimmed his sides. Large, purple bruises marred his skin, indicating the damage within his body.

"Where are we?" he grunted. He began swaying where he sat, and she hurried to steady him with her arms. Only when he gained control of himself did she dare to let go and sign.

"Home."

He squinted against the light of the sunset. "You are not speaking again? Why?"

Despite how much she longed to speak, to converse with him for hours on end, she knew she couldn't. The wind traveled in the direction of the fields, and her voice could easily ride it in murderous waves. She didn't dare utter a sound.

"Home," she signed again, gesturing to the fields surrounding them.

Finally, he blinked his eyes into focus and glanced around. "How did we get here?"

His attention moved from the sky, to the fields, to his bare chest, and to his shirt she wore to cover herself.

And then he noticed her feet.

"You walked all this way."

She nodded and placed a hand over his heart, not caring as much as she thought she should when the shirt she wore lifted enough to reveal her upper thigh. He had already seen this much of her skin and more. It didn't matter. What mattered was his health.

Releasing a long breath, he covered her hand with his and closed his eyes for several moments. "I feel absolutely awful, but I'm still alive. Let's find out how your sister is faring."

He surprised her by grabbing onto her hand and lifting her onto the horse in front of him until she rode with both legs draped over one side of the creature. His arm wrapped around her waist, and his chin rested on her shoulder as if he struggled to remain upright.

A frenzied rhythm pulsed through her veins, heat blazing through her cheeks at the familiar way he held her.

Trying to ignore her heated cheeks, she took the reins and led the shadow horse down the main road of her hometown. Slowly, the sky darkened, and stars prodded out the sunset hues in favor of a quiet night. Crickets greeted them in a symphony of synchronized chirping. The horse's clomping hooves joined the chorus, followed by several bleating sheep and lowing cattle.

A surprising amount of dread gathered within her like dark storm clouds as she spotted the family home. Lanterns flickered to life within the windows, a couple of shadows crossing the main room.

What would her parents think of her return? Would they turn her away? Would they send her back to Katalle rather than welcome her into their home?

"Perhaps I should talk to them first," Killian murmured tiredly into her ear. "I can help them understand."

When her hands stilled with fear, she allowed her emotions to speak for her instead. Her parents didn't want her anymore. What if they were angry at her return?

She stopped the horse in front of the house and slid to the ground, wincing when her injured feet struck the dirt. Ignoring the pain, she hurried to help Killian down. He swayed for a few moments after his feet touched the ground.

"Stay right here," he instructed, pointing to a spot in the shadows just beyond the door. "Hopefully, we will be well-received."

A pounding drum took control of her heart as she watched Killian stumble toward the door and knock, barely holding himself upright. Several moments later, it opened, the light in the house creating a silhouette of her father.

Pain and happiness pricked her soul, but she remained still.

"Hello?" Her father's eyebrows furrowed.

Despite his obvious fatigue, Killian smiled. "This is an incredibly awkward way to meet you." He held out a hand. "Lord Killian Graves."

Her father gawked as he shook his hand, his mouth hanging open as if awed. "The archmage? What are you doing here? Is Lyyli all right? We haven't heard from her yet."

Her mother soon joined her father at the door, her gaze raking over his unclothed upper half. Dark circles lingered beneath her eyes, weariness in every crinkle around her puckered mouth.

Killian grimaced. "I swear there is a logical explanation as to why Lyyli is wearing my shirt. May we come inside?"

Heart in her throat, Lyyli hesitantly stepped into view, her hands pulling the hem of his shirt as far down as possible. Still, most of her legs were visible. She was a tall woman.

"Lyyli," her father sobbed. He pulled her into a crushing embrace, quickly joined by her mother, who whispered apology after apology as she showered her cheeks in kisses. They ushered them inside.

She inhaled a deep breath of farm and freshly baked bread. She was home.

24

A relentless heat scorched Killian from the inside. Every fiber of his being gasped for relief from the heat, from the pain. But as if he suddenly found himself trapped in a dry desert, he found no cooling relief.

He watched as Lyyli ducked into another room, only to return wearing a flattering peasant dress cut in the human fashion. She handed his shirt to him, the glass of his potions clinking together as he pulled the garment over his head.

Worry puckered Lyyli's forehead as she signed to her parents. Slowly, as if giving him a chance to catch onto her words. She spelled out A-S-T-R-A and he recognized the word for "sick."

Mr. Ives nodded, casting a hopeful glance toward Killian. That glance turned to worry when Killian lowered himself onto a chair at the kitchen table and rested his head against the wall. Everything hurt. Especially his pounding head. What was he to do? He couldn't think of anything that might heal what damage a siren could do. Was this it? After all his efforts to save his school, his title, his mother… This was how he was going to die?

This couldn't be the end.

"Yes, Astra has been sick ever since…" Mr. Ives grimaced as he shared a look with his wife. "Ever since the incident at the pond. I suspect hearing your voice had more catastrophic effects than we originally realized. The doctor doesn't know how to help. We don't know what to do."

Grief filled Lyyli's face as she waved her hands frantically again. He didn't follow, and his weary eyes and mind didn't want to try. Perhaps someone might interpret for him.

He glanced around the house, taking in his new surroundings that Lyyli had grown up with. This was her life.

The farmhouse was small, only one story tall. The kitchen shared a space with the table, the fireplace, the sofa, a rack for coats, and a basket for shoes. Down the hall, he spotted two doors, which he assumed were a couple of different rooms. A pantry was tucked in the corner of the kitchen next to a wood-burning stove. Garlic and several herbs hung over the sink. A couple of lanterns lit up the small space, casting soft glows across everyone's faces.

Even in the semi-darkness, his eyes struggled to pick up the faintest details.

"Lord Graves?" Mrs. Ives asked softly as she set a steaming cup of tea before him on the table. "Lyyli thinks you can help Astra. Do you think…" The woman trailed off as if noticing his own haggard appearance.

He glanced toward Lyyli to find her holding her hands to her heart, her eyes pleading and hopeful.

Ignoring the cup in front of him due to his severe loss of appetite, even for the sake of polite appearances, he rubbed the ache from his temples. He should be trying to find a way to help himself first, but he didn't know how. "I will do what I can, of course."

Mr. Ives shot out a round of questions, speaking out loud and with his hands at the same time. "Tell us everything. Did you get to the archmage's home safely? What have you been doing since? Why did you show up the way you did?"

An ache rippled through Killian's ribs as he stood, forcing himself not to groan. He answered for her. "There is a lot you don't know about Lyyli. Your daughter is..." So many words came to mind, but he settled on one. "Exceptional." He turned to Lyyli, the warmth of gratitude in her eyes to match his own. "You can decide how much you want to tell them. I'm going to see to your sister."

He probably should have asked, but he hadn't the strength to do so as he dug through the kitchen pantry and drawers to locate a wooden bowl and spoon. He struggled against the dizziness bouncing through his head as he took one of the lanterns from the main area and ambled down the hallway. He stopped in front of one of the doors, raised his eyebrows questioningly at Mr. Ives, who nodded.

When he entered the room, a waft of cold air greeted him as it drifted through the open window. The light of the lantern revealed a small room with two beds—one empty and the other occupied by a writhing and shivering small form of a girl. The girl was tiny. He knew humans were often shorter than Shadow Fae, but she seemed unusually small tangled up in the bedsheets.

Quietly, he set the lantern on top of an armoire and untangled the sheets from Astra's legs before tucking them back in around her. A flush filled her cheeks, her skin hot to the touch. She wore a long, white nightgown. Careful to respect her privacy, he made sure the sheets covered her as he lifted the gown just enough to inspect her ribs. The skin of her torso was discolored like his own, and judging by her rasping breaths as she slept, she struggled to breathe.

He pulled the nightgown back down and sat at the small vanity beside the bed. The chair wobbled against his weight, and he worried it might snap altogether.

"Fever, broken bones, night sweats, chills, and who knows what else," he mumbled as he watched her breathe for several moments. He didn't know how to heal her, but he could at least take away some of her symptoms.

"How is she?" Mr. Ives asked quietly from the doorway.

Killian frowned as he took out all of his vials from his pocket and placed them on the bedside table. He must have brought *something* to help with Astra's immediate suffering. "I am no physician, but…this looks bad. From what information I've collected, I can assume she has a little longer than I do. I was closer to Lyyli than Astra was when inflicted with her magic."

"Just how close, exactly?"

With a grimace, he glanced over his shoulder to find Mr. Ives' raised eyebrow, a heated glare burning slowly in his eyes. He released a long breath before turning back to the potions and inspecting each one. He'd labeled the outside of the vials with their corresponding color to make things easier on himself.

"As close as you think," he finally replied in a regretful tone. "Will you close the door for a moment?"

The door clicked shut, though Killian placed the majority of his attention on the task at hand as he began to mix several drops of one vial with another until it smoked inside the wooden bowl.

"Well?" the man demanded.

"I'm not sure how much Lyyli told you."

"Everything. Though she failed to mention your romantic involvement."

He sighed wearily. "Right. She likely failed to mention my ultimatum as well." He plucked one of Astra's blonde hairs and mixed it in with the potion before he turned in his seat, his hands clasped as he gave Mr. Ives his full attention. "The Shadow Lords have decreed I must marry, or I will lose my title. I...I..." He ran his hands down his face, finally admitting his feelings out loud. "I love Lyyli. Though, I completely muddled my attempt at a proposal. Perhaps it was for the best."

When the man's jaw hung slack for a moment too long, Killian turned back to his concoction when it began to hiss and stirred another ingredient in.

"What do you mean?" the man asked quietly. At least he wasn't yelling. Or choking him to death. "You changed your mind? Does Lyyli know how you feel?"

"No, she doesn't know. Things keep going wrong. Maybe we're not meant to be together. We're just not working."

Silence.

The elixir bubbled and hissed as he stirred it with the spoon, and he added the final ingredient to cool it down.

Finally, Mr. Ives spoke. "You mean making it work is too difficult."

His hand stilled as the realization hit him in the gut. Was he truly giving up? After everything? It went against every fiber of his being to give up on *anything*. But so many things whirled around him in a dizzying fog, out of his control.

To give himself a few moments to think, he gently lifted Astra's limp body to a sitting position. Mr. Ives leaped forward to help keep her steady while Killian slowly poured the elixir into her mouth, little by little until nothing remained. In minutes, the flush disappeared, and her fever lessened. It wouldn't last, but it would buy him some time.

A grateful smile lifted on Mr. Ives' face as he ran a thumb along Astra's cheek. "Lyyli may not be my flesh and blood, but she's still my daughter. If she makes you happy, maybe you will consider not giving up yet. You don't realize how hard life has been for her. No one does, and no one will."

Not knowing how, exactly, to reply, Killian gathered up his things, scratching the stubble on his chin on his way out. "I need to make another potion, but I don't have all the necessary supplies on hand. I'll go scavenging for ingredients outside. May I also peruse your pantry?"

"Of course. We are very grateful for your presence."

His heart and mind heavy, he didn't stray far outside as he searched for what he needed to improve Astra's—and his own—condition. He hoped he could find a way to help the girl. But without his books or supplies on hand, he wasn't sure how much good he could do.

He could only try.

"I'm writing down everything else I know about mermaids," Killian said at the kitchen table a few minutes after administering another elixir to Astra, one that seemed to help ease her symptoms even more than the first had. He'd already explained as he'd written, constantly wincing against the pain he must feel while struggling to sit. "Sirens, especially. Perhaps something will jump out at you, and we can use it to reverse your magic's effects. No one knows you better than you know yourself."

Lyyli shook her head and pointed to his chest. Her mother translated as she signed. "I didn't even know I was a mermaid until I met you. You figured it out in less than a minute."

Killian's mouth twitched as if fighting a smile, though he didn't glance up as he wrote. "It's a good thing you came to me then. I only wish Auer didn't get to you first."

Biting her lip, she watched as Killian fell into a working trance. Concentration lay on his brow, his pupils dilating the slightest bit as ink splashed across the page in a mixture of words and images.

She wasn't the only one to notice his eyes.

Both her parents stared as if faced with a completely foreign object.

"Stop staring at his eyes," she signed to her father, Killian oblivious to their silent conversation.

"I can't help it," he signed back. "I've never seen anything like them."

"Me neither. But I'm rather fond of them."

His expression softened. "You love him."

Her cheeks heated as she glanced back toward Killian, who still scrawled across page after page. After she'd confessed her feelings for him, he'd kissed her. But he'd never mentioned it again. "Yes," she admitted with her hand. "I'm worried I muddled things. I don't think he loves me back."

Her father smiled, his eyes glinting with amusement as if he knew something she didn't.

Gently, he squeezed her hand before continuing their silent conversation. "From what I've gathered, he's a very focused and straightforward man. The way to deal with his type is to get him to put his strict focus on you instead of his work."

"How?" She huffed a breath of frustration, barely restraining herself from rolling her eyes. It wasn't like she hadn't tried often since they'd met.

He gestured to the door. "Go for a walk? Get him away from his books and his potions and his magic. But mostly, take him away from his worries."

Her mother cut in with her own signing, a grin on her face. "Draw attention to yourself. Wear your hair down. Ask him a question that makes him really look at you. Feign an injury."

Her father frowned. "Really?"

She patted his cheek. "It worked on you, dear."

Lyyli glanced in Killian's direction, watching as he winced in pain before his lips pressed tightly together, the end of the quill tapping against his temple. A tendril of hair slipped over his eyes, and he brushed it out of the way with his shoulder. He was adorable. She loved his intense focus, his high ambitions, his vast knowledge, and his desire to always learn something new. "I can't just force his affection. It doesn't work like that."

"It's not forcing it," her mother said as she brushed a hand against her cheek. "It's focusing on what's already there. Sometimes men need a push. That man right there," she nodded her head toward Killian just as he looked their way, "he needs a bigger push than most."

Killian set down his quill and crossed his arms, speaking out loud to break the silence. "Are you three talking about me?"

Her heart pounded, and she clutched her hands to her heart as she stared at him wide-eyed. This might be her only chance to get him alone, and she needed to get it right.

Overly aware of her rampant emotions, she signed, and her father interpreted. "My parents thought you looked tired. Will you take a break? Come outside with me."

She worried over his broken ribs, hoping fresh air might do him good.

An intense silence charged the kitchen as he rubbed his ribs and grimaced before he glanced toward his work.

Please. Please. Please.

"I suppose I can spare a minute or two. I'm having a hard time recalling a particularly evasive page in my mind anyway."

"I'll go grab a shawl." She ran to her room, tugged her hair free of its braid, and watched in the mirror as loose waves fell across her shoulders. When she reached for her lipstick, she hovered uncertainly. It would make little difference when Killian was unable to see color. So instead, she threw a white shawl over her shoulders. She paused, torn between setting him free of her and claiming what she wanted. But her parents seemed to think they could make this work. Couldn't she at least try?

When she emerged from her room, her father smiled, and her mother signed, "Beautiful."

She took a deep breath and glanced around for Killian. Nowhere in sight. When her father nodded his head toward the partially open door, she smoothed her skirt and bit her lip.

"I can't do this," she signed after staring at the door too long. "I can't do this to him. He's dying because of me. Nothing will change."

Her parents shared a look, but her mother answered. "I know the look of a man in love when I see it. You will break his heart if you run away."

He loves me?

She wasn't sure if she believed it.

Before she managed an answer, her mother spoke quickly. "Go out there and have an honest conversation with him. And maybe by the end, you might get a proposal."

She doubted that as well.

Hesitantly, she slipped out the door and closed it softly behind her. The night bathed her in darkness. A wave of nostalgia hit her as she breathed in the fresh country air. The scent of hay, horses, and dust.

A brief glance around the yard revealed Killian sitting on a fence post that overlooked a field of cows. His shoulders were hunched, and his face lay in his hands. He appeared exhausted and upset.

His weary posture remained as she approached, slipped through the bars of the fence, and climbed so her feet rested on the bottom post and her arms on the top. She nudged Killian with her elbow, which earned her the faintest twitch of his mouth.

He opened his mouth as if to speak, closed it again, and when words escaped, they cracked. "I feel like I'm breaking." His shoulders hunched even more as he dug the palms of his hands into his eyes. "Everything is out of my control, and I can hardly do anything to fix it. I feel so powerless."

Heartache—and guilt—rippled through her at his candid confession. While she had been worried about their relationship, he had the weight of the entire world on his shoulders.

She tilted her head to rest against his elbow, as she had no other way to speak but her actions and emotions.

Killian dropped his hands from his face to reveal the deep sadness within his eyes. "Will you speak again? You have already proved you can do no further harm to me."

With a resolute shake of her head, she glanced toward the house. A curtain dropped quickly over the window as if her parents had been watching them.

"You are afraid of your family hearing your voice?"

She nodded. Near her family, she refused to even whisper to Killian. She wanted to prevent anyone else from suffering from her power.

"You don't know I can't still hurt you further," she signed. Frustration trembled within her bones when he gazed back at her in confusion. She'd left her notebook lying in a heap on the floor in Killian's archmage quarters before she'd fled to the ocean. A foolish, hasty decision fueled by hurt and devastation.

"Listen, Lyyli..." He gently placed a hand on her shoulder. "Let me explain myself. I can only do so much by trying to teach you how to control your magic. But if you go home with your aunt, you will have no walls. I may be a teacher, but I'm not the best one for you."

She turned her head to stare out over sleeping cows rather than at Killian to hide her hurt. No doubt, he saw it spinning over her head like a flashing beacon anyway. How many times in twenty-four hours could she be rejected? Her heart might shatter if he spoke even one more word.

"I have a confession to make," he said slowly. "Two, actually."

Please don't hurt me anymore. She refused to turn her head to look at him. He continued speaking anyway.

"I brought you to the school to propose to you in my most favorite place in the entire world."

All at once, her entire body froze, and her breath stuttered in her lungs.

"I am not sure why I thought it would go well. I have not had much practice courting lately. I said all the wrong things and did all the wrong things in the wrong order. I was a nervous wreck. I truly wanted everything to go perfect." He lowered his voice to a husky whisper. "I love you, Lyyli."

Surprise shocked her to the core at the unexpected confession. She lifted her head and carefully studied his expression. Only nervousness and honesty lived within his eyes. This was not the rejection she had been expecting.

Several long moments passed in silence as she tried to make sense of his words. They didn't match his actions. She asked with her hands, "Why are you sending me away then?"

Another long pause as his eyebrows furrowed as if trying to dissect her words. Finally, he answered. "Because all your life, you have lived in silence and loneliness. I do not want that for you. I would go to the ends of the earth for you to speak freely and live happily. This is the only way I know how to do it."

Warmth touched her heart, reminding her how much he had already done for her and showing her how much more he was willing to do. "If I go, you will marry," she spelled out the name with her fingers, "J-O-H-A-N-N-A."

"Ah." He released a long, labored breath before leaning forward to rest his elbows on his knees. "I finally see the issue here. I'd imagined you would be happier when given an opportunity to learn more about yourself and your abilities." He turned his head to look her in the eye. "You are reluctant to leave me."

His smile echoed the same warmth burning in her chest.

She dared to lean her head against his leg to confirm his assumption. Crickets chirped calmly in the momentary silence between them, followed by a couple of lowing cattle. Her heart settled into relief that he finally understood. Nothing held her back except him. She would gladly give it all up if it meant a future together.

"You know we can," he coughed, "work something out, Lyyli. We—" When he coughed again, she glanced up in alarm to find perspiration dotting his brow, his skin paler than ever. He clutched his side and began to pitch backward. Panic bolted through her, and she reacted instinctively as she slipped through the wooden slats and barely managed to catch him beneath the arms before he took her down with him, landing on top of her. Pain flared in her side, but she ignored it as she unpinned herself from beneath him and knelt over him.

Killian groaned deliriously as blood dribbled out of his nose and the corner of his mouth.

All the breath left her lungs as if crushed by a boulder. His broken ribs. They must have pierced him from the inside.

Her father slammed the door open and rushed toward them, her mother at his heels.

"Help! Please help," she signed. Her hands hovered uselessly, not knowing how to help him. Her magic was killing him from the inside, wreaking havoc within his body.

As her father elevated Killian's head, Killian struggled to breathe as he mumbled incoherently.

"Let's get him inside," her father said in a serious tone as he hefted the front half of Killian's body while she and her mother lifted his legs. "We'll send for a physician."

"Look at him!" her mother gasped as they struggled to carry him inside. "He's not going to last long enough for a physician to get here. It could take hours. Maybe more."

They lowered him onto the floor, and the moment her arms were free, Lyyli crashed to her knees beside him and placed her hands on either side of his face. She willed her magic to return to her, to leave his body. But he continued to bleed and mumble nonsense as he rasped in breath after labored breath.

She kissed his bloody mouth and kissed it again, hoping the act might drain her magic from him.

He continued to die before her very eyes.

Wiping the taste of metallic blood from her lips with the back of her hand, she stood abruptly and rushed toward the kitchen table where Killian's notes lay. Pages upon pages lay sprawled on the rough wooden surface, each covered in his familiar scrawl.

Panic trembled through her knees, threatening to collapse her legs, but she forced herself to maintain a level head. Killian's life depended on it.

While her parents attempted to help Killian, Lyyli scanned his notes for anything that might help. What could reverse mermaid magic? Or what was strong enough to counter its effects? Even more importantly, what was potent enough to heal the damage done by a siren?

Her Aunt Eliel's words came to mind. *We exist to heal, to comfort, to inspire happiness in times of grief.*

Heal? But how?

In a moment of despairing rage, she swiped the entire stack of notes off the table when nothing jumped out at her. She couldn't do this. She couldn't heal. Nothing could stop her magic.

Tears cascaded down her cheeks, blurring the flurry of activity as her parents desperately tried to keep Killian from drowning in his own blood. Red cascaded from his mouth and nose, covering his entire face. His body convulsed, the skin on his face becoming paler and paler as he lost blood. If only she could share his pain. If only she could take it away entirely and suffer in his stead.

Her eyes widened as she spotted the last sentence Killian had written about siren tears being capable of miracles. Her thoughts struck a chord. A memory. She had shared Killian's grief at his estate by consuming his tears. What if tears could do more than just share pain? What if they could heal as well?

When her voice was inaccessible in front of her family, even to try to use it to heal, she dropped to her knees and used the next best thing.

She swiped the tears from her cheeks but paused when blood continued to flow out of Killian's mouth. It was not possible for him to consume her tears. But perhaps she could heal in the very place she had caused damage.

Prayers leaked from every inch of her heart as she dripped her tears onto his bloody lips and waited. And waited. When her tears continued to flow ceaselessly, she smoothed more over his bottom lip as her father held Killian steady.

She waited some more.

Slowly, Killian stopped convulsing, and blood ceased leaking from his mouth and nose. His body became limp, his head falling to the side.

No! she screamed inside her own head as she grabbed his face and brushed her thumbs along his cheeks. *Please, no. I beg you. I love you. I love you so much.*

When heartache threatened to rip her chest open, she rested her forehead against his and squeezed his hand.

His hand squeezed back.

Her head shot upward in shock, only to find him wincing. He groaned and murmured her name. She clutched his hand harder and rested her forehead on his chest as relief overwhelmed her. Blood covered him. She didn't care. He was alive. Her tears had healed him.

"Thank the stars," her father muttered under his breath moments before he stepped outside, his hands on his hips as he gazed into the darkness.

"Your magic is gone," Killian rasped before he released a breath and fell into a deep slumber.

Lyyli felt his pulse beat through his wrist before she smoothed each of his eyebrows and wiped the blood off his face with the hem of her skirt. Quietly, her mother joined her with a bowl of water and wet rags. They cleaned him up together and changed him into a borrowed shirt in silence.

No words came to mind as they finished cleaning him up, and the three of them transported him to her parents' bedroom. She tucked the sheets around him and felt his forehead. Cool. No fever.

A numbing shock coursed through her veins. All her life, she had believed herself to be a monster. Cursed. But she had just healed someone with her tears. Aunt Eliel was right. She was capable of so much more than death and destruction.

She kissed Killian's hand and then left a lingering kiss on his forehead, not caring that her parents stood nearby and sure that the display of affection wouldn't harm him again. The terrifying night had proved something vital—she couldn't let him go. Ever. He meant too much to her. Everything.

Straightening, she signed, "I'm going to try to heal Astra as well."

Her father nodded. "I'll watch over the archmage." When she turned to leave, he grabbed her elbow. "Did he at least propose?"

"Father," she signed, followed by an exasperated sigh.

"Well, did he?"

"No." She shook her head but smiled softly as she glanced toward Killian's sleeping form. "But he told me he loves me. Nothing could make me happier."

He beamed and kissed her forehead before shooing her toward the door. When she entered the room she used to share with Astra, she paused near the doorway as sadness washed over her. Her sister writhed in the bed, her face red and covered in perspiration.

"Can you help her?" her mother asked beside her as she wrung her hands together. She sighed. "I know you didn't mean to do this. I shouldn't have gotten so angry at you. Please forgive me, Lyyli."

"There's nothing to forgive," Lyyli reassured with her hands. "I'm just sad she has suffered for so long, and I had no idea."

Her mother's voice trailed behind her as she approached Astra's bedside. "We were worried when we hadn't received a letter from you for months. We knew you were hurt and upset, but we were beside ourselves with worry. I only wish we would have inquired into the situation. You say there is nothing to forgive, but there is so much to forgive."

Shaking her head, Lyyli placed the back of her hand against her sister's forehead. Scalding hot. Dripping her tears onto Killian's lips had worked. Astra had heard her voice instead. Could her tears heal through Astra's ears?

Thinking of all the hurt and all the pain she had caused her family inspired enough tears for her to swipe them from the corners of her eyes and drip one at a time into Astra's ears.

They waited.

Slowly, Astra stopped writhing. Her skin transitioned from scalding hot to feverish to warm, and finally, it cooled into a normal temperature.

Lyyli stepped back as she watched her mother rejoice, gathering Astra into her arms and kissing every inch of the little girl's face. Father soon joined them in the embrace. Her chest warmed with gratitude. The warmth brought peace and comfort, and as if to keep it there longer, she pressed her hands over her heart. All her life, she had killed and destroyed and caused pain.

Well, no longer.

She strode across the room, opened the armoire, and pulled out a brown cloak.

"Where are you going?" her mother cried out in alarm, finally noticing her.

Lyyli threw the cloak over her shoulders and clasped it at the neck. She signed, "If Killian will go to the ends of the earth for me, I can do the same for him."

"What will you do?"

"Try to heal his mother." There wasn't much time left for her. "When he wakes, tell him where I've gone."

Purpose guided her feet forward as she stepped outside into the darkness of night and strode toward the shadow horse munching on a rat. Or at least she assumed it was a rat. Blood oozed between the creature's teeth, a long tail dangling from the edge of its mouth.

She grimaced. At least they didn't eat people.

"Wait." Her father grabbed her elbow to stop her. "It's too dark. At least wait until dawn. It's not safe out there."

Perhaps not for a regular human, but she was a siren.

"I can't wait. If I do, it might be too late."

After a moment's hesitation, her father pulled out a sheathed dagger from his back pocket and handed it to her. Emotion bubbled up in her throat as she stared at the plain leather brown hilt and the shiny silver sheath. Her family was not wealthy by any means. This dagger was one of the few nice things her family owned.

And her father treasured it.

No words needed to be spoken between them as she clutched the weapon to her person. In his eyes, she could see regret. He wanted to accompany her, but leaving the farm and the family could be catastrophic, even for a day or two.

The silence of worry prodded her in the back as she approached the shadow horse. Flecks of blood flew from its mouth as it snorted, pelting her cloak. But otherwise, it laid down for her to climb on.

She took hold of the reins, steadying herself as the creature stood. Taking one last look at the house she loved and treasured, with more people she loved and treasured inside, she kicked the horse's flanks and sped away at a gallop.

Birds twittered. Horses snorted. Cows lowed. And an intruding, unwelcome light pierced Killian's eyelids.

He groaned and turned over onto his stomach to hide from the offensive light of day but paused at the feel of the unfamiliar straw bed beneath him. His eyes flashed open as he inhaled a flowery scent that reminded him of Lyyli.

Too quickly, he spun around in the bed, half expecting to find her beside him. Pain rippled through his ribs at the sudden, jerky movement. But rather than the sharp stab of broken bones, his body only felt bruised.

He blinked several times as he took in his unfamiliar surroundings. No one lay in the bed with him, neither did he find anyone in the room. The bed was big enough to fit two people, and both men and women's clothing and belongings lay scattered about the room.

"Where am I?"

The last thing he remembered was the ocean. And Lyyli. And—

Oh!

Memories of meeting Lyyli's family came to mind, followed by the reminder of excruciating pain, and then…nothing. He remembered very little, and by the looks of it, he lay in someone else's bed.

Wearing someone else's shirt.

Shifting on the bed, his feet touched the floor, the stockings he wore the only barrier from the scarred wood. His entire body protested as he stood, tired and achy as it was. He kept one hand on the wall to steady himself as he exited the room and slowly made his way down the hallway. Usually, he would sleep at this hour, but he needed to know where Lyyli was and if she was safe.

He stopped short at the end of the hallway at the sight of a small girl sitting at the kitchen table, her legs swinging as she ate bread and cheese. Astra.

The girl tilted her head to the side, studying him as he did her. A flush no longer marred her tanned face. She breathed steadily, not a single wince of pain following each breath.

"Your ears are funny," she said finally.

Amusement lifted his mouth in a smile as he touched one of his pointed ears. "I am fae."

"I saw a fae woman once with *really* long ears. Very pointy. But my ears are boring. They are just round."

Before he managed another word, Astra prattled onto another topic.

"Mama said you were a fae prince."

"Me?" He laughed out loud but regretted it when his ribs squeezed painfully. At least nothing else hurt except a slight pounding in his head. "I am a Shadow Lord. I don't consider myself a prince, but I am in a position of power."

Curiosity streamed out of her as she tilted her head again. "Mama also said you know a lot of magic. Can you teach me?"

Teaching humans was not impossible, but it came with plenty of risks a child wouldn't understand.

"I'd love to one day. If your parents would let me. Humans don't often trust other humans who practice magic. You might have to learn and practice in secret."

"Hmm." The girl snatched a piece of cheese from the plate and stuffed it into her mouth, revealing the painted plate beneath it. Curious, he opened a cupboard and sure enough, each one of the wooden bowls and plates was painted.

He picked up one of the bowls and marveled at the steady, intricate strokes of each design. At least five different shades stared back at him, but he wasn't sure what colors they were.

"Did Lyyli paint these?" he asked, remembering she said she liked painting bowls.

Astra nodded. "She paints them and sells them on market day. Papa is sad that the bowls she painted for market are almost gone. But that's okay. She can paint some more."

Flipping the bowl over to study a magnificent painted flower in bloom, he decided Lyyli was far too talented to only paint bowls and plates. When they were married—and he would see to it as soon as possible—he planned to give her a room filled with paints and canvases and whatever else her heart desired.

"Where is your sister?"

The girl shrugged. "I don't know. I haven't seen her in two days."

"*Two?*" he choked. How long had he been asleep?

With urgency in his stride, he burst outside and flinched against the bright light piercing his eyes like rods of lightning. He squinted against the brightness, but he was halfway blind during the day. Through the haze of light, he spotted silhouettes from horses, cattle, and a lone dog panting beneath the shade of an apple tree.

His magic cowered beneath the unforgiving warmth, out of reach. Relief escaped him on an exhale. At least his magic was recovering, slowly rebuilding itself within his well.

He paused with one foot in the shadows, the other in sunlight. How had Astra recovered from hearing Lyyli's voice? How had *he* recovered? And why was he only barely asking these questions?

"You are finally up," a sing-song voice said, and he turned to find Mrs. Ives approaching him with a bucket of water in her hands. The dark circles beneath her eyes had disappeared. She seemed lighter as if unburdened by life's trials.

Was he dream walking?

He pinched his own arm, wincing when it hurt. No, this wasn't a dream.

His voice stuttered. "How? What? Where?"

The woman's mouth twisted as she produced a handkerchief, dipped it in the bucket of water, and swiped something from his cheek like a mother might. The cloth came back with some color on it. Blood?

She lowered her voice as she spoke. "Lyyli used her tears to heal you and Astra."

Tears? He nearly choked on the realization. How could the solution have been so simple? How had he not thought of it?

She continued. "If you are wondering where she is…" She grimaced apologetically. "My daughter is not here. She left in a hurry after your recovery."

Not again.

Closing his eyes, he took a deep breath and let it out as he braced himself for what she might say.

"Did Lyyli leave to meet with her aunt?"

"No. She said if you were willing to go to the ends of the earth for her, she would do the same for you. She traveled back to your estate to try to heal your mother."

"What?" His eyes flew open in alarm, both with the realization that her tears were the cure to her own voice and because the roads were dangerous. "Please tell me she didn't go alone."

"She took that carnivorous horse with her. There was no one else who could accompany her."

Killian rubbed his temples as he muttered to himself. "With several powerful people and dangerous beasts out looking for you, what could go wrong? Honestly, Lyyli."

Mrs. Ives grimaced apologetically. "She couldn't wait for you to wake."

Because he'd been unconscious for two days. He couldn't blame her. In fact, he admired her courage and bravery. And he couldn't deny the hope blossoming in his chest, hope he hadn't felt in weeks. Lady Auer's enchantment on his mother and Charlotte was strong. But was it strong enough to withstand a siren's magic?

"What will you do?" Mrs. Ives asked as she worriedly bit her lip. "Will you go after her?"

"Obviously." He sighed wearily. The woman he loved always kept him on his toes, no doubt. "I can't shadewalk the distance until sundown. Is there something I can help with around the farm in the meantime?"

Her face lit up with a smile as she hooked her arm through his. "We would love your help. But first, you need food in your belly. Scared us, you did, with your near-death experience. Come. I'll prepare something for you inside."

****

Lyyli pulled her mount to a stop, both of them worn and exhausted after what was supposed to be just over a one-day journey by horse. The unfamiliar path and surroundings had slowed Lyyli down, and more than once, she'd found herself traveling in the wrong direction. She'd scared off a creature with large eyes, sharp teeth, and a fluffy tail while the horse had snatched several bat-like beasts from the air and gobbled them down in a single bite.

Otherwise, their journey had been more or less uneventful.

She released a weary but relieved sigh at the distant sight of Killian's estate in the darkness. Lanterns from within illuminated the shape of several windows while wispy flowers twirled with the slight breeze.

Everything was quiet.

Lyyli kicked the horse to move closer to the estate, but the creature refused to budge. Its ears flicked backward as a nervous snort escaped its nostrils. It stamped its feet and backed up.

She recognized a spooked horse when she saw one.

Gently, she attempted to bring the creature to a standstill, patting its neck soothingly to keep it from either rearing or bucking her off. But the more she handled the reins, the more she lost control of the animal. It fought against the reins, backing up even more.

She slipped off the horse and scrambled out of the way of its hooves as it reared. A frightened whinny-like growl escaped it before it thundered off into the darkness, away from the estate.

Her eyebrows furrowed in confusion as she wiped the dirt from her palms on her dress. Perhaps it smelled the other shadow horses in the stables? Or maybe Killian housed another type of beast that had frightened it?

The horse didn't return, so Lyyli made her way toward the estate by herself.

Only to pause within the shadows of the trees.

Horror licked its way up her body like flames growing steadily across a stake. Bodies littered the yard—soldiers judging by their weapons and armor. They wore Killian's family crest on their breast pins.

Blood oozed from holes within their armor as if they had fought something with sharp claws—sharp enough to pierce metal.

Her heart pounding in her ears, she hugged the shadows as several people exited the estate. A soldier wearing Auer's crest dragged Johanna out of the building by the hair as she kicked and screamed and struggled. Several other soldiers roughly handled Mia and Laureen, both stumbling down the steps until Mia lost her footing and crashed onto the gravel.

And then Lyyli's heart dropped to her toes as dread rained down on her. Lady Auer followed the others outside, her back straight and her hair in perfect condition. The woman's expression remained blank as she glided down the steps and stopped in front of Johanna, who now knelt as she tried to free her hair from her captor's grip.

Even from her hiding spot in the trees, Lyyli heard every word.

Lady Auer lifted Johanna's chin. "Where is she?"

No...

The blood rushed out of Lyyli's face as she realized who they were looking for. Somehow, they knew where she was staying.

"I don't know!" Johanna sobbed. "We never had a guest here. Killian is gone on business."

"You are lying," came Lady Auer's smooth reply. "I know she's here. Where are you hiding her?"

Johanna shook her head, which resulted in a look of annoyance passing through Lady Auer's thick, unemotional mask.

"I see I need to refresh your memory." Lady Auer produced a long, wickedly sharp dagger and placed it over Mia's heart. Mia whimpered, turning her head away. Johanna screamed unintelligible words as she sobbed and thrashed against her captor. The woman meant to kill Mia, and after her experience as Lord Auer's prisoner, Lyyli knew she would.

Picking up a large rock from the ground, Lyyli rushed out of her hiding place and threw it toward the others so it skittered against the gravel, announcing her presence.

If they wanted her, they could have her. Just as long as no one else had to die.

All heads turned in her direction. Lady Auer's lips turned upward into a smirk. Johanna ceased shrieking long enough for her eyes to widen in horror.

"Run!" Johanna screamed. "Otherwise, they will unleash a horror unlike anything we have seen for a thousand years."

Lyyli didn't run. Instead, she stared Lady Auer down with as much courage as she could muster. She used her hands to sign. "Let them go, and I'll come willingly."

Although Lyyli wasn't sure if the woman understood, Lady Auer's smirk grew wider as she signaled for two guards to seize her dagger and then each of her arms. She didn't resist.

"Where is Lord Graves?" Lady Auer asked, craning her neck as if to look behind Lyyli.

Again, Lyyli signed. "I don't know."

The woman laughed. "You are lying to me. No matter. As long as he's not here, he can't cause any problems. Load her into the carriage. The sooner we get to Bramwick, the better. The Shadow Emperor wants his bride."

All the breath squeezed from Lyyli's lungs, her feet suddenly numb as the soldiers dragged her to a carriage down the road. They shoved her into the darkness, Lady Auer following behind, before the door slammed closed.

Silence.

Only when the carriage lurched forward did Lyyli's thoughts tumble inside her head. She didn't know a lot of history, but she knew enough. The Shadow Emperor was said to have conquered many lands, slaughtering many innocent men, women, and children in his conquest to rule.

However, he was dead. A thousand years dead. Why did it sound like he was actually alive?

Lady Auer forcefully grabbed Lyyli's chin with buttery soft hands, her thin pupils growing larger and gleaming slightly in the darkness like a cat's. "Your voice may be able to hurt my men, but it can't hurt me, nor will it cut through my magic. If you fall out of line, I will send my men back to eradicate what is left of the Graves line. Understand?"

Fear stuck in her throat, Lyyli nodded. She didn't know what was coming for her or what to expect, but the uneasy pit in her stomach grew larger with each passing minute.

She glanced out the window and stilled as if ice closed around her body. In the sky flew a large, familiar beast with black feathers and symbols on its beak. All this time, she had been hunted. And once again, her enemies were successful.

Her only regrets were what she might be forced to do from here and that she hadn't been able to save Killian's mother.

The energy spent shadewalking from the Ives' home to his own taxed his body, draining him as if his magic were porous rather than held within a sturdy container. Recovery from Lyyli's magical effects might take at least a few more days. Perhaps even a week.

His essence slithered through the last stretch of shadows before he stumbled onto the path in front of his house.

He came to a shocking halt as his mind struggled to keep up with his eyes.

A couple dozen bodies lay strewn about the yard, the vacant eyes of guards staring up at the night sky. Each of the men carried the same wounds, blood escaping punctures the size of coins.

Without taking a closer look at the wounds, he knew what had done this—the bird creature that had attacked Lyyli.

The horror of the gory scene displayed before him strangled the breath from his lungs. His soldiers! His servants! His family! What had happened to them? Where were they?

"Killian!" someone screamed, and he turned just in time to be tackled into a fierce embrace by Laureen, who sobbed into his chest. Mia joined her sister seconds later until two blubbering women latched onto him for dear life.

He swallowed the lump of dread in his throat while also inhaling excruciating relief as he returned their embrace, murmuring words of comfort into their hair. At least two of his family members had survived this massacre.

Another trembling breath of relief escaped him when Johanna rounded the corner of the estate. A haunted look lived in her eyes. Blood dripped from her hairline. Her chin wobbled at the sight of him, but otherwise, she remained stoic.

He escorted his other two cousins onto a bench before he spoke to his eldest cousin, the only person not broken down into a blubbering mess. "What happened here? Who did this?"

And why hadn't he been here to stop it?

Guilt ate at him as he moved from one soldier to the next, checking for pulses and any signs of life. Dead. Dead. Dead.

They were all dead. Every last one of them.

Servants were not among the dead, though he feared what he might find should he step foot inside the estate.

His cousin followed him as he finished checking for signs of life. "Lady Auer came while you were away. She demanded we release the siren into her custody. I didn't immediately realize she meant Lyyli."

A dizzying fog momentarily clouded his mind as he fought to keep his balance. He reached out to the outer wall of the manor to steady himself. If anything happened to Lyyli, his soul would be crushed and then quickly wither and die.

His words struggled to escape his mouth. "But she's all right. She hasn't arrived here yet."

However, the regretful look in her eyes contradicted his hopeful words. His knees buckled, and to keep himself from collapsing, he leaned his entire weight against the wall. While his head spun, she explained.

"I activated the enchantment barrier around the house just as you had instructed me to do in the case of a hostile attack. Lady Auer's magic burned right through it. I've never seen anything like it. And then her beast attacked the soldiers. When they were all dead, they broke into the house. We tried fighting them off. It did no good. They demanded to know where Lyyli was. Somehow, they knew we were keeping her here."

"And the servants?" he managed to get out through the grief beginning to sprout in his heart. "What of Charlotte? My mother?"

"They are alive. But Lady Auer almost killed Mia to make us talk." His cousin shivered, running her hands up and down her arms. "Lyyli saved Mia by offering to go with them willingly. She came out of the trees, out of nowhere. She shouldn't have been here. Listen, Killian! They are going to use her to do something terrible."

A chill pierced his bones. "What?"

Instead of answering immediately, she led him into the house, followed by his other two sobbing cousins. She disappeared into her room, only to return with a book opened near the middle. When she turned it to face him, every last breath squeezed from his lungs, replaced by horror.

Staring back at him from the page was an altar. On the altar lay a mermaid, but it wasn't just any mermaid. It was a siren, and she was singing as she lay dying. On the next page, standing beside the altar, was a figure of legend. Not quite man, not quite beast.

But he recognized it from his dream. No, not his own. Lord Auer's dream.

Johanna's voice escaped as barely a whisper. "Lyyli will resurrect the Shadow Emperor."

A flash of anger heated Killian's entire body, mingling with dread. "No!" In his rage, he kicked over a washing bucket, sending it flying across the room and splashing water over the floor. "I've seen how this ends." He gripped Johanna's shoulders. "I've seen how this ends! Everyone dies. My family. Servants. All the Shadow Lords. Everyone."

He recalled the gruesome dream, realizing it hadn't been a dream at all but a premonition. Bodies strewn about. Eyes staring vacantly at the sky. Crumbled buildings. Smoke. Death. Decay.

Tears slipped down Johanna's cheeks as she closed her eyes and nodded. "I told her to run. She saved Mia's life by going with them instead. But I fear she has only delayed the inevitable."

Killian released his cousin's shoulders. Lyyli couldn't have known why Lady Auer wanted her because he only now understood himself. The blood Lord Auer had forced her to spill? The people sacrificed? They were to resurrect the Shadow Emperor's demon companions. First, the galiphor. Then the bird-like creature.

And now Lady Auer planned to resurrect one of the most powerful and dangerous beings to have ever walked the land.

"What will we do?" Johanna asked quietly.

Even in the face of danger, she possessed a skill many did not—a calm inner strength no matter how difficult their circumstances.

Taking a deep breath, he attempted to reflect her calm as he cleared his thoughts to make room for a plan. "This involves all of the Shadow Lords. I think we must contact each of them and ask for aid."

"Are you suggesting…" Her words trailed off as she stared at him. "You will need all ten Lords to summon that kind of power, Killian. Lord and Lady Auer are out of the question."

"Yes, but their heir and my friend, Lorenz, can take Auer's title and power."

Johanna shook her head. "He must receive the power willingly or if his father dies. Do you really think he would work against his father? Against his mother? He won't do it."

"He will. He has to."

Her voice dropped to a hoarse whisper. "I hope you are right."

Without further argument, he reactivated the protective barrier around the house before climbing the stairs two at a time. He first peeked his head inside Charlotte's room to find her breathing in her unconscious state. Next, he burst into his mother's room. She also breathed, but she almost seemed weaker than she had only the night before.

"Mother, are you all right?"

A collage of mixed emotions lifted from her. They did nothing to reassure him, but at least she was alive. "I am glad to find you still here after what has happened." He turned to leave, but his voice quavered as he glanced over his shoulder. "And by the way, the proposal went terribly. You'd better stay alive long enough to hear the tale."

The door clicked closed behind him before he rushed up to his tower. Johanna followed at his heels, leaving her sobbing sisters behind downstairs. His weary body protested against climbing so many blasted stairs, but he forced himself to keep going until he entered the tower through the door.

A white sheet covered an object in the corner. He pulled it off to reveal an oval-shaped mirror within an intricate frame. The design swirled like bouncing shadows, pulsing with power.

"How long ago did Lady Auer leave the estate?" he asked Johanna without turning around as he dug through a chest of vials. He swore under his breath when he couldn't see any of the colors. Which one was filled with clear liquid?

"Perhaps an hour ago."

"Good. We should have enough time."

One by one, he placed each vial on the desk, each a varying shade that, to him, ranged from lighter gray to darker gray. "I can't see color for the life of me," he said as he briefly flashed the swirled design of the curse on his arm as a reminder. "Will you place the clear vials right here?" He pointed to a spot on the desk before turning back to the mirror.

Vials clacked behind him as if his cousin sifted through them. "All this time… Why didn't you tell me? You know you can trust me."

"Of course, I can trust you. But just look outside!" He grunted as he lifted the mirror and placed it in the middle of the room. "Knowledge is power. But it is also dangerous to know too much." After a pause as he tipped the mirror backward at a slight slant, he explained further. "I went to see the witch on the mountain. This is the bargain we struck. She took the color from my world and gave me the ability to see everyone's emotions."

The clacking stopped, and he turned to find her eyes wide as she stared at him in horror. "You can see my emotions."

"Unfortunately, yes. I can't turn it off."

She squeezed her eyes shut, took a deep breath, and then opened them again. "Listen. I am happy for you and Lyyli. I truly am."

"I know."

Another pause before she handed him a clear vial. He swirled the contents for a minute to make sure everything mixed together correctly.

Johanna bit her lip as hesitation crossed her features. "Would you have ever chosen me? Without Lyyli in the picture. And given enough time."

The conversation had taken a sudden uncomfortable turn, but he owed her this answer. Her advances had always been subtle, but he'd caught on. At least by the end, with the help of witnessing her emotions.

He met her gaze in the mirror. "You were the logical choice. Yes, I would have chosen you. Life would have been comfortable and easy. Familiar. But I love Lyyli. And you deserve more happiness than I can bring you."

"We could have been happy."

"True, but after realizing just how happy I *can* be, I want the same for you."

She nodded, saying nothing as he readied the vials and the spell. After a minute, she said, "After this is over, I want to marry well. Perhaps you might formally introduce me to Lord Galish's son, Paul."

His lips pressed together with uncertainty. It was hopeful wishing. If they didn't stop Lyyli, he might never get the chance to try. "I will."

Just as he unstopped the vial, his cousin's voice made him pause. "What about Lyyli? She will be killed if anyone finds out what she truly is."

"I know." His hand trembled as he dumped the contents of the vial over the mirror. "*Accersi Lorenz Auer.*" Then he glanced over his shoulder at Johanna as the mirror rippled. "I will do everything in my power to prevent the information from spreading. Otherwise, she will not be safe as my wife if she isn't killed before then."

He forced his expression into a mask to hide his discomforting emotions. The image in the mirror rippled more and more, the light gray turning to a darker gray. A blur solidified into a shape, which became a person.

The man staring back in the mirror held his hands clasped behind him, his hair slicked and his back straight.

A servant. Not Lorenz.

"Lord Graves," the man greeted as he bowed.

"Good evening. I need to speak with Lorenz."

"He is not available at the moment."

"It was not a request."

The servant paused as if contemplating his words. But finally, he dipped his head in a brief nod and disappeared from view of the mirror. Killian fought the itch to squirm where he stood as several minutes passed, knowing every minute wasted was another minute disaster could seal their fate.

"Come on," he said quietly after another few minutes passed. Not only did he fight against squirming, but he also fought against the foolish desire to shadewalk into Lady Auer's moving carriage, grab Lyyli, and shadewalk out. He had no doubt the woman expected such a thing. She likely had a trap laid out for him, one that could seriously maim or kill him.

Finally, Lorenz stepped in front of the mirror. Dark circles lay beneath his eyes, his expression solemn instead of his usual mirth. He wore all black from his neckcloth to his gloves to his shoes. At least Killian suspected it was black. The shade was very dark.

The realization struck a twisted kind of relief through him. But also a sadness for his friend. "Your father."

Lorenz nodded wearily. "He passed last night. His heart has been bad for some time now. But it still seemed so unexpectedly fast."

Killian frowned with sympathy. He remembered what it had been like after his own father had passed. Agonizing.

Confusing. Plenty of mourning as he stumbled into the new role of Shadow Lord.

"I am sorry to hear it," he said at last. "I hope I might somehow help with the uneasy transition."

Again, his friend nodded. Although his expression remained blank, relief and gratitude made an appearance above his head.

"Why have you called on me?" Lorenz asked. "If not to express your condolences."

"I know this is poor timing."

"You attempted to save my father from that creature. In the end, it didn't matter, but I appreciate your efforts. Anything you need is yours if I can give it."

Now came the tricky part. He was not the most tactful person. He could either make an enemy or solidify their friendship. He glanced toward Johanna, who nodded her reassurance.

"Do you know where your mother is?"

Lorenz shrugged, but he didn't miss the red anger and green-yellow annoyance streaking out of him. "She claimed she needed time to grieve on her own. I don't know where she is. I only hope she will return in time for the funeral."

Killian clenched his fists, anger driving him as he scooted the mirror toward the window and tipped it to give his friend a clear view of the dead bodies strewn about the yard. When he tipped the mirror back, horror filled the man's eyes.

"What happened?" Lorenz gasped.

Killian glared, not at his friend, but because he was angry. "Your mother happened. She slaughtered my soldiers and nearly killed my cousins. I ask you—no, I *beg* you—to help me. Your parents are involved in some very dark, very sinister magic." His glare melted, his hands falling limp at his sides. "Please help me. I know they are your parents, and what I'm asking you to do is not fair. Just…please."

For several long moments, Lorenz paced back and forth across his view of the mirror, running a gloved hand over his stubbled chin. Finally, he stopped and said, "Tell me everything."

So he did, with the exception of Lyyli being a siren and the power she held within her. He would take her secret to his grave, and he knew his cousins would as well. He only hoped that whatever was to happen, he could still maintain her secret.

After his explanation of recent events and the task required of him, a thunderous anger also filled Lorenz's expression. "What is my mother thinking?" He paced again and then stopped. "I will help. On the condition that my mother will live. I want to hear what she has to say."

"Deal. Thank you, my friend."

After Lorenz agreed to contact four Lords and Killian the other four, they ended the communication. He reached for another clear vial and began to swirl its contents.

"What can I do?" His cousin's stoic voice wobbled momentarily.

He paused as he bit his lip in contemplation. He didn't dare leave his family here without him. He didn't dare take them with him. "Pack up your bags and flee with your sisters when the sun rises. No one will find you at the hidden cottage."

"What about Charlotte and my aunt?"

Clenching his jaw, he turned back to the mirror. "Leave them. There is nothing we can do to save them. I'll leave a few servants here to care for them. If Lady Auer returns and she finds you here, I have a feeling you won't be so lucky. Take care of your sisters."

"Where will you go?"

"Into the heart of the battle."

His jaw ached with trepidation as he poured another vial over the mirror. He'd seen how this ended. But Lord Auer had been in that premonition dream. The man's death meant the future could be changed. He only hoped this was the way to do it.

The carriage bounced and swayed before it rolled to a stop in front of the foreboding fortress—the nightmare Lyyli had been all too eager to escape. Invisible shackles seemed to clamp around her wrists as if the terrifying structure slowly pulled her into its dark depths. Perhaps not the structure itself, but whatever lay deep within.

Watching.

Waiting.

The footman opened the carriage door and helped Lady Auer down first and Lyyli next. The other woman slipped her gloves off, revealing the large red stones set in the rings on four of her fingers. The color pulsed with light as if they were alive.

"I expected Lord Graves to chase after you," Lady Auer said with her hands on her hips, surveying the area around them. "I wish he had. The enchantment on the carriage would have killed him."

Her words punched the air out of Lyyli's lungs. She held a hand to her racing heart, reciting a silent prayer of thanks.

When Lady Auer led her toward the thick wall of gray stone, she realized they were entering through a back entrance rather than the front. Trepidation created an ominous chill within her bones. Lord Auer had terrified her. But something about his wife struck a chord of foreboding louder than deafening thunder.

She took one step up the rough gray stairs and froze. If she entered within the walls of the fortress, she might never again see the light of day.

"Come along," Lady Auer said over her shoulder. "Don't make me remind you what will happen without your cooperation."

Breathing out her fear, she continued to climb the short set of stairs. The moment they entered the fortress, someone stepped in their way. Brunette hair. Serious, chestnut eyes. Tall, but not as tall as Killian.

Lorenz.

The man's eyes hardened as his gaze passed over Lyyli and then next, his mother. "Mother. I wasn't sure if you were going to show up for Father's funeral."

Funeral?

A strange mix of sorrow and relief stirred within her, taking her by surprise. How was it possible to feel both at the same time over a man who had forced her to do awful things against her will?

Sadness filled Lady Auer's expression, but Lyyli wondered if the emotion was genuine. "You know I would never miss it.

My husband is gone. It hasn't quite sunk in yet." She dabbed her dry eyes with a handkerchief before motioning Lyyli forward again.

Lorenz's hand clamped tightly around her arm, startling her. "I see our guest has returned. I will personally escort her to her chambers. To give you time to rest after the journey," he added for his mother.

Lyyli cautiously stared at the hand gripping her arm. This man was Killian's friend. But he was also Lord Auer's son. At least Lady Auer was a familiar evil. She didn't want to find herself alone with a man she knew nothing about.

When she pulled her arm free of him, his eyebrows furrowed in response. Displeasure and a flicker of worry moved across his mouth but disappeared quickly.

"I cannot impose on you like that," Lady Auer continued. "Continue with your new duties. I will see our Lyyli safely settled."

Our Lyyli?

The woman grabbed her wrist and pulled her forward. She dug her feet into the ground instinctually. But after a warning glare, she succumbed to the fate awaiting her within the dark hallways. She glanced over her shoulder to find Lorenz watching her with furrowed brows.

As they turned the corner, he vanished.

A numbness crawled up Lyyli's body, first claiming her legs, and then her limp arms, and finally entering her heart. The numbing ice finished its job within her mind, effectively silencing her thoughts as they continued through the maze of dark hallways with the occasional flicker of a torch to keep her from tripping over her own feet in her blindness.

When they reached a staircase, and she began trudging upward, thick apprehension broke through her numbness like mud trapping her in its sludgy substance.

Thoughts of Killian infiltrated her hopeless reserves. All his sweet smiles, kind touches, and heart-stopping kisses. She cherished them all and would hold them close to her heart for the rest of her life.

You know we can work something out.

He'd wanted a future with her and was willing to sacrifice to get it.

I would go to the ends of the earth for you to speak freely and live happily.

No one had ever helped her as much as he had. He could have turned her away. He was a busy man with his own problems, yet he had set aside his own worries to focus on her.

I love you, Lyyli.

She closed her eyes and pressed her hands to her heart. *I love you, too, Killian. So very much.*

Lady Auer led her down a silent hallway, two torches flickering on either side of an ornate door etched in green and silver with the Auer family crest burned into the wood. Two heavily armed guards stood in front of the door, bowing and stepping aside as they approached. In unison, the guards opened each door to allow them inside.

In any other situation, Lyyli would have gawked at the high, painted ceilings, the rich threaded tapestries hanging from the walls, and the beautiful carved furniture. In any other situation, she would have marveled at the enormous red rug spread out in the center of the room and admired the beads of glass hanging in circles from the chandelier overhead.

But instead, the red rug reminded her of spilled blood. The tapestries fluttered against the wall like dead bodies hanging from a noose. The chandelier lay in wait to trap an unwilling victim in a cage of glass.

The moment the doors closed behind them, leaving them alone in the too-large space, did she speak out loud. "Why are you doing this?"

The woman crossed the room and tugged at the steel bars covering each window before turning around, a look of satisfaction in her expression. She closed the space between them and rested the back of her fingers against Lyyli's cheek. The touch was cold. Hungry. Possessive.

"I have been planning for this day for many years," Lady Auer said, her fingers moving to her hair where she resumed touching her possessively. "The Shadow Emperor will rise again. I will sacrifice you and your blood to resurrect him, and when your soul has withered within your body, mine will take its place. *I* will be his new bride, taking your siren magic in the process. And *you* will cease to exist."

Lyyli took a horrified step backward. What the woman spoke of was sacrifice and possession. No wonder she did not seem remorseful over her husband's death. Perhaps she'd even arranged it.

"What about your family?" she whispered.

"They will be spared. All of the Shadow Lords will have to be killed, but my Lorenz will keep on living." Lady Auer flexed her fingers, flashing the red of each ring she wore. "For years, I have quietly collected souls in these stones. Mostly people who will not be missed. Thousands of souls live within them, along with their accompanying magic. I am more powerful than you realize. You will sing the Shadow Emperor back to life, and I will restore him to his former self."

A shiver raced down her spine when Lady Auer ran her hands down her arms. She jerked away from the woman. "You admitted you will kill Killian. You have no leverage over me."

"Then make me a deal." Lady Auer grinned wickedly like a woman who was about to get everything she'd ever wanted. "What I want is your full cooperation. Until the very end."

A heaviness weighed on her shoulders as she crossed the room and stared out the barred window into the darkness. Somewhere out there was the man she loved, likely still recovering with her family. What would he say? What would he have her do?

"What will the Shadow Emperor do once resurrected?" She continued to speak quietly to avoid risking the guards outside hearing her voice.

"It is not your concern." The wicked smile on her lips and the gleam in her eyes revealed something awful. Evil. Unfathomable.

People would die. A lot of them.

Could she sacrifice the lives of dozens, perhaps even thousands of people, to save one life?

Her gaze traveled down to the ground. A fall from such a height would kill her. What Lady Auer seemed to need was a siren. But what if there was no siren to use?

"You will be watched closely," the woman said as if knowing the direction of her thoughts. "The windows are reinforced. Everything in the room is bolted into place. You will have guards tailing your every move. Your every decision." She trapped Lyyli's chin in her fingers. "I can make this much harder on you than you could ever realize. I will have your full cooperation. End of discussion."

"No."

The word shocked her, and she knew she should grovel on her knees and take it back, but she stood firm. Killian would not want this. Johanna hadn't wanted this. Should Lyyli die from singing the Emperor to life, she had no guarantee they would be spared. It was a fool's agreement.

"No?" Lady Auer's eyebrow arched high as anger flashed across her eyes. "I see you will need a little more...*persuasion*. I will make another visit to the Graves residence to solidify your cooperation. When I return, I fully expect you to comply."

Lady Auer swept out of the room, leaving a sticky horror in her wake. The moment the doors slammed closed, the terror of the situation gripped her insides and squeezed with a death grip.

"Stop!" she screamed as she ran across the room and pounded on the door, yanking at the handles with all her might. The doors didn't budge. "Please, stop!"

On the other side of the door, metal sang like swords unsheathed from scabbards. Two grunts followed by thumps against the ground, one after the other. Lyyli's eyes grew wide in horror as blood seeped from beneath the door and soaked the fabric of her slippers.

Lady Auer's voice was muffled from the door separating them as she spoke. "How much blood will coat your hands after this is finished?"

Without another word, her footsteps echoed down the hallway and disappeared.

Silent sobs shook Lyyli's shoulders as the strength fled her wobbly knees. Her legs collapsed beneath her, and she hit the ground with a sickening splash as she landed in the pool of blood growing larger with each second.

She should have gone with her aunt when she'd had the chance. Now it was too late.

Much too late.

By the time Lady Auer returned, she feared how much more blood might coat her hands by the night's end.

illian casually rested his elbows on the table with his fingers laced together, his chin resting on top. A strange calm wrapped him in a cool embrace despite knowing what was about to happen to him. Lorenz's words from an hour ago floated through his mind.

My mother is coming for you.

Good. Let her come. It meant Lyyli refused to comply. But the next hour would test Lyyli's strength of refusal. If the situation was reversed, he would have no strength at all.

A frosty chill entered the silent, empty dining room. Shadows slithered across the ground like angry vipers. The candles sputtered out around him as if suddenly too damp to sustain their light. The extinguished fire created tendrils of smoke wafting upward toward the ceiling like a bad omen.

Darkness bathed the room.

Yet, he remained calm.

Lady Auer stepped into the room, flanked by two guards. He had lowered the magical ward around the house to let her in, though he'd strengthened the wards around Charlotte's and his mother's rooms.

Although no emotions escaped the woman, the guards were terrified on either side of her. Terrified. Hopeless. Sorrowful.

"Lady Auer," Killian said, staring a hole through her. "To what may I owe this visit?"

For a single moment, her confidence dropped, and she hesitated. "You knew I was coming."

"Will you stomp on my intelligence so easily? You are not always the smartest person in the room."

She regarded him carefully as he did her. This woman was as patient as she was formidable. She'd waited years to see her plan to resurrect the Shadow Emperor to fruition. She held most of the cards, but she had also laid most of them down face-up as well.

The woman glanced around the dark room, seeming to notice the empty silence. "Where are your cousins?"

"Gone." His attention dropped to the rings on her fingers, and his gut churned with acid. How long had she been collecting souls? It was possible she may have an endless supply of magic sitting on her fingers. No wonder she was much more powerful than any Shadow Fae ought to be.

"How fortunate for them." Her expression took on a mask of indifference. With the slightest nod of her head, she beckoned one of her guards forward.

Killian attempted to shadewalk, but his power sputtered out like the candle on the table as if Lady Auer's presence dampened his magic. The guard grabbed the back of his hair and smashed his face into the table.

Once.

Twice.

Blood gushed from his nose. His right temple throbbed. His cheek burned at the bruise forming around the open wound.

The man heaved Killian to his feet and pushed him toward the second guard, who smashed his fist into his face. His body crumpled against the overwhelming dizziness clutching his head. An incessant ringing filled his ears.

When the first guard hooked his arms beneath his, he didn't fight it. The second guard smashed his fist into his gut several times until he choked on his own blood.

"You are not fighting back," Lady Auer commented.

Killian spat out a mouthful of blood, straining to look at the woman through swelling eyes. "A smart man knows when he is already beat."

"Fair enough." She held up a hand, and together, the men heaved Killian to his feet and dragged him into the shadowy black abyss of a dark portal.

The sensation was nothing like shadewalking. He felt as if he were tumbling headfirst into a deep cave with no bottom in sight. His stomach lurched. A feeling of weightlessness. Of falling. And then he stumbled when his feet touched the ground, landing hard on his knees.

One of the guards wrenched his head back by the hair, forcing him to look at someone with lovely eyes and shock written on every inch of her face.

"Lyyli," he gasped, and then he disappeared again. When he reappeared this time, he landed on chilly stone. The fabric ripped at his knees, scraping his skin hard enough to bleed. His shoulder thumped against metal bars, adding to the aches and pains growing within his body.

He blinked several times as he attempted to survey his surroundings through his bruised and battered face. He knelt in a small cell, a row of bars separating him and Lady Auer. The two guards flanked her, both feeling guilt and sorrow.

Despite his hopeless position, he couldn't help the surge of satisfaction from shooting through him. The fool of a woman. He was in the heart of her home. He likely wouldn't have been able to enter the fortress otherwise.

Now, he only needed to stay conscious. Otherwise, his plan wouldn't work.

"What have you done with Lyyli?" he growled, though he only managed to spatter blood across the metal bars with each word.

"Nothing yet."

Killian took the momentary silence to wipe the blood from his mouth and face with the hem of his shirt while surveying his surroundings. He found himself in a dungeon of sorts, but one void of other occupants. Cell after cell lay empty in the endless gray darkness. Only a small, lone window blocked by metal bars near the ceiling gave any indication of the time. Still night. Perhaps early morning.

He'd never seen this part of the fortress. A part of him wondered if Lorenz was oblivious to it as well.

He turned his attention back to Lady Auer, who continued to watch him cautiously. "What are you going to do to me?"

"That all depends on Miss Ives."

She said nothing more but rather continued to stand still as if waiting for something.

Or someone.

Several minutes later, a door creaked open on the far side of the dungeon. A third guard entered, forcefully dragging Lyyli into the room. The moment their gazes locked, shock, fury, and devastation whirled out of her. The guard released her elbow, and she flew across the dungeon and into his arms.

Although bars separated them, he was relieved to hold her again. If only for a short time.

"Enough!" Lady Auer snapped. "Step away from the cell."

Killian glared at the woman. "You will have your turn with the Shadow Emperor. Just allow me this last goodbye."

Her eyes narrowed. "Make it quick." Although she moved several feet away as if to give them privacy, her hawk eyes never strayed from them.

He threaded his fingers through Lyyli's hair and kissed her cheek, then her jaw, before whispering in her ear. "Something horrific is about to happen to you. I can only do so much, but I will try." His lips feathered across her lips and grazed her second cheek before he whispered in her other ear. "Get me as close as you can."

Her eyes shimmered. She clearly wanted to speak but was unable to do so. He read her emotions instead. She was afraid. For him. He pulled her closer to wrap his arms around her through the bars.

"We can only hope I am immune to your power now. If not, life, as we know it, will never be the same."

A questioning look loomed in her eyes. He could not tell her. Not without risking Lady Auer hearing him. The Shadow Emperor was already halfway summoned. Perhaps more. The only way to defeat him was to contain him in a tangible form.

Through the bars, he kissed her lips several times. She didn't seem to care about his bruised and bloodied face. He was also surprised she let him do it after what had transpired between them earlier after she'd nearly killed him.

"Trust me." His last words feathered across her lips, barely audible.

"I believe I've given plenty of time to say your goodbyes." Lady Auer stepped closer, eyeing Lyyli. "I want your full cooperation. Otherwise, we will give Lord Graves a further taste of torture."

A shiver ran through Killian at the cruel suggestion. Torture? Especially done to a Shadow Lord? The woman truly did not care about the consequences of her actions. Because she knew she could get away with it.

Lyyli grabbed onto his wrists, her eyes closed and her head bowed as if fighting tears. Finally, she turned to Lady Auer and signed. "I want him there with me." Or at least, he translated it as such. He was still missing half the words.

"No, Lyyli," he said before Lady Auer got in a word. "I don't want to be in there. I don't want to watch you die."

She ignored him and signed again. "I need him."

He clenched his jaw for appearances. "Let me have this last memory of you. Please. I don't want to come."

The woman shrugged, still eyeing him cautiously. "He can do no harm with his magic suppressed. But if he comes, what the Shadow Emperor does to him is out of my hands. If you don't kill him first yourself."

Lyyli hesitated as she glanced at him. But then she nodded.

He tried hard to hide his relief.

His relief was short-lived as two guards opened the cell, dragged him out, and clamped a cold, metal choker around his neck. It buzzed against his skin, rattling his entire frame as the shock ran through him. One of the men slammed his knee into his gut. He grunted and doubled over, barely seeing Lyyli's frantic form rush toward him through his swollen, bleary eyes.

The guard accompanying her held her back.

Lady Auer ran a finger along the choker around his neck, smug satisfaction in her eyes. "I know you know what this is. It will tighten around your neck every time you use magic until it strangles the breath from you completely. Only my blood can take it off."

Lyyli signed, "I'm sorry. I'm sorry. I'm sorry."

He attempted a smile, but it likely looked more like a grimace fighting through the bruises on his face. "I'm all right. You'll be all right."

"There is no sense in lying to her," Lady Auer said, taking the lead out the dungeon door, across a dank, stifling hallway, and down a flight of stairs. "She is doing this for you. She knows what will happen to her." She nodded to one of the guards. "Take her back to the room. If she steps out of line once, let me know. Lord Graves will pay the price."

Killian reached out for Lyyli's hand as they were dragged in opposite directions. Only the tips of their fingers touched before she disappeared from view completely.

All at once, his aches and pains crashed onto him at full force. Everything ached from his face to his neck to his stomach to his knees. He was vaguely aware of being dragged into a pitch-black room several degrees cooler than the dungeon. One of the guards patted him down rather invasively before pulling out each of the vials from his breast pocket. One by one, they shattered across the ground in a heap of glass and liquid, sending a pungent aroma throughout the room.

Next, cold irons clamped around his wrists and ankles, chaining him to the wall.

Once his eyes quickly adjusted to the darkness, he noticed the altar in the middle of the stone room. It was covered in blood.

His stomach dipped to his toes. Lyyli's blood would join the fray. He wished to stop this. He wished to whisk her far away from Katalle, where no one could find her. But he couldn't.

And the knowledge nearly killed him.

"Keep a close eye on him," Lady Auer ordered her guards while still watching him suspiciously. "And I mean close."

The woman's skirts swished around her legs as she turned on her heel and exited the horrifying room. He slumped against his chains, watching as his broken potions oozed across the ground in a mass of black and gray.

Hold on, Lyyli, he thought to himself. *This will work. It has to.*

****

Lyyli stood with stillness rivaling a fence post as she stared sullenly into the mirror. Servants rushed about the room, one washing her hands, feet, and face. A woman washed Killian's blood from her cheeks, and with each wipe, effectively scrubbed the man himself from her body completely. But they could never scrub him from her heart. There, he remained safe.

Lady Auer oversaw the servants as they dressed her in regal red garb with a long train splayed out behind her. Golden designs were embroidered into the dress from her hips to the hem. Long, tight sleeves hugged her arms while the bodice dipped low enough to reveal cleavage pushed up in the most uncomfortable fashion.

She'd never worn anything so…suggestive. Thoughts of what Lady Auer planned to do with her own body sickened her. Would Lyyli's soul die and allow the woman to inhabit her body? Or would she still be present and conscious of everything around her without being able to control her own limbs?

She shuddered.

What was Killian thinking? With his magic bound, he could do nothing to help her. She preferred he stay away rather than witness this, immune to her power or not.

After pinning up Lyyli's hair, a servant placed a long, red headdress on top of her head. The fabric draped down to her waist in a similar fashion to the train, also embroidered and beaded with gold.

For the final touches, they darkened her lips with red lipstick and shadowed her eyelids with a dark gray substance. One of them brushed rouge across her cheeks.

To some, she might have been considered beautiful. But she thought herself hideous. The woman staring back at her in the mirror was not her. It was somebody else.

Lady Auer stepped closer, standing in front of her as she ran her hands down Lyyli's arms, her waist, and then she cupped her face, turning her head every which way.

The woman smiled with satisfaction before stepping back. She lifted her hand, and the red stones of her rings began to glow. A shadow formed several feet in front of her, slowly becoming less translucent by the second. Black eyes flashed red, and a deep voice escaped the shadow's mouth. "I am pleased, my bride."

Lyyli's heart shot into her throat, and she took a fearful step backward. The shadow became a solid beast at least two feet taller than her, with ashy gray skin mixed with red like flowing lava, a thin black tail whipping behind him, and horns curving from his head like an animal's. When he smiled, his teeth gleamed an onyx black, each at a sharp point.

Fear quivered in her bones as she stared back at the creature looming over her. She was torn between passing out at the fearsome power leaking from his every pore and running away.

But she remained still. For Killian.

The Shadow Emperor's long, sharp fingernails captured her chin, his palm nearly as large as her face. He crushed his mouth against hers, and she grunted in shock.

All around her, chairs toppled, glass shattered, and several cries of pain echoed in the room. She attempted to break free from the creature's grip, but he held on tighter, nearly crushing her face as his kiss became more brutal, more demanding. He bit her lip, tasting her blood.

The room silenced into nothing.

Tears fell from her eyes.

"I have been waiting for you," he said in a gravelly tone when he broke away, his red eyes searing into her. With his relaxed grip, she caught a glimpse of blood spilled across the floor before he forced her to look at him again. The very act of his fingers traveling through her hair and holding onto her waist left her almost feeling more defiled than his kiss.

But she behaved. For Killian. She would do anything to keep him safe. Even endure this.

Heartache weighed on her soul as she once again caught a glimpse of blood. How much blood stained her hands now? How many lives had she accidentally taken because of what she was?

The Shadow Emperor snapped back into Lady Auer's rings. The woman dropped her hand to her side, an air of haughty indifference in her expression.

"Come," Lady Auer beckoned. "The Shadow Emperor refuses to wait any longer."

Killian's wrists throbbed painfully with each pulse of his heart. The manacles clamped around his wrists dug into his skin, drawing blood whenever he shifted. He tried not to move at all, but his discomfort increased as he waited a half hour, and then another half hour for Lyyli to reappear while the two guards watched him closely.

Too closely.

One of the guards hovered over him, standing only a foot away. The other took up his position near the altar. Neither of them glanced away for a moment. Although they appeared menacing, their guilt never lessened. They didn't want to do this. They didn't want to be here.

Perhaps they had little choice.

Footsteps echoed down the hallway, growing louder with each passing second. The wooden door creaked open, and Lady Auer whisked inside and began to set up a circle of crystals around the altar. Lyyli followed at a slower pace. His heart skipped a beat in surprise as he watched her tall, elegant form step into the room, a long, exquisite train following in her wake. A matching headdress covered most of her hair, her eyes shadowed with dark kohl. It was as if he'd stepped into an alternate time, gazing at an empress rather than the woman he loved.

Lyyli met his gaze and then quickly glanced away. Her cheeks darkened, and shame billowed out of her.

Hurt.

Shame.

Guilt.

What had happened in the hour of her absence?

"Lyyli, look at me." His gentle voice seemed to coax her to lift her head. When she met his gaze, her shame fanned brighter. She lowered her gaze again, and only then did he notice the faint trail of black running down each cheek. As if she had cried. He didn't know what had transpired, but he wanted to ease her conscience. "It's not your fault. It's all right."

"It's not!" she nearly screamed at him with her hands. He caught the words "killed," "five," and "people." And then she signed "kiss" and pointed to the cut on her lip. Blood slowly dripped from the wound as if someone had bitten her.

Who would have done that? He wanted to break their nose on his fist.

"I'm sorry," her shaking hands said. "I'm sorry. I'm sorry."

And then she began to silently weep.

He slumped in his chains, unable to do anything more. He wanted so desperately to fold her in his arms and soothe her pain away. What a burden her siren gift must be on her shoulders.

Again, he reiterated, "It's not your fault." He waited until she looked at him again. "I love you. So much."

She held her hands to her heart, the faintest smile of grief and happiness lifting on the corner of her lips.

"Quiet," Lady Auer snapped as she finished arranging the crystals around the altar. One by one, she lit each candle next to the crystals. "We're nearly ready to begin."

The woman gripped Lyyli's elbow and steered her toward the altar, inside the sphere of crystals. Magic rippled through the sphere, ripe for creation.

Blindingly fast, Lady Auer whipped out a dagger, grabbed Lyyli's hand, and sliced her across the palm. Lyyli winced in pain, but she uttered no sound.

"Place your hand on the altar," Lady Auer instructed, "and sing."

Lyyli's chest heaved up and down with each fearful, labored breath. She shook her head, more black trailing down her face with her tears. With a startling realization, he realized *who* might have kissed her so violently. But he didn't understand *how*.

After a nod from Lady Auer, one of the guards punched Killian in the gut. "Oof!" He winced when pain rushed through him with the next breath.

Again, Lady Auer nodded to the altar. "Place your hand on top."

Lyyli glanced back and forth between him and the altar, her eyes wide. In her hesitation, Lady Auer nodded again. This time, the guard struck him across the jaw. His head spun. His face ached. A cut bled on the inside of his lip. Through his hazy vision, he noticed Lyyli shaking and crying silently into her hands.

Stay conscious, he warned himself when his head spun sickeningly, and the black dots in his vision threatened to drag him under.

"As much as I'm enjoying these beatings..." He spat out a mouthful of blood, wincing when the action agitated the cuts in his mouth. "I ask that you dismiss your guards. Enough people have died. You don't need to lose three loyal men as well."

If Lyyli accidentally killed anyone else tonight, it would gut her. He couldn't allow it to happen.

Lady Auer paused as if considering his request. Finally, she nodded, and the guards scrambled out of the room as if relieved to flee the scene. "The next beating will be from my knife. Get her to cooperate, and you won't see the blade up close."

Across the room, Killian met Lyyli's terrified, grieving eyes. He must have looked awful because her sorrow nearly drowned her in its blue hue as her gaze passed over his face. "Do it, Lyyli. All will be well."

When Lady Auer turned her head toward Lyyli, Killian spoke again, this time silently. Despite his bound hands, he attempted to sign. "Trust me."

Black streaks of kohl continued to drip down her face, but this time instead of hesitating, she nodded. Her fingers trembled as she lowered her bleeding hand to the altar.

A dark power pulsed through the room like an explosion of shadow, slamming him back against the wall. His head hit stone, followed by a fiery burst of pain. The black shadows in his vision swarmed like angry bees. Buzzing. Stinging. Blocking out any source of light.

Stay conscious!

He gritted his teeth and fought against the powerful pull of darkness. His eyes watered as he squinted through the shadows. His entire jaw ached from the effort to grind his teeth together.

Within the darkness, a single sound floated on the shadows' thunderous wing. A sweet, melodic voice. A song. It started out small and hesitant and quickly stretched over him like a blanket of beautiful desire. He wanted nothing more than to bask in the lovely melody.

Focus!

He bit his tongue hard enough to make himself bleed. The metallic taste brought him back to reality.

He dove deep within his own well of magic, deeper than he'd ever ventured in his life. He swam far beneath the surface and into the inky depths of the bottom of the pool. He reached out with his fingers for the magic that was his birthright. Deep. Dark. Forbidden. All-consuming power.

When he latched onto the snaky tendrils, the magic returned his strong grip. The ancient magic coursed through him, raging through every pore, every vein in his body. His eyes tingled as if melting to onyx like they did when he shadewalked. His body thrummed alive with power, swelling within his core. Stronger. Stronger. Stronger.

Until he could no longer hold it inside him.

He released the magic, the surge of power filling the room to combat Lyyli's own magnificent power. The clash of magic sent a pillar of black spiraling toward the sky.

And then the metal band around his neck began to strangle him.

Panic bolted through him when he could no longer breathe. He instinctively fought against his chains before rational thought kicked in, and he forced himself to relax as the life slowly faded from his eyes. He ignored his desperate need for air and focused on keeping the stream of magic steady.

The Shadow Emperor flashed in and out of existence as he stepped out of Lady Auer's rings, his eyes blazing bright in the darkness. He swatted Killian's magic away with a clawed hand, but Killian increased his efforts until the magic shrouded him.

One by one, the magic flickered in response to the other Lords as they also unleashed their ancient power around the outside of the property, like a ten-sided star, all points connecting.

One. Two. Three. Four. Five. Six. Seven. Eight. Nine.

Where was the tenth?

The metal band clamped tighter around his throat, squeezing hard enough for stars to shoot across his vision.

"You!" Lady Auer thundered, her expression murderous. "You did this."

Through the nearly blinding stars, he noticed a mirror created from Lady Auer's magic showing the Lords standing around the fortress, releasing their birthright of power like a cage trying to contain a beast.

As if the concentration of Lady Auer's power wavered, the band loosened the slightest bit for him to suck in a breath of air and then grunt out a sentence. "I told you not to assume you are the smartest person in the room."

Blindingly fast, her hand struck him across the face, rattling his entire jaw and leaving behind a festering burn. "There are only eight Lords outside. You are in here, quickly dying. And my son would never turn against me. Your efforts are in vain, Graves."

He grimaced when the band tightened and loosened again the slightest bit, only to clamp tighter than before.

The stars won out. His power flickered out as he lost consciousness for mere moments. His body slumped against his chains. His surroundings faded slowly.

"You are wrong, Mother," a voice said through the haziness of his mind.

"Lorenz," Lady Auer gasped. "You must realize this is for the greater good. It is what's best for our family."

Killian didn't hear the next part as his subconscious flickered out entirely.

Only for a rush of air to enter his lungs. His lips tingled as he sucked in gasp after gasp. Darkness turned into shooting stars until his surroundings slowly came into focus. The band that used to strangle him lay at his feet in two halves soaked in a pool of blood. Lorenz stood protectively in front of him, his own hand dripping with blood.

Killian's eyes widened when he realized Lorenz and his mother shared blood. Hers wasn't the only one able to free him.

His gaze dizzyingly darted toward Lyyli. Magic continued to swirl around her like a dark storm. With every passing moment, the Shadow Emperor became more solid.

Lyyli continued to sing as if unable to stop.

And…Lorenz didn't die from hearing her voice. Instead, a ruby ring around his finger glowed brightly as if heat raged within its depths. Lyyli's voice would eventually break the stone.

"Lorenz," Killian grunted as a warning, shaking away more stars from his vision.

Without moving from his protective stance, Lorenz's magic shot out from him. Killian's followed suit as he gave it his all. His well of magic depleted slowly, exhausting him to the very core. He wanted to collapse in sheer exhaustion. He wanted to succumb to the fatigue in his body.

But he refused to give up now.

Ten tendrils of shadow began closing in around the Shadow Emperor, who snarled and attacked each bar of his shadowy cage with a vengeance. The power zapped him with each attempt.

Lady Auer blasted powerful magic in their direction, but the potions spilled across the ground provided a protective barrier from her magic. The translucent, glimmering ward shot up between them and the destructive magic, protecting them if only for a short time. He'd prepared the potions beforehand, only hoping they'd become useful.

The Shadow Emperor shouted his rage before he lunged toward Lyyli. Still bound to the wall, Killian released the last of his magic in a powerful surge.

Silence.

And then Lady Auer's heavy breathing echoed in the room. Hair had fallen out from its bun and into her face. Her glare penetrated through his very soul. Startling each of them, her rings shattered in a miniature explosion of stone shards. Lorenz leaped toward her and seized her remaining rings, as well as bracelets, earrings, and necklaces. He knew for a fact Lady Auer was not capable of much magic other than the shimmering barrier around the fortress. The rings had provided her with more power.

Killian's fatigued body pulled against his restraints as he searched frantically for Lyyli. He found her sitting with her back against the wall, staring at a small birdcage resting in her hands. An onyx fog pounded against each side of the cage, the Shadow Emperor's essence trying to break free.

She met his gaze across the room, and it was as if their hearts intertwined despite the short distance. Despite the silence. Gratitude, love, and relief pooled around her. For once, he only wished she could see his emotions as well, as he didn't think he could speak through the swelling in his face.

Lorenz dug into his mother's pocket, produced a key, and unshackled Killian. He fell into a heap on the floor without the agonizing support keeping him upright. He attempted to pick himself up, but then a pair of gentle hands wrapped around his arm and helped him. On shaking feet, he sighed when

Lyyli's comforting touch lightly trailed across his jaw, followed by sweet, tender kisses around his swollen eyes and cheeks.

He captured one of her hands in his own, struggling to speak. "Don't you worry about me. I will recover."

"Unhand me!" Lady Auer shrieked, struggling against Lorenz's grip as he pinned her hands behind her back, her shoulder against the wall before tying rope around her wrists. "I am your mother. I refuse to be treated with such disrespect."

"And that is my friend," Lorenz said, nodding toward Killian. "You deserve just as much disrespect as you've shown him. Besides…what you have done here is worthy of execution, but I have asked for your life to be spared. You will have a fair trial."

Killian winced as he tried to speak through his cuts and bruises, grabbing his friend's elbow as he made for the exit. "Thank you," he murmured quietly to keep Lady Auer from hearing. "And please…keep what you know about Lyyli a secret."

Lorenz paused to glance curiously at Lyyli. "I couldn't see much, and I didn't hear anything. As far as I know, she wasn't even here."

He sighed in relief and nodded, unable to do anything more. Quite frankly, he'd never felt more beat up in his life than he had in the past several days. Not even after his run-in with the basilisk.

Yet, Lady Auer must have heard anyway.

"I will tell everyone what she is, Graves!" she shouted, completely losing her carefully constructed mask.

"No, you won't." Lorenz tightened his grip on her wrists. "Do you realize how much leverage I have on you, Mother? If you want to keep from joining Father in the afterlife, I think it's best you remain silent."

Lady Auer gave one last attempt to struggle against Lorenz before she settled on a glare. He led her away.

When Lorenz disappeared with his mother, Killian stooped to pick up the birdcage. It fit inside one of his palms. The Shadow Emperor was trapped inside, along with his beasts of darkness. For eternity. In order to rise again, only all ten Lords could free him just as all ten had trapped him.

"Forgive me," Lyyli whispered so quietly, he had to lean closer to hear. "For so much."

Another wave of relief washed over him when her voice had no effect on him. At least, no dangerous effects. He still wanted to bathe in the sound.

He pulled her close, her head against his chest. "There is nothing to apologize for."

They remained in each other's arms until his legs started shaking. If forced to stand much longer, his knees would collapse.

Without a word, Lyyli latched onto his arm and led him out of the room, her strong grip helping to keep him upright. They stopped at the bottom stair of a staircase that spiraled upward, making his knees shake at the mere thought of climbing it. She turned to him and ran a hand over his chest as if searching for something.

"I apologize." He winced against the agony of moving any muscle on his face. "I don't have my notebook. I couldn't risk getting caught with it. It holds too many secrets."

Her hand settled over his heart, and they shared a quiet moment of relief, gratitude, and love. No words needed to be spoken. He didn't even need to see her emotions to understand them. They reflected his perfectly.

Leaning against the wall, he sighed and closed his eyes as he placed his hand over hers. He hadn't been looking for someone to love. By the shadows, he hadn't even wanted it. But she had entered his life and shaken it up a good deal.

He couldn't be more grateful.

Lyyli kissed his jaw and whispered in his ear. "You are going to fall asleep on your feet. Let's find you somewhere comfortable to sit."

elieving herself of the makeup and thick curtains Lady
Auer had called a gown felt like peeling off a layer of
dirt and drudgery. Dressed in her own clothing,
although plain, made Lyyli feel as if she were cleansed from
the horrors of earlier that night.

Daylight broke through the windows of the great hall, all
ten Lords sitting around a circular table with haggard
expressions. One had fallen asleep. Killian had dozed off
perhaps one or two times.

She didn't dare retire for the day, unable to sleep when he
sported a good beating on his face.

Lord Galish struck the table with a fist, and a resounding
boom echoed across the room, startling everyone upright in
their chairs. She even jumped where she sat in a comfortable
armchair near a window.

"We need to make a decision before the day's end," Galish
said wearily. "Lady Auer has broken a dozen different laws,
many of them severe. In any normal circumstance, she would

face execution for her deeds." The man turned to Lorenz. "She is your mother. What will you have her punishment be?"

Lady Auer had refused to give a statement nor admit to guilt or innocence during her short trial. She now slept in the dungeon with the rats.

Lorenz stood slowly, drawing every eye in the room. "She brought about my father's death. Although he was no innocent bystander in all of this, she cannot walk free again. Exile in prison. She will not be seen in Katalle again."

Murmurs ran around the table.

Finally, Galish asked, "All in favor?"

Instead of a few hands raised here and another few raised there, all ten Lords lifted a hand in favor of the decision.

Galish nodded. "The decision is made. Now let's discuss the Shadow Emperor."

Groans echoed around the table. Lord Blom even dropped his head on the wooden surface, the sound banging loud enough to likely leave a mark.

"Fine. Fine." Galish held up his hands in surrender. "I'll keep the cage he is locked in for now. We'll discuss the matter in three days' time. At..." His gaze scanned each Lord. "I believe our next meeting place is yours, Lord Graves."

Killian dipped his head in agreement. "I would prefer it. My mother doesn't have much longer left. I want to be nearby when..."

He trailed off, but she sensed the deep sadness within his words. Lord Blom stood abruptly, swiping a hand across his face at the mention of Killian's mother. Without a word to excuse himself, he strode out of the room. Killian stared after him as if seeing the man's distraught emotions. It was clear he cared for her greatly.

"Meeting dismissed," Lord Galish said.

Murmurs of relief made it around the table, though she suspected one of the Lords had fallen asleep with his head buried in his folded arms. She didn't know the man's name.

A servant approached her and bowed, startling her. She glanced over her shoulder, but no one stood behind her. "Miss Ives. Allow me to escort you to the bedchamber provided for you."

"Oh," she mouthed silently. Her gaze darted toward the table. More specifically, she sought out the man already staring in her direction. She shook her head and signed to the servant, though she didn't think he understood. "There is something I need to do first."

The man bowed again. "Then just follow the west wing corridor. Your chambers are in the fifth door on the right."

As if pulled together by an invisible rope, she and Killian met in the middle of the room. She tucked her arm in the crook of his elbow before they veered off down another hallway. Instead of escorting her to chambers, he led her into the east wing, glanced both ways down a vacant hallway, and then pulled her into a dark, empty bedroom.

Surprise sent her heart hurtling to the top of her ribcage, and as she glanced around the lavishly decorated chambers, she realized they belonged to him.

"I cannot let you go for a single moment," he murmured as his hand trailed down her arm and clasped onto her fingers. "Not after everything. I fear if I let you out of my sight, something might happen to you." He bit his lip as uncertainty flickered in his eyes but winced as if the action pained him. "Do you object to staying?"

Involuntarily, her gaze darted toward the bed large enough for two people, plus some. A thick, velvety fabric draped over the bed, pulled back at four large corner posts with intricate designs etched into the wood.

She shook her head and returned her gaze to him, only for sorrow and worry to pass through her at the sight of him. Cuts and bruises covered his face, his eyes swollen along with his cheeks. His bottom lip was split on the left side, and small flecks of blood still lingered on his jaw.

"I apologize. I look like a nightmare."

No, she had lived the nightmare. He looked like a hero.

"Lorenz gave this to me," she signed, producing a vial of blue-tinted liquid. She softly cleared her throat, remembering she could speak in his presence without repercussions. Out loud, she said, "I think it will find better use with you."

Killian sighed as she gently guided him to sit on the edge of the bed while she sat beside him. "I want to listen to you speak all day."

She smiled as she unstopped the vial and dabbed the elixir onto the tip of her finger before spreading it across the wounds on his face. "Someday, you can."

Heaviness lingered in the words unsaid as she continued her administration. The cuts closed little by little, though not quite all the way. The swelling in his face died down until she could see both of his eyes clearly. Purple bruises transitioned to a yellow-green color. When the vial of liquid ran out, she only wished to procure more in hopes that his injuries would heal completely.

Also, she desired to understand the properties of the elixir, the ingredients within it, and how magic played a part. There was so much she wanted to learn. But so little time.

Setting the empty vial aside, her shoulders slumped. "Killian, I need to stay with my aunt for a while."

He sighed again, this time with sadness. "I know. You leaving is inevitable. I just don't like the idea of not seeing you."

"I won't be gone long, I hope." She trailed a finger down his cheek, his jaw, and her touch lingered on the soft skin of his neck. Although he stared at the wall ahead, his throat bobbed up and down as he swallowed.

Desire.

Her lips twitched as she fought off a smile. His self-control was admirable. But she didn't want it. Not tonight. She wanted this amazing, brave, selfless man for the rest of her life. She wanted to be his and for him to be hers. For the rest of their days.

She softly kissed the base of his throat. His eyelids fluttered closed. She kissed the smooth skin at the top of his shoulder peeking out of his shirt. His hands found her waist. And when she moved to straddle his legs, a breath shuddered from his lips.

"Perhaps one last, sweet parting before I go." She nibbled softly on his ear. "Unless you are too tired."

"A man is never too tired for this," he chuckled. Warmth traveled up her thighs beneath the caress of his hands.

"Accompany me to Skaad first before you go. My mother will want to say goodbye."

"I will. But I have a feeling we won't have much time together after today." She raked her fingers through his soft, blond locks. "I want to take advantage of what time we do have."

He released a warm breath against her neck before trailing soft kisses from her jaw to her collarbone. Her fingers clasped tightly to his shirt as a delightful tingle traveled down the length of her spine.

"Try not to suck the life out of me this time." He smiled at his jest, though he'd not only built up immunity to her voice, but her tears seemed to protect him from her power entirely.

Despite the terror of that night, she couldn't help but laugh quietly at the teasing lilt of his voice. "If I can speak to you, I don't think I can harm you. But you *will* tell me if it's too much?"

A smile grew across his face. Despite his fading bruises, despite his healing cuts, he was still as handsome as ever. "I promise I will *try*. You don't quite understand the effect you have on me."

"It's only the siren part of me."

"No," he murmured against her neck, and she gasped when his hands trailed higher up her legs and then up her back. Starting at the top, he began unbuttoning the dress. "It's *all* of you. Being a siren is part of who you are. I wouldn't change it for anything."

"Truly?"

His fingers paused as he gazed with sincerity into her eyes. "Truly. You are everything to me."

She answered him by throwing her arms around his neck and pulling him into a loving, passionate kiss. Her fingers made quick work of unbuttoning his vest and then his shirt before she trailed her hands over the muscles of his chest and over his broad shoulders.

When his fingers tangled in her hair before he laid her back on the bed, she inhaled sharply at the passionate fire burning through her veins.

She broke the kiss and studied him through half-lidded eyes.

"Are you dying?" she whispered.

His lips twitched in amusement as he shook his head. "Not as far as I can tell. Your power doesn't seem to affect me anymore. I must have built up immunity."

Tears escaped the corners of her eyes and trailed down her face. Happy tears. Grateful tears. Tenderly, she trailed a finger down his cheek and across his bottom lip. "I love you, Killian."

"I love you, Lyyli. All of you. Always." His voice escaped as a husky whisper as he wiped her tears away before reclaiming her lips in a searing kiss, which she wholeheartedly returned.

No one had ever wanted all of her—the good and the bad. But he did. And she wanted all of him too. She loved him with her whole heart.

O ne by one, the Shadow Lords began to arrive.

Lyyli wrung her hands as she stood at the window in the drawing room, watching as Lady Feist descended from her carriage and walked toward Killian's estate. Several servants and guards accompanied her.

Five more Lords had yet to arrive, though Lord Blom had made an appearance earlier last night and had stayed sequestered in Dowager Graves' room for much of the time. On more than one occasion, she'd heard the man weeping.

From the corner of her eye, she watched as Johanna rose to her feet and exited the room to greet their newest arrival, her footsteps heavy with burden despite her pleasant, friendly expression.

Now was Lyyli's only chance.

She slipped out of the drawing room and rushed up the stairs, her slippers quiet against the lush carpet. Several times, she glanced over her shoulder for a sign of anyone within view or signs of pursuit.

No one followed.

Candlelight flickered in sconces on the wall as she snuck down the upstairs hallway. A servant rounded the corner carrying a bundle of sheets, so she quickly ducked into a window alcove, pressing herself against the wall until the woman passed.

Her heart raced within her chest, each pulse thundering in her ears as she peeled away from the wall and hurried down the length of the hallway. At the sound of laughter downstairs, she quickened her pace until she reached one of the doors, turned the handle, and slipped inside.

And she locked the door behind herself.

Fire crackled and popped in the hearth, the warm glow casting light and shadows across all four walls of the room.

As well as on the person lying on the bed, as still as death.

Dowager Graves' face was nearly as pale as a piece of parchment. Dark shadows lined her eyes. Her breath rasped in and out of her lungs.

The woman would likely die today. Killian would be devastated.

Unless…

Lyyli swallowed the fear and uncertainty rising in her throat as she slowly approached. She had been able to heal Killian and Astra with her tears. But with Dowager Graves, it was different. Lady Auer's enchantment had been so strong that even she couldn't break it. What chance did Lyyli have?

Unpleasant memories of her time in Lord Auer's imprisonment flashed across her mind. But one memory, in particular, tickled her consciousness. Her voice had been able to break the strongest of spells. It had been able to resurrect a powerful being from the dead. Would it be enough to shatter the enchantment before her?

The distraction of new arrivals downstairs would only last so long. She closed the drapes around the woman's bed to block out some of the sound before climbing up herself. Dowager Graves' lungs rattled with her next breath.

Taking her hands, Lyyli signed, "This will either cure you or kill you. Forgive me."

And quietly, she began to sing.

Immediately, Dowager Graves' body lurched violently as if fighting against restraints. She shuddered and thrashed and bucked.

Snap!

Lyyli's chin wobbled as the woman's rib cracked, but she kept on singing.

Snap!

Another rib broke. Her body continued to thrash, and then blood leaked from her nose. Lyyli's heart ached, tears trailing down her face as she watched her dangerous, deadly magic try to rip Killian's mother apart. This felt far too much like purposely attempting to kill someone.

Yet, she continued to sing.

Snap!

Lyyli's trembling hands rested on either side of Dowager Graves' head to keep it steady, and she focused on the magic pouring out of her. She told it to heal rather than hurt. She begged it to help rather than destroy.

The thrashing became wild, and Lyyli pinned the woman down by the arms.

Dowager Graves' eyes snapped open.

And Lyyli wasted no time as she stopped singing and scooped her tears from her own face and into the woman's ears. The wild bucking and thrashing became a half-hearted struggle until she ceased fighting altogether.

Blue eyes stared back at her. Confused. Panicked.

Curious.

For several long moments, Lyyli waited, her eyes wide with hope. Dowager Graves didn't throw herself out the window, on a knife, or bash her own skull against the wall. Instead, she just blinked and stared until her eyebrows furrowed.

"Lyyli?" the older woman finally croaked, and she nodded. "You...you saved me."

A relieved breath coursed out of her as she hung her head as the tension escaped her body. Silently, she climbed off the bed where she pinned Dowager Graves down, picked up the full glass of water on the table, and helped her sit up to drink.

After downing half the glass, Dowager Graves watched her curiously with intelligent eyes. Eyes like Killian's, missing nothing. "You are a siren."

Lyyli bit her lip as she debated what to say. Finally, she nodded.

"Does Killian know?"

She nodded again.

Surprisingly, Dowager Graves chuckled and rolled her eyes, wincing as she sat up further and draped her legs over the side of the bed until her feet skimmed the floor. "That explains so much. Killian couldn't go for the sweet, timid, aristocratic woman. He went for the most dangerous fish in the sea."

Not entirely knowing what to say, Lyyli simply shrugged her shoulders and smiled sheepishly. Killian would be so happy that his mother was awake and healthy, the enchantment broken. Nothing else mattered now. Except attempting the same feat with Charlotte.

The woman studied her curiously, warmth spreading through her blue eyes as she reached for Lyyli and held her at arm's length. "My, you are beautiful. Though, it takes more than beauty to turn my son's eye *and* keep it there. You must be special."

Not daring to speak again, she signed, "He's the special one. He helped me when no one else could. Besides, I'm not all that special. Just a farm girl from a poor family."

"I know my son's worth." The woman smiled and patted Lyyli's hand. "Killian has a hard time finding women who match him intellectually. Either he finds them dull to converse with, or they care more about his title than what he has to say. It is part of the reason he has given up on courting. Until now, it seems."

She coughed and took another sip of the water. "I suppose I must find a way to put Lady Auer behind bars. It has been terrible to not be able to move yet feel every excruciating moment pass by."

"She is already in prison," Lyyli answered with her hands, much to Dowager Graves' obvious surprise. "Killian has a lot to tell you."

"Will you not expand?"

Shaking her head, Lyyli pulled out two vials and handed them to her. Her own tears filled one while her mermaid scales filled another. Surely, Killian would love the gifts to use in one of his potions. "Give these to Killian for me. Please."

Dowager Graves stilled, her gaze slowly lifting. "You are leaving."

"Yes," she signed. "For a short time. I know for a fact that if I see Killian, I won't have the strength to leave. And I must. It is for my own benefit and his, too. So, no goodbyes."

"Do you love him?"

Lyyli smiled softly, recalling Killian's beautiful blue eyes, always full of wonder for the world around him. "Very much." Without another word, she stood, crossed the room, and unlocked the door. Before exiting the room, she turned around to say one more thing with her hands. "Lord Blom is downstairs. Perhaps you might put his grieving heart to rest."

And then she left the room and smiled to herself. She felt lighter than she had in a very long time. Leaving was the right decision. And quick while she still had the strength to do what was necessary.

****

A terrible somberness had hung over the Graves estate since Killian's return. The bodies of the soldiers who had protected his family had been buried and put to rest. He had personally visited each of their families.

It had been one of the hardest things he'd ever done.

And his mother…

Barely alive. Hanging onto the strings of mortality. She would die today. Lord Blom seemed to know it as well, as the man had hardly uttered a word since breakfast earlier that night. It was a shame. Lord Blom would have made his mother happy. But now, he didn't have the chance.

As Lord Lang arrived last, Killian's gaze scanned the ballroom where they were holding the meeting. Lyyli was *still* nowhere in sight. He'd been hoping to see her for hours if only just a glimpse.

Now rejuvenated from the demanding task of imprisoning the Shadow Emperor, eight of the other Lords talked and laughed. Even Lorenz managed to make a joke or two despite the sadness, worry, and frustration escaping him in blue and yellow billows.

Killian's footsteps were drowned by the noise in the ballroom as he approached Lord Blom, who sat in a secluded nook. Three empty chairs kept him company around a table where men often liked to play cards during large social events at his home.

"Mind if I join you?"

Lord Blom gestured to an empty chair across from him, nursing a grayish liquid within a small glass. Drinking this early while a meeting was about to begin?

Where could Killian find a glass?

"Where's your woman you stole from Auer?" Blom asked as he stared deeply into his glass.

"Lyyli? I don't know."

"You better marry her quick." He nodded toward a group of three Lords on the opposite side of the room. Lord Beelek stood beside his daughter, who dripped with nervousness from her wringing hands to the sickly yellow emotion pooling at her feet. "Lord Beelek is about to make a foolproof recommendation that you marry Miss Flora Beelek." The man leveled him with a stare. "By the end of the week."

"This again?" Killian sighed wearily as he closed his eyes and rested his head back against the chair. "Why the rush?"

"Politics."

They sat in companionable silence for several minutes, finding respite from the noise, the people, and for a moment, their responsibilities as Lords.

At least until Lord Blom gasped, his eyes wide as he stared at a place just over Killian's shoulder. Eyebrows furrowed, he turned to look as well.

Only to freeze in his chair.

He blinked several times, but the image remained. His mother entered the room wearing a light-colored dress, her hair pinned neatly to her head. Her already slender frame appeared thin and gaunt, the frock nearly falling off one shoulder. She clasped her hands in front of her, eyes darting about.

"Mother," he choked, unable to draw air when he realized she was really there and not a figment of his imagination. He stood abruptly, and in his haste, knocked the chair onto its side. It crashed to the ground, drawing many stares in the room. He rushed toward her, closing the distance between them in long, hurried strides until he engulfed her in a tight embrace.

He couldn't stop himself from sobbing in relief, and as if his emotions influenced her, she buried her face in his chest and sniffled too.

"Look at you," she finally said, eyes shining with unshed tears as she gently touched the bruises on his face. "What happened?"

"So much. I—"

Lord Blom pushed him aside and pulled his mother into his arms, unabashedly kissing every inch of her face despite their audience. Killian gazed up at the ceiling to give them a moment of privacy as they kissed and while Lord Blom whispered something into her ear. Out of the corner of his eye, Killian saw his mother smile and nod.

His knees shook at the realization that his mother was alive. And on the mend, it seemed.

The entire room crowded around them, expressing relief and wonder at her miraculous recovery.

Only a minute later, Charlotte entered the room in her nightgown, her eyes glazed with confusion. Another round of surprised exclamations and weeping took place as Johanna's aristocratic mask fell. The four sisters embraced, though Charlotte's confusion never abated. He wondered for a moment if she hadn't been as lucid as his mother in her unconscious state.

"How?" Killian asked, unable to speak anything more past the frog in his throat.

His mother shrugged, though her eyes sparkled with knowledge. "Lady Auer must have released me from her enchantment after all." She pulled him into a firm embrace and murmured in his ear. "Lyyli."

He reeled back, shocked as his gaze traveled over his mother. He took her elbow and led her into the hallway, away from listening ears, and turned to face her. "What do you mean?"

She glanced back and forth down the hallway as if to make sure they were alone before she answered. "I know what she is. She sang to me. Broke the enchantment. And healed me." Happiness sparkled in her eyes as though oblivious to his shock. "You have yourself an incredible woman in your life. I hope you don't let her go."

A waterfall of relief gushed over him, and to try to hide his rising emotions of gratitude, he turned to gaze out the window. Torchlight flickered in the darkness of night as his soldiers made their rounds. Lots of soldiers. He didn't dare leave his estate as unprotected as he had during the massacre. Never again.

"I'll never let her go," he finally croaked.

"Hmm." She approached the window beside him and also stared out into the darkness. "You told me the proposal went terribly. What happened?"

He ran a hand down his chin, glancing briefly toward his mother to find curiosity and a slight amount of sympathy trailing out of her. He stared out the window once more. "I messed up. A lot. And then she nearly killed me. It was a disaster."

"Hmm," she said again. "I assume the second time went better?"

Confusion knitted his eyebrows together as he scrutinized his mother, who simply watched him in that way she always did. As if she knew something he didn't. As if she were trying to wheedle information out of him.

"Second?"

Her eyes hardened. "You are officially engaged to Lyyli, correct?"

He paused, thinking back on his words over the last several days. He winced when he realized he hadn't officially proposed. "Well…it's an implied understanding between us."

His mother huffed, slowly letting out a long breath as she always did when he tried her patience. He suddenly felt like a child, waiting anxiously for her sharp tongue to lash sense into him. He tried to beat her to the chase.

"It's not a big deal. I'll propose officially later tonight."

Another huff escaped her. "And how will you do that?" She dug into her pocket and pulled out two vials, plopping them into his hands. The glass clinked together in his palm. He immediately recognized the contents—mermaid scales and tears.

His face paled. "Lyyli didn't leave. She wouldn't."

"Well, she *did*. She's gone, Killian. She didn't want to say goodbye."

Unable to keep his shaking legs from collapsing any longer, he plopped down on a bench against the wall and buried his head in his hands. "She wasn't supposed to leave yet. Not like this."

Unfortunately, his mother wasn't done chastising him. "A man of your station needs that stability and assurance." She counted on her fingers. "You let her go without a ring. Without a promise. Without an official date for the ceremony. Killian, my son, I love you very much. But you are foolish at times."

His shoulders drooped at her berating. She was right. He was horrible at this courting business and even worse when it came to marriage. "What am I supposed to do? Lord Beelek will demand I marry his daughter at tonight's meeting."

Her tone softened as she touched his shoulder. "Hold off the Shadow Lords for as long as possible until Lyyli returns. But in the end, they may try to force you to marry someone you do not love."

"I won't let that happen."

"Neither will I. Come. Let's attempt to salvage some of the damage you've done."

He released a relieved sigh. "What would I do without you?"

She squeezed his arm. "This is what mothers are for."

Together, they entered the ballroom, and as if lying in wait for her return, Lord Blom slipped his arm around her waist and led her away, though not far. Killian called the meeting to fruition and joined the others at a long, rectangular table. Servants rushed in to provide drinks and refreshments before he ordered everyone out except the Lords and relatives. All at once, doors shut tight with soft *clicks* on each side of the room.

Torchlight flickered across the walls as if touched by a faint breeze. All became quiet. Still. Until Killian broke the silence.

"I call this meeting into order. Our first item of business? The Shadow Emperor. What shall we do with him and his trapped beasts?"

For an hour, they argued about what to do with the Shadow Emperor. Someone proposed to bury him deep underground. Another proposed to let the cage of shadow collect dust in a crypt. No one wanted such a dark power to linger anywhere in their own provinces, especially not in their homes.

Finally, they agreed to bury the Shadow Emperor in a crypt deep beneath the Skaad mountains, with an entrance that could only be sealed as well as opened by the ten Lords together. They wanted to take every precaution possible to avoid someone stumbling upon the Shadow Emperor, even in his imprisoned form.

Lord Beelek steepled his fingers together, his gaze swiveling across the room until it landed on Killian. His face blanched.

"Lord Graves," the man said with conniving, calculating eyes, "I believe we have been more than patient with our request that you marry or lose your title. Due to recent circumstances, we will forgive your lack of efforts to wed. But I am speaking for all of us when I say it is not smart to wait any longer. Should you have died in our battle against the Shadow Emperor, Skaad would have been without an heir."

Killian let out a long breath as he tried to dig within his mind for an excuse, but Lord Beelek spoke over him.

"I propose we arrange a marriage between you and—"

His mother stood abruptly, the action cutting off the man's words. She seemed to float rather than walk as she stood behind Killian and placed a single hand on his shoulder. "Impossible. As my son is already engaged."

Mother?

His eyes threatened to widen, but he forced himself to keep a neutral expression. He was not engaged. Not officially. But he supposed no one else knew it.

Continuing, she said, "Lyyli Ives is descended from a powerful line of merfolk, and we wanted to make a strong alliance with the mer to also strengthen the Graves line. The wedding is already set in motion. We will need three months to make the marriage official."

Lord Beelek scowled. "One week."

"Two months," she countered.

"Three weeks. We cannot afford to wait any longer. If he is not wed by then, he will wed my daughter."

A hundred different curse words floated through Killian's mind as he tried his best not to glance toward Flora Beelek, though he attempted to keep a calm mask. "Fine. The date is set. I expect each of you to be here on the last day of the month to attend the ceremony."

A murmur of assent circled the table, but Killian could only think about how he could possibly contact Lyyli before then. Surely, she would return before the three weeks were up. Right?

He frowned when he replayed her words in his mind. She'd sounded as if she'd planned to be gone for a long time.

But…

His heart leaped into his throat when he realized he could still intercept her in time before she joined the ocean for who knew how long. He could still make this work.

Excusing himself, he exited the room before shadewalking as fast as his magic would carry him. In his ethereal form, he slithered from shadow to shadow, his surroundings transitioning from familiar trees and dirt to rivers and sand.

And then he stopped short within the trees bordering the beach where he had first taken Lyyli to teach her how to swim. Clothing lay discarded on the sand, making a trail containing a dress, undergarments, and finally slippers with several yards separating each as if she'd hastily kicked them off her feet.

His gaze darted toward the ocean just in time to witness two tail fins splashing the surface of the water before disappearing altogether.

"Lyyli!" he shouted.

No answer.

He didn't bother discarding his own clothing as he splashed into the ocean, kicking up water in his clumsy attempt to follow. The heaviness of the water tripped him, and he dived face-first into its frigid depths.

He abandoned his attempt to run and started to swim in the direction he'd last seen her. The rising tide choked him and clawed at his hair. It latched onto his clothing and pulled him under. But he refused to stop.

When he could no longer touch the ground, he opened his eyes beneath the water.

Only to stare back at the dark, murky depths.

His eyes burned. His lungs cried out for breath. But still, he searched for any glimmer of mermaid scales.

Nothing.

Finally, he kicked to the surface and gasped in a breath of air, turning every which way as he carefully watched the choppy water. Yet, he found no sign of mermaids, only fish and a sea turtle swimming by.

When his body tired too much to keep himself afloat, he swam toward a rock jutting out from the water and clung on tightly, still watching the water. Nothing. Lyyli was gone.

A tingling sensation shot up his left arm, like pins and needles after a limb fell asleep. He hissed at the pain before swatting at his arm, convinced something had stung him. But when he rolled up his sopping wet sleeve, he inhaled sharply.

Slowly, the black designs etched into his skin began to recede, the visible curse disappearing in a matter of minutes. His eyes widened when the smallest bit of color seeped into the black and grays of his vision. Dark gray trees burst into colorful greens and reds. The gray ocean water transitioned into dark blue and a hazy green. And his clothing...

Brown, red, and black popped into his vision, nearly startling him into releasing the rock. And when his arm stopped tingling, the ocean drowned his ears with its waxing and waning, suddenly much more noticeable when his world was no longer muted.

Instead of feeling overjoyed that the color returned to his world, despair crashed into him as he stared out over miles of ocean, his heart heavy. The one person he wanted to see in full color had disappeared. A part of him feared she might be gone forever.

"You win, witch!" he shouted into the air in the direction of the mountains. Lyyli had disappeared. And she had taken his heart with her. "Are you happy?"

No answer. Then again, he hadn't expected one.

If he didn't figure out how to get in touch with Lyyli, their future together would be nonexistent. But even his knowledge of the ocean and Ocean Fae was limited. Three weeks. It was enough time. It *had* to be enough time. Otherwise, the woman to stand by his side would not be a choice of his own making.

33

The gentle ocean water stroked her hair like a mother's soothing touch as Lyyli lay in a bed of soft seagrass, sighing against the tickling sensation brushing her skin. A world that had previously felt so foreign only less than three weeks ago now felt like home. A part of her never wanted to leave. Another part of her held another home within her heart.

Her stomach twisted violently, and her eyes flew open. She kicked her tail into motion, just barely reaching the green coral in the corner of the underwater cave before she retched. The clams she had eaten the night before came back up, along with a good amount of bile. The coral eagerly consumed what she expelled, acting as a waste exterminator.

A groan escaped her as she rested her head against the cool, rocky wall, her eyes closed.

"Sick again?" Aunt Eliel's tone held mirth rather than sympathy. "I was never sick this early with any of my pregnancies, but your mother was sick within a couple weeks of conception."

She spoke in mer tongue, and Lyyli understood it from having learned it as a child. Speaking it took practice, however.

Lyyli groaned again, wrapping her arms around her midsection. Her fingers brushed the strands of pearls hanging from the seashells covering her breasts. She'd missed her monthly bleeding a week ago, and her aunt's waterstone had turned pink in her hand to confirm the pregnancy.

"Killian will be so upset," she murmured, fighting off another wave of nausea. "It took a lot of convincing for him to agree to marry. He will be so unhappy to learn about the child."

"You don't know for sure."

"I do!" she cried but winced when her siren power escaped with her voice. She took a moment to control her emotions before speaking again. It took much effort to keep her magic from clinging to her voice, but at least when it did escape, it no longer killed. She had her aunt to thank for that. "He won't marry me now. I don't have a chance."

"Do you really believe that?"

Finally, Lyyli opened her eyes to find her aunt gazing back at her with a similar shade of green eyes. Her red hair floated in the water, unadorned with her usual seashell accessories.

Her shoulders slumped. "No. Killian is a good man."

Speaking felt very different beneath the water than it did on the surface. Although she still didn't entirely understand it, Eliel had said it was possible because of the mermaid magic that helped them transform.

Absently, she swam around the cave, her mer eyes seeing everything as clear as she might above the water. Bobbles and seashells she'd collected lay on a shelf made of pink coral. A map etched onto a slate rested in a nook nearby, which helped orient her within a vast ocean. And a mirror attached to the corner of the rocky wall. Her mer image used to shock her. Now, she loved it.

Her skin was a light blue, her fins also blue with a silvery tint in the scales. Shimmering silver streaked through her copper strands. Several new earrings climbed up one ear in the mer tradition of piercing one's body.

She reached out and touched the surface of the mirror with webbed fingers. It rippled like the top of a pond after a lone leaf grazed it.

Eyebrows furrowed, she touched it again, only to dart away in shock as the mirror continued to ripple. Eliel swam to her side and gripped her elbow tightly, her mouth drawn in worry as she wielded a knife.

"No magic is strong enough to find us. I'm worried. Go!" Eliel ordered, pushing her toward the cave's exit. "If someone comes through that mirror, no matter what, you must survive. *No matter what.*"

Her aunt's tone struck a chord of fear in her heart. Were they under attack?

Knowing how valuable she and her unborn child were to the hope of siren survival, she swam toward the exit, only to freeze when she heard a garbled but familiar voice speaking from the mirror.

"Lyyli, can you hear me? Lyyli?"

"Killian!" she gasped, kicking back toward the mirror. Her aunt didn't stop her as she placed her hands on either side of the rippling surface. "I'm here. I can hear you."

His image continued to ripple and distort as if the ocean between them provided too great of an obstacle.

He sighed. "I don't think this is working."

"I'm here!" she cried, but his image only wavered more, his words becoming disjointed sentences.

"My tenth attempt...news...frustrated." The ocean swallowed up his next sentence completely before she heard a distorted version of the following sentence. "Wedding...tomorrow night...marrying her. Ugh. Drat this communication. I can't...and put this off any longer. The...Skaad church. Goodbye, Lyyli."

When Killian's distorted image rippled once more before leaving the surface flat, she stared dumbly at her own reflection. Her mind blanked. Her heart beat with cold numbness as if trudging through layers upon layers of ice.

Absently, she rested her hand over her belly, over his growing child. Her eyes smarted. Her chin wobbled. Her aching heart broke through the ice and tumbled into despair.

"Does he not want me anymore?" she stuttered, glancing away from the mirror to her aunt. "Three weeks is not at all that long. Did he misinterpret that I planned to return? Or am I not good enough for a Shadow Lord?"

Empathy filled her aunt's eyes. "You will have the baby. That's what's important."

Lyyli shook her head and swam to the mouth of the underwater cave. "It's not enough. If he expects me to sit back and allow him to marry another, he will be more than surprised." She glanced over her shoulder. "How long will it take me to reach Skaad?"

Eliel's expression drooped with sadness. "A day. Plus traveling on legs. You might not make it in time. Especially because we don't know how old his message is or when he tried to send it."

"I must." She began to move forward when her aunt's voice called her back.

"You cannot travel the sea alone. I will accompany you. But I haven't stepped foot on land in a long time. I would only slow you down at that point."

She nodded, and after gathering a couple bags of provisions and more weapons than Lyyli knew what to do with, they set off at a brisk pace. After only a half hour, her body began to ache, not having yet developed the muscles she needed to make a quick journey. But she fought through the ache. Through the pain. Through the worry. She refused to give up Killian so easily. Not without a fight. Even if it meant making a scene on someone else's wedding day.

Miles of ocean passed by on all sides of them from the deepest of blue to the blackest of black. A wide range of colors of fish, plants, and merpeople crossed their path, from green to blue to pink and more. Usually, she loved to admire the beauty of the deep sea.

But today, she had a wedding to stop.

By the time they reached a well-trafficked area filled with all manner of merpeople, her gills burned, and her fins protested against traveling any further.

Eliel moved closer to her, always keeping a suspicious, watchful eye on other merfolk. They were friendly enough. But if any of them caught a whiff of their siren blood, they would be gutted faster than a fish on a line.

"I can't keep going," Lyyli wheezed as they entered a current that would take them many miles further without so much effort on their part. "My body can't do this."

"Yes, you can." Her aunt took her shoulders and gently squeezed. "There is enough time. The night is hours away yet."

Closing her eyes for a blissful few moments, she nodded. Killian was worth it.

For hours, they traveled until the water darkened as night approached. At last, her head broke above the surface of the water just as the sunset twirled its golden gown along the horizon. Her lungs drew in a painful breath of air while her gills lay momentarily dormant.

She fought tail and fin against the ocean trying to drag her back into its depths until she finally dragged her weary body onto the sand. Her body collapsed, and she found herself staring at a pink, yellow, and orange sky on a secluded beach. Her and Killian's beach.

The air felt foreign in her lungs, and as her fins slowly dried, the transition back to legs startled her.

"Hurry!" Eliel called from the water, breaking her out of her tired, fatigued state. "The sun is almost down."

Lyyli picked herself up off the ground, but unused to her legs, she swayed and crashed sideways into the sand. The gritty substance coated her skin and clung to her wet hair, layering each of her eyelashes.

She gritted her teeth and tried again. She swayed a second time but managed to keep her balance.

Her gaze darted toward a cluster of rocks, and her heart skipped in surprise. Her old clothing lay folded neatly on top of a rock, her slippers pinning them down.

As if someone was waiting for her to return.

Killian.

Hope bolstered her courage and her strength. Now all she needed to do was figure out where the Skaad church was. And also how to get there.

****

Killian paced.

And paced.

And paced some more. Until the soles of his shoes sank against his weight with every footstep as if they might fall apart entirely. Exactly three weeks had passed since Lyyli's departure. And despite his eleven desperate attempts to contact her using magic and even her mermaid tears to summon her, he couldn't get in touch with her.

He ran his fingers through his hair, overly aware he likely looked like a mess after his hours of frantic pacing. String instruments played softly in the other room as more guests arrived to witness the nuptials. Family, friends, and Lords from all over Katalle and beyond waited just beyond those double doors.

As if taunting him, he opened one of the doors and peeked inside the chapel. The majority of his guests had already arrived. He spotted King Calle Everdon in the back corner with his new fiancée, Skaja. They were to be married in two months at the start of winter. Johanna sat beside Paul Galish, her expression full of adoration as he spoke animatedly with his hands. The man was deaf, and Johanna was perfect for him, already able to speak sign language, and they got along well. Killian hoped their relationship would work out.

His gaze traveled across the room to find all other nine Lords in attendance, including Lord Beelek and his daughter, Flora.

Killian couldn't help but frown as he watched the young woman for a moment as she fiddled with a yellow handkerchief in her lap, desperately hoping she would not become his bride tonight. Sure, she was pretty. But she had no real personality of her own. Conversation with her so often became dull and lifeless. She would hang onto his every word without trying to understand anything he said. Her hobbies included embroidery and training to run a household. She didn't care about magic or books, and she zoned out whenever he spoke about the Darkest Star Arcane.

Behind him, his mother sighed as she touched his elbow. "I'm sorry, Killian. I had hoped she would be here."

The lump in his throat prevented him from replying as he scanned the chapel for the dozenth time, his gaze missing nothing as he took in the guests, the dark brown pews, the crystal sconces on the walls. He wasn't entirely sure what to look for, as he'd never seen Lyyli in full color. However, no redheads graced the building.

"Just a few more minutes," he croaked.

"A few more minutes won't make a difference. You either march out there and accept being stripped of your title, or you marry Flora."

Killian blinked several times as he fought off his emotions. He glanced at his mother and then at his four cousins sitting in a pew beside the Galishes. It was possible that Paul Galish would marry Johanna, and maybe Lord Blom would marry his mother. But for now, all five of them depended on him. If he didn't have his title, he would have nothing to offer them and no way to support them.

He opened the door wider and stepped into the chapel with a heavy heart. Many heads turned in his direction, and the musicians played even softer than before. The lights seemed to grow brighter with each step he took. Blinding. Nauseating.

He stopped in the center aisle, terrified of taking even one more step. But for his mother, he must do this. For Johanna, Charlotte, Laureen, and Mia, he had to follow through.

So, he took one more step but froze when the chapel doors swung open and banged against the wall. The momentum blew out several sconces nearest the door, revealing a woman breathing heavily, her hair and clothing bedraggled, and a look of pure weariness and desperation on her face.

His eyes widened. His mouth dropped open.

Golden copper hair. Jade green eyes. A pert mouth. Tall, shapely frame.

And absolutely beautiful.

The sight of Lyyli struck him speechless. Although he hadn't seen her in only three weeks, it felt like years. And the version he found himself gawking at hardly resembled the black and white version he had come to know. Instead of uncertainty and hesitation, she carried herself with confidence.

Locking eyes with him and still breathing heavily, she took several steps forward...

...and careened to the side, landing directly in King Calle's lap.

"My apologies, sir," she said. *Out loud*. No one died after hearing her voice. Magic didn't line her words but rather stayed within her well. "I mean, Your Highness?"

She climbed to her feet again, stumbling to the left, and then to the right. "I promise I'm not drunk. I swam here as fast as I could. I don't have my land legs yet."

A rumble of laughter.

But he could only watch her with wide, mystified eyes. She was here. Really, truly here. And he couldn't breathe.

At last, she took one last stumbling step into his arms, and he clung on tight to her as if she might disappear at any moment. She searched his eyes, a look of rising panic on her face. "Please tell me you aren't married."

He barely managed a shake of his head.

The action didn't seem to console her, as she glanced around the room until her gaze fell on Johanna. "I beg you. Don't take him away from me."

Killian blinked several times in confusion. Why was she asking Johanna and not Flora? And didn't she know how desperately he wanted her here? To marry her and only her?

"No, no, no," he murmured in her ear when he finally found his voice. He turned her face toward him to kiss each of her cheeks, her nose, and then lightly kiss her lips. "The message must have gotten distorted by miles of ocean. I said Johanna desperately *didn't* want to marry me. She's rather fond of Paul Galish."

A raging blush spread across Johanna's face, which only seemed to grow darker when her sisters began their relentless teasing. He grimaced when he realized he'd revealed something he shouldn't have. At least Paul couldn't have heard it, and her secret was safe.

Wanting a moment alone with his, hopefully, future bride, he whisked Lyyli into another room and shut the door behind them. The air rushed from his lungs as he faced her again. In black and white, she was beautiful. In full color, she was breathtaking. He wanted to bury his face in her golden copper hair and inhale her flowery scent. He wanted to gaze into her gorgeous green eyes all night long. He wanted to bask in the sound of her voice like a shadow cat lying in the moonlight.

Lyyli gazed at him in confusion, but she waited for him to speak first.

"I was a fool." He watched as her initial worry turned to surprise. "And my mother let me know it, too. I let you go without an official proposal. Without a ring. Without a date set for a wedding." Heart pounding in his chest, he reached into his vest pocket and pulled out the rectangular box with the unicorn tapestry embroidered on the top. When he opened it, he pulled out a ring made of deep blue sapphires.

She gasped, and the sound slammed into him, burning into the onyx ring on his finger. As if aware her magic had escaped, she took several moments simply to focus on breathing.

"Marry me, Lyyli. Today. Not because I need you to keep my title. Not because I am pressured by the other Lords. But because I can't handle the uncertainty of you never stepping foot in my life again. I selfishly love you too much to let you go one more time without knowing for a fact you will return. I desperately want you in my life."

As if at a loss for words, silent tears streamed down her face as she pointed to the top of her head.

He shook his head. "I can't read emotions anymore. My curse is gone. I can see you. All of you. You are beautiful." Even with her rumpled clothing, her hair stiff with salt, and cheeks red from exertion.

Her lips flickered with a smile, and rather than speaking, she nodded and held out her hands, signing, "Forever yours."

Relief gushed into him, worry melting off of him like a mudslide as he slipped the ring onto her finger. He began to pull her toward him to kiss her when she breathed out one word.

"Wait."

He froze.

She continued, a distraught look on her face as she turned the ring around on her finger. Her lips moved silently as if debating what to say. Finally, she glanced up to meet his gaze. "I am with child. Your child. I just thought...you needed to know before...before we knelt at the altar."

A baby?

The color drained from his face. A frigid cold swept through his body. And then a sudden nausea churned in his stomach.

"I think I might vomit," he wheezed as he doubled over, resting his hands on his knees. After a few moments, he tried to straighten, only to double over again. He had almost married the wrong woman and forfeited what life he might have had with his own child. The realization of what he'd almost lost created more nausea in his stomach.

Her gentle hand touched his shoulder. When he glanced up, he found worry and immense distress in her eyes. Green eyes. Oh, they were so beautiful. Although he missed being able to see emotions, he was so glad to see her in full color.

She signed instead of speaking. "Are you upset with me? Are you changing your mind?"

"No!" he gasped. "Never." He smiled when he realized he'd understood what she'd said. He'd been practicing sign language. A lot. "You are simply really good at keeping me on my toes. Just when I'm over one surprise, you manage to tackle me with another."

With a sheepish shrug, she signed, "It takes two?"

A laugh escaped him, but he instantly regretted it when his stomach violently protested. He rushed for an exit, and unable to keep the contents of his stomach inside any longer, he retched into the nearest bush before swaying on unsteady feet.

Lyyli quickly joined him outside with a glass of water, which he gingerly sipped, her expression full of worry.

This time, she spoke out loud, a comforting hand on his bicep. "I am supposed to be the one vomiting. Not you. Now I'm worried you will pass out at the altar."

His eyes widened as he envisioned the horrific scene. "I would never live that down. Ever." The cold liquid soothed his throat as he took a long drink. It gave him a few moments to think. To clear his head and approach the newest obstacle rationally. "The child will be a siren."

Slowly, she nodded her head. Several moments passed of crickets chirping in the autumn night darkness. "No matter if the child is male or female, yes. Are you angry?"

"No." Not angry. Just surprised. And a bit uncertain. Perhaps a little scared. He wrapped his arms around her waist and pulled her closer until their lips met in a hungry, starved kiss. He couldn't refrain from touching her any longer. "We'll make this work," he murmured against her throat, slowly working his lips along her jaw. "I signed up for this. I knew exactly what I was getting into." His face only inches away from hers as he gazed into her eyes, he offered a solemn promise. "We will keep your race from dying. Sirens will flourish again. Not immediately. But one day."

"Thank you," she breathed. "I love you so much."

Those words filled his heart with immense joy and relief. They met in another passionate kiss as if he were her sunshine and she his moonlight. He kissed her like a starved man, drinking in her sweet taste. Needing more, more, more.

Someone knocked on the open door, and they both jumped apart when his mother stepped outside with a shocked, disbelieving expression, which quickly transitioned into amusement upon their fluster.

"Are you two going to get married? Or will you continue to force us to wait while you create sparks on sacred property?"

Lyyli stepped in while he remained rooted with fluster. "Just a few more sparks?"

His mother laughed and rolled her eyes before motioning with her hand. "Your mother is waiting to help you dress. You can leave Killian to pace just a little bit longer."

"My mother is here?" Lyyli followed her inside, their voices becoming more distant.

"Mmhmm. And your father and sister. It was lucky you showed up when you did. A minute later, and events would have turned disastrous."

When their voices disappeared, Killian leaned against the church walls, his eyes closed as he breathed out the shadows of relief. He listened to the soothing rhythm of chirping crickets, the gentle breeze floating through the trees, and the melody of the music emanating from the chapel. He had been minutes away from making the biggest mistake of his life.

He wanted to weep with gratitude, but nervous flutters of excitement won out. Excitement to marry the woman he loved. Excitement for the unknown variables of the future.

Excitement, but mostly nervousness, for his unborn child.

The realization knocked the air out of him. He was going to be a father. To a siren. He had no idea how to be a father. He didn't even know how to be a husband.

Warmth gathered in his chest as he glanced toward the door Lyyli had disappeared behind. Although he didn't know how to be either of those things, he knew a beautiful, kind, interesting, magnificent young woman who would help him.

And stay by his side every step of the way.

****

When Dowager Graves led her into another room where her mother and Astra waited, Lyyli broke down into tears as she embraced each of them. There had been a time when in Lady Auer's clutches that she thought she might not see them again.

Her mother held her at arm's length. "You are speaking now," she said with wonder.

Lyyli touched her throat and signed, "I am learning. I will need to spend more time with my aunt to control my magic better."

"Which brings me to this point..." Dowager Graves grinned with unrepentant mirth. "You will not leave this church until you are properly married to my son. He's a smart man when it comes to magic, and even he couldn't figure out how to contact you. The Shadow Lords gave him a date to marry right after you left. He was beyond himself with worry."

She bit her lip. "Sorry," she murmured. "I wasn't thinking about the Lords when I left."

But the woman waved away her apology with her hand, disappeared behind a folding screen, and reappeared with a gorgeous gown in her arms. Blue like the color of her mermaid skin, with intricate lace and fabric as soft as downy feathers.

When words failed her, she signed, "I cannot wear this."

"Why not?"

"Because I'm—"

"—about to marry one of the wealthiest, most powerful men in the country?" her mother finished for her. "You will practically be a queen, and you deserve to look it."

Dazed, she allowed the two women and her sister to dress her and fix her hair until it was pinned elegantly to her head. When she faced a mirror in all the foreign splendor, her heart stopped.

The image staring back at her was not the scared little farm girl she had grown up to be. She was confident. Elegant. Beautiful. Regal. She looked like a woman who could stand beside Killian.

She trailed her fingers down the soft, lacy fabric of the bodice and gently fisted each side of the silky skirt before swishing the fabric around her legs. The gown was beautiful—the most beautiful thing she'd ever slipped on. But underneath all the fabric was a bundle of nauseous nerves. "What will Killian think of me?"

Dowager Graves fussed with the bottom of the skirt as she replied. "Quite honestly, he will be awestruck. You'd better put him out of his misery and fast. He's been fretting non-stop over the past three weeks. He's been almost too distracted to open his school."

Her heart tripped in surprise. "He started classes?" she asked out loud but reigned her voice back in when her magic seeped out. She finished her thought with her hands. "I didn't realize I missed that."

Dowager Graves smiled and nodded. "School started two weeks ago. Killian has been half a mess. I've rarely seen him so stressed out. Your presence here will put him back to rights."

"I hope so." Or perhaps she only managed to stress him out more by telling him about the baby. She hoped he wasn't vomiting again. Or even passed out cold somewhere.

Astra pressed a handful of white flowers into her hands and stood on her tiptoes to kiss her cheek. She was going to miss her family. Even more than she did now. She hoped she would get to visit often.

Without further preparation, they led her into the chapel, where Killian waited at the front of the room. His hair was only slightly less messy than it had been when she'd first arrived, though he was handsome in his regal red and black clothing. He was handsome. Tall. And his beautiful blue eyes gazed at her with immense love and adoration.

The music grew louder as she walked toward Killian and his outstretched hand. And when she slid her hand into his, the entire world fell right into place.

cratch. Scratch. Scratch.

The chalk in Killian's hands raked across the chalkboard with each of his words, giving off the scent of dust and learning. It was one of his favorite smells in the world, next to old parchment and the flowery aroma of Lyyli's hair.

His heart ached at the thought of his wife. He hadn't seen her for eight weeks and two days. It had been too dangerous to birth the baby above land where its wailing cries could kill anyone within the vicinity. Including himself. At least until she learned how to protect others from its power until it learned how to do the task itself. But to think she had to birth the baby alone with only her aunt as company?

He shook the thought away and finished the detailed drawing of a rare plant found within the tundra further north. Without turning to face his students, he pointed to the plant with his chalk. "This is the chamellia nivalis. The extract from its roots can be used to create very powerful healing potions.

But if you harvest it wrong, it can also create a very powerful poison. In tomorrow's class, I'll take you to the greenhouse and teach you how to harvest it, as well as how to prepare it for a healing draught."

"Do you know how to make a love potion?" someone blurted out.

The entire class tittered while whispering in hushed tones to one another. He chuckled as well to find that one of his brightest students, a Forest Fae, had asked the question. She twirled her dark, braided hair innocently, though she kept glancing toward another student on the opposite side of the classroom. The Sun Fae grinned back at her through tired, bloodshot eyes. He obviously wasn't used to waking up in the dead of night to attend one of Killian's lectures.

"I do," he answered when their tittering died down. "Several, actually." He twirled his chalk between his fingers and sat on the edge of his desk while facing the fifteen students. "It may not seem like it, but love potions are one of the darkest of magic spells. It takes away a person's will for a time. And no. I will not teach you how to make one."

Groans filled the room.

"At least not in this class." He chuckled before dismissing them, each packing up their things and filing out of the classroom. As his last class for the night, he began packing up his own things when he heard a quiet *scuff* in the doorway.

He glanced up, expecting to find one of his students. But when he instead found a beautiful woman with golden copper hair and green eyes that rivaled the most beautiful plants in

Katalle, he dropped his chalk in his surprise. It shattered across the floor.

"Lyyli," he breathed.

In only a few strides, he crossed the room and pulled her into a sweet embrace. Her floral scent teased his nostrils as he buried his face in her hair, clinging on tightly to her as if she might slip through his fingers like water. When she released a sob, and then another, he kissed her cheeks, her nose, her lips, and finally the top of her head as he held her close.

"I missed you so much," she sobbed into his shirt. "Remind me to never leave for such a long time again."

"How long were you in the hallway?"

"Maybe fifteen minutes," she sniffed. "I enjoyed listening to your lecture."

Again, he kissed the top of her head, and in response, she held him tighter around the waist. But with only one arm. Was she injured?

He peeled away just enough to glance down at her, only to inhale sharply. She held a bundle of blankets in one arm.

His entire body froze, rooted to the spot, as his gaze fixed on those blankets.

And the gurgle that came from within.

Slowly, his frozen body melted until his limbs thawed and his eyes began watering. "Is this…"

She nodded, smiling softly as she pulled down the blanket to reveal the baby's sleeping face. Blond hair like his, long eyelashes, and skin not quite as pale as his own. The nose and mouth shape resembled Lyyli's.

Her voice quieted, almost reverently. "Killian, meet your son."

He swallowed as emotion clogged his throat. He hesitantly reached out and touched the child's plump cheek. The boy opened his mouth in a large yawn before lying still once more. "May I hold him?"

"Of course." She helped situate the baby in his arms.

He was so tiny. His head fit snugly in his palm, his small body easily supported by one arm. "I've never held a baby before. I feel so awkward."

"You won't for long." She smiled up at him, her eyes glistening with happiness. "I haven't named him yet. I wanted to wait for you to meet him first."

He tenderly stroked the top of his child's soft, fuzzy head. "How about we name him after my father and your adoptive father? Marcel Jonathan Graves."

"It's perfect," she whispered as she rested her forehead against his as they held the baby between them. He basked in the beauty of having his small family within his arms. "I think the name is perfect."

ABOUT THE AUTHOR

Sydney Winward is a fantasy and paranormal romance author who dabbles in the occasional historical fiction. She loves building complex worlds filled with magic, strong characters, and emotional stories that can make you laugh and cry.

Sydney is the author of the Sunlight and Shadows Series and the best-selling Bloodborn Series, and when she's not writing, she's reading, thinking about stories, or going on adventures with her children. She lives in Utah with her husband and three amazing kids.

www.sydneywinward.com

9 781737 485438